a keeper of sheep

"Like life, the novel wheels around every time you think you have it figured out, revealing a new facet of itself and offering a more complex point of view."

Washington Post

"Carpenter's plush prose is evocative and to the point, as is his most consistent subtext, the idea of evolution. But the most compelling evolution is Penguin's. Witty, harrowing and heartfelt, hers is a journey worth taking."

San Francisco Chronicle

"A new stepmother, a local drug-running Vietnam vet, well-meaning reactionary neighbours and the devoted gay couple next door are collectively made vivid in prose that manages to be unobtrusive and gorgeous at the same time."

New Yorker

"The basic plot is familiar: the separate lives of women college friends. But the variations on that theme, replete with lush descriptions, are enchanting; few male writers have so sensitively depicted a female protagonist."

Library Journal

Also By William Carpenter

Poetry
The House of Morning
Rain
Speaking Fire at Stones

William Carpenter

a keeper of sheep

An *Abacus* Book

First published in the United States of America
by Milkweed Editions 1994
First published in Great Britain by Abacus 1995

Copyright © William Carpenter 1994

The moral right of the author has been asserted.

A CIP catalogue record for this book
is available from the British Library.

ISBN 0 349 10664 9

Printed and bound in Great Britain by
Mackays of Chatham PLC, Kent

Abacus
A Division of
Little, Brown and Company (UK)
Brettenham House
Lancaster Place
London WC2E 7EN

For Donna, Daniel, Aura, and Matt

a keeper of sheep

1

The reason I am called Penguin is that it mutated from Penelope, which is my real name, via Penny, which I can't stand, in a process so far back that I don't even remember. The reason I set fire to the Beta Sig house is because I am an only daughter and it's always been easy for me. They gave me a book one day without pictures, just writing, and they said *read,* so I read a few words and they clapped their hands for me as if I had played a sonata. And so it went. I would perform and they would clap. I did get a flute, and I did play sonatas after a while, with Katherine sitting at the piano and Richard watching, and although my heart wasn't exactly in it they clapped then, and they clapped when I memorized ten poems by Emily Dickinson and recited them one after the other before the parents and graduates of the Eighth Grade. I began with poem number two hundred and fifty-eight, "There's a certain slant of light," and I ended with number seventeen hundred and thirty-two, which ends "and all we need of hell."

Nobody clapped when I wrote DIVORCE in Katherine's lipstick on the bathroom mirror, and when they finally got one I was packed off to Morrelsex, which of course the boys shortened to Oralsex, where I learned something better than applause. That was to write something and rewrite it until they gave you an A. No comments, no red words at the end of the last page. Just an A, preferably with a period after it that meant there's nothing more one can say about this. A. The feeling an A gave me protected me for up to a month, or until the next A, whichever came first. It protected me from field hockey and cross-country and from my classmates Lance and Victor, who would attempt to prowl around under my shirt after the Friday night bonfires in Founders' Field.

Most of all the As protected me from the Divorce. When it came anywhere near my room on the fourth floor of Rawlings I would brace the As up against the door like a row of furniture, right back to the opposite wall, and the Divorce would snort and rut around out in the corridor like the Thing, but it could not get in.

I should add that at twenty I was probably the only virgin at Dartmouth College. Or I should say ex- at Dartmouth, because I was also Expelled. They never expel anyone. They want your money too much at the end of the line, when you make out your will. You're not going to leave them your millions if they expelled you. So usually it's suspension, which is what they got for burning the Effigy, but this was arson, it was real, there were real plainclothes detectives in from the State Police in Concord, there was a real trial in Superior Court, which I will get to, with real lawyers. And the strange thing is, we got suspended sentences, then they zapped us in the fake-chicken Dartmouth student kangaroo court, with bogus student attorneys and no Law in any coherent form whatsoever. It made the biggest headline in the *Dartmouth Daily* since the destruction of Pearl Harbor.

FOUR WOMEN EXPELLED

I am also a Feminist. I lived off campus in a feminist household with two other women and one guy, Bondo, who was a feminist too, which is not to say *effeminate* but just that he understood. Bondo would pull me aside to discuss love and romance from time to time but anything like that would have made our living conditions impossible so I paid no attention. Besides, he was our mascot. Bondo was my height exactly but amazingly strong for his size, so when the TV or bookcases needed moving he would do it. He could somehow pick up a bookcase with all the books in it and move it unaided to another place. We would sit and watch Bondo move things while all the time he was explaining why men are stronger, how the percent of muscle to fat differentiated over the centuries as man hunted while woman sat and watched. Love was unthinkable with anyone, particularly with Bondo. But he was a friend.

We did not go home for Christmas vacation, and because we lived off campus, they couldn't throw us out when they went through and fumigated the dorms and cleared out the suicides that had been decaying in the rooms since midterms. We didn't go home because we had a Project. None of us had ever sewn anything in our lives but we sat there night after night when it was twenty below outside sewing a quilt. We were like old New England women sitting in a row and stitching and listening to the Talking Heads.

In this quilt there was a winter scene with three men skating on a frozen pond. The skaters wore those black formal cutaways they used to skate in, with their hands held behind their backs, like the portrait of Parson Cockburn Skating by Sir Joshua Reynolds, or Sir Henry Raeburn. I forget. But I knew it when it counted, on the test. Around the edges, in nice nineteenth-century letters cut out of black velvet, we sewed CASTRATE THE CAPITALIST PATRIARCHY. We were just going to say castrate the patriarchy but Jennifer's father is a vice president of Merrill Lynch and she wanted the word Capitalist so we voted and she got it three to one.

Bondo sewed too. His actual name was Martin Bond but if anyone had called him Martin it would have gone right through him and come out the other ear. He was an angel and was doing his honors paper on Julia Kristeva, which is totally acceptable as far as politics are concerned, but of course his fingers were like stumps and he was getting around one-fifth as much done as we were on the quilt. Then Bondo went home on Christmas Eve to Connecticut so it was me, Rebecca, and Jennifer, whom I've mentioned. Jenny and Rebecca were ex-athletes who both used to be on the women's crew. Jenny was a large wholesome generous-looking woman with a large kind cariboulike face. Rebecca was diminutive and quick. She'd been the cox on the freshman crew and I used to see her perched on the back of the boat like a nuthatch, shouting through a megaphone attached to her mouth. She had the face of a nuthatch, too, sharp and symmetrical, with black nuthatch eyes that were always open as if she had no eyelids, and a sharp nose. They were both Lesbians, which I had considered once also, at Morrelsex, but did not actually take the plunge. If I were to find someone it would have to be a man, probably, or at least not another woman, since I believe in the opposites, which lead to the Dialectic, which is what makes us human beings.

Although Jenny and Rebecca were my friends and co-conspirators, I could not imagine them together in any physical sense of the word. They looked like two separate species. They were so different in size that it seemed impossible to have a democratic arrangement, which love should be. Besides, they were both anthropology majors, which means they also knew the same things, which adds up to silence as far as I'm concerned. Give me somebody who can teach me something I don't already know, even if it's science. Some of my best friends were premeds who knew everything about the body, I mean the interior of it, which is a complete mystery to me, like the inside of a TV.

It was Christmas Eve. Bondo was gone and we had a bottle of Mescal tequila with a worm in it that Jennifer had brought back from Mexico on a little weekend jaunt with her family. Much as she hates them she allows herself to devour a slice of their affluence from time to time.

We called Michelle Rabkin. She was the editor of the *Id*, which was this underground newspaper supported by nothing and without any office or money, but it had to exist because of the *Digest*, which was a right-wing newspaper supported by all these conservative alums. The *Digest* was racist, sexist, elitist, Reaganist, and Bloomist. The writers made full-time salaries and the ads came from places like Starkweather Investments in New York, which is a well-known neofascist front. No one advertised in the *Id* if they could help it, and it printed anything it could get, which was at the time mainly from us. The *Id* went down along with the Expulsions and that is probably another reason that the school wanted to get rid of us; the paper was such an embarrassment from the point of view of journalism. But it told the truth.

We saw Michelle coming up the walk with her green-and-white ten-foot scarf wrapped around her head like a cocoon. When she unwrapped it, her face was down and she said she had bad news.

That spring there had been a rape at the Beta Sig house, or really a gang rape, since about four football-size men had gotten a freshman woman into a corner of the Beta Sig basement and had repeatedly entered her in turn and without her expressed consent, to say the least. Two of the guys had been tried and sentenced to a year, which was a victory, only now Michelle was here on Christmas Eve saying she heard they got off on an appeal, which meant that that young person had been raped for nothing. We were all miserable and got into the tequila right down to the worm. Looking back on it, I believe that I was not truly radical until that point.

The strange thing is, we didn't even think of burning the Beta Sig house at the time. We got drunk and wrapped the half-finished quilt around the four of us and tried to dance but one or the other would keep falling and drag everyone down in a heap. We got out Virginia Woolf's *The Waves* and read those beautiful italicized chapters about the ocean. We talked about all the great women who had killed themselves, from Ophelia on down, including Diane Arbus and Sylvia Plath, and a few others like Djuna Barnes, who no one knew whether they killed themselves or were still living in some kind of terrible obscurity. We vowed never to be old women with bitter histories and that we would all take our own lives when the time came, and we fell asleep more or less involuntarily and more or less at the same time.

It was the next morning when we were making the eight-egg omelet that Jennifer said it required an Action.

—We talk and talk and talk, she said. She held her arms kind of stuck out like an osprey and hovered over Rebecca, who was working the omelet off the bottom of the pan because the Teflon was half rusted away and it would stick.

—We have our Dialectic, Jennifer went on. It includes women

and blacks and the Third World and the Bag People and the Migrant Workers, and we write our hearts out in articles for a paper nobody reads. Meanwhile the educational Machine turns out little Xeroxed Clones for the medico-legal-investment Machine, which sustains the political-military Machine that oppresses people from birth so that they're not even human. And one after another there in the corner of a fraternity basement behind the pool table, four males stick themselves into a person who they have gotten so drunk that she doesn't even know what is happening and when they cross-examine her in court she can't remember details and she breaks down and cries. And what do we do? We major in History, which is a chronicle of greed and injustice. We major in Anthropology, which is our own little mirror of myopic ethnocentricity. We major in Political Science, which is the applied science of oppression. And English, which is the Primary World Language of imperialist domination. We write papers the way we're told to and condition ourselves like experimental rodents to get the As, which are the little pup tents that protect us from reality.

—The omelet is done, Rebecca announced. Sit down and eat before it gets too cold.

It was then, sitting with the quilt over my lap and drowning my hangover in black coffee, that I saw it like a vision. A also meant Action. We would start the fire in the basement and the famous circular staircase of Beta Sig would do the rest. It would promote the fire like a chimney. We would begin at the old wooden pool table and purify the region of the Atrocity. We would get in there, somehow, before vacation was over. We would pile up the old mattresses that the brothers fucked women on without even bothering to ask their names, we would splash them with kerosene and we would light them. The house would be To The Ground by the time the volunteer fire department got their trousers on and slid down their Vaseline-coated pole.

We quartered the omelet and poured the grated Gruyère over it and ate it. We had to figure how to get in, and of course there were brothers living there over vacation. Not many, but some. We didn't

6

want any immolations, even of men. The human body is priceless to women, beyond concepts and ideologies, no matter who happens to be inside. It is the principal reason for which we live.

Of course, private property is another question. It is on the far side of the Dialectic and totally expendable. But how could four known feminists get into a Dartmouth fraternity carrying a bottle of kerosene and not get caught?

We formed the plan that Christmas morning with the icicles lengthening outside the window like the bars of a cage, darkening the sunlight but also refracting it into rainbows that crept slowly across our beautiful quilt, which was nearly done and hanging on the wall over the couch. We put the kerosene into the tequila bottle. The worm, which was still at the bottom, turned a nauseous green and curled up like a doughnut when the kerosene hit it. The bottle sat on the shelf till January third.

It was the coldest day so far. We put a thousand sweaters and tights on and many pairs of socks. We put the bottle in a green book bag, along with the page from the Freshman Green Book that had the rape victim's picture on it. She had a small round face and had been president of the Latin Club all four years at Newton High. Plus she was Valedictorian. All those As and they didn't protect her from a thing.

We walked over to the athletic complex across from Beta Sig and waited at the entrance to the indoor tennis courts where we could see the house. We didn't say anything, just stomped our feet and breathed steam and squinted at the sunlight over the crusty snow. Around ten, the brothers came out and got into this big station wagon, which scrunched down almost to the ground from their collective weight. Jenny went to the pay phone and called the house.

—I let it ring fifteen times, she said. There's no one in there.

Our feet made that extreme squeaking sound from the dry snow, but no one heard it because no one was around. No cars, no people. It was perfect. Just for a moment, no one existed in Hanover but us, as in those dreams when you're the only person in the world.

We took the path up to the Copley dorms and cut sharply into

7

the frat from the back door. There was a stuffed female moose with a cigar in her mouth facing us as we came in. There was a pile of cross-country and downhill skis and a number of bikes piled on each other like skeletons. And there was the door into the basement.

I have to say that at this point I was scared. Not scared of getting caught, but that it was a moment of truth and I might fail, more scared about the strange courage I was feeling than by anything outside. It was like getting another personality, someone much bigger and braver than I was entering my body so I didn't even exist, just this other being who was neither a man nor a woman and who scared me even while it gave me the courage to go on. One moment I was a normal student and my duty was to write each of my parents occasionally at their separate addresses and to get As in everything I took. The next moment I was a terrorist carrying a bomb. It was like being one of those snails who leave their shells so that a totally different animal can take over, like a Hermit Crab.

The Hermit Crab had taken over when the Divorce came and it inhabited my shell for nine months, then gave it back. I don't know where I was during that period. I don't know where the regular Snail goes when the Hermit Crab comes in. But when I entered the Beta Sig house carrying the green book bag with the kerosene bottle, there was my shell with my ridiculous name on it, Penguin Solstice, but now there was someone else inside.

—*Penguin*, Rebecca said. *Down here.*

We went down and Michelle turned her flashlight on the room. It smelled of beer-on-mattresses, which is the worst. I thought those mattresses would be too wet to ignite, even with the kerosene. They carried the accumulation of decades of unthinking vice: whiskey and sweat and sperm. They weighed more than three tons apiece. We dragged them one at a time, each taking a corner, and built them into a pyramid over the Beta Sig pool table. I wasn't scared because I wasn't there. The Hermit Crab had come into the shell and was acting with a strange indifference of its own.

—Do you know what has been done to women on these mattresses? Michelle whispered.

It was a rhetorical question. She meant that women have been brought here and have been made drunk so they weren't even human. That they have vacated themselves so things could be stuck into their bodies while they were oblivious or asleep. They have awakened not knowing whose semen was congealing inside them or who or where they were.

I thought of the underground sanctuary of Eleusis where by torchlight a priestess had held up a single grain of wheat to commemorate birth and springtime and regeneration. And then I thought of how women were sacrificed like ewes here on Homecoming weekend and Houseparties weekend and particularly in the blood rut of Winter Carnival when this floor of mattresses would witness another gang rape consecrated by the pig-men whose fathers owned not only this country but the Third World and who would come to possess it themselves when their time came.

I thought: *The generations of men violate the people of the earth one after the other exactly the same way that the Beta Sig brothers lined up with their erections before the involuntary nakedness of the little Valedictorian in the Freshman Yearbook.*

I took the bottle out and sprayed it on one mattress. The kerosene smell drowned out the other smells. I gave the bottle to Jenny, who poured and passed it on. It was the same bottle we had drunk from on Christmas Eve when Michelle told us the brothers had been acquitted of their crime.

My eyes adjusted to the pit darkness and I looked around. The walls were covered with paddles that had the brothers' names on them and that they used in their homosexual rites. I pulled two of the paddles off the wall and added them to the pile, then more, a whole armload, and Michelle added an armload. We had found the symbols of the sodomitic male power structure who in this secret poolroom lowered their trousers for each other and assumed attitudes of submission in a profane mockery of the relations between man and woman. The paddles were wood and they would smell wonderful as they burned, just like a campfire in the night.

We had put a long string in the bottle for a fuse. We pulled it out

9

and dumped the worm into the pile. We stretched the wet string out over the floor and lit a match. Our four hands held the match at the same time and lit the end of the string in absolute solidarity. I felt something come into those hands that would connect us forever with the hands of Trotsky and Kropotkin, of Fidel Castro and Daniel Ortega, and with the slim suicidal hand of Virginia Woolf.

For all the Anarchists, all the Revolutionaries, all the great women who understood everything from the beginning but were not permitted to act, we touched the match to the string and ran upstairs. We composed ourselves for a second in the mirror underneath the moose. We pulled the cigar out of her mouth and threw it down the cellar stairway right where the fire was beginning to take root.

2

I wish I could say that I had a perfect physical appearance. But the other reason I am called Penguin is that I have this somewhat livid birthmark stain across my shoulders and upper back that was so dark in infancy that Richard said I looked like a penguin when he tried to stand me up. Over the years this has lightened, but in my adolescence it kept me in T-shirts and basically kept me away from the beach. On the Cape I was a sailor and rower but I only spent time in the sun when I was alone. My purple back tans faster than my white front so that after a while I look like two different races that have been bonded together by glue.

My neck is similar. It looks at first like something is wrong with the mirror. It makes a line from the right corner of my chin down into whatever garment I have on to join with the body mark, like one of those geological veins where one kind of dark rock cuts into the lighter rock around it. Dikes. For this reason all photos of me from ages eight to fifteen show only my left side, which I would turn like a sunflower toward any cameras that happened to come around. Then I stopped caring. The picture in the Morrelsex Quill shows the mark clearly. The school photographer called me specially to ask if I wanted it "burned out." We could make you appear absolutely natural, the photographer said. He was a world-class lecher. I told him no. Then I found myself crying on the way back to the dorm. I wish I could reverse myself in time and tell him to make it darker so it would really show.

I used to think I had been given somebody else's body, but it's now come to be more or less who I am. If I were asked to draw a picture of myself I might even forget to include any marks at all. Given enough time people get used to anything. There was one time, though, before I established my comradeship with Bondo, that he'd actually tried to kiss me. "Look at me, Bondo," I'd told him. "I'm not an attractive person. I'm disfigured." I pointed the right side of my chin at him like a weapon. I also tilted my face up a bit because at the right angle my profile is not inconceivable to look at if the light is behind me and you can't see the details of the skin. "There is no excellent beauty that hath not some strangeness in the proportion," Bondo had said. I wish I knew where he ever came up with that.

I also wish I could say that the Beta Sig house burned to the ground. I have had many dreams in which it stood there like a flaming wedding cake and in it the brothers were burning in their beds.

We tromped back through the snow to 36 Chestnut and sat down like four women simply opening a bottle of red wine. Michelle unwrapped the green-and-white scarf from her neck the way you would undo a bandage, slowly, as if it covered a layer of burned skin.

We heard the sirens and we said, They're putting their trousers on. They're sliding down the pole.

It was all on the TV news from Concord. There was the Dean of Students standing in front of the Beta Sig house in a little Tyrolean hat. His breath made clouds that seemed to come right out of the screen into the living room like a trompe the eye painting by René Magritte.

—Attempted arson, the Dean said on the TV. Probably a rejected pledge. Ten years ago someone tried to ignite the Deke house when they didn't pledge him, then tried to set himself on fire. The boys take these things awfully seriously. It's common in the sophomore year.

A cop came up and the Dean shook the cop's hand and smiled.

—It won't be hard to find him, the Dean said.

Then a fireman came up, dressed in yellow like a man just off an ocean-going yacht.

—We contained the blaze, said the fireman. The cellar took the worst of it, and there was smoke damage. But the building is structurally intact. And what's best, there were no injuries. Nobody was home.

The news switched to Littleton, where a three-hundred-pound black bear had walked down the main street of town. The bruin threw residents of that small community into a temporary panic...

We had failed. We had tried to act, we had actually acted, but it didn't matter. Intentionality was nothing. What counted was Results. The Beta Sig house was still there and the brothers would be swarming all over it fixing it up and the pile of charred mattresses and the blackened pool table would be out in the snow waiting to be hauled off and replaced. We needed new ones anyway, the brothers would say.

The students came back from vacation. Winter term began. I was taking Sociobiology of Humans and Anthro 12, which is Shamanism and Witchcraft. I passed the freshman woman who had been raped, walking right in the center of the Green with a couple of huge textbooks in her arms as if nothing at all had happened.

You don't know, I thought. *You don't know what we almost accomplished in your name.*

Of course the *Digest* carried the whole story as it went on. The cops went through the list of Beta Sig rejects and questioned them. Then they started on the left wing and the radicals, antifraternity people, which wasn't a great number, so pretty soon they got to the *Id* staff and questioned all the men. The men. They didn't even interrogate Michelle, who was the Editor. Even though it was a Fraternity, where a person had been raped, they did NOT QUESTION ANY WOMEN.

In their eyes we were incapable even of the action that was absolutely inevitable for us. If you ever want to accomplish an act of terrorism get a woman to do it. No one will suspect her even if she succeeds.

We had let Bondo in on the secret, even though he was a male. Michelle, Bondo, Rebecca, Jenny, and I had a beer at the Dungeon and talked it over. What good was a political action if no one knew who had committed it? It was absurd to sit around being anonymous when the whole point was to show Justice could still be carried out when the judicial system had failed. It took us less than five minutes to decide to end the investigation and confess. We put on the yuppiest clothes possible and we walked into the Hanover police station and turned ourselves in. I wasn't in the least scared and I was the spokesperson for us all.

—We set the fire at Beta Sig and we did it because one of our own kind had been violated in that basement and the System did not provide for her anything that faintly resembled equal protection under the Law.

The minute I started talking a large-eared woman came out of nowhere in a police uniform with a navy blue necktie and started to take notes on everything we said.

In about three hours Jennifer's father had one of his lawyers flown in from New York. He said we were not to say anything to anyone. We told him we weren't worried, that we'd intended to burn the Beta Sig house to the ground, that we didn't regret anything, had nothing to hide, and that we were willing to suffer all consequences. Which obviously wasn't what the lawyer wanted to hear.

—You could earn sentences in a women's prison, he said. You can imagine what your father is thinking about this.

All of which was addressed specifically to Jennifer, as if the rest of us didn't exist. I could see he was thinking of ways to detach Jenny from the group, that maybe he'd been instructed to think that way. Jenny could see that too.

—We're all in this together, Jenny said. I support what Penguin said down to the letter.

I ran forward and hugged her. We all kept our arms around each other while the Corporate Attorney stood outside the circle, waiting for us to get done.

The worst of it was the three-month wait for the Trial. Plus, we were suspended from campus and couldn't even live in our own home because it was controlled housing, which was an example of guilty before proven innocent if I ever saw one.

We went to Jennifer's summer place on Lake Winnipesaukee and kept ourselves warm at the huge granite fireplace while we read to each other from Dostoevsky and Kafka and a book called *Lives of the Great Anarchists*, which Jenny's father amazingly had in his library.

Mr. Kaiser in fact came up one weekend and talked to us. Jen had expected complete psychological and every other kind of disinheritance, but he took us out to dinner and asked us all kinds of questions as if he was truly concerned. The Dialectic would be easier if all capitalists were assholes but sometimes even when you see one you can't tell. Mr. Kaiser drove us back to the lodge and we all stood there in the snow stamping our feet and looking up at the stars, which there were so many of that the entire sky looked white from starlight with no dark matter anywhere in sight.

Mr. Kaiser told Jenny he was proud of her and he even looked at the rest of us, Rebecca and Michelle and me, as if he were half proud of us also, though not for the same thing. Maybe for supporting Jenny.

Then there were *my* parents, which was another matter. Katherine, my mother, lives in Brussels with her second husband, who is in the importation of Furs. I didn't want to paint her the entire picture, especially with the husband who is conservative, to put it mildly, so I had written something vague about dropping out of school for a while and let it go.

My father is Richard Solstice, the sculptor. He comes into the story later in a large way, and of course earlier, but for now you just have to picture what he looks like so you can see him. Richard is a physically gigantic man whose head looks like he had sculpted it himself in some kind of fleshlike metal that will not change for a thousand years. He's fifty-five. His face is covered with planes or facets that might have been cut with a chisel working against aluminum plate, and the skin is like raw metal too. You are afraid you might cut yourself if you ever touched the skin of that face, and it is not from aging because it has been that way since I can remember. It wasn't even softened when he had his beard. The beard had facets and planes in the same way. Richard inherited from me the shell-like exterior in which he hides the more vulnerable parts. If I try to think of myself not as his daughter but as a woman meeting him for the first time, the way Dorothy Dvorjak must have, I would think: this man is handsomer than anyone I've ever seen, but because he is impenetrable I am not going to be attracted to him, not in the least.

Only Dorothy must have seen it some other way, since she was allegedly in love with him and they were living together and the word "marriage" had begun to creep onto the scene. He had also sent me a photo of a wiry stainless steel female sculpture that was in all probability her. I had never of course met her but I knew the type.

I've always called my father Richard. And that's how I wrote to him on February first. I said, basically, Dear Richard, we are all suspended. We tried to burn down a Fraternity because someone was raped there and they got acquitted on technicalities. We have our own trial coming up in April and we are all waiting in a big house outside of Laconia.

Love. Penguin.

He sent five hundred dollars and an exhibition catalog from the Hirshhorn Museum in Washington and a note. Not a letter of explanation but an announcement, as if there were nothing that could be done. He was going to marry Dorothy Dvorjak in early June. No date.

The only thing wrong with the Kaisers' lodge on Lake Winnipesaukee was that the plumbing was shut off and Mr. Kaiser had put the liquor cabinet off limits. I read this letter and opened the cabinet and unscrewed a bottle of Jack Daniels. I drank a glass of it without ice or water and went out and threw up into the snow.

16

At the Grafton County Superior Court we entered a plea of Guilty and received the prearranged six months' sentence to the Women's Reformatory in Concord. It was a plea bargain. Like us, the sentence was also suspended. I will spare details of our bourgeois dialogue with the judge. He asked us if we "felt contrition" and "recognized the irresponsibility of our actions" and we basically said no.

Michelle answered that our action was inseparable from the rape of Jesse Greenfield, that whatever we had done had to be looked at in light of the whole situation and in terms of a Justice higher than the New Hampshire statutes.

—The law of the land separates each charge and treats it individually, said the judge.

Michelle was eloquent. She was a Poli Sci major and she had studied people like Burke and Paine.

—All human actions are interrelated, Michelle said. The crime was against us as women, not against you as a man or the State as an impersonal entity.

—You are speaking of vigilante justice, young lady, the most primitive form of revenge. A world where the ruthless and powerful dominate the weak.

—Do you mean we are the ruthless and powerful? Michelle asked. That poor victim Jesse Greenfield is the ruthless and powerful? And the Beta Sig brothers are the weak?

I thought Michelle was going to get the sentences unsuspended on the spot. I pictured the four of us in blue denim jogging around the prison courtyard. I pictured Richard in the visiting room handing me cigarettes and candy bars under the barrier.

I was also proud, and I stood straight beside Jennifer and Rebecca as Michelle spoke for us to the judge. Mr. Kaiser's attorney was sitting down beside Michelle looking as if he'd eaten one of those clams with salmonella. He'd spent half his spring in New Hampshire and arranged everything perfectly. He'd accomplished his mission in keeping Mortimer Kaiser's daughter out of jail, plus he had not even had to sacrifice her friends, which he would of course gladly have done, if it had come to that.

And now these girls were displaying their gratitude by badgering a judge who looked ready to go back on the whole deal and send them up the river. The Merrill Lynch lawyer stretched the expansion band of his watch right to the breaking point and let it crack back against his wrist. I thought the bone would shatter on the spot but the judge only looked down at him and cleared his throat.

The courtroom windows were shuttered on the lower half but through the higher panes I could see the treetops of Lebanon, New Hampshire, which were just coming into full leaf. A flock of black starlings were fluttering nervously in the upper branches, pecking at each other, pushing each other around, making little flights into the air to land right on top of another bird. It was probably their version of an orgy, the orgy of spring, which we were decidedly not participating in this year.

We were conscious of everything we did, what it meant, how it fit into the Dialectic. We were the terrorist wing of the upper middle class, and I kept a picture of Yassir Arafat on my mirror, yet even in our moment of declaration it wasn't quite right. Watching the starlings in their sex-and-decadence rites, I just wanted to be unconscious again. I wanted to be a human being, free and alone. I wanted to get the usurper out of my shell and welcome the basic Snail back, its eyes on long stalks, its body leaving a simple trail of slime.

When the judge finished with Michelle, he turned to me.

—Do you recognize the severity of your crime?

—Yes, I said. But we had intended to do a better job.

—Do you realize the sanctity of Private Property in a free and democratic state?

—We didn't know Private Property had anything to do with a democratic state. We don't believe in the violation of people's bodies against their will.

The judge leaned over his podium as if he were going to crawl forth, robed, into the courtroom like a huge black slug.

—Perhaps you weren't listening when I explained the Law.

Another case, which may have been heard already in this judicial system, has no bearing whatsoever on this charge. You are accused of the felonies of Criminal Trespass, Arson, and the Conspiracy to Commit Arson. You have pled guilty. These are crimes that you yourself have agreed on through the system of representative legislation.

—There is also something called Justice, I said, echoing Michelle. It takes over where Law leaves off. I don't see how an action of any kind is separable from any other action. That's what the Gaia Hypothesis means. The world is a network. Our act was related to the fraternity's. We did what we had to in the freedom of our beliefs, I said, and we are willing to take the consequences.

Rebecca and Jenny didn't even have to speak. The judge read us our sentences. He paused to let them sink in, then said *suspended*. We sat down together and we held hands for a minute, not hugging, because in a way it wasn't right. We had a sharp lawyer and he had gotten us off, just like the brothers of Beta Sig.

The judge picked his robe up like a black skirt and walked out through a doorway in the oak paneling that I hadn't even noticed. It seemed as if his body passed right through the wall.

Back in Hanover, the Dartmouth College Committee on Student Standards was altogether different. The judge was played by the same Dean of Students who we had seen on TV. The lawyers were prelaw seniors, the courtroom was in the cellar of Snidle Hall, where they stored stuff for the Outing Club. There were canoes lying around the floor on either side of the seating, and mildewing canvas shelters that hadn't been used since the nineteenth century.

There was another moose, also, only this one was a male with ten-foot antlers and with dark reddish eyes that looked like they had been turned around so they faced the inside of its head. He made me think how acceptable Death will be when it arrives. The dead have this tremendous patience because they are not waiting for anything in the future. They are already there. The moose could care less about the Dialectic and the Contradictions. Even the worst thing in the world, even if it was the moose's spouse over there in the Beta Sig house that got incinerated, if you are dead it has already happened and you are no longer eligible to be hurt.

I thought, That's what a real judge would be like. That moose. He would sit there with his head sticking out and the rest of his body invisible behind the wall, and he'd just grow wiser and wiser and would never pass judgment on anyone but himself.

The prosecuting student was a fraternity man, and asked for Expulsion right away. The defending student, who had been assigned to us, just asked for suspension, but he was a fraternity man too, and you could see that he wanted the Final Solution as well. So did the Dean, which you could see from the beginning. There was half the Beta Sig brotherhood in the room and only a few women and some hangers-on from the *Id* staff, which had mostly disbanded since they lost Michelle.

We had acted for the women of Dartmouth and for women everywhere who are taken and fucked in the dark with rags stuffed into their mouths so they cannot cry out. Now we were here in this phony courtroom getting expelled and there wasn't anyone to back us up, there wasn't anyone to say that was the way fascist governments everywhere handle dissent, to silence it, censor it, scapegoat it out of the community. In the back row, their clothes dark as Nazis, the editors of the *Digest* waited in quiet supercilious glee.

The Dean passed the sentence of Expulsion and the *Digest* staff applauded. The handful of women with black armbands walked out one door and the Beta Sigs out the other. The Superior Court had freed us and the kangaroo court gave us what amounted to its Death Penalty. There was a thousand feet of no-man's-land around us when we walked home from Snidle Hall across a campus we were never supposed to see again.

3

We broke up the household and actually got some money back from the bursar for not having completed the term. Jennifer was going up to the lodge again for the summer and to figure out what would happen after that. Michelle was taking a Vista job in Arizona on an Indian reservation. Rebecca's family, like mine, had a summer house on Cape Cod, so we decided to travel down from Hanover together.

We of course missed the six A.M. bus and had to sit in the lobby of the Hanover Inn watching the old grads grope their way into chairs made from the skins of poached animals and unfurl their *Wall Street Journals* to see how their fortunes were accumulating. The eight o'clock bus pulled up to the doorway of the Inn a half hour late. The time mattered because we had to change buses in Boston and even from there it was a long ride to Squid Harbor. Three or four women my age got off, looking groggy from having slept in a bus seat and also looking like blind dates coming up to spend the weekend in the frats. Good luck, I wished them. God be with you. You may never be the same again.

The driver loaded the two boxes containing everything I owned into this hole in the underbelly of the bus. The side of the bus said *Vermont Transit* but his hat and shirt had embroidered greyhounds on them, and beneath the lettering on the side of the vehicle I could make out the faint shadow of a running dog. Things seem normal at first, I thought, then you begin to sense the connections beneath the obvious that are the synchronistic mysteries of the world. The

21

relation between Vermont Transit and Greyhound is one of these, and there are many more. Things are linked together, just like the wires under the electric train Richard built for me one Christmas back when we were a family. The train had a little village with lighted houses plus street lamps and a crossing gate that flashed and lowered and stayed down while the train went past. It had a white dairy car that stopped at a green platform way over on the other side of the layout, much further than I could reach, but if I pushed a certain button a man would come out and deliver eleven cans of milk and then he'd close the door and the train would leave. All that winter—which must have been 1976—it had seemed like a miracle to control from such a distance the dairy man and the crossing gate and the tiny red moving buckets of the coal elevator. But one spring evening after supper I lifted the canvas skirt under the train table and looked in and saw the webs of wire that linked everything together. It wasn't magical after that, and the train began to bore me within a week.

It was the only time I saw Richard sad that I hadn't been a son.

The whole process had worked out in a crazy way. I still saw the world as an illusion, like the top of the train layout, with the appearance of individual humans and animals and houses. But I knew, also, there were invisible structures under the ground that connect us to things and people we don't even know we know. If I got the train now, the first thing I'd do would be crawl under the table and expose those wires, which contain the subplot of the world.

The wires go into the future, too. I knew the Fire was going to connect to something and I knew no matter how far we might get scattered in time and space—Jennifer, Rebecca, me, Bondo, Michelle—we would stay linked by the grid of wiring under the electric train that once puffed innocently around its oval track.

I took up cigarettes on that bus ride with Rebecca Crowell down Interstate 93. We climbed and descended through the New Hampshire hills. The little towns inhabiting the valleys swam in a chlorophyll-colored haze surrounding everything that was green:

patches of forest, tree-shaded houses, the green geometrical squares of farms.

It was good just to sit next to Rebecca in silence. There had been so many words—days and weeks and months of them, in the *Id*, in the *Digest*, in the courtroom and in the interminable kitchen dialectics at 36 Chestnut and in Jen's summer house up at Lake Winnipesaukee. The words were like individual tree leaves or blades of grass, but they added up to this ocean of undifferentiated green that you could drown in exactly the way our little bus drowned in the Connecticut Valley as we rode south. I vowed to myself that when I reached Squid Harbor I would not say anything for at least a week.

Every once in a while a church steeple would stick up through the haze as a sharp definite point that organized all that green randomness and made sense of the landscape in the way our own Action had made sense, a definite point that couldn't get blurred or erased, a fact of history, a fire.

—We'll never get into another college with this on our record, Rebecca said.

She pulled a pack of Merits out of her bag and tore off the gold band and the cellophane and pried loose the first cigarette, lit it, and offered it to me. I took a deep inhale. It felt unhealthy and pleasant and rawly ticklish inside. It seemed like the right thing to do at the right time.

—What do you think? Rebecca asked. She pushed her face close to mine when she talked, with the sharp beak, the black nuthatch eyes.

—I like it. I think I'm going to be a smoker from now on.

—No. I mean about the future.

I didn't think anything at all about the future. It was a blank stage in which Richard Solstice and Dorothy Dvorjak walked out in wedding costumes, made this elaborate bow to each other, then disappeared.

—I've had it with formal education, I told her. It does the exact opposite of what it's supposed to. It's supposed to make you think for yourself. You read these original thinkers like Foucault and Derrida. You learn to deconstruct things and put them back together again, and look what happens. You get out and you never have another idea as long as you live. They don't teach you original thought in college, they teach you obedience to someone else's original thought. That's their little secret, they make you think you are learning to think when you are actually learning to obey. Look at your father. He was a Rhodes Scholar. He joined the First National or whatever bank it was, and he will die in the First National Bank. He read Plato, too, once upon a time, and Locke and Marx.

—Probably not Marx, Rebecca said.

—And look at my father. He never graduated from anywhere. He dropped out of high school and got thrown out of the Korean War and dropped out of NYU and then dropped out of art school. But his mind is his. He is original and he thinks.

—That's your problem, too, Rebecca said. You think too much.

She leaned her head on my shoulder and slept for a half hour, which felt good. I was a little drowsy myself. Maybe love is an answer, I thought, love of anything, it didn't matter whom, just so you could get rid of yourself. Then I remembered Richard and Dorothy and I woke up.

In Boston we had to change buses. We waited an hour in those black chairs that have a small coin-op TV attached to them. Rebecca actually put a quarter in her TV and watched it. She must have wanted to tune everything out. She was scared to face a tribunal of parents who didn't know anything but Success and couldn't interpret anything else except as Failure. Especially attempted arson, criminal trespass, conspiracy, and nonreproductive sexual experimentation. Those words were not in the Crowell family thesaurus.

Besides the few travelers there were about fifty homeless men in the bus station and a few homeless women, too. They were like me in that they had bags and parcels containing all their belongings, but I had a home to go to, a home of sorts anyway, though I didn't exactly know what to expect of the new occupants. I tried to imagine

24

my father's wedding to Dorothy Dvorjak taking place in a bleak justice of the peace's office that looked like a police station. I couldn't form the picture properly. I could see them sleeping together with no problem, and riding surfboards or whatever they did in Jamaica, but marrying would not come into focus.

This one homeless old derelict shuffled across the bus terminal with some kind of blanket over his shoulders like a robe, the blanket he probably slept in and went to the bathroom in and wrapped around his body when he went begging outside the station. When he came by, though, I saw that he *wasn't* old. He was maybe thirty-five or forty at the most, only his eyes looked as if there was nobody in there, like he'd vacated his shell at some point, like me, only nothing had come in to take his place.

Which is what the Crowells of this society do to you if you don't succeed, if you don't get a job and struggle with it until some point when you and the job perish simultaneously. That's what they were doing on the top floors of those high-rise bank buildings, they were keeping watch over the city like a kid looking down on her electric railroad, making sure that there was at least one derelict for every success. Most people lived in ordinary houses, which was all right, but some lived in elaborate dwellings with eight rooms for every person and for every one of those rooms there was a person trudging their bag or shopping cart along the street.

It wasn't the Sixties anymore either, when they had a counterculture and you had the option of being a Hippie Freak. This guy walking across the terminal and now stopping to ask another derelict for a quarter might have been a Hippie in his time, then when the Hippies all dressed up and became stockbrokers he might have chosen not to change. It was like The Last Judgment by Michelangelo. God came down and He said, The following Hippies will become stockbrokers, like Jerry Rubin, and I'm sorry but these other Hippies have to become derelicts and finish out their lives in the bus terminal.

The underground connections are not only wires but tubes draining off one person to feed another so that there is always an equal balance of injustice. If you look closely enough you can see the tubes leading right down through the air of Boston from the top of the Prudential Center to each individual derelict asleep on his heating grate. Now women are invited to join in, too, so there can be women bank presidents and women derelicts, and the natural equality that has bound women to each other for centuries can shrivel and drop away in the competition like an umbilicus. *You think too much,* I could hear Rebecca saying. Which is what men have always told women and when there weren't men around, the women have said it to themselves. I thought a lot. I thought my head off. This world is not going to change if we don't think.

On the bus for Hyannis, Rebecca was totally awake.

—I decided what to do with myself, Rebecca said. I'm going to apply to the U of Mass.

—All that time I thought you were watching TV, and it turns out you were deciding on your life.

—That's the only time I can make decisions, Rebecca said, when I'm watching *Search for Tomorrow.*

—Anyway, I thought we couldn't get in anywhere. With our records.

—You can always get into your State University, Rebecca said. It's home. U-Mass. When you have to go there, they have to take you in. Besides, I can't see living with those people for longer than a week. Even if they make me live in an institution, I'll go to classes with a keeper.

—Hey, that's something, I said. Maybe we can get ourselves declared insane. Then they'd have to take us back because we're not responsible for our actions. Plus equal opportunity. The insane are a minority.

—I'm not so sure about that, Rebecca said.

Rebecca was always the weakest of us, and without Jenny beside her, Jenny her old boatmate and roommate and God knows what else, she often tended to fold up.

—Do you think you'll be seeing Jenny soon? I asked her.

—Sooner or later, she said. It doesn't matter.

Her tone surprised me.

—You seem inseparable, I said.

—We're all inseparable. I'm as inseparable from you as I am from her. Maybe more.

She spoke with her eyes so close to mine that I couldn't focus and each of my eyes was forced to look into each of hers. Her face had somehow softened as if the bones had melted inside it. This must be the woman Jennifer sees, I thought, not the nuthatch-eyed, sharp-nosed Rebecca, but someone made of a pliant material like a rubber mirror that could be changed to any shape you want.

She was also offering something that I didn't know how to want to take.

—Comrades, I said. Comrades and co-conspirators. Partners in terror to the end.

—You know what Jen says about you, Penguin. She says you have no feelings. You think but you don't feel. And not to feel is a kind of stupidity itself.

—I don't want to make any mistakes, I said. Women go through life with their hearts leading them around by the nose. We go from one bad situation to another. We're not going to evolve unless we change.

I searched around my mind to see if I felt anything. I disliked Fritz and my mother, I hated the Beta Sigs and Dorothy Dvorjak, whom I didn't even know. Those were certainly feelings. And for Michelle and Jen and Rebecca I felt a deep revolutionary bond.

—Of course I feel, I said. If we'd been really sentenced back there in the courtroom I would have gone off to prison with you and Shelly and Jen for the rest of our lives. Happily. As long as you guys were there.

—That's not what I mean, Rebecca said. You don't even know what I'm talking about. It's like you have something missing, Penguin. You're like a *man*.

With that ultimate insult she stood up and pushed past me to get out in the aisle. She struggled to lift her heavy backpack from the

27

overhead and walked to the rear seat. Some Hispanic-looking boys were back there smoking a joint. She sat down among them with the backpack on her lap, looking straight ahead past me out the windshield of the bus. The boys passed the joint to each other right in front of her face, but she didn't even blink.

The bus swung off Route 3 to make its stop in Plymouth. I would have gone back to her but I didn't want a scene among those kids. When we stopped in front of the Wendy's in the Pilgrim Mall, Rebecca hoisted up her pack and marched right out of the door. I opened the window.

—*Rebecca,* I shouted over the heads of a hundred people with suitcases. *Wait!*

She heard me, but she didn't turn her head. The bus clogged with people stuffing their luggage into the overhead racks and taking their coats off, and I let her go. Maybe she was right about not feeling. Maybe my heart had grown numb from too much ideology. I tried to find it in my chest, but I couldn't recall what side it was on, right or left, so I gave up.

The bus pulled out of Plymouth into the strange desert country approaching the Cape Cod Canal. My mind felt like a sand dune: billions of grains of basically unconnected minerals. Maybe I had misunderstood everything. I thought we were four classmates engaged in a political struggle for the freedom and equality of women at Dartmouth and in the World. I thought we were an oppressed minority in a conservative, male-dominated college that manufactured leaders for the multinational phallocracy.

I was completely innocent and yet I felt I had eaten the Apple. I remembered that painting from Western Art where they get expelled from the Garden of Eden and the look on Eve's face as she covers her eyes out of shame. That's what I felt like as the bus circled the traffic rotary just before the bridge. I was being expelled from Paradise into a country where there were no maps and nobody had gone before. But Eve and Adam were still a married couple. They had themselves anyway, whereas I all of a sudden was alone.

4

As the bus peaked at the highest point of the Sagamore bridge I could see the canal extending out on both sides and beyond that, the open waters of the Atlantic. A couple of sailboats were passing right under us, and a big freighter or tanker called the *Aphrodite* was heading up towards Boston, followed by a train of gulls that were drawn along behind it as if on kite strings.

It had always meant freedom, crossing the Cape Cod Canal. It meant the freedom of getting out of school, plus as we used to drive up and over the big bridge I would always hope for a truce between my parents, as if their struggle had been a profession that had its vacations just like any other job. Even in the midst of the separation we managed to come here as a family, and when we crossed the canal it was always summer again and anything had seemed possible, even the reconciliation that never quite took place.

After supper, Katherine and Richard would walk down to the pier and try to hold hands. I'd be up in the loft where they both slept, watching from the skylight over their bed. They would move closer to each other and try looking at the sunset. I would squeeze my fists between my knees and pray for them to grab hold of one another and start to kiss. Kissing seemed like a nauseating practice at the time, but for them I would have made an exception. Sometimes they even did. Then something would happen and they would return with their faces set into two grim basalt masks. Richard would stalk out to his studio while Katherine would lock herself into her room and type. Once I saw what she wrote after one of those romantic evenings at Squid Harbor. I uncrumpled a page from the wastebasket and looked. It was composed of totally random characters, nothing but consonants, formed into words like *bvftpq* all the way down the page.

Hyannis. West Yarmouth. Chatham. Orleans. Brewster. Our driver called out the towns as the Greyhound crept eastward along the bicep and around the sharp elbow of the Cape. The low sun illuminated the little tourist cabins along Route 28 with a quality of light that made them look painted by someone like Edward Hopper, their shadows forming mysterious geometric shapes in which anything could be lost. The cabins were anachronisms that hadn't quite been replaced by motels. Around their hibachis and barbecue grills the tourist families gathered to listen to the Red Sox and drink beer and eat soft-shelled crabs. These things were eternal and seasonal, like the migration of birds. They were inside me. I was eating or playing frisbee with them and riding the Greyhound home at the same time.

The bus stopped at the Red Heron Tavern, a couple of miles from Squid Harbor. I tried to call Richard, but he wasn't there. He was probably drinking somewhere with Dorothy Dvorjak, since the Squid Harbor cocktail hour lasted from three in the afternoon to right around midnight. It was the way Richard had lived his summers ever since I could remember. He'd get up at sunrise and spend the whole morning in the gray-shingled studio up behind the cottage, the arc welder hissing and the sparks rising like the Fourth of July. I wasn't supposed to look, but I'd hide under the window or peer through the crack in the big barnlike door and stare at the arc's white center until my eyes burned. The sparks started off as fire but they'd change in the air and land on the floor as red embers, then cool to little metal chunks like meteorites. Then I'd be allowed in to gather them in a coffee can and add them to my collection. I pretended I had been on the Apollo mission and was bringing back little samples of the moon.

Richard would pick up chunks of still glowing metal for me with his tongs. He used to compare them to the stars, which started as white dwarfs and then became red giants and ended as cold dark hulks floating around in space. We only see the living ones, he'd say, but think how many dead ones are up there, stars nobody can see because they've lost their light.

And of course later on, in the Sun and Planets class we took for the Science distrib, they did tell us about dark matter and how it outweighed by thousands all the visible stars. Richard couldn't have known that at the time, but he was an artist and he knew light and dark had to balance somehow so he invented something that turned out to be actually true. I don't think either of us had heard of black holes at the time. Even if black holes didn't exist people would have had to invent them. We need something that is the complete opposite of light.

I can remember during the litigation praying to God that Richard would get Squid Harbor even if my mother made off with everything else, which she basically did. She would have got it, too, except she was going away to live in Belgium forever. She was already involved with Fritz Sprauter, who as I said is this plutocrat living off the trapping and marketing of endangered species. If Katherine and Fritz had ended up with the cottage it would have been lost as far as I was concerned. I never would have set foot in it again. But as it turned out, the summers after the divorce were idyllic, it was father and daughter. We would canoe up into the Swamp or sail the Laser, and as soon as I was sixteen he even let me go to cocktails. I'd dress up to a certain extent and he'd take my arm gallantly as if I were a Date.

At that point I wasn't a child any longer and I put away sailing and tennis, as well as my contemporaries, who had grown preppy beyond belief. The boys already had that destined look in their eyes that would not change until they retired and it became the trancelike stare of old age. I remember thinking that if I ever let a man get near me he would have to be at least twenty years older and he would have to be an artist, because they were the only poor people at Squid Harbor, and I knew that handling too much money could possibly give you a disease.

It was still early in June and they wouldn't all be down yet. I took Rita's Taxi to the cottage, and Rita asked how my year had been at school.

—Uneventful, I told her.

I figured they'd find out soon enough.

—No events here either, she said. The season's just starting up.

Rita drove the taxi all day in five-inch heels. She was the center of Squid Harbor gossip and little bits of it flew off her like sparks from the arc welder, white hot and dangerous.

—The Varnum boy is down alone with his two daughters, she said. He'd be a good catch for someone like you. Better than winning the Bay State Lottery.

—Not interested, I said. Have you seen my father yet?

—He's at the Steins' tonight. Or I should say the Stein-Mallows. I always forget. They're having the party. And I've seen the new wife, too. Tell me, Miss Solstice. What do you think it will be like having a mother younger than you are, or are you both the same age?

—We were born the exact same day, I told her.

That would give her something to think about. I didn't know how old Dorothy was precisely, twenty-six maybe or twenty-seven. She was one of Richard's students at Cooper Union and probably a Disciple. There had been a long line of disciples, and they made little versions of whatever Richard was sculpting at the time. Sometimes he'd bring one to West Fourth Street for supper when I'd be there and I'd have to endure it. They would gasp when they saw Richard's studio, and they'd run their fingers over his latest piece. They would call on the phone a few times with these fading, desperate-sounding voices, then they would disappear, only to be replaced by another. There seemed to be an infinite supply.

—You'll have a great summer, Rita said. I can't see you being alone for long.

I stopped short.

—What do you mean? I asked.

—There's a few people around who would like to know you better.

—There's no one around. People haven't come down yet.

—There's some who never leave. We're people, too, you know.

—Such as?

I was curious.

—I'm not the Personals column, Rita said. It will find you if it's meant to happen.

She patted my good cheek and took my duffel bag over her shoulder. She carried that burden through the sand amazingly on the spike heels and slung it on the deck. Rita had been one of my female role models during the motherless years after Katherine moved to Brussels, and she still was. She was alert and independent and drove her taxi like a maniac in every variety of weather. She dressed like a torch singer yet I never saw or heard of her being with a man.

I reached in to get something to pay her.

—Forget it, honey, she said. Remember me when I'm old. That's when we'll need each other. Till then it's every man for herself.

It was almost nine P.M., but the sun had just finished setting over the marshes and our living room still carried the day's heat. I opened a window and just sat. I could hear night herons croaking to one another and the whole population of spring peepers like a million electronic alarm clocks going off. In the dusk I could barely make out the last swallows scooping up mosquitoes over the flats. As the night came the swallows would become bats; then when it got light again the bats would disappear and the swallows would return. It was the rhythm of summer, like the kids in their Lasers out on the water, interminably racing, their shouts coming across the harbor as they collided at the windward mark, like the gulls picking crabs out of the shallows, lifting them high over the sand flats, dropping them, swooping down to peck out the soft parts while the legs would writhe helplessly around. I had come here for every summer in my memory and it was always the same, year after year, the same row of cottages with their front feet right on the tide line, the mothers

33

loafing and gossiping on the sand, their infants wandering into the shallows with miniature clam baskets and rakes.

I had been one of them, too. I had put on a T-shirt to cover my bodily imperfections and gone out there barefoot to feel for the squirts of quahogs between my toes. I had dug desperately as they tunneled for their lives. I had returned home with my fingers sliced up from grasping their sharp shells. I had been a kid, I had been a feminist, and I had been expelled.

And now what?

Life was out of balance, like that Hopi word in the movie, *Koyan-nisquatsi* or whatever it was. Last year I had arrived here from Hanover, climbed into my thoroughly unrevealing bathing suit, and hit the beach. My friends Robin and Sue, whom I'd grown up with, had also been home from college and we'd sat around talking about majors and careers. Now I was someone who had set a building on fire. What could we possibly discuss?

The future was infinitely long and empty: a house with no furniture, or not even a house, an open field with no structure and no geometry. It wasn't enough to be a woman. Anyone could do that. I needed to be a Native American or a Sikh Terrorist or a Rastafarian or a Palestinian Revolutionary, something with an ethnic identity or a Cause.

Our house was like all the old shore cottages at Squid Harbor: Uncle Joshua's cottage next door and the Stein-Mallows' beyond that, and so on around the curve of the bay: one glassy open living room with the ceiling going to a peak, then a corridor with bedrooms off either side. It was understated, neat, modern, and functional in kind of a Bauhaus way and exactly as old as I was. The capitalists, who came later, built gargantuan ornate residences back in the dunes, but they weren't right on the water like ours, and I was proud that we had never sold out. I grew up thinking that art was better than money because although the homes of the Varnums and the Schlessbooms were like estates, it was the minimalistic little boxes of the artists that sat right on the shore so you could hear the tide lapping at your feet.

Of course the sculptures made ours different from anyone else's. There was a Calder that Mr. Calder himself had actually given my father, which hung from the ceiling with red and black ovals that moved even when the windows were shut and there was no breeze. Richard used to tell me it was responding to the movements of the Earth.

In the far corner there was one of Richard's *Poems,* which are like rows of writing welded in stainless steel. It makes you try to read them. You think they must mean something in some language, but they don't. They are literally poems without meaning, and they show you how beautiful words can be if they don't have to stand for anything but themselves. It's not words that get ugly and distorted, it's just their meaning, if you see what I'm trying to say.

Richard loves poetry and there were always poets around our apartment on West Fourth, scrounging meals and cigarettes because they were forever broke. Once one of these poets lived for a week in the little closet off our kitchen. He was the man who taught me to play chess. He never said much, he just drank wine and smoked cigarettes and read European books whose pages he would cut apart with a little silver knife. "Poetry is nonverbal," he would say. I'd ask him how it could be nonverbal if it was made of words. The poet would light a cigarette off the one he had just been smoking and stare into the cloud of smoke. Later he killed himself, only at the time I was just told he was on a grant. Those are the euphemisms that make death harder for children when it really comes.

It was around that time that Richard started to make the *Poems,* one of which is in the Museum of Modern Art.

There is also a piece by George Rickey that cantilevers out from the breakfast nook, a long gold and red rod that always made me feel physical pain when I looked at it, and it still does. I am not an artist myself, and anything I try to draw looks like I made it with my feet. But when you grow up in the same house with one, you learn to think that way and the pieces of art become more real than pieces of the world. Even my own house and furniture would seem like shadows compared to those objects that were almost like human beings

35

and had a life and language of their own.

It's a good thing that Richard collected sculpture, because we have so many windows that you can't hang anything on the wall. We do have one painting by Hans Hoffman, an abstraction painted with a house-painting brush and greener than any green in nature, a sheer acid color that comes into my dreams sometimes and with its pure courage defeats all the shadows of darkness and death.

Amidst the changes, the house was the one unchanging thing. Richard had been separated and divorced and had changed apartments and brought home over a dozen girlfriends. Now he had married one. I had been fingerprinted and tried and expelled and placed on probation, so that I had to call my parole officer once a month and tell her I was still living at home. Meanwhile the house stood there year after year, vacant in winter with the snow drifting over the deck and exposed to the torrential rains of spring. We would come down expecting the windows to be smashed by vandals or the roof caved in or the whole structure to have been carried off on a hurricane tide. But it was always there, the gray weathery shingles and the silver Pyrofax gas tank with its tube leading right into the wall.

And now it was the same as always, or almost the same, anyway, because one thing was new and different. On a dark wooden stand off in the corner near the fireplace was a spidery wire sculpture like nothing else in the house. It was not Richard's or by anyone else I knew. It looked alive, and although it was small, a small thing woven of wires in a little web, it seemed to threaten every sculpture in the room, every piece of furniture, and even the house itself. It was the only nonliving thing I had ever seen that looked like it was about to grow. I turned off the spotlight that lit it up and turned on every other light in the room, but it was still lurking there in its corner and it gave me the creeps.

The sinister sculpture somewhat invaded my feeling of being home. I decided to check out my room. First of all, I was surprised to find the door closed. Nobody closed their doors at Squid Harbor, even when they slept, so that was strange. This is my first taste of the new Regime, I thought, the reign of Dorothy Dvorjak. And when I looked at the space where my bed had been, and my Navajo rug and my books, it was full of the same spidery sculptures.

They were in different stages of construction. One was just an abdomen in a vise, one had half its legs on and was dangling from the ceiling like a mobile. They were of all kinds of metal and some had the legs or feelers cast in a different metal than the body. They were individually quite interesting if you forgot what they were supposed to represent. But their collective effect was one of absolute weirdness. And they were hers.

So where were my own things, I thought, what happened to my bed and my bookshelf and the sculpture Richard had made for me back when we were a family? The new woman had held a yard sale with them, or melted them down into liquid to cast more spiders. I looked in the one remaining room, which was a semi-closet where we used to throw all the life preservers and the oars.

And there it was. My room had been taken apart and moved and reconstructed like one of those antique bedrooms in a museum. There was my bed with its old quilt that had been handed down from Katherine's grandmother and we somehow salvaged from the litigation. It had little scenes sewn by women in different styles and had inspired the Castration Quilt at Dartmouth. There was the Harvard Classics' "five-foot shelf of books," which I used to stand on end and measure myself with, looking up. And there, between the bed and window, was Richard's *Penguin: 1975,* which was of me, a penguinlike construction of welded cubes with a conical welded beak, a child and a penguin both at once. Although you couldn't exactly hug it because you would get hurt, it was my stuffed animal during the middle years when things were hardest and I used to sit there in the dark with one hand on its cool aluminum wing. And now, though I was a grown woman and a hardened criminal and at least a foot taller than it was, I was glad to see it and I gave it a moderately affectionate kiss. If it could endure the presence of all those spiders then maybe I could too.

5

The cottage next door to ours belonged to Uncle Joshua. Of course he wasn't a biological uncle, but he was around Richard's age and to me they had seemed almost like brothers. I can remember climbing down from the sleeping loft in pajamas with feet on them in the middle of the night and finding the two of them in conversation over a bottle of brown whiskey next to the cut-glass bowl of ice cubes that would start swimming around in water as the time went on.

Uncle Joshua was a bachelor, which had struck me as more and more intelligent as things got worse between my parents. My mother would say "Joshua never married" in an arch way that made it sound as if any normal person should get married as soon as they possibly can. To my mind, though, Joshua lived free and alone and was therefore invulnerable to such things as separation and divorce. When things got bad at home I would just go next door and there would be Uncle Joshua on his porch: dependable, dapper, dressed and groomed like a senator made up for TV. He would offer me my choice of animal crackers from a box that had wheels and bars on both sides like a traveling circus cage.

Later I came to know more. Joshua Brand was one of the first generation to summer at Squid Harbor. He came down with the artists and poets who had built their little studios at the high-tide line. And it was Uncle Joshua who arranged Richard's exhibition at the Fogg Museum and wrote the essay in the catalog that called him "the most promising younger sculptor of his generation." I remember that phrase because I was in the middle of learning to read and Katherine helped me sound out those polysyllabic words.

Uncle Joshua wasn't actually an artist himself. I dimly made that distinction even in the beginning. When the artists would be setting up their easels on the sand or arranging fruit bowls on their porches or posing a naked model on a dune behind their house, Uncle Joshua would be in his smoke-filled study gazing at reproductions and writing his books about art. I learned early on that some people are in charge of making things and others are in charge of writing about them, and that these two activities are genders apart. I used to think of an afterlife that Richard would go to when he stopped living, and all the great artists would be there. I had a clear picture of them in togas, hiking around on the clouds with sketch pads or sitting in cloud-colored Appalachian chairs and talking about the light. Uncle Joshua would go to a different place, I thought, and there would be great people there too, but of the scholars' heaven I had no clear image, except they would all be smoking, surrounded by books, and indoors.

I learned about Professor Joshua Brand in the slow osmotic way kids learn about the adults around them, mirroring their own changes as they grow. He stopped being Uncle Joshua with an animal cracker hidden in his pocket and became a professor from Harvard, who would leave one morning to fly to someplace like Teheran and come back much later, often not till the end of the summer, and always bringing me a bright piece of clothing or a miniature toy. This would be presented to me in a ceremonial manner, along with the story of how he bought it from a man on a flying carpet hovering five or six feet above the colorful Persian bazaar.

He once brought me a little silver lion and had me look at it with a magnifying glass under the blazing sunlight on his deck. I was sitting up on his lap. The lion's mouth was open and you could count the individual teeth. Behind the tongue, in the hollow of the lion's throat, there was an infinitesimal red jewel. As I turned the animal under the magnifying glass, it seemed that its body was filled with fire, which made my own stomach burn inside with something like a lion's hunger. I remember turning to look at him, twisting my head as always and looking sideways to conceal my bad side, and Uncle Joshua taking my head and turning it straight again as if to say he accepted me exactly as I was. Katherine judged me explicitly, and I always felt the unspoken, ultimate judgment of my father behind her, but Uncle Joshua seemed like a man who would let someone follow their own desires.

In those years, before Richard Solstice got famous, Joshua Brand was already buying sculptures from him and installing them all over his house. Most of these he had lent to the Fogg Museum, but one had been standing out on his deck at Squid Harbor ever since I could remember. It was as big as an ordinary full-grown man, though nowhere near Richard's own height, and was composed of two steel cubes, balanced diagonally one over the other and touching at their points. It was called *Chance*. And after all the years it was still there.

I stood outside for a long time looking at this sculpture, allowing its clear geometry to drive out the evil accumulations of the year. It seemed to brighten as the dusk came on, as though it had gathered the day's light into itself and would keep holding it and giving it off all through the night. I sometimes found it easier to relate to my father's work than to Richard himself. "A man should never be concerned with his existence as a person," he used to tell me. "He should live entirely in terms of his work." I wish he had used "you" instead of "a man," but he didn't. It left me wondering in what terms *I* was supposed to live.

A moment with this radioactive statue was a way of greeting him before we actually met, or of meeting my father alone before I had to face him in the context of Dorothy Dvorjak.

In the late evening darkness Joshua's cottage looked deserted. Maybe he hadn't arrived yet for the season, or maybe he was in Venice or Iraq. His windows were dark and the only light seemed to come from those two radiant cubes. So I was surprised to make out someone's shadow standing on the far corner of the deck, opposite the sculpture. That shadow was looking, as I was, into the dark. The only human sound was the distant chatter of the cocktail party, which blurred into a nonlanguage like the sound of the spring peepers or like one of Richard's *Poems* without words.

My first impulse was to say Hi, if it was Uncle Joshua standing there by himself, but I didn't really know how to address him. A couple of summers ago, when we last met, I called him Uncle Joshua the same as always. Now I was in college and I knew who he actually was. He even appeared on the Bibliography handout in World Art. Brand, J. *Persian Illuminated Manuscripts.* Cambridge, 1975. I had turned to the woman next to me, whom I didn't even know, and said, "Look. That's my next-door neighbor on the Cape."

I couldn't have addressed him as Joshua like an equal or Professor Brand like a complete stranger and certainly not Uncle Joshua like a child. I was not a child. I was a twenty-year-old woman with a criminal record and at least three criminal friends. So I decided to not disturb him. It might have been someone else anyway. People came and went at Squid Harbor, and maybe he had rented out his place. So I headed for the party on the road behind his house rather than on the beach.

The minute I started walking I wished I had taken a vial of Cutter's Insect Repellent from the house. Squid Harbor is the mosquito capital of Massachusetts, and they are the size of vultures with about a quart of blood in them already before they even strike. They draw from many sources before they are full. I had jeans on and low Reeboks with no socks and I could feel them finding my ankles in the dark and taking aim. The first bites of the season are the worst. They swell up and itch for hours, and the red afterspot lasts for a week. Later on, as Labor Day approaches, it is possible to grow somewhat immune.

You could always find where the party was by following the Japanese lanterns. Rita exaggerated when she said no one was down yet. It was early in the season but I heard the hum of many voices as I neared the glow of the lights. The gathering was at the Stein-Mallows'. Bob Stein and his third wife Marsha Mallow had accumulated about eleven children between them because they were both so nice that whenever either of them had been involved in a divorce, they'd get the kids. So their household grew at a geometrical rate, like Bangladesh. I could already hear them whooping and shrieking over the drone of conversation. At one time I would have fallen into that troop and grabbed a squirt gun or a gorilla mask, but for the past five summers I had of course avoided them to the extreme.

I looked for Richard but I couldn't see him. Daniel and Lydia Adler were there, who are both theater people from Boston, and a painter, Daphne Lazar, who was very sinuous and always sidling up to Richard, and the Varnums, who are rich and have about five cottages in a separate imperial compound, plus George Whipple, the real estate man who used to own the whole cove and sold everybody their plots in the beginning.

I should mention that Squid Harbor was a Land Trust, which is a kind of communal holding where your house is yours but the land is held in common like in the Middle Ages. The trust was called Squid Harbor Associates and it met once a month during the season. Of course it was also meeting every evening at cocktails because the members are ferocious about who gets to live there and especially about what is done with the common land. Although you can't legally exclude someone, it all goes through George Whipple, and he either sells you a house or he doesn't. This is not to discriminate by race or gender, but to keep out "developers" along with people with loud animals or boats. In a sense it was like a fraternity, only the principles were not supposed to be evil but in favor of tranquillity and nature, and who could ever quarrel with that?

There is also about a cubic mile of primordial swamp that no one gets to build on or fill in. The swamp is owned by everyone collectively and held in what they call Easement, to be kept forever wild. You can go into these marshes with a canoe. They include many varieties of ducks, blue and white herons, ibises, and also bitterns, which are so quiet and camouflaged they are almost never seen.

That was the one thing Katherine did for me before she migrated to Europe. Her father, Grandpa Forbush, had been this big ornithologist and starting from when I was first old enough to hold the binoculars myself she had taught me the names of birds. At one point I tried to forget them so I could just see the creatures themselves without the labels, but I couldn't, and even the birds in my dreams have little identification tags as in a museum. Now I accept it. They remind me of Grandpa Forbush, whom I never exactly knew, but sometimes when I'm really focused on some natural object he seems so close he could be looking through my eyes.

The marsh is also where the mosquito population breeds, and if you go in there you have to have either some miracle repellent on or be wearing a net from head to foot. I would ask my father how they got enough blood for the millions of mosquito nests with so few human bodies around, and all of them wearing insecticide.

—They get blood out of dogs, Richard would say. And cattle.

But there were about two dogs at Squid Harbor, and no cattle around for miles, so it seemed that most of that blood had to be coming from us.

In those days before I knew better, I would sometimes worry about the mosquitoes having so many enemies and not a single species that could be called their friends. Once in a while if I thought their offspring were in fact starving, I used to let one bite me deliberately while I watched. It's all right, I would say to them, I have several pints of this stuff and all you want is a few drops for your kids.

—Only the females bite, Richard would say.

Of course the Stein-Mallows had a Bug Zapper with a purple fluorescent tube that would go *zert* every few seconds and a mosquito would keel over into this deep trough under the light. The troughs filled up over the summer with dry lifeless mosquito carcasses, then in the fall they'd get cleaned out by tropical storms. I still felt sorry for the insects. Their destinies seemed to be so human. You're drawn to some attractive light and then it kills you. That neon glow was so intense against the blackness of the harbor that I felt like flying into it myself.

Standing right next to the Bug Zapper was my father, with

Dorothy Dvorjak naturally close beside him. Their faces were somewhat spectral in the ultraviolet light, as if maybe they had died instead of getting married. I had seen Dorothy only once, when she was just one of the disciples in a typical black dress. Now she was wearing a man's white V-neck undershirt with of course no bra and white painter pants with loops all over the thighs for holding her many tools.

I stepped out of the darkness into the purple illumination of the Bug Zapper. It was Marsha Stein-Mallow who saw me first.

—*Richard,* she cried. Look who's here.

—Penguin.

I ran into his arms and held on.

The first thing I recalled was how much larger my father is than even the memory of him. You have to jump up in the air to be anything like an equal, and he may catch you and hold you there or he may not. In which case you're down to your own embarrassing level again. And you can't get your arms fully around him either, so you end up clinging to the front of him like a rock-climbing enthusiast or one of those clinging marsupials like a lemur.

I hugged Dorothy, too, who had a fairly svelte appearance but was quite fat around the waist when you actually encircled it. I have my doubts about hugging as a means of communication, but it does give you a sense of what people are under the skin.

—You're alive, Dorothy said. I was so worried for you. We heard such awful reports.

—We were both worried.

—It was an ordeal, I said. But it's all over.

Dorothy pulled a dark woman over to us, with tight braided hair. She could have been Greek or Armenian or Turkish, or from one of those gypsy nations on top of Greece. She was definitely exotic, and I was surprised when she talked in regular New York English. Dorothy took us both by the shoulders and sort of pushed us together.

—This is Penelope, but we call her Penguin. She's Richard's. Penguin, this is Pura. She's with the *Village Voice.*

—Freelance, Pura said. I sell what I can. You're the one at Williams?

—Dartmouth, I said. Only not any longer. I'm freelance too.

Richard smiled down at the three women from his large, sculpted head. He was still holding my arm. I could feel the individual bones of his fingers as in one of those X-rays where they show the hand bones inside the flipper of a whale.

—Penguin attacked a *fraternity*.

Dorothy whispered this like a conspirator, or like someone who would like to have been part of a conspiracy except that she feared no one would trust her. She was probably right. I tried to imagine Dorothy among us in Hanover; even at twenty-six she was too old. I tried to imagine her my age, but she looked like she'd skipped my period of life and went directly to her own. I knew that by twenty Dorothy had already been divorced, which did make me feel closer because divorce is also a kind of arson in its own way.

—Which fraternity? Pura inquired.

—Beta Sigma. One of the worst offenders.

—You should thank God it didn't burn down, Dorothy said. You would be spending the summer in prison.

—That wouldn't be such a bad thing for her, Pura said. She'd learn more from three months in prison than from four years in a country club cloister like that.

Richard pulled me out of the flickering ultraviolet circle and we stood together in the dark. He took my chin in one hand and turned my face in different directions the way a connoisseur would evaluate an object of art. He trusted only touching and seeing. I was like Katherine in that if I trusted in anything it would be words.

—Have you stopped at the cottage yet? Richard asked. Dorothy's using your old bedroom for a studio.

—I noticed.

—Then you saw her piece. It's one of her *Arachnids*.

—I didn't turn the light on, I lied. Is Joshua here?

—Off and on, Richard said. He's not here at the moment. He wasn't lucky enough to have been expelled, so he still has papers to

45

grade. And he has to put on his alchemist's robe and hood for commencement.

—That's very strange, I said. I thought I saw him standing out on his deck.

—Well, it was dark. You probably imagined it. There is a sure way to tell. When there is a cocktail party in progress Josh Brand will be there with a martini in his hand. You can set your watch by him. At six Josh is having his first martini. At twelve he is turning out the light.

Pura Batrachian found us and dragged us under yet another Bug Zapper. She seemed to like being next to them and she gave a little smile of delight each time an insect burst into flames. At one point a sizable moth immolated itself on the grill, which took several seconds and evoked from Pura a long whistle of appreciation. I guess she didn't get to observe raw nature very much in New York City.

—Tell us about Dartmouth, Pura was saying. I understand there's a women's movement up there. I may want to do a piece on it.

—There's no movement any more. We had a newspaper, but I think it's defunct. And so am I.

—Dorothy tells me you want to write.

—Well, not exactly, I said. I get bored sitting that long in the same place. It's just that I don't like money, and I haven't got any specific talents, so that's what I'll probably end up doing.

—Great, Pura said. Those are just the right reasons. So what if you got kicked out of school. Look at what's-his-name from *Catcher in the Rye*. Holding. He got expelled and he made a book out of it. It's your life. It's your material. Readers don't want happiness. They have more than they can deal with already. They don't know what to do with it. They graduate, they get some pointless mercenary job, and then they die. Big deal. Take you, for example. You've done something unique. You ought to write it down and sell it.

—I don't know. Isn't that kind of like prostitution, selling your own life?

—It's not prostitution, Pura said. It's marketing.

—I haven't written much. Term papers. A few hysterical columns in the *Id*, which was our tabloid. Nobody read it. We gave it away for nothing and people used it in their walls for insulation. It was too political.

—Politics, Pura said. Great material.

—It wasn't material to us. It was our way of life.

—You have to separate your life from your writing, Penguin, or you'll never get off the ground.

There was something about this Pura Batrachian, though, that I kind of liked. She was about Dorothy's age and she had a job already that she lived for. She knew what she was doing and who she was. She was overly made-up and she wore painful-looking military boots and her earrings, on closer inspection, were little golden rats whose tails looped up through her ear holes, but that was all on the surface, and underneath she was a woman who had made for herself a viable way to live. It didn't matter what she looked like. It's possible to be a journalist without having to decorate yourself like that.

A short distance away, Richard and Dorothy and the Stein-Mallows could be heard talking about venereal diseases, which seemed incongruous for honeymooners in the lingering romantic summer twilight but was, I suppose, one of the subtopics of love.

—Syphilis, Richard was saying. It's such a sibilant word, one of the purest in the language. It's too bad it had to be wasted on a germ.

—As I understand it, Robert Stein-Mallow said, Syphilis was a character in a classical Greek play. A shepherd. He got the disease from one of his flock, back in the period of the Greeks.

—Syphilis, my father repeated.

He enunciated each individual syllable as if you could see their sounds written in the air. He didn't care what it meant, just the way it sounded and felt on the tongue. Which I was coming to see was the best and the worst thing about him, a phrase I also remembered from Katherine's tirades in the old family days. Richard does have a magnificent voice. It seems to be loud but it isn't. It just exactly fills the space he wants it to fill. He used to read to me on Sunday

47

mornings when Katherine was allegedly in church. He'd throw my children's books on the floor and read poems from Vachel Lindsay and Hart Crane. Those were his favorites.

—It's true with AIDS, too, Mr. Stein-Mallow said. Didn't that come from monkeys in the first place?

—African green monkeys, his wife said. I read it. But the Africans weren't sexually involved with them, the way the Greeks were, I mean, with their sheep. It wouldn't be possible. The green monkeys are tiny creatures, the size of a human infant. In the beginning it came from eating the monkeys' brains.

—Syphilis would make you a genius, Pura said, then it would kill you. If you were lucky, like Schubert, you got five good years.

—That's why there are no great artists anymore, Richard said. No more Schuberts. No Nietzsches, no Shakespeares, and no Van Goghs. The great creative diseases were killed off by penicillin.

—Shakespeare? I said. They didn't teach us that in English 12.

—It's right in the sonnets, he went on. It's a hidden meaning. The Dark Lady got it and gave it to Shakespeare. His rival had it too. She gave it to both of them. I can imagine the two men at the Mermaid Tavern when they discovered it. It must have been one gloomy evening.

—And if he hadn't contracted it?

—No *Hamlet,* Richard said. No *Antony and Cleopatra.* He never would have gone beyond *Love's Labour's Lost.*

Dorothy Dvorjak was getting distinctly nervous about this conversation. She moved closer to him and kind of insinuated her hand into his waistband.

—Richard darling, you're not saying he deliberately contracted it, to make him a better artist?

He gazed at my new stepmother with a certain ambiguous look that I knew well.

—He knew what risks he was taking, getting involved with a muse.

—That's because he was a man, Dorothy said. Women don't

think that way. We don't like to sacrifice the human body for anything. Except maybe religious extremists, sending their sons off to the Jihad.

—All artists are extremists, my father said.

Bob Stein-Mallow, the host, tried to divert the conversation back to a neutral subject.

—It's terrible about AIDS in Africa, he said. In some countries a fifth of the population has it now.

—That would be fitting, Richard said, if our beginning and our end evolved from the same place.

Marsha Stein-Mallow always had this exaggerated reverence for what Richard said, completely missing the flickering self-irony that made it worth hearing, besides the fact that he took sculptor's license and invented half the facts, like that stuff about Shakespeare and his girlfriend. If Marsha had been younger and single, she might herself have been one of the disciples. But then I guess anybody would.

—Oh. Death, Marsha exclaimed. You're not thinking it will kill us all?

Maybe that's what happened to the dinosaurs, I thought. Maybe it wasn't the comet hitting Siberia, but some incurable disease that also got distributed through love.

Dorothy interrupted.

—Richard's too modest to say this. But he's been commissioned to do an AIDS monument. Like the Washington one, only in New York, down by Canal Street. Tribeca, where the big Serra piece was.

—The size requirements keep changing, Richard said. It's not like the Vietnam monument. I have to make it with expansion modules that can be bolted on.

—A generation of orphans, Marsha said. We have to watch how we live now. We were excessive in the past.

Some of the Stein-Mallow kids could be heard mauling each other back in the cottage.

Richard went over and poured a large drink and another for

Dorothy, then looked at me and added a third.

—Some of us continue to be excessive in the present, Dorothy said.

Daphne the painter drifted up to us in her velvet pants. She had a shrill curlewlike voice and was always after Richard anyway, so when she heard him actually talking about sex, she was drawn right over.

—AIDS is a dead subject, Daphne said. The epidemic is slowing down. They'll control it and they'll find a cure.

—They won't, someone else said who I didn't even recognize. It mutates so fast, as soon as you define one strain it changes into another.

And so it went. The words dissolved into the night air and became as invisible as the microbes they supposedly described. There were places that words couldn't reach, though, like the actual sickness of a real person, African or American, words and numbers couldn't reach that. Richard would try with one of his immense constructions of welded steel, but how could that even begin to communicate the suffering of a single victim or of the person who they loved?

I felt somewhat infected myself, not from the disease but from the conversation. Words were like viruses, too. They could get into your brain and you wouldn't be immune anymore and you'd believe anyone's version of the truth.

I walked off towards the table under the bug light where the Stein-Mallows kept the liquor and ice. Richard went with me and created two more perfectly transparent martinis, just like the old days. We clicked glasses together.

—To the road of excess, Richard said.

—To the palace of wisdom.

For better or worse, there I was back at Squid Harbor with my father, where I had more or less begun.

6

I stood apart from the group with my drink and just observed. With the Japanese lanterns around it and the triangle of Bug Zappers in the middle, the party was an island of artificial illumination in the deepening night. Overhead there were stars, and I thought of each one of them as a cocktail party sending its fragile verbal energy into the chill of space. Dorothy Dvorjak got more and more animated as the other guests quieted down. Waving her arms around, smoking as many as two brownish-colored cigarettes at a time, she was telling some story about a sculptor who pushed his wife over a cliff.

—You risk your life, she was saying, when you marry one of these people. The best of them are irresponsible narcissists, and the worst are beyond belief.

I moved forward to stand beside Richard at the table. Maybe instinctively I was preparing to protect this new woman from her own remarks. I wondered if she knew what she was getting into. If my mother had ever said anything like that, he would have poured a Manhattan over her head. That's how it always started, Katherine making some remark in public and Richard tipping the table over or walking fully clothed into the sea. This new one amused him. He broke into an unprecedented smile that totally rearranged the planes of his face.

—So what's it like, I asked him, living with another sculptor?

—She's not a sculptor yet. She's still a student. She makes the same thing over and over. But she does have the energy of youth.

She can drink till midnight and go into her studio and then work twenty hours straight.

—Which you used to be able to do yourself.

—Used to, he repeated. I used to turn out four pieces a month. I used to carve stone all morning and when my hands got too tired for that I would go out and weld some steel.

—You're in the sunset years, I said. Plus you're letting the competition right into the house. A woman, too. I thought sculpture was strictly for men.

—There aren't any men anymore, Penguin. I haven't had a good male student in years.

—Thank God, I said. You would have gone off and married him.

—No bitterness, Penguin. You wouldn't want me to spend the rest of my life alone. Bachelors don't last very long. It's a known fact. The prostate gland expands, then one morning you wake up dead and nobody finds you for a week.

—Come on, Richard. You're immortal. You're like the mastodons. You'll outlive us all.

—The mastodons are extinct, Richard said.

—I'll say one thing for Dorothy. She certainly outshines Fritz.

Of course Fritz had been a huge threat to Richard during the separation, but by now he was a household joke. Mom's Belgian millionaire with his Afghan hounds. My father kept a photo of them in his studio with the dogs and Fritz in equestrian costume holding a riding whip.

—But what about you? Richard asked me. Are you still traveling alone?

—Nobody's in my life at the moment. It's a hiatus.

—A hiatus? A hiatus between who and whom?

—Between anarchy and unemployment. So I came home.

I put my arm around him at that point and was amazed, as always, that it only reached halfway. When he stood still he was like a sculpture, a sculpture of a sculptor, but when he moved he was a piece of heavy construction equipment specially evolved to handle large plates of steel, to fabricate them against their will like the pieces of his own excessive life. He solved all problems through monomania. He excused himself with it as if it were a handicap or a disease. Nothing mattered for him but sculpture. People could come and go. He would be in his studio regardless. He was my model, him and Rita. Do the task you're supposed to do and forget the rest. As soon as I found out what my task was, that's how I'd be.

—I thought we were sending you up there to find a man, he said. All those dormitories up there and you couldn't find one to bring home?

—I've got one here already, I told him. What would I do with two?

He put his arm over my shoulder and we fell in step. Richard sang "Long Way to Tipperary" in his dinosaur baritone as we strutted past Joshua Brand's house in the dark.

—Drunk again, Solstice? someone asked. And more women. Is it never going to end?

So Uncle Joshua was here. We couldn't see him, but it was his own cultivated voice. The porch light flicked on and there he was, dapper as ever, leaning on my father's sculpture with a martini glass lifted in his hand. He had a dark blue shirt made of some shiny metallic fabric that echoed the starry night, plus a pair of lime-yellow slacks with a red belt. He looked skinnier than I remembered, a bit like a fad dieter, but even in the shadows you could see the deep tan that counterpointed his almost-white, somewhat monastic hair. There was always something of the monk about Uncle Joshua, a monk maybe who spent his vacations in the Caribbean. There was a monk's austerity in his hairstyle and something of a monk's decadence in the trim, mink-colored beard that did not yet have the slightest hint of gray. I made a note to look up the word *tonsured* when my head was clear.

—You haven't forgotten each other? Richard asked.

—Penny. Penelope, Joshua said. The faithful housewife of Ithaca. Your father and I had been reading Homer when we named you.

—We've settled on Penguin, Richard said.

—A flightless bird of the Antarctic, Joshua went on. There are no more trees at the South Pole, so its wings have evolved into paddles.

—Not at all, Richard argued. A penguin is a fish on its way upward, with so much desire to fly that its scales have already become feathers and its fins are stretching themselves out into wings.

I don't think I'd been inside Uncle Joshua's house since I was twelve. The porch was as far as one was ever allowed, though he wandered over to our house all the time. But he didn't have any insect protection whatsoever, no porch screens and no bug-zapping light, so we went in. On the outside, the Brand cottage might have seemed small, gray, and shingly like our own, but the interior was more like a palace of the Moguls than a Cape Cod summer camp. The carpet had obviously been ripped off from the Cloisters museum, covering the entire floor with its narrative tapestry of a pack of hunting dogs biting the legs of a deer. The drops of blood coming from these wounds refracted the light like jewels. A couple of tables flanked the couch we were sitting on, each of them holding a jade mountain with little jade Buddhist hermits climbing towards sanctuaries at the top.

Unlike our own wall of ocean-facing glass, Joshua had small windows even on the side facing the sea. Maybe he preferred interior privacy to a view of the harbor. Or maybe he needed wall space to exhibit his objects of art. The Persian miniatures between each window were surrounded by gold frames with Arabic characters carved into them. The effect could be either lovely or decadent, depending on your point of view.

On one corner of the carpet Joshua had a baby grand piano with the music open to a Schubert sonata. On the other corner was an amazingly lifelike gigantic sculpted dog, that to my knowledge never had been let out. I felt sorry for it. I saw its ear move, then it stood up and yawned. It was a fully alive Great Dane the size of a Lippizaner stallion, which looked us over for a minute then sat back down.

—That's Cosimo. He's really much more sensitive than he looks. Cosimo, this is Penguin.

—How long have you had him?

—Years.

—How could I not have noticed?

—Stealth dog, Richard said.

I moved over closer to my father on the couch. He had been there enough so Cosimo didn't bother him at all, but I wondered why in all that time he never told me Uncle Joshua kept a dog. Did these men have secrets between them that even a daughter wasn't supposed to know? How many?

Joshua brought me a martini with a little silver toothpick piercing the olive through its heart.

After a couple of these nightcaps we found our way next door. A car arrived at the same time, which was Pura dropping Dorothy off. My new stepmother looked a little unsteady on her feet, and so were we.

—At long last, Richard said. The nuclear family.

—Postnuclear, she answered. It's going to be fun.

Richard climbed up to the sleeping loft and left his two women to finish the evening by themselves. Dorothy had brought a drink back from the party and I still had half a martini and the silver toothpick minus the green olive. Dorothy sat down on the floor next to her spider with her legs and body forming a perfect right angle in the white clothes. The posture looked cramped and yogic, like someone schooled in causing themselves pain.

After the drinks I could begin to understand Richard's attraction to this woman. She had wide-spread eyes and still something of the innocent adolescent around her mouth, more I think than my own, despite her extra six years of experience. The skin of her face was perfect as far as I could determine through its layer of apricot-colored cosmetics and the slight flush of our extended cocktail hour. From Richard's point of view she could seem quite fetching in an unformed and vivacious way, which might possibly make up for the difference of thirty years.

—When I was your age, Dorothy said, I didn't know what I was going to be. I'd dropped out of three schools, I'd been married, battered, and divorced. I assumed life was over.

—So when did you start making sculpture?

—The day after my divorce came through. I was a Reichian at the time. My therapist told me to get some clay and sculpt something I hated and then attack it. I went and made a seventy-five pound penis. I took a hacksaw and sawed it into equal slices like a pepperoni. The next week I saw the big Gaudier-Breszka show. I went home, reworked the clay, and made a seventy-five-pound head. Right out of nowhere, I just invented it. It was my inner Platonic ideal. I lugged it through my period of homelessness after the divorce. I'd sit there listening to *Sgt. Pepper's Lonely Hearts Club Band* and the only thing with me in those bare rooms would be the head. One day I brought it in to Cooper Union and said, "Here. Admit me." The admissions lady laughed out loud. "You're some kind of friend of Richard Solstice," she said. "I've never heard of him." "Well, that's him," she said. She was pointing at the head. I couldn't have got a recommendation at that time if I had bribed them. But I got in. The first day I saw your old man in the hall, with that face, that head, I almost lost it. That's the man, I said to myself. That's him. I was a *freshman* taking basic required this and that. I was beginning over, in my fourth school. I carried the head around in a TV carton with one of those carrying handles made of wire. One day in the fall term I dragged the box into your father's office and said *Look*. He thinks I'm a delivery person with a Sony. He looks in the box and says "What the hell's that?" He takes a blade out of his desk and cuts the box open so the front drops forward and there he is, facing the thing itself. "You won't believe what this started as," I tell him, "but I transformed it."

Dorothy reached into the locker under George Rickey's sculpture and took out the gin bottle without even looking. This is her home, I thought. I better get used to it. She splashed it into both our glasses and continued.

—They put me in Graduate Sculpture before I knew it. There I am knowing nothing, no technique, twenty-three years old, my head a complete mess from many years of not living correctly, and I am in the studio dropping things on the floor and bending my fingers around with pliers and who walks in. "I've got two tickets for Pina Bauch tonight," he tells me. "You're coming with me." I had about ten minutes to get the brass filings out of my hair and some clothes on. The Pina Bauch is terrible, all this decadent sex and sadomasochistic innuendo, but your father eats it up. We go to the Corner Bistro in the Village. "Tell me for what reason you like something like that," I say. "Tell me so I can understand it. I am trying to learn." So he starts in about structure and postcontemporary formalism and in about six minutes I realize I am a complete vacuum, that I've never known anything in my life and if a thought ever found its way into my brain cavity, it would starve.

She fixed us both another substantial gin and tonic.

—"I'm not getting my work done these days," he tells me. Here is a fifty-plus-year-old man with so much notoriety that people come up to him in Greenwich Village restaurants to get an autograph. He has sculpture in the Metropolitan Museum of Art. He has sculpture in the Peggy Guggenheim collection in Venice. Right now he has a show at the Hirshhorn Museum that they take groups of schoolchildren to see, just like the Lincoln Memorial. And he is sitting in this Village bar with sawdust all over the floor, saying to me he feels like he is through. He has sculptor's block. "What about your family?" I ask. I don't know anything about him. "I'm self-supporting," he says. We split up the tab. Somehow we get into the same taxi—I know I'm telling you everything, you have to forgive me—and end up at his place on Fifty-One West Fourth. Your place, I should say. I was overwhelmed to an extreme. There's the little Giacometti on the coffee table. There's the red David Smith with the numbers all over it. There's the loft full of his own work. *Sheer Locomotive* is sitting there half done in the middle of everything. And there's no one to see it. I mean everybody sees Richard Solstice's finished work but nobody sees the process, which is much more important than the result. You need an audience, I told him. I went and got my possessions and moved in. That's the whole story. That's how your father met his second bride.

She decanted the last drops into my glass and peered up into the bottle as though it had a model ship inside. I tipped it up to my mouth and this random memory flashed in on me. The family was in Maine or someplace on a hilltop and there were wild juniper bushes all over. Richard picked one of the berries and split it open with his thumbnail under my nose. The sky was blue and there were clouds running through it like a flock of escaped sheep. Mom and Richard were breaking the berries open and laughing about something and I laughed too, though I had no idea why. I'd wanted to eat one of the juniper berries, but they took it out of my mouth and we climbed down. And in the middle of the night it came back like a home technicolor movie as Dorothy Dvorjak and I finished Richard's gin.

Ever since the Divorce I'd imagined some kind of a mother in my life. Now I had this.

7

Green monkeys surround the cottage. They occupy the high cranber-ry bushes, chattering, drawing closer. They have discovered fire and they are going to try it out under our house. Each of them has a single live coal on a fraternity paddle. I hear the flinty sounds of Bic lighters under the floorboards. I hear the flames.

It is a wicked night. A dull feathery gray blocks the window as if someone were smothering the entire house with a down pillow.

Now a choking person giggles in the sleeping loft right above my head. Somebody whispers Quiet. A heavy bureau shudders and shifts its weight. Splok. Somebody rolls off a foam mattress onto the floor.

Quiet. Do not disturb.

Jingle jingle jingle jingle jingle. As if they've hung one of those little elephant bells beside the mattress specifically to ring people awake.

Wake up, it says. We're married. We're making love.

Ring ring ring ring ring ring ring ring. RING.

Wake up. We're done.

Outside, radar squeaks of bats tracking mosquitoes. Inside my stom-ach, way down, a single bat chewing his way out. I open my legs.

Go ahead. Gnaw, I say. Gnaw yourself out of there and fly.

One of those postdream mornings I stayed awake listening until dawn. Someone came down the stairs. Dorothy, not Richard. She plugged the coffee in. It boiled. I heard the file scraping at metal in her studio. It was too light. I'd never get back to sleep. I put on my

Synchronicity sweatshirt and my most-destroyed clamming sneakers and invaded her room. My room.

—Let's take the canoe out, I said. The tide's up. We can go up into the marsh and I'll show you the heron rookery.

—I can't. I'm working.

—Come on, I said. Nature is more important than art. Everyone knows that. We need the Cutter's Insect Lotion, though.

—All right. I'll need a minute to finish bending this one leg.

I'd been at Squid Harbor for exactly a week. Richard was welding every afternoon out in the studio, and Dorothy had become for all practical purposes my friend. She was sometimes too drunk and quite frequently too sober, but in between she had an extraordinary lightness and energy. I admired her capacity for talking while she was doing everything else, cooking, repotting the geraniums, blasting at a brass rod with her acetylene torch, or following me right into the bathroom. She was the only person I had met who could carry on a complete conversation while she was at the same time actually reading a book. I began to suspect that she had two brains, or was maybe one of those people whose brain halves are separated from each other by a space, so that their eyes look in different directions and their hands fight with each other over their food.

I brought the Cutter's and a thermos for the coffee. Dorothy packed something into her bag and brought it. Probably a small bottle of Seagram's, I thought. Dorothy is capable of starting in early.

It was still dark enough to show the moon, tilted up like a wine glass and very high, almost in the exact center of the sky. We swung the canoe into the marsh, then it got too shallow so we poled. Our paddles sank way down into the ooze.

Quock. A night heron rose directly in front of us. Its feet were still dripping at the end of its long legs as it flew.

—Nature is beautiful, she said. But not important. It's too perfected. It doesn't have possibilities, it doesn't have anywhere to go . . .

I jabbed at her back with the end of my paddle to turn her off.

We were coming to the heron rookery, which was basically three massive prehistoric trees wound around with vines that had become white from bird droppings. The wood itself must have long ago rotted away, leaving the shells of excrement like limestone casts. It was the most sacred and mysterious place I'd gone to in my childhood. The egrets and herons stood on the lime-white limbs like guardians of the dead, their beaks pointing down at us from those long motionless necks. How do you know what another creature is thinking? I tried to look down at Dorothy and myself through the fixed monochromatic eyes of a snowy egret. Maybe we were the long canoe of death coming for their eggs and children. Maybe we were white hunters coming for their plumes.

A thickening cloud cover obscured the sunrise, so that it got darker rather than growing light. For once, Dorothy was completely silent. A brown moth materialized out of nowhere and landed right between us on the rail of the canoe. It flapped irrationally, gripping the wood strip with its numerous woolly feet, which it alternately lifted and put down as if in a ritual dance. Another moth landed on the floor, flapping around between us near Dorothy's pack. They were fugitives from the night, confused by the experience of brightness.

—They're huge, Dorothy whispered. What are they?

—Polyphemus, I said. We called them elephant moths. Look at the eyes.

The blue eyes on the backs of the moths' wings looked like the eyes of a great horned owl.

—That's called offensive coloration. Something attacking them to eat them would be deceived into thinking they were a bird of prey.

—That's proof there is a God, Dorothy said. I always knew it.

—God doesn't have anything to do with it. It's evolution. The ones that didn't have the eyespots got eaten and therefore they did not pass on their genes.

—I can't imagine anyone wanting to eat one of these things. Who would do it?

—Bats. Nighthawks. Screech owls. Shrikes. All the night

hunters. Human beings would probably eat them if we were hungry enough.

—Let's hope it never comes to that, Dorothy said. By the way, Penguin, how come you know so much?

—My grandfather was an ornithologist. On Katherine's side.

—My father fixed refrigerators, Dorothy said. So don't expect to learn anything from me. Hey! Maybe that's why she went off with the fur man. She's working her way back to nature.

—It's a distinct possibility, I said.

All the moths over the swamp must have been signaled by the silent dance of the first, because they kept appearing, from above us and behind our backs and from both sides at once. Now there were fifteen or twenty of them flapping around the rails and the inside of the hull. One had gripped onto Dorothy's back, which she did not see and I did not bring up. They all had the same inebriated flutter, as if their brains were being destroyed by the oncoming light.

—Moths are disgusting, Dorothy said. Let's go back.

I brushed a huge specimen off my paddle and turned around so I was in the bow and the canoe's direction would be reversed. There wasn't room in the thin channel to turn the canoe around. I felt a distinct urgency from the sternperson to get out of the marsh as soon as possible. I poled harder and the paddle sank deep in the mud. It clung heavily to the blade, which I had to swirl clean after every stroke. I could feel Dorothy behind me doing the same thing, only with a desperation that was basically counterproductive. I felt the canoe drawn backwards as her paddle was sucked in and she tried to pull it out. Once the bow leapt forward and I looked behind. Her paddle was stuck in the mud a boat-length in back of us, sticking straight up out of the channel with three elephant moths batting against it and trying to hang on.

We weren't going back for it. I switched to my stronger arm and poled for the two of us. I sensed Dorothy behind me reaching for whatever she had stashed into her bag.

—This is a sign, she said. We are not supposed to be in here.

—Nature's revenge, I said, for your priorities. I used to come here all the time when I was a kid. By myself. And nothing like this ever happened.

—That was different, she replied. Back then you belonged in here. Now you don't.

I wondered if she was right.

We got clear of the marsh and changed seats so I could use our one paddle in the stern. It looked like a heavy rain might come eventually, but we were in open water and we could relax. Dorothy handed me the flask.

—Breakfast, she said.

I hadn't even brushed my teeth. I swirled the whiskey around in my mouth to get rid of the moth taste and spat it out over the side.

—It's a bit early for that, I said.

—All sculptors drink at all times. Your father, for instance, has been seen not long after sunrise . . .

—It's so damn masculine. Drinking all day, so you never have to know what's going on around you.

—All sculptors are masculine, Dorothy said.

I took a whole mouthful of Seagram's and swallowed it down.

—Are you saying you're not a feminist?

—They're full of shit, Dorothy said. They sit around all day and talk about how oppressed they are. It's one more way of procrastinating their lives away and not getting any work done. Feminism was invented by men to keep women in their place when we started looking like a threat. Of course your case was different. You found something you needed to do and you did it.

—I don't know if it's my "work," I said. There aren't many career opportunities for arsonists.

The outgoing tide swept us back to the cottage without paddling a stroke. There was no wind, and the Cutter's had begun to wear off. I got a bite on one ankle and found four or five bites on my hands that I hadn't even felt. They weren't big gaping welts anymore, either. They were dainty painless red dots that looked like the prick of a needle. I was getting my seasonal immunity. By August they could attack me like vampires and I wouldn't bat an eye.

It looked like a serious rainstorm was about to come in. We'd drifted almost down to the Stein-Mallow's cottage, the last one before you really went out to sea, and it was time to turn back. Dorothy took a last swig and screwed on the top of the silver hunter's flask. Her hands were tiny and fragile, with short undeveloped fingers like a little girl's, yet they were cut in a hundred places from metal shavings and scarred like rawhide from the burns of the acetylene torch. She was twenty-six and she had already built more than two dozen bronze spiders. How could you get to be both male and female? A masculine feminist. I had six years to learn. I stabbed in my paddle and pushed backwards so the canoe stopped and turned around in its own length.

It was still early on a Sunday morning and there was no sign of activity anywhere in the harbor. People would be sleeping it off, lying in bed listening to *Morning Pro Musica* while their Mr. Coffee machines turned themselves on, grinding and percolating without ever being touched by human hands.

We passed close to Uncle Joshua's house in the soft rain that had just started to fall. He was up already. I could see light around the edges of his small curtained windows. Everyone else at Squid Harbor lived a completely open life in terms of being seen from the water. A person passing in a boat could watch you staring out the window in your bathrobe, frying your eggs, brushing your teeth at the kitchen sink. But Uncle Joshua was different. All those summers I'd lived next door to him without even knowing he kept a dog, let alone a Great Dane that was not ever allowed to bark or to leave the house. He was a public figure in Cambridge, as Richard always said, but a very private citizen on the Cape.

Dorothy was lying in the bow of the canoe at this point with her eyes closed. I stopped paddling and raised the binoculars to watch a gull drop a quahog with deadly accuracy over a rock. It failed to split and the gull simply flew off to find something else. The quahog was free to dig back into the sand and resume its life. Summer was like that, a lapse in the struggle for existence, a space for silence in which no excessive effort had to be made. The whole harbor was free of mechanical sounds, not even an outboard, just a few plaintive bird calls and the flap of herons changing their feeding spots. So it was startling to hear a car thumping along the washboard-surfaced Squid Harbor access road at this hour of the morning and to see it pull up beside Uncle Joshua's house. I lowered the binoculars to get a look.

Uncle Joshua appeared on the porch in his dressing robe, then ducked in and in about fifteen seconds emerged fully dressed.

The car was an official-looking gray van with some kind of insignia on the door, maybe from Harvard, only the sign wasn't crimson, it was green. Dartmouth? Two men got out and opened the back. They took a long panel out and placed it down as a ramp covering the steps to his porch.

I nudged Dorothy with the paddle. Two men were guiding a wheelchair out of the van and along the path to where they had put up the ramp. Joshua got between them and the three of them wheeled someone up and into the house. There was an exchange of papers, then Joshua went in alone. The van drove off.

—He must have a relative, Dorothy guessed. Maybe a parent.

I couldn't imagine Joshua Brand having parents. I couldn't imagine him ever having children, or a wife. Even the Great Dane was incongruous. He was a self-sufficient person, which I respected. People sprawled all over each other with their needs. Jennifer and Rebecca, Richard and Dorothy. I could see them reaching for anyone around like an octopus. Rebecca had put out a tentacle on the bus ride, and I could still feel the row of suction cup marks on my right arm. With Richard and Dorothy it was like living with two octopi in an undersea cave, though those two were so entangled in one another that I felt safe.

Uncle Joshua seemed like such a singular person. I wondered who could be riding a wheelchair into his home.

8

Dorothy was scooping the yogurt into three bowls and slicing a banana into it and adding a tablespoon of vanilla and a tablespoon of Bacardi to each portion. The sky was already clearing into a high satiny silver and beyond that you could see the cloud fringe and scraps of Venetian azure. I was grateful for having taken Western Art because I knew who Giovanni Tiepolo was and the memory of his colors made the sky even brighter and more blue.

Out in the studio I could hear the arc welder sputter and die as Richard shut off the current. We sat down to breakfast. The Seagram's had already worn off. Our dawn expedition seemed like a week ago, let alone Hanover, which seemed like another life belonging to a totally different person. I'd written to Jennifer up in New Hampshire, telling her Dorothy was manageable and that having a mother six years older than oneself might possibly turn out to have its advantages. Which was not to say that I knew what they would be.

We told Richard about our escape from the moths. He got this indulgent look over his face as if we were children.

—You girls are going to get in trouble with that canoe.

At that Dorothy suffered a hand spasm and spilled half her coffee over the yogurt and bananas. She wasn't exactly drawn to the idea of becoming his eldest daughter, though I rather liked it myself. A second mother was unnecessary. But who knows what might come up when having a sister would come in handy? I put an arm around her shoulders and tipped her breakfast stool closer to my own.

—I'm getting a camera, Richard yelled. We have to immortalize this moment.

—Forget it, said Dorothy, straightening herself up. No pictures. Enough fooling around. Half the day's gone and nobody's done any work.

—Speak for yourself, Richard said. I've been up working since eight.

—Count me out, too, I said. I don't have any work. The question does not apply.

The living room was filling up with new sculptures from both of them, as if they were competing in some kind of art race. Richard had almost finished *Smart Locomotive* and its sleek cylinder and black steel cubes covered most of the rug. Dorothy had so many spiders in so many corners of the house that you had to keep both eyes on them every minute to make sure they didn't move. I'd been in a sling chair for days trying to read *Being and Nothingness,* but the book pressed on my stomach in such a way that it put me right to sleep. I had read about nine pages in a week.

—Your father and I are worried, Dorothy said. You're out of school. You don't seem interested in getting a job. You're going through that book just like a snail. You're at the same place you were at on Wednesday.

—What day is today? I asked.

—Sunday.

—But it's summer. The days are supposed to drift by like this.

—It's going to be fall. It's going to be winter before long. I'm in my studio ten hours a day.

—You see work as salvation. That's how they control the middle classes. Haven't you heard? Work hard and all your problems will be solved.

—You should get into politics if you're so committed.

—Around here? The Cape Cod Republican's Club?

—You could do it at home. New York could always use an honest politician.

—Home? I said. This is my home. I never lived on West Fourth.

I went to boarding school and came here summers. I went to college and I came here summers. This is it. I'm from Squid Harbor.

—Maybe there's something in Provincetown, Dorothy suggested. Some feminists. You could be among your own kind.

—No thanks. I'm an ex-feminist and an ex-student. I don't care about money. I'm not gay. I'll never be a yuppie. I don't even like drugs.

—You're a total washout, Penguin. You better start over. Maybe you should begin by finding yourself a man.

—Forget it, I said. Love is like being joined at the hip. I saw enough love in this house to last a lifetime.

—I give up, Dorothy said. Do nothing. I'm going back to work.

I showed up in Richard's studio smoking one of the brown Balboa cigarettes Dorothy bought in Perera's, which was this little Portuguese market in Truro that smelled of salt fish and had opened a gourmet section for the summer. Richard looked at me disapprovingly, but he couldn't say much. They were his wife's cigarettes. It was her habit, not mine. I only smoked a couple a day since the big bus ride with Rebecca and I wasn't hooked. My whole generation is quite wary about addictions.

Richard was lifting a slab of aluminum plate with the ceiling hoist, then moving it into place using the long chain. Another plate was already welded to the base, making an inverted V like a tent. In the tent was a metal animal with nail heads sticking out of it at all angles, like a sheep that was in the process of being struck by lightning.

—Is that the AIDS thing you were talking about at the party?

—No. That one is still in my head. It may never get built, either. Some of the money was supposed to come from the government and they won't fund anything homoerotic.

—It doesn't seem very erotic, a wall of dead men's names.

—It's a cemetery of eroticism. Jesse Helms himself couldn't get aroused by that.

—So what's this?

—I'm calling it *Scapegoat*. It's a sacrificial animal that carries the sins of the tribe off into the forest.

—How can it collect the sins if it's inside a metal tent?

—I don't know, Richard answered. I only make them. I don't figure them out.

—Did Dorothy tell you what we saw at Uncle Joshua's this morning? They were taking someone into his house in a wheelchair.

—Who?

—Who knows? Whoever it was was wrapped up in a blanket.

—I'll be able to tell you tonight. I'm going to Josh's for a drink.

—With Dorothy?

I was hoping to tag along.

—Sorry, Penguin. No women invited.

—That's pretty retarded. Professors are supposed to be examples of enlightenment. Not to mention artists.

—Josh is a man of the old school.

—And you go along with it? You let yourself go over there under those sexist conditions? It's not medieval. It's neanderthoid.

—Take it easy, Penguin. It happens once a summer. Joshua and I reminisce about the old days, and you get a chance to be alone with Dorothy.

—Speaking of Dorothy, I said, did I tell you she's getting on my case about not working? I'm supposed to be on vacation.

—Maybe she's right, Richard said. Maybe you *should* work. It is the human condition. It doesn't count as vacation if you've been expelled.

He lowered the aluminum plate onto the base and let it lean gently against the other half of the tent. He dropped the welding helmet over his face so his eyes were just barely visible through the dark window, then turned up the current. He looked like a savage in the obsidian mask of a God. I thought of the Orozco mural back in the Dartmouth library, where the Aztec is cutting the victim's heart out with a stone knife. I studied underneath that image for my Math 5 final, and I will forever associate calculus with human sacrifice.

—Take a helmet if you want to watch.

I took one of the welder's masks from the shelf. Richard turned up the welder and adjusted the arc. The dark glass made the spark scarlet, like an explosion of blood working along the metal seam, sealing it for all time. The studio could come down and the dunes shift and cover us all, and when they dug up this piece it would be intact. The sacrificial victim—goat or sheep—would be lodged safely inside the tent, awaiting its hour to come around.

I had tried to destroy something I hated, and it almost worked. I thought of the Beta Sig brothers staying over the summer to repair the Hou, as they called it. They would be tearing the walls down, erecting new studs, plastering them, smoothing the finish, painting it white again just the way it was. They would be over in White River Junction searching the flea markets for another moth-eaten moose. They would be laboring collectively to build something up again that we had wrecked. I would never be sure whose victory it was.

Richard came home from Joshua's that night at eleven and sat down between us on the couch. Dorothy and I had been drinking Irish coffees and watching the TV news. They were interviewing an East Berliner who wanted to reinforce the Berlin Wall again so they could keep the AIDS virus out of the GDR.

—How was it at men's night? I asked.

—We discussed philosophy. Then we put on elk antlers and danced around the room.

—Did you find out about the person in the wheelchair? Who was it?

—Oh, someone is visiting, some old friend of his. Whoever it was was in the guest room asleep when I got there and never emerged.

—Strange. He didn't say anything? He didn't introduce you?

—How could he? The guest seemed to be asleep the entire time.

—Was it male or female?

—If you don't see them, it's rather hard to tell.

9

A few mornings later, I was out picking the first tart pinkish strawberries at the edge of the driveway that separated our land from Uncle Joshua's, when suddenly he appeared out on his deck. He wore the same salmon-colored dressing robe that he had on the day before when he greeted the men in the gray van. He didn't call to me or even say hello but motioned me over to join him with his hand. He had brought his Italian espresso maker out on the deck table and had set out a couple of elegant ebony-colored cups.

Uncle Joshua seemed to want to talk about my generation at Squid Harbor: Eliot and Robin Adler, Sue Love, Adam and Nick Whipple, Chester Schlessboom and this high SAT prodigy called Newton Yin. I was surprised he knew so much about them. Here was this international scholar knowing all our schools, even our majors. Especially the boys. He knew Chester Schlessboom was a year behind me at Dartmouth, and I had never seen him on campus and didn't even know he was there. He knew Newton Yin had already graduated from MIT, even though he was younger than all of us, and that he was working for some weapons laboratory on the West Coast. Of course education was Uncle Joshua's business, but I never imagined it would extend to us.

The ears of the Great Dane showed in the window for a moment, then disappeared.

—You'll have to excuse me, Joshua said. Cosimo hasn't had his breakfast.

Joshua didn't invite me in, so I had to imagine him pouring the

Gravy Train into Cosimo's red bowl, the cigar-butt tail vibrating in gratitude. When I got settled somewhere maybe I'd have a dog.

He returned to his deck chair and leaned forward as if to study my face. He looked a lot older in the morning light. The deep tan he had on the first night we talked to him seemed to have vanished, leaving a skin that was creased and pale, with dark furrows making a tent over both sides of his mustache, one deeper than the other, which came from the fact that he smiled on only one side of his face. His lips looked unnaturally red, as if he had applied some kind of coloration, not lipstick exactly but the dye they might use to give a dead body the appearance of life. In this light even the mink-colored beard seemed to be dyed. At fifty-five my father was just growing into the destiny of his face, while Joshua's already seemed artificially preserved.

I also noticed a ring he hadn't been wearing the other night, which had a skull pressed out of pewter or silver. And he had a small pendant around his neck carrying the same figure, which was a great logo for scholars, who spend so much time over the bones of the dead.

—Now, Penelope. Penny. Penguin. Richard tells me they're worried that you'll be idle all summer. Which I don't agree with. It's a grand time to read and observe.

—Why don't you tell Richard and Dorothy that, I suggested. They never get out of the studio. They're obsessed by the Puritan ethic, which I for one do not want to inherit.

—Well, I have a proposal, Joshua said. I have to be away for a long weekend, three or possibly four days. I have to attend a workshop in Boston.

—And you want me to feed Cosimo?

—I do want you to care for Cosimo. He is somewhat temperamental and inclined to be lonely when I'm away. He is a large animal with a very gentle heart. Do you have any experience in caring for dogs?

—None whatsoever, I said. I've never been responsible for anything except a goldfish.

I didn't tell Uncle Joshua that the fish had a tragic outcome; the thermostatic heater failed and it got boiled. It wasn't my fault exactly, but it did happen in my room and was therefore no one's responsibility but my own.

—Do you think you would be willing to learn?

—I can learn anything, I said. I have a liberal education. Almost.

—I wouldn't have asked you if I didn't think you were the right person. I have always thought of you as someone one could trust should the need arise. Along with Cosimo, I would also like you to look after a human friend who is not in the best of health. A family matter, just between the three of us concerned.

At first I couldn't figure out which three he meant.

—I don't know how you can keep a secret in *this* community, I said. Everyone knows everything at Squid Harbor.

—It would mean a great deal to Arnold and myself if we could have a summer of privacy.

—Arnold? I asked.

—My companion, Arnold Fratorelli. He is a composer, a musician, a former athlete, and a friend. And my closest companion for the past year.

That must have been the shape we saw in the wheelchair. The man even my father didn't get to meet. Then it struck me that there was only one category of sickness which, if you had it, you might not want anyone to know. Though I couldn't have imagined anyone even noticing at Squid Harbor. It was a pretty sophisticated place.

Uncle Joshua turned his face slightly while I thought, so that it appeared in a different slant of light, with the sun directly behind it, and I could see the skull outlined beneath the thinning gray hair and the onion-gray transparencies of his skin. What if this was a sexual disease? What if it was AIDS or syphilis, and this man had some kind of codependency with Joshua Brand so Joshua had to take care of him for life? That would explain the sense of doom that even on an incandescent summer morning enveloped Uncle Joshua like a shawl.

No one was unhappy at Squid Harbor. It was one of the

unwritten rules of paradise. You weren't supposed to bring your problems across the Cape Cod Canal. Seeing this sudden history in my father's friend, a man his age, this uncle, this family friend, brought on a chill, not to my skin but the skin of someone inside, maybe the little girl with a jewel-throated lion in her hand.

My first thought was to get out of the situation as gracefully as I could and then work on forgetting the whole thing. I wanted to remember Uncle Joshua exactly as he had been for me in childhood. I wanted to stay the way I'd been. Then I realized that Joshua already wasn't as he was and neither was I. Even if you had no interest in knowing something, there was no possible way to unknow it once you knew.

—But why choose me? I can't take care of anyone. Why don't you try to find a professional nurse?

—We may be forced to resort to that. But first we would like to try a friend.

—So how am I supposed to explain my existence?

—You'll be my research assistant. I'll give you a room and a desk.

For some reason known mainly to Uncle Joshua, it was a condition of the job not to tell anyone I was doing it. It would mean having to lie to my new mother as well as my old father. It would mean exposing myself to someone with a disease I knew very little about, only that the Dartmouth Alternative Health Caucus had passed out pamphlets saying it was spread by sex or needles or contact with contaminated blood. There'd been a condom in my pamphlet, which I'd opened and unrolled and tried to stretch on over my foot but it ripped open and the toes came out. I had political sympathy for gay males as an oppressed minority, though that still didn't erase the fact that they were men. But personal sympathy was something else. Why would I do this for the sake of someone I had never even met? They could get a nurse. She'd know what to do from the beginning. It could even be a male nurse in plain clothes who wouldn't arouse suspicion, if Uncle Joshua was so worried about his image.

Of course it would ease things at home for me to have a job. And there was this other thing: someone was calling out to me for help, someone who had been set adrift from the rest of us by a random combination of germs and passion. He needed a bridge to connect him to the regular world again. He wasn't a relative or even a family friend, this Arnold Fratorelli, not even a member of the Squid Harbor Association. My relation to him was a total coincidence. We weren't the same age or I suppose the same sex and God knows what his politics would turn out to be. All that we possibly had in common was that we both happened to be human beings, and perhaps also marginal outcasts but for totally different reasons. It was a major decision.

I did what I did as a child when I had to think something over. I smeared Cutter's into the fabric of my blue nylon warm-ups and I took the canoe up into the marsh. It was totally different from when I took Dorothy there. The sun had dried out the grasses so the wind ruffled them like someone blowing across a stringed instrument. Every few feet I would come on a marsh wren singing its heart out from a cattail stalk.

I lay down in the hull of the canoe and looked at the center of the sky. There was no question about what was wrong with Joshua's friend, though the term wasn't actually pronounced. It was a word always written in capital letters, like the scarlet neon sign over Abe's diner at the corner of Twelfth Street and West Fourth: ABE'S. It was a word always spoken in a certain tone, like one of the secret names of God.

Not to mention the question of Health. I was a health freak by nature. We all were. That's one of our strategies: Victory Through Outliving. We ate raisins and yogurt. We ate eggs because eggs attack men and not women. I was a relatively chemical-free human being and of course the male organ of reproduction had not come into the picture yet at all. "Mrs. Natural," Katherine had called me in Brussels once, when Fritz the Fur Merchant had tried to stuff smoked goose livers down my throat. "I know how those geese are killed," I had told him. Which goes for all animals. People who eat

75

living creatures carry a terrible karma and will be condemned to starvation or cannibalism in their next life. Even the Dartmouth Food Service had been on a vegetarian trip. In many ways, health was our form of immortality and our religious belief.

I was also a complete virgin as far as death was concerned. My parents were both living. My nonbrothers and nonsisters were already victims of contraception and could never die because they had never been born. Three of my grandparents were even alive. The fourth, Grandpa Forbush, the ornithologist, had flown cleanly away on a little engraved card that looked like a wedding invitation. We might have been responsible for a Beta Sig or two cremated in their beds during the fire, but we had made the pay phone call like good citizens, and they weren't. My body was perfectly healthy except for the wine stain on my neck and the Florida-shaped blemish on my back that except in a mirror I would never see.

No one anywhere near me had ever died. Joshua's proposal was a call from the direction of death, into the totally unknown. The one thing I had done in my life was to destroy something. What choice did I have but to say yes?

10

The canoe rode a bit lower and heavier in the water with the weight of my decision lying in the bottom of the hull. I stopped and rested the paddle. The tide was up high with the new moon and there were seals playing in the harbor, their heads sizing me up, then their backs humping up through the surface as they flipped and went under.

Maybe it was because all seals look the same that they seemed immortal. But how would you know if a venereal epidemic ran through the seal colony? One by one they would die and sink to the bottom, and a human being even living right on the shore wouldn't know what was going on. They'd be noticed only among their own kind, bubbling down through the water as they sank past. They would copulate and pass on the affliction and would not guess what was happening to them until they became extinct. For some reason I heard Bondo's crazy amphibian voice talking about condoms for seals.

Putting their rubbers on without using any hands.

I'd have to write Bondo. Of course I wouldn't say anything about my new job.

A seal appears right on the flat green boulder in front of the cottage. It has tried to climb the seaweed-covered rock and fallen back. It falls back again, and then finally makes it.

They've come out on the porch: Richard, Katherine, and their eleven-year-old daughter, Penny. The girl walks down to it, seeing how close it will allow her to come. The seal doesn't back off or get overalert the way wild animals get when you're too near, and she gets closer to it than to anything she has approached before in nature, even a chipmunk.

She can almost touch it. Her mother whispers Come back, but she can hear Richard up on the deck, calming her down. The seal sways its head from side to side, the way she has seen old men pray to themselves without speaking, just moving their lips.

She sees something wrong with one of the seal's eyes. It is closed over by a greenish-gray membrane and is weeping green pus. At first she thinks it has been crying, then she thinks: Infected. Nothing out there among the water species would be able to help it, not its mate, not anything with a seal's brain. It is seeking help where it has been afraid ever to come, from the strange white creatures that live in overgrown lobster traps along the beach.

The seal bows lower and sways its head further in each direction. It is losing energy and hardly seems able to keep itself up on the rock. She reaches out to touch it. She thinks it might help to know someone was concerned, someone out of the water where there are veterinarians and antibiotics and animal hospitals.

She reaches out and at the same moment hears Katherine scream no! from the deck and this time her father calls too. You have to come back now, he shouts. You could get hurt.

They've called the Massachusetts Fish and Wildlife Station in Chatham. The state biologist was just sitting down to his supper. The seal was probably injured by a propeller, he says. He would come afterwards but it would be too dark. It's a forty-five-minute drive. He'll come first thing in the morning if the seal is still there.

She watches the seal all during dinner, as the tide rises to surround its rock. At eight o'clock exactly it slips back into the water as if something has given way under its weight.

That was the summer before the first bleeding, two summers before the separation, three before the Divorce. And Eliot Adler had said, *Shit, Penny, it could have given you rabies.*

I had begun lying to my mother early in life and had kept it up on a fairly routine basis in letters and phone calls after she moved to Brussels. Since everything I told her would go right to Fritz, and since Fritz was not to be trusted with any version of the truth, lying to Katherine was both ethical and appropriate. Besides, it gave me practice in keeping up a second character, the daughter she would have wanted, a daughter who actually existed in the data I supplied her with. This provided me with something of a twin, to compensate for the children she had assassinated by smearing their unborn little bodies with spermicidal jelly so they would never be able to draw breath.

I tried to avoid lying to Richard. With Dorothy I had not yet had the opportunity, so I didn't know what it would feel like. On principle I would not have lied to Dorothy as a friend, but I would have had to as a mother. A mother can overwhelm you if you don't separate yourself from her plane of truth. But if you lie to your friends you are in trouble.

Dorothy was at her spinning machine when I came in. This strands the bronze filaments into the kind of stiff cablelike wire she uses for the legs of her spiders. She didn't like me pestering her at work, but I sat on the white plastic chair anyway, took one of her Balboas, and put my feet up on the workbench.

—I've found something to do, I announced. Over at Uncle Joshua's.

—What?

—Feeding Cosimo while Joshua's up in Cambridge.

—Cosimo?

—The dog. A Great Dane.

—That will take about ten minutes a day. Unless you are planning to feed him with a medicine dropper. Is Joshua going to pay you?

—Better than that. He's going to let me use a room to write in. I'll have my own studio. Just like you and Richard.

—Write?

79

—Yes. Write. I'm assisting Uncle Joshua with his new book. Also I'm doing a narrative on the year in Hanover. I'll just put down all the events, starting from the beginning. From the rape. Even before. I'll go back to what it was like when it was all male. The first coeds, all the problems with sexism, then the Beta Sigs and the Jesse Greenfield affair, then us. Jennifer and Rebecca and Michelle and the *Id*. I'll just put it down as it happened, ending with the fire and the trials.

—What will you do with it?

—Somebody might want it. Pura said I should do it. She's been asking so many questions, if I don't write it I'm afraid she'll do it herself. People are interested. It made the news when it happened. Both the rape and the fire were in the *Globe*. FEMINISTS AT DART-MOUTH. That's what the headline read. It's catchy, that's what Pura said. It's incongruous.

—Incongruous, she repeated, cutting and coiling a strand of bronze wire. You're very verbal, Penguin. Maybe you can do it. I could never write anything. I have the ideas, I sit down to write them and nothing happens. Eventually they come out as another spider.

—Joshua's giving me a typewriter and a desk.

—You're moving over there?

I wasn't, but Dorothy seemed somewhat pleased with that idea. Not that we weren't getting along, but my presence did pour something of a wet blanket on the honeymoon bed. During their lovemaking scenes in the middle of the night I could hear her start making these embarrassing lynx noises and scratching at the wall. Then I'd hear Richard put his hand over her mouth to quiet her down. "Shh. Penguin will hear you," he'd say. "Wait till she falls asleep."

Besides, Dorothy was turning out to be a somnambulist. She would start talking in her sleep. Then she would walk around the sleeping loft in these funny uneven paces, like someone with three legs. I would hear Richard stand up and lead her back to the bed. She'd say, "I was dreaming about Greece," or "I was dreaming about

Morocco." Richard would say, "You'll walk right off the balcony. Besides, Penguin will hear you." The whole time Dorothy being sound asleep.

—I think it's a grand project, she said. But you should talk to the others. You ought to get different points of view, not just your own. You know Peter Schlessboom. He went to your college about ninety years ago, and he has some amazing stories about old Dartmouth frat parties and the busloads of women they used to import when it was all men.

Now that I had lied even a little, we had entered a territory of fantasy that could be played out ad nauseam. Meanwhile I could keep the actualities to myself. I was establishing Dorothy as future parent, not as friend, which felt right. One might need a mother in this world, after all.

I would, however, need a friend to confide in. If Joshua was going to trust me, there had to be someone I could trust myself. Trust is a chain, that's the way it has to work. Jennifer had started waitressing in some restaurant at her Lake. Rebecca was off limits. Michelle was in the Southwest with the Indians. Which left Bondo. Bondo had written that he was already sick of stringing tennis rackets at Willensky's. I'd write to him and get him down to the Cape. He would eat very little and could live in the back of his jeep. Even though he was male, Bondo was housebroken and could be more or less trusted to the end.

When Joshua opened the door for me, Cosimo was already standing erect. The dog's eyes were on an absolute level with my shoulders and its ears angled out of the sides of its head like giant ferns. I extended an arm straight out so it would eat just my hand and not the entire body.

—He won't hurt you, Joshua said. Steady, Cosimo. Nice dog. You can refer to her as Penguin.

—We never kept animals, I said.

There was a slight dog smell in Joshua's house that I hadn't noticed the night I stopped by with Richard. They must never let the thing out and I wondered what it used for a bathroom. Maybe they had trained it to use the toilet. In some ways, Uncle Joshua was a highly disciplined man.

There was also a hospital smell. The sounding board on the piano was raised and the bench was moved over underneath the window. There were blank music sheets and half-written scores on the stand. There were also two microphones bending over the piano as if they were peering down into the strings, and one of those old-fashioned tape recorders with the two big reels.

—Arnold is resting. He works an hour at a time, God only knows how, then it exhausts him. How about something to drink?

I took a Mount Gay and cranberry juice, which mixed out to the color of antifreeze. As he was opening the refrigerator I could see medical-looking bottles and some gallons of 2 percent milk.

—He's now on liquids exclusively. He seems to be able to hold them down. Milk, liquid yogurt, and this enriched solution that looks like stagnant pond water covered with frogs' eggs. Arnold says it tastes just like Crab Florentine.

—How do we give it to him? I asked.

—Arnold is drinking in the regular way. At this point. What may startle you is how swiftly food passes through his system. He has more bacteria inside than you and I, and they break down the nutrients before he can use them. You'll see the result when you meet him. He used to be an all-state runner as well as a musician. He has lost nearly fifty pounds since we first met. So far it's been easy to care for him. It may get more complicated later on.

—What do you mean?

—We may have to pipe food directly into the stomach, if he loses his throat and esophagus functions. Then we'll have to increase our level of care.

—I don't know anything about the body, I said. I eat vegetables and brush my teeth. That's the extent of it.

—I didn't know anything either, Joshua said. But I'm trying. You learn when you're forced to learn. I've spent a week at the clinic already, and I'm spending three more days this weekend. I'm learning to give him oxygen and to administer injections.

—I don't understand why you took him out of the hospital. They can do all this stuff professionally. I know they can't cure him, but they are equipped to sustain him better than this. Better than leaving him in my hands anyway.

—He was in the hospital off and on for a year, Joshua said. They were maintaining him physically, but he was dying from within. His vital functions were stable, as they put it, but he wasn't composing a note. Which for Arnold was a fate worse than death. Since he's been here he's been writing superbly. You'll hear it tomorrow and you can judge for yourself.

—Are you saying you'd sacrifice his life to his music?

—He has made out a living will, Joshua said, that places all final decisions in my hands. We are carrying out his own specific desire to be at home.

—Just don't abandon me, I said. I've never even been responsible for a hamster.

—Don't worry. When I come back, I'll take over the care. You can go. Or if you've gotten involved, we'll talk about your staying on.

—But will he go to a hospital eventually?

—We've been to the hospital. I've seen him in a ward with forty other victims of this disease. We've decided that Arnold won't be going there.

—Until much later, you mean?

—He won't be going there at all. What must be done can be done here, and we will learn how to do it. And, when the season is over, if there is still any need for it, we can move back to Boston.

You can hear even the quietest person walking around in a house, but you can't hear a wheelchair even when it's right on top of you, so when one comes it is like the approach of a ghost. There was a space in the corridor behind Joshua and there, in the space, was a man's head.

Joshua turned and looked down when he saw my expression.

—This is the person I have told you about, Arnold. This is

Penelope Solstice. Penguin. She is a student at Dartmouth.

—Was.

Joshua spoke to him with the exaggerated slowness and volume that you use on the deaf. Arnold's hearing must have been starting to go, which would, I suppose, be like a painter going blind, despite the legend of Beethoven's deafness, which somehow I had never quite believed.

Arnold looked at me for a long moment, then out the window at Richard's *Chance,* as if the sculpture and I were products of the same hand.

—Maybe I'll have the pleasure of meeting him, he said.

—You should have come out when he was over here for cocktails. He didn't even realize you were here.

Arnold had the face of a young man who's been suddenly surprised by age. His eyes, still untouched by sickness, held a look of astonishment that probed right through us into the machinery of our cells. He was staring at me the way someone gazes into a mirror when they are alone. And I realized that he actually was alone. Already we weren't quite there for him.

There were also these small multiple nicks or lines around his mouth that he had probably got by cutting himself while shaving, or maybe while Joshua was shaving him. And he was smiling at me and Joshua as if he had caught us at something indecent. I couldn't imagine that someone could smile like that who was vulnerable to every medical disaster of humankind and who would be ending his life within a finite, foreseeable amount of time.

I felt I was in the presence of a person who had in some way already died, which also seemed to affect me and Joshua, as if we were all now somehow in the category of the dead.

—Penguin will take over the chores for the next few days. She'll be staying at her parents' and coming over early in the morning. She'll have the room opposite yours for a study. She's going to be helping me with the Persian book and in her spare time she'll be working on her memoirs.

The blanket jumped suddenly in Arnold's lap as if he had a small animal under there. Over in the corner Cosimo's ears lifted, then relaxed.

—We'll be getting some work done, Arnold said. I'm sure. There's so little time in a summer. Before you know it, you turn around and it's gone.

—So you don't see us sunning ourselves on the beach, Joshua put in.

I didn't. But then I didn't spend much time on the beach myself.

—You're working on something? I asked Arnold.

Joshua answered for him.

—It's called *The Keeper of Sheep*. He's setting three poems to music. They're by Fernando Pessoa. Are you familiar with his work?

—My whole education was a waste, I answered. I'm trying to start over. That's why I'm here.

Arnold threw off the lap blanket with a gesture that startled me. He'd look ready to die, then he would make these rapid movements, as if he were saving up energy to be released in spasmodic little bursts. It was no living creature under the blanket, it was a book, which he opened to one of its first pages and then handed to me, squeezing both my hands as I accepted it, as if it were some kind of sacred text.

—He's a Portugese poet, Arnold said. Read this. Read it out loud.

I was afraid it was going to be in a foreign language. It wasn't. I read slowly, looking up in the spaces between the lines at Uncle Joshua, who was leaning down beside the wheelchair. I couldn't yet bring myself to look Arnold Fratorelli in the eye.

And if something's in my fancy
I desire to be a lamb
(Or the whole flock of sheep
So I can go over the hillside
And be many happy things at the same time.)
It's only because I feel what I'm writing when the sun sets
Or when a cloud's hand passes over the light
And a silence runs off through the grass.

—That's what I'm working on at the moment. I'm setting it for mezzo-soprano and piano. Pessoa's a favorite of ours. We found him on a very romantic trip to Venice. I thought it might be the right thing for a last work.

—Not "last," Joshua said. Don't even say it. You know they've had remissions. You could have years. They are working on cures night and day, in every civilized country in the world. There's the AZT. Look at you. The AZT is holding the thing at bay.

Arnold made a face at me like a kid being forced to eat their Brussels sprouts.

—AZT. Bluk.

Up to this point Joshua Brand had been as cool as I've seen anyone. Now he was agitated and it showed. He bent over the wheelchair, almost touching his face to his friend's face.

—No illusions, Arnold reminded him. You promised us one summer without illusions.

Arnold had two copies of the book, so I took one home. I thought it best also to befriend Cosimo on the way out. I reached out my hand to its furthest extension, like a telescope, and waited for him to tear it off at the wrist. He just put his nose on it. It felt leathery and black and cold, like a Reebok, and it was dripping a little so I pulled my hand away wet.

They say it came from African monkeys in the beginning. They say dolphins have caught it from floating hospital garbage and are beaching themselves in despair. I left Uncle Joshua's wondering if perhaps dogs couldn't get it too.

11

I woke early and pulled Fernando Pessoa out from under the base of my aluminum penguin, where I had tucked him when I went to sleep.

I feel my whole body lying full length in reality.
I know the whole truth and I'm happy.

My body was lying full length, but I wasn't sure if it was in reality or not. I didn't know the truth. I wasn't particularly happy. I had dreamed that my fingers were welded together into a single stump that I had put a latex glove over that had only one opening, like a contraceptive. Then someone had put Mikhail Gorbachev in my arms and told me to lift him, and he weighed nothing, like a balloon, and I realized he was dead. I've always felt close to Gorby because of his skin markings, which are somewhat reminiscent of my own.

Joshua was leaving at nine, and I would be in charge. There wasn't a sound yet from the newlyweds upstairs. But, in the alder thicket between our cottage and the road, a hermit thrush called, then stopped, then called again from another direction. Or maybe it was a second bird answering, a rival competing for the right to breed.

In the complete silence between thrush calls I could hear piano chords from the next cottage. Joshua had said Arnold never slept, he worked at all hours, day and night, trying to finish his piece. *The Keeper of Sheep.* Now perhaps with his existence revealed at least to one neighbor, he could let his work out of the closet to some extent. I knew even less about music than I knew about Portugese poetry, but I knew what dissonance was and these notes were dissonant to the extreme. He would play a chord and wait, the individual tones struggling with each other in the fogbound morning distance between our two cottages. Arnold's chord would tense up the air, then the thrush would sing its harmonious multiple flute carol and things would be released. They went on without knowing the other existed, and I lay in my bed under the open window, listening to them both, bird and human, not quite knowing which I was supposed to be.

It was a wonder that Richard and Dorothy hadn't heard this predawn music, or never mentioned it at least. Maybe they thought it was Joshua playing, or a stereo. Or they were too busy in their erotic little nest of a sleeping loft directly over my head. The world of a couple is very small, while the world of a single person extends as far as she can hear.

So I lay there a long time listening to the thrush and the chords growing more and more discordant until you'd think something would break and I thought *what?* What more was there to be broken, what in the universe remained to be destroyed? I had been born into a world disassembled by war, then dissected by universal divorce. Now, in this so-called time of peace, it was being eaten by a disease, a disease we thought we could save ourselves from through straight behavior or armor-plating ourselves with rubber shields, so that only the evil or reckless ones would be exposed. My father was right, though. We're interconnected. As long as one person is suffering from this, we are all suffering. You couldn't protect yourself by being a woman, either, or any kind of division into we the healthy and they the diseased.

Joshua had told me that Arnold's mother was dead. I was glad of it. I wouldn't want to think of her somewhere waiting, I wouldn't want to think of her sharing the strange countdown that composed his life.

The one thing I had learned in college was to resist the male gender from the center of my heart, and I had tried to burn down one of their major headquarters. So at first it had seemed like a kind of justice that the penis would have an incurable fatal malady all its own. But I was now face-to-face with a sickness that transmitted itself specifically through the male organ and nowhere else except maybe the slim phallus of the heroin needle. It wasn't fair. A tooth for a tooth was all right, but not an eye for a tooth. Men brought discord into the world. Arnold's music was discordant to the point of violence. A woman could not have composed it. It was too unnatural. It could make a person wish to be deaf, especially next to the thrush. Yet it was his music that was calling to me, personally, and not the thrush's. His strange chords replayed themselves in the articulation of my spine and I felt their discord in the discoloration of my back, which in the mirror was shaped like the state of Florida: not an island but a peninsula. Maybe it takes an epidemic to know what the lines meant about for whom the bell tolls. No person is an island, no matter how hard they try.

I opened the book.

I never kept sheep, but it's as if I'd done so.

The poet was writing in the name of another poet, a fiction. And the fictional poet was imagining he was a shepherd. And I was reading it, imagining myself as a man, a Portuguese poet from the turn of the century, a lover of Walt Whitman, a homosexual.

Yet how could you know what it was like being inside another person? Somebody who woke up with music or sculpture or poetry in their head and spent the day or night trying to get it through the barrier of their skull and out into the actual world, somebody who was another sex or from another generation or another language? Somebody so sick that death ate and slept with them like a Siamese twin.

Or you could just sing your heart out like the bird that woke up out of its nest to find itself a hermit thrush once more and sang the notes over and over that were prestructured in its brain.

And the only innocence is not to think.

Arnold had marked two of the three poems he was setting to music. One was the one about the lamb which I had read to him in the wheelchair. The other was about the Oxcart.

I'd give anything if only my life were an oxcart
Squeaking down the road early one morning
And later returning to where it started
Toward nightfall down the same road.
I'd have no need of hopes—I'd need only wheels.
As I grew old I'd have no wrinkles or white hair.

When I'd be of no further use they'd pull off my wheels
And I'd lie there overturned and broken at the bottom
    of a pit.

And it was a strange thing, I wanted to write a paper about it and hand it in and get it corrected, not for an A but so that someone would read it and understand what I had tried to say, or maybe hand the paper over to his wife who would shut off the TV and read it and understand it too.

Maybe I could go back to school under another name.

I got over to Uncle Joshua's at nine sharp and found him packed and ready to leave. He'd left a page of instructions written in his precise scholarly script. Arnold, in the wheelchair, was at the piano but not playing. Evidently they'd said good-bye already because Joshua simply waved, wished us luck, and drove away in his off-white Volvo sedan. I wondered if they slept in the same bed: the two tenses of being human, the sick and the healthy, wrapped up for the night in one another's arms.

I wondered if Joshua had it also or would come down with it and what would happen to him if he did. You could carry it and it might not show up for years, then you could pass it on to someone and in them it would show up in six months and they would die.

Eventually, though, the odds were a hundred percent.

Joshua had laid out a pair of hospital gloves along with the instructions on the counter over Cosimo's dog bowl. They looked like condoms with fingers. The sight of them scared me, as if they had hands in them already. For the first time I imagined an infection, which would take the form of my whole body becoming a uniform livid purple. I thought of my own death as a man with a purple face, purple hands, purple body, coming just before sunrise into my room. And not because I had taken any sexual pleasure, but because I'd helped someone I didn't even know.

Cosimo was sleeping in his corner. I put the gloves on and walked over quietly and calmly and touched him on the ear tip. With the gloves over my hand he didn't scare me. You could walk through the world like this, I thought, fearless. I peeled the gloves off and folded them and put them in a drawer. Maybe I'd use them if things got bad. For now life was too precious to go around wearing an artificial skin.

Arnold was replaying his morning chord sequence on the tape deck, writing it down on lined paper. Amidst the notes I could clearly distinguish the voice part, which would carry the words of the poem. He shut it off, but the music remained a while longer in the air.

—Is there anything I can get you? I asked him.

—A cup of coffee. And Cosimo hasn't been fed. Josh was in a rush.

I doled out about twelve pounds of Mighty Dog and a half package of raw hamburger, which brought last night's scalloped oysters right back up into my throat. Maybe I'd wear the contraceptive gloves just for handling Brother Cosimo's red meat. I put some coffee through Joshua's polished steel espresso machine, then steamed the milk in the two cups for cappuccino. I made Arnold a mixture that was one-tenth coffee and the other nine-tenths milk.

His hands were so weak, so shaky in taking the little cup that I wondered how they could have produced the extreme chords I'd been hearing since before dawn.

—You were playing at sunrise, I said.

—I work early, when I can work at all. So as not to disturb the community with music they might not want to hear.

—I read two of those poems. They're easy. I hate poetry when it's obscure, so it takes a professor to tell you what it says.

He pulled a handkerchief out of the pocket of his robe, coughed into it, and put it away without looking. If he had been alone, I knew, he would have stared at it. He would have read it as a message from the world that was self-destructing inside him, like one of those necromancers reading the entrails of a goat.

—So what is the third poem? I asked. I read the ones about the lamb and the oxcart.

—It's the last poem in that group: "I go indoors, and shut the window." That's what I'm working on now. I just have to stay here long enough to get it done.

—Also, how can you write a song without hearing the voice? I asked. Do you just know what it's going to sound like? Can you actually hear it in your head? How could Beethoven have composed if he was deaf?

If anyone had the answer to that one, it would be Arnold, whose whole body was in the process of going deaf. He spilled a little of the cappuccino on his blanket and looked away, out the side window. He was trying to keep up an exterior dignity while he was shrinking away inside, like a man carrying something that gets heavier and heavier until he has to put it down. Although Arnold was sitting at the piano, penciling in the notes, you could sense the tension, and the further tension from his knowing it could only get worse. That was the tension that I heard in the notes of his work, which gave it this anxious jagged quality under the simple and lovely words. The music disturbed me. It was like the disease itself, spreading by stages into the outer world. It was the first time I'd understood the reason for dissonant music, which is not just modernist weirdness but addressed to the envelope of sadness in which we live.

—No, I don't hear it in the air, he said. And I don't know what it's going to sound like and I don't think it's previously composed up in heaven so that you just have to write it down. I make it step by step, like a mathematical equation. Each chord leads to the next, determines the next, and the next should inevitably follow from the one before, and yet they are all free and you might choose any one of them completely at random.

—So you don't know how it's going to come out when you begin?

—Tell me, if you could be given a drug that would allow you to see the future in exact detail, would you swallow it?

—People try everything to get into their futures, I said. I wrote a paper on that. They get their tarots read. They get their palms studied. The Haitians cut off the heads of chickens and tell the future from their blood. The old generals used to have dream interpreters in their tents. They'd wake up and the interpreter would be right there. I wrote a paper on this for Anthro 12. The *I Ching*...

—You're overeducated, Arnold said.

—I never heard *that* before.

—I meant, if you could find out the exact time and location of your death, would you accept that information?

—I see what you mean, I said. I wouldn't do it. I only keep going because I don't know what's going to happen. Look at this, for example. Who would have thought I'd end up here with you?

—That's the difference between you and me, Arnold said. I already know how it's going to turn out. The only thing I don't know is my next note. Even death isn't in the future any more. It's already happened. It's in the past. All I have for chance, for a future, is the end of this work. That's the only place where chance can enter into my life.

—I know what chance music is, I said. That's like that guy letting the cat walk on the piano keys.

—It's right on the tip of my tongue, Arnold said. I'll think of it in a minute. Chance. Dice. Aleatory. Bird. Flight. Prison. Cage. My friend John Cage, who is tragically misunderstood. Did you know that aleatory comes from the Latin *alea,* which means dice? I should say die. One of them. Chance is everything. If you know how something is going to come out you are not an artist but a factory worker assembling a product.

—There's nothing wrong with factory workers, I said.

—There's nothing at all wrong with factory workers. They are making things, just like artists. The only difference is that they know what the thing they are making is going to look like and we don't.

He suddenly reached out and struck a chord and held it. Over in his dog basket Cosimo howled, a low falsetto that he let out like a ventriloquist, without opening his mouth.

—Cosimo is my best critic, Arnold said. He doesn't know anything about music but he knows what he likes.

—But what about Beethoven? I asked.

—Beethoven wasn't deaf inside.

With an energy that seemed to come from someplace outside of his wasted body, he played a sequence of two or three more chords. Even though it was pure summer, with a dozen multicolored spinnakers out in the harbor, the chords had a complex discordant weight that made me feel older and created a cool wind that made the weather all of a sudden seem like fall. In one sense Arnold was right. Workers were precious because they were human beings, but one note of this music was worth the whole output of a truck or mayonnaise factory, because it could shed some light into the swamp of feelings where things usually move around in confused darkness. A man was dying. I looked into my politics to understand it and found nothing there. I needed something or someone to be angry with, but there was no enemy in sight, no place for politics or anger, just this sadness that already had the odor of wet leaves.

Arnold coughed again into the handkerchief, a long low sound like a bellows blowing on a live coal in his chest. When he brought the cloth away from his mouth it was not dark menstrual crimson but a bright phony red like dyed maraschino cherries or stage blood.

12

Uncle Joshua was at a training program for home carepersons at a private clinic in Boston. He had started the program before they came down, interrupted it to establish Arnold on the Cape, then he'd gone back. He called to say he would be another day, or at the most two. That meant I'd be alone with Arnold for the better part of a week.

Avoiding my hyperactive parents, I spent most of my time writing my narrative, with one ear always open to Arnold's needs. He would rest for an hour, then rise up coughing and I would help him into the wheelchair and steer him up to the piano. Like Gorbachev, he was so light I could lift him bodily into the air. He had no flesh at all and his bones felt as if they'd been already digested from within.

The minute he started composing he was a different man. The coughing would stop and you could feel this intense concentration radiate from his hands as he played, penciled in the notes, then reached over to switch on the tape deck and replay the chord sequence through.

He could only work for an hour, then I would wheel him to the bathroom and help him in and out of the chair.

—You should have those gloves on, he said. I'd be wearing them myself if I were still alive.

The strange thing was, I wanted to touch him. I wanted to feel the slightly fevered outer warmth of the skin and the hollow avian bones. It was almost supernatural to be able to lift someone like that, it had the magic of a ballet like the Nutcracker where people can lift one another into the air.

He'd sleep for a couple of hours, then wake up and start again. When Joshua was there he'd been writing only in the early morning. For some reason, with me he wrote in these short bursts all day long. Sometimes he'd play something and ask me "Is that going to work?" half to himself and half to me. I couldn't of course comment at first, I was trying to think about it too much, then I got bolder and I'd say yes when it felt right. I found a new sense in myself, a vestigial musical organ right beside the heart.

Sometimes I'd check my responses out with Cosimo, who paid utmost attention to every sound.

In the evening we'd play a couple of rounds of Boggle, which is this game where you try to make as many words as you can while the sand runs down in a little yellow hourglass. Arnold slaughtered me in the beginning—he was really a genius in all areas—but our scores were more and more even as the week went on.

—You're getting smarter, he would say. You must be studying the dictionary while I'm asleep.

But I wasn't. His verbal skills were deteriorating right before my eyes. It was like playing with a person who got a year older and closer to senility every night. He began having these trance passages in which his eyes came unfocused and wandered in two directions. I'd have to say *Arnold* and he'd shake himself out of it to find his last grains running through the pinched neck of the glass.

He was growing smaller inside his body and his hands were getting even longer and thinner. They made me think of the long, fingery flight bones inside the wings of a pterodactyl, especially when he spread them over the piano with the summer blanket still drawn over his arms. I had been with sick people before. Bondo had pneumonia in December, just before the fire, and had stayed motionless in bed for a week. Rebecca Crowell had the Bangkok flu and spent three days in a coma with a 103° fever, watching daytime TV shows with the sound off. I had seen the battle going on inside them between sickness and health. Even at the worst of it, when they were convulsing and throwing up, you could sense their bodies striving to restore themselves and you knew they would get through.

But now, with Arnold, there was no dialectic of invasion and immunity, and no interior health asserting itself with a program for the future. That was why he was so strangely calm. The cottage was like a haven of peace, a shrine, a country cemetery like you see on the back roads of the Cape, compared to Richard and Dorothy's frantic place next door, which was wired with ambition and sexuality and desire.

Each morning a section of *The Keeper of Sheep* would be started, and Arnold would develop it as if in slow motion, chord by chord, over the entire day.

Every so often he'd say, "Penguin, it's time for the next course," which meant I was to produce one of his nutrients in the sequence of milk, yogurt, apricot juice, mint tea, and Crab Florentine Concentrate. These were prescribed in Joshua's list of instructions, which I had taped to the refrigerator door. He asked for them without hunger and sipped them apparently without satisfaction. The hunger Arnold did not feel was, I guess, transferred to me since I would get ravenous about every two hours and nuke up a haddock portion or a bagel, things I would never have allowed into my mouth, except what sense did health food make when you were with someone who was never going to get well?

Cosimo would then stand up and salivate over whatever I was eating, so I would have to pour some more Mighty Dog into his bowl. Then I would let Cosimo out and he would go back to sleep and I would start feeling numb and hazy and have to lie down in my study for a nap. In counterpoint to my cycles of hunger and fulfillment, Arnold rested and went to the bathroom and composed: striking a chord, writing it on the staff, then striking another as the score to *The Keeper of Sheep* accumulated on the page.

I would stare at the jade carving on Uncle Joshua's end table with its three tiny philosophers halfway up their mountain. I hadn't noticed it before, but at the base of the jade mountain was a miniature city of Chinese huts, which must have been where they lived.

Two of the philosophers were already in the hut and another was about to join them. He was carrying an umbrella to indicate that it was raining, but there was no feeling of urgency in his posture. He would arrive when he arrived. If he was soaked from the rain his friends would give him a dry robe and some tea. Then they would look down from that height on the busy universe of men in the valley beneath them. Later on perhaps they would all climb to the uninhabited summit. But for the present they were content, they were resting and talking at a point where a mountain brook emerged from the rock, a point halfway between the sky and the city, death and life.

That was the ambiance at the Brand cottage while I was alone with Arnold. The only thing in that home that moved or changed was the slender trail of notes finding their way over the blank lines of the music paper, which was like a miracle because those combinations of notes had never existed before and now they did, they were produced from nothing and they would continue to exist after Arnold himself died. Anyone who could read music could play them and bring him back. He would never have any children, but these marks were like his DNA: his body was laying a trail of inheritance in some secret place because it was scheduled to perish before its time.

And I was working too. The chronicle that I had fabricated as an excuse to live there was actually taking shape. It was a microscopic event in the annals of womankind, but it was real and I knew it from the inside out.

I had also started something else. On alternate pages I was keeping a journal or diary about Arnold, what was happening to him and what was happening to me as a result. It didn't seem like they had much to do with each other, the story of women at a men's college and a man wasting away in a beach house, but maybe at some point in the history of the future it would make sense.

Sometimes Arnold and I would stop working at the same time and I would wheel him over to the window and draw back the shades so he could look out at the harbor where the kids would be sailing their Lasers, or maybe some visiting schooner would have come into Squid Harbor and lowered its sails for lunch. We wouldn't even say anything. The glass was a hundred feet thick that separated us from the crew scrambling on the deck and the wind heeling the little boats almost into the water. Arnold had found his way to the place halfway up the mountain, where the Chinese philosophers were, and for that period anyway he had taken me along.

I was startled one afternoon to see Sue Love and Robin Adler walk by on their way to the beach. Sue had on a Mount Holyoke sweatshirt. She was less anorexic-looking than usual and so tan she looked like an Indonesian. Robin was white and delicate and urbane. They threw a glance at the cottage but of course they couldn't see in because of the bamboo shades that were always drawn over Joshua's window. I felt like a separate species and turned back to work.

I was getting along great with Dorothy, being out of her hair, and Richard was at his happiest, which is when he is in his studio day and night. Every couple of days he would make a trip to his fabricator in Braintree and he would unload another aluminum section out of the van. My new parents liked to copulate in the afternoon sun down on the daybed, and with me occupied next door they could do it whenever they wished. Their enthusiasm for each other kept them from wondering what else I was doing over there. I wasn't even jealous of Dorothy Dvorjak since I had in my own way also taken a man into my life.

After I came home from Joshua's we'd have a Sombrero and I would read my parents the material I was writing about school. But I'd leave out the other stuff. All in all, it was a good week, and I was making a friend to replace all the lost friendships of the year, perhaps a temporary one, but knowing that only made the time more precious.

It was also preposterous. I was devoting my life to a man who did not officially exist, so in a way I didn't have an existence either. Dorothy wasn't curious, and even seemed happy for me as I slipped off to work before her exhausted husband was awake. I didn't perhaps have my hands on a prospective Groom, but at least I wasn't wasting my life on the beach like Susan and Robin.

—College kids are supposed to work in the summer, she'd say. But look at those two.

On that we agreed.

Then came the night of the big Squid Harbor Fourth of July's Eve party at Peter Schlessboom's mansionlike cottage up on the hill, which was oriented directly above the entrance to the marsh.

—Come on, Dorothy said. You can quiz Peter Schlessboom about his college days.

So we all went. Richard was letting his beard grow again and looked handsome, though it did obscure the planes of his face. Beards make men look essentially alike, which was perhaps intended by nature so they'd have a uniform appearance, while women would be the individuals of the race. Dorothy was dressed in these curious medieval-looking olive pants with about a fifty-inch waistline and a drawstring, plus an olive drab vest.

—You could be an extra in a Miracle Play, Richard told her.

I wore my ordinary clothing, which was combat boots and a sweatshirt with Lenin on it just so I would feel right at home at the Schlessboom estate. Richard of course said nothing concerning my appearance at all.

Peter Schlessboom greeted us at the door with his big belly and his totally bald head, which looked like it would be soft if you pressed it, like one of those Chinese mushrooms or the head of a huge newborn baby before the fontanelle plates have closed up. He put out for our inspection a hand that was just like an inflated surgical glove. Everything about Peter was so rounded and smooth that you felt he was out of his element in the air and should have been a marine mammal such as a dugong or manatee. He owned a chain of dry-cleaning establishments around Boston and his house was like an advertisement for Clorox bleach. It had overstuffed white upholstery and bleach-white polar bear fur rugs. The only thing that was not white in the Schlessboom house was the long green Dartmouth banner stretched over the ivory-colored couch. He was a true alum.

Peter pointed the top of his fetal-looking head straight at me and talked down towards my feet.

—You're one of the Big Green too, I understand.

Evidently the word hadn't reached him about the Beta Sigs.

—I got a dishonorable discharge this spring, sir. I am out.

—Oh yes. You were involved in the troubles. You're not one of the expelled women, are you? Heavens, I should have been told. I'm a Class Agent. Something can be arranged. There are no unforgivable sins. No, no. Not here on earth.

—You seem to know a lot about it. Was it in the alumni magazine?

—No, no, Peter Schlessboom said. That's one organ I never touch. Just obituaries and demands for money in that thing. They're afraid to print any news. Afraid the old grads will stop coughing it up. No, no. It was all reported by my son.

—Sleezy? I said.

—Chester.

I guess that's what they were calling him around the house. I couldn't believe Chester Schlessboom even got admitted to Dartmouth. He went to the thirteenth grade after high school, then the fourteenth grade. I suppose if your father went there you were a Legacy no matter what.

—Chester's a Phi Delt, his father said. As I was, and my brother Dunc and my father and my father's brother, Preston Schlessboom the third.

—I want to talk with you about Dartmouth, I said. You were there when it was all men. What was it like? I mean, did it get weird? Is that why they let in women? I heard the men used to bang their heads against the walls. I heard some of them died that way.

—It was Cro-Magnon, Peter said. We cooked wild animals over bonfires of human bodies on the college green.

He was wrong about the Cro-Magnons, but I didn't correct him. They were quite decent and humane, more so than us.

—What do you think about coeducation? I asked.

—Serious mistake. Girls distract you from your educational purpose. Emotional entanglements cloud the mind. Discipline crumbles. Our boys suffer from protein loss and the teams go down in defeat. As you can see.

Even I knew the Big Green were in the cellar again last year. Peter Schlessboom looked like he was about to cry. At which moment Sleezy himself stepped up. The transformation was starting already: the manatee stomach, the head, the perfectly pressed clothes smelling like they'd been boiled in carbon tetrachloride.

—I've never seen you around, I said.

—I've seen *you,* Sleezy said. You had your picture in the *Digest.* I've got it on my wall.

The *Dartmouth Digest* had printed all of our photos with rifle targets superimposed over our chests.

—You probably used it for a dartboard, I remarked.

—No, no. It's because I knew you from Squid Harbor. In fact, it's too bad you didn't go all the way. The Beta Sigs are assholes.

—Chester was never one to mince words, his father said. My boy.

Sleezy pulled me aside.

—If you want to take the Land Rover over to the back shore, he suggested, we could do some surf-casting for striped bass.

Pura Batrachian came up all in black, with dangly little chain-link earrings and a chain necklace to remind us she kept at least one foot in New York.

—Are you writing that article? Pura asked.

—I'm writing something. I don't exactly know what it is.

Peter Schlessboom came up with about eight cans of Darlings that he managed to hold between the fingers of both hands like some kind of scarlet fruit-bearing plant.

—As I was saying, I'm sure we can do something about your separation from the college. Nothing is ever final. If it were, we'd all be dead.

He laughed with a weird inward sound, like someone laughing

with their head completely underwater.

—I don't think I'd be welcomed back, I said. I'd be assassinated.

—Wait a couple of years, Mr. Schlessboom said. Enjoy the world, then go back. Your opponents will all have graduated. You'll be the only one left.

I talked to Chester Schlessboom and I had to say he'd turned out better than you might have expected, given his genetic limitations. He had a simple philosophy. He separated the world into two camps, the assholes and the nonassholes, which is an apolitical division having to do with neither the right nor the left but what I suppose you would have to call the center. Maybe after Joshua got back I'd take Sleezy up on the idea of the surf-casting trip. I had been fishing a few times but had never caught anything in my life.

Pura turned out to be at the party with Jerry Perera. The Pereras were this huge Portuguese family that owned Perera's, the mini package and grocery store out on the Truro Road. They had kept the store since the time of Vasco da Gama. Jerry had taken over the patriarchy when old man Perera had died, who was just a children's legend by the time I came around. The Pereras had by this point sold enough Scotch and smoked oysters to the summer people that they could buy their own place on the Cove, though you would never know it from looking at Jerry, who still ran a lobster boat and wore survivalistic old army fatigues or lobsterman's yellow or the grease-stiffened overalls of a mechanic. Jerry was about thirty-five and generally orchestrated the family in its daily routine at the store, which involved at least ten Pereras at all times, up on ladders reaching things down or passing crates from the cellar through a hole in the floor. The Pereras were decidedly not into population control.

Jerry was dark with a short dark Marine style haircut, and I'd heard way back in my childhood that he had gotten into college someplace and had dropped out after two weeks and volunteered for Vietnam. When I was sixteen years old and at the cottage by myself I tried to buy a six-pack at Perera's and Jerry Perera had said, "Penny, if you're old enough to buy alcohol, you're old enough to fuck." I didn't think I had heard him correctly so I asked him to repeat it. He did. It was my very first proposition and I'd gone home and thought about it for five hours and written him an elaborate letter saying no.

There was also a rumor that Jerry Perera had something to do with drugs, which was maybe the real reason his family lived so well, with a steel-and-glass year-round house on the second row of dunes that was the same shape as the Schlessbooms' if not quite so grand. Putting it all together, he looked just about right for Pura, and I could picture them in the dark after the store closed, with all the groceries around, sniffing a few lines of coke, then tying each other up with leather thongs.

Dorothy was at my side, holding my hand, whispering in my ear.

—You have to help me. I still don't know everyone yet. Who's that?

—Those are the Loves, I said. Susan's parents. They've been divorced and then they got remarried in a big ceremony on their boat. It rained and everybody was in oilskins. He's called Pig and she's called Corkie. I've never known their real names.

—Pig and Corkie Love, Dorothy repeated. It's nice to come up here from New York and meet some normal people. And who are the Oriental couple?

—That's Smokey Yin and his wife Daisy. He's in computers. He is a genius. They say Smokey invented one of those artificial languages. They have a kid, Newton, who used to come over all the time. He went to MIT right out of the ninth grade. That kind of thing is inherited.

—I don't know, Dorothy said. This is quite a preppy group. How'd your father get mixed up in this?

—It used to be totally artists. Hans Hoffman lived here, and Milton Avery. And before that, Edward Hopper had a place out on Route 6A. He was the first, then everyone came. Then the prices went up. Most of the artists got squeezed out, but not us. We were so poor we used to rent it out and only come up for two weeks, but

Richard never sold out. People would come right up to the door and ask to buy it. Of course Katherine's lawyer tried to get it, too.

—Don't talk to me about Katherine, Dorothy said. The subject is off-limits. Who's that over there?

—That's Bailey Varnum.

—Oh, he's the one they call P. T.? With the castle?

—He runs a beer company. Darlings.

I took Dorothy over to meet P. T.

—Penny Solstice! P. T. bellowed. You're a grown woman. You must be over twenty-one.

—Twenty, I said.

—Another year, he said, and you can be one of our consumers. By the way, you know who wants to see you. Virgil. He has the twins this summer.

—Child care. I'm not exactly designed to be a nanny.

I imagined scrubbing my hands after lifting Arnold out of his wheelchair, then running over to take charge of P. T.'s little grandchildren. Somehow it didn't seem to fit.

—Child care nothing, P. T. said. My son has an eye for pulchritude, if you'll forgive an old soldier for using a word like that.

Pulchritude. Virgil Varnum was about eight years older than me. He had chosen me as crew for his Laser once and had exposed himself to me right in the middle of the race. It was so small that I hadn't recognized it and at first I thought he had some kind of a snail in his lap. When I finally saw what it was I let the sheet go and the boat righted and we both fell out. They'd had to come and get us in the launch and when they pulled us out Virgil was still unzipped. Now he was divorced and had twin daughters and custody of them for the whole summer. God protect those little children. There should be a third sex, self-reproducing, like the creatures in Plato with the four arms and four legs, so we would all be saved from men, the best of which are only half there.

—It sounds like he's interested in you, Penguin, Dorothy whispered.

—I'm sure he is.

—He'd be a prime one. You wouldn't have to work for the whole rest of your life.

—Just what I need. Lifelong unemployment. And all the beer I could drink.

She changed the subject.

—Joshua Brand isn't back yet, is he? From Cambridge.

—No, I said vaguely. Monday or Tuesday.

—So will you still be able to work over there? I suppose not.

—Uncle Joshua said that would be up to me. Their house is bigger than ours. *His* house, I mean. There's still a couple of spare rooms. The one I'm working in won't be in use.

—It could get crowded over there, if he gets too many people.

I wondered how much Dorothy knew. How could she not? It was all going on a couple of hundred feet away.

—What do you mean?

—I mean what with you and Joshua and that giant dog you say is over there, that I've never laid eyes on. Only males are allowed in the Brand household. Male men and male dogs. And you. You're the exception. The female caretaker in the male harem.

And right in the middle of the Schlessboom's party she put her arms around me and kissed me right on my neck beneath the earring.

—I'm sorry, she said. I'm having too many of these gimlets. And it's the Fourth of July. So I get to say what I want. And another thing, Penguin. I worry about you.

—What's there to worry about? I'm an employed person. Or at least I have been.

—I had a dream about you.

She had moved in close to my face, whispering. And, of all people, Virgil Varnum himself was heading for us, which made Dorothy press closer as she continued, almost as if she were flirting with me, or flirting with Virgil indirectly by getting close to me. People are strange.

106

—I had a dream that you died. We were out on the water in the canoe, off Joshua's cottage, where we were when we saw the man in the wheelchair. You remember? We were in the canoe and this door opened in the floor of the canoe, like a trapdoor, and you went down through it. It was a nightmare.

I did remember Dorothy screaming in her sleep a couple of nights before.

—Penguin, you've got to be careful.

At that point a voice broke into the conversation from behind.

—Careful of what?

The voice belonged to Virgil Varnum. Virgil had become a tall, yuppie-haired, close-shaven, undistinguished late-twenties male except for his nose. The bone or ridge inside his nose was so sharp it reminded you of a weapon. I remember when I was a kid and Virgil was probably in prep school—before the incident in the Laser—I used to ask him if I could touch it to feel how sharp it was. And as he aged it had grown even sharper, so that it seemed to occupy only two dimensions, and if you thought of kissing him, for example, the nose would either lacerate your cheek or it would get bent over against his face and break.

—Penguin's a risk taker, Dorothy said. Out in the swamp alone with the canoe, attacking a fraternity house, God knows what else. She lives right on the edge. And she hasn't got anyone to restrain her. I worry.

—You're her new mother, Virgil said. That gives you the right to worry. Right, Penny? If not the right to restrain her.

—Penguin, Dorothy insisted. Penguin the Daring. The disappearing stunt woman of Squid Harbor.

Dorothy was drinking a lot. She was focusing in on Virgil Varnum, who was just a bit older than she was and pointing his nose right at her, Virgil the Flasher with his predatory organ pointing like a shrike right at the space between her eyes.

—We are all risk takers at this point, Virgil was saying.

—All? Dorothy asked.

—Anyone who lives around here. Nude beaches just over the highway. A town full of the gay and the restless just across the bay.

—The AIDS virus doesn't fly, I reminded him. It walks. You have to have intimate contact.

—Penguin the medical expert, Dorothy said.

—I don't know, Virgil said. Maybe it does fly. If you can get it from a drug needle, why can't it be carried in the nose of an insect? You slap a mosquito full of someone else's blood. It gets all over you. Say you have a cut in that spot. Why couldn't it get into the bloodstream through the sting hole? I did it just this morning. I killed a fat bloody one. I said to myself, "That blood could be anyone's." The rain falls, you know, on the just and the unjust alike.

Even as a kid Virgil had these irrelevant Bible quotes. I used to think he'd had his mind twisted in Sunday School. "They toil not," he used to say, "neither do they spin." Which was the basic history of his life.

I had this vision of Virgil Varnum evolving into a mosquito with its aggressive little proboscis sticking right out in front.

—Insects can't carry it, Dorothy said. Everyone knows that.

—They do in Africa, Virgil said. Virgins get it, children, boys and girls both. How else could it happen? They are all naked and covered with biting flies.

Dorothy held her bare arm out and backed away from it as if it contained an anthill.

—Viola is worried, too, Virgil said. She called from Poughkeepsie.

—Who's Viola? Dorothy asked.

—My ex. She called from Poughkeepsie. She's worried about the twins. She doesn't want them exposed to anything on the beach.

—You mean you told her about your mosquito theory, too?

—It was her idea in the first place. She takes it seriously. Viola is quite the alarmist when it comes to the children's health. Of course it's also her excuse to get them back. She'd like me to have no visiting rights at all. She has an entire law firm watching over the twins whenever I have them. She has a private detective living in a motel in Wellfleet. I know my phone line is tapped. There's no end to it.

—Little children, Dorothy said. Everyone. But how far can a mosquito fly?

—It would only take the distance from me to you.

Virgil pointed the Nose towards her at a mosquito's angle and started to tiptoe around her and buzz. Then he stopped short, held his hand out, and waited for one to land. He slapped it and its little body lay in a red smear. He was trying to scare her, God knows why.

—I wonder where that load came from, he said.

—That's horrible, Dorothy said.

—It's bullshit, I said. He's just provoking you. I've been bitten this summer a million times.

At which Dorothy gave me this spidery look as if she had eight legs under those balloon-shaped pants.

Now P. T. Varnum himself joined us, shorter than his son, with a little less nose but with the same gold-tinted eyes. P. T. wore a navy blazer with large purple buttons that said "D" on them, I guess for his company, and maroon Bermuda shorts. His calves were huge, hairless, hard-muscled, with random little nodes on them that looked like extra sub-muscles for specialized motor tasks. I could see him as a wrestler or an athlete in his time. I could see him in boxer shorts or even naked, oiled, wrestling with the president of some other distillery in the oak-paneled gymnasium of a club for men.

—What's horrible? P. T. asked.

—AIDS, Virgil said. You know Viola is worried about the girls.

—Oh. AIDS, said Virgil's father. I'll tell you what they should do about that. The Center for Disease Control should create an AIDS reservation in the southwestern part of the country where the weather is pleasant and there are still federal lands. Like they did in the tuberculosis days. It's the only rational approach.

—Dad, this is a serious problem, Virgil cut in. You can't move a million people around like that.

—We did it on D-day, P. T. said. We did it with the Indians. And now we have computers. Get the CIA doing something useful with themselves rather than selling opium down in the jungle. What do you think, Solstice? You're the creative type.

Richard had been listening quietly since he came in, with that little smile on his face that says in the long run it doesn't matter because art will transcend everything, even us. In some way I had been fighting that smile all my life.

—The way things are going we may all have it someday, Richard said. It will be part of the human condition.

—Not all of us, P. T. said. Some will and some won't. That's what it will shake down to. Some will be eliminated and some will survive. Which is the way Darwin intended when he set it up. Survival of the fittest, which in this case means those who manage to control their desires. If they happen to have them. That's what the word civilization means. Western Culture. Have you read the book by this fellow Bloom? When people are taught to gratify their extremest impulses you can kiss civilized life good-bye. My Christ. What are we coming to? It's like the last days of Pompeii.

In the ultraviolet light of the Schlessbooms' Bug Zapper his gold eyes had become completely invisible, like the drilled-out pupils of an Egyptian statue, a pharaoh.

—Bloody Jesus, P. T. continued. Everyone has appetites. We all have. And everyone can learn to deal with them. The ones that can't have to perish. You can see it in nature. Look at the giraffe. How do you think they got that way? You think they evolved those necks by giving in to every unnatural impulse that came their way?

I had to escape P. T.'s lecture on evolution, so I traipsed after Dorothy, who was following Virgil Varnum into the darker zone of the Schlessboom terrace. She was craning her neck up at him the way you look at the World Trade Center, as if she wanted to evolve like the giraffe. Her throat was bright red from the gimlets, a triangular patch just like a rose-breasted grosbeak.

—My father certainly has his moods, Virgil was saying.

—But your wife may be right, Dorothy said. How old are your two daughters?

—My ex-wife has never been right. Not once. Not about anything. She is a certifiable hysteric, wanting to keep the kids off the beach because they might get AIDS. The twins have just turned five.

—She probably just wants to keep them away from you, I said. Dorothy persisted.

—I don't blame your wife for being concerned. Ex-wife. What was her name?

—Viola.

—I knew it was a stringed instrument, Dorothy said.

My new stepmother was maneuvering Virgil away from the party, away from the ultraviolet light and into the rock garden, where the Schlessbooms had some fake Buddhist dragons with big fangs and their tongues hanging out. We used to catch frogs and stuff them down their mouths. Dorothy and Virgil stood in the shadow of one statue so it looked like the dragon was taking part in their conversation. I didn't know whether to join them or go back to P. T. Varnum's theory of human rights. So I stood on the bank of the patio like an eavesdropper and listened in. Dorothy was standing on tiptoe trying to whisper in Virgil's ear, but she wasn't tall enough and Virgil wasn't bending down. He was making her stretch, which forced her chest to within about an inch of his belt buckle. The buckle was made of some kind of metal that glowed even in the dim light and had a B on it, probably for Beer.

—What if I were to tell you something, she whispered to Virgil. What if I were to tell you something really frightening? Could you keep it a secret?

—My lips are sealed, Virgil said. He pursed up his lips and touched Dorothy with them at the hairline.

—No. I need someone to consult with. You said you were a lawyer.

—Went to law school, Virgil corrected her. And passed the bar. That was enough to please P. T. I have not practiced one sentence of law. A profession of parasites.

—Well, I need some advice. What if you found out there was someone with AIDS right here at Squid Harbor?

—I'd think you were getting paranoid, just like Viola. Who would it be? We know everyone here. That's what a community means. And there they all are, normal, boring, and healthy as a herd of seals.

Virgil indicated the party with a slight turning gesture of his nose: the big circle around the liquor supply and the small sub-groups clustered under the bug-zapping lights. He smoothed Dorothy's hair back from her forehead and scrutinized her eyes like an optician. She turned demurely away from him and headed back toward the party.

Good for you, Dorothy, I thought. He is an asshole. But you also know more than you're letting on.

She walked me back to the table with all the half-empty gin and Scotch bottles and the ice bucket full of melting cubes.

—I like the Adlers, Dorothy was saying. I always hated theater people before them.

Dan and Lydia had arrived late but had picked up the thread of the evening and were talking about the big subject of the last few summers—a proposal to spray insecticide over the major mosquito breeding areas, especially the Great Marsh.

—I'm against it, Dan announced. And I'll tell you why. The whole ecology of this area—which we have spent a lot of money to preserve—is based on insects. They're the root of the food chain. We should all reread *Silent Spring*. It's truer now than it was when Rachel Carson wrote it. We'd wake up one morning and there wouldn't be any birds.

—Plus putting all those chemicals into the marsh, added his wife. They would just stagnate in there and kill everything off. There's no end to it when you start tampering with the environment. We've worked to conserve this place as it is and that means insects along with everyone else. It's nothing new. Every time somebody moves in they bring up the idea of spraying the marsh as if no one had ever thought of it before.

—This thing is different, Peter Schlessboom said. I've lived with mosquitoes every summer of my life and by August I get so immune I don't even feel it when they bite. But if they snort blood out of some heroin addict on his drug boat and then come after me, that's another story. It calls for a special meeting of the Association, if you ask me.

—To spray or not to spray, Dan Adler said. We've had that debate before.

—The stakes were somewhat smaller in the past, Pete Schlessboom said.

—Come on, Dan said. It's a dead herring. It's been studied and disproved. You're not going to get AIDS from an insect bite. Every summer the scare comes up. It's like *Jaws*. Even the Surgeon General says it's a myth.

—We'll all be dead herrings, Peter Schlessboom said. You think this government is going to tell us what it knows? Look at the atomic radiation tests in the forties. They haven't declassified that information yet.

A mosquito, perhaps intoxicated with Squid Harbor blood, made a large boiling *zert* as it got electrocuted by the purple light. Here are these grown men, I thought, afraid of the air itself. If they only knew what I did every day with my bare hands.

Dorothy had polished off about her twelfth gimlet and had the thirteenth in her hand. She pointed her glass at the Adlers.

—If there is any question, Dorothy said, we should be on the safe side. Lydia, you ought to know that. You're a mother. You know what it is like to have children and worry about them. There is absolutely no comparison between a human life and a cluster of birds and lizards in a swamp.

—We might have someone come down from the state and test the mosquitoes, Dan Adler suggested.

Dorothy squinted right into his weekend growth of beard.

—The problem is closer than you know.

I grabbed Dorothy's sleeve to shut her up. I was a little bit blurry, but what she was about to reveal instantaneously sobered me up.

—Richard's gone back already, I hissed. We've got to go.

I put a hand on her shoulder and pulled up the side of her vest that had slipped down. One of the things about Dorothy was that when she drank, her clothing started to come undone of its own accord. I was trying to push her in the direction of home when Virgil himself came up and offered to help. Over our heads a single skyrocket was arcing up from somewhere on the mainland and burst into a flower of red and white embers that floated down over the marsh like burned-out comets.

—Look, it's the Fourth of July, Peter said. It's midnight. Let's go home and get some sleep and tomorrow we'll really celebrate. Then we can look this whole thing over.

—I'll drive you home, Virgil said to Dorothy. Penny can come too, if she wants.

—I'd rather walk, I said. There might be more fireworks.

I let Virgil open her side of his car and help her in, then I started to hike back. Their taillights bounced irrationally over the sharp ruts and disappeared.

It felt cool and there was a night breeze that kept the blessed mosquitoes away from me, so I took it easy and looked up at the stars. No matter what happened on the Earth, plagues and wars and people turning against each other in violence, the stars looked down at us with a beautiful indifference. It will be good to be dead, I thought, to be up there with the unchanging ones in their cool starry beds. But as long as we're here we have to be working, in a small way, for what we think is right. In my terrorist days I'd tried reforming the public sector and I got burned. Now I was a private citizen making her miniscule effort to help out.

I finally turned the last curve in the road and stood there for a second hesitating between Joshua's place and ours. Virgil's car wasn't in the driveway and he hadn't passed me on the way back. They must have continued on up towards the beach. I didn't want to encounter Richard with my indecent suspicions concerning his new bride. Besides, after what happened at the party, I was not about to turn around and go home.

I felt for Uncle Joshua's key under the deck post where he hid it and went into his house, where it was dark. Arnold must have actually been asleep. Cosimo came up silently and licked my hand. I let him out and, a few minutes later, I let him in. I stroked him on the left ear and unwrapped the aluminum foil from a two-pound hamburger package and put it in his bowl. Then I went into my study and drew the extension out from under the daybed and lay flat on my back in all my clothes. It was the first night I'd slept over at Arnold and Joshua's. If this was the leprosarium, then I was an inmate like the rest. No better and no worse. I passed immediately into a dream in which it was freezing cold and there was a family living in an igloo like Nanook of the North. It was Richard and me and Katherine and the three of us were wrapped up in the whole red leathery skin of a giant fox.

13

When I woke up I had to think for a moment to remember where I was. I'd been having this dream that I was a Vietcong woman and the Americans were systematically blowing up my village. I popped awake before they got to my house, but the explosions kept on. It was the Fourth of July morning and already the kids were shooting off firecrackers down at the pier.

Arnold was up and had wheeled himself into action without my help, which was a good sign. He wasn't composing but playing something classical on the piano that sounded like Haydn or Mozart, a delicate touching lyric that spoke of a civilization where life was gracious and orderly because everybody knew who they were supposed to be. The dog was up, too, looking into my room, his mouth opened in a yawn so you could inspect it all the way back to his wisdom teeth. Cosimo blocked the doorway like a horse.

I had a splitting hangover and I ground both fists into my eyes to make it stop. Then I thought of last night's conversation and the headache came back, doubled in strength and throbbing like a brain tumor. Dorothy would tell Richard. She would tell everyone. If she didn't divulge everything immediately then she would the next time she had a drink. It wasn't that I cared who knew what I was doing for the summer, but I had made a promise to Uncle Joshua that I wouldn't expose his life.

I needed some special assistance at this point. Luckily Joshua had an extension in my room. I grabbed the phone off the hook and pushed the buttons for 36 Chestnut up in Hanover. I had completely forgotten that we didn't live there anymore. The voice on the phone was a total stranger but the man knew where Bondo could be reached. I pushed more buttons, and evidently I got him out of bed. Bondo was yelling at me on his end and I was whispering on mine, so Arnold wouldn't hear.

—All right, Bondo. Just drive down here anyway and help. It's getting out of hand.

—Jesus Christ, Penguin. It's six o'clock in the morning on the Fourth of July.

—It doesn't matter. You have to get in your car and come down.

—I'll have to quit at Willensky's. I have to give some notice. I have five rackets to be strung. Give me a few weeks.

—Fuck them, I said. They are small town bourgeois capitalists and there is no reason to dignify them with two weeks' notice. Bondo, how many times do I have to tell you that they're the Enemy? Tennis rackets are their weapons. You are working in an arms factory.

—I'll get there when I can, Bondo said and hung up.

He could get a better paying job down here.

I fed Arnold and Cosimo. The three of us looked out the window and watched them prepare for the Regatta out in the harbor. The kids were pairing up in their sailboats as the adults anxiously observed them from the float. Already the boys were all captains, at the helm, while the girls were all holding the sails as crew. Twenty years of revolution and nothing had changed. It began in diapers on the Squid Harbor beach and would not end until they were pensioned from their company and their widows watched them get lowered into the earth.

Arnold was energetic and he almost seemed better in a physical sense. I wanted to tell him he looked good, but I didn't dare. Any overt mention of improvement could bring bad luck. I caught just a hint of how striking he must have been in his time. He had let his beard grow in enough to start hiding the violet skin eruptions that had spread to cover his left jaw from just under the ear almost across to his mouth, marks that were coming to look strangely like my own.

117

I moved the two chairs so the window sunlight would fall on both our faces. Bondo would undoubtedly have been working on his tan for a month or more, whereas I looked like a turnip that had been in the ground since fall. A little ultraviolet radiation might do Arnold some good also. Even Cosimo joined us sitting in the summer light.

—Who's that blond boy in the green boat? Arnold inquired.

—I lose track, I said. There are so many kids.

—No. You couldn't miss this one. He's very attractive. I've seen him walk by. You'd think he was too young.

The boy he referred to was about eleven years old. Yet it was the first sign of erotic desire I'd ever seen in him and it made my heart start up and race to think that the life force was coming back to him and that there might be a chance. Maybe it was because Joshua was due back the next day, or maybe it was because the organisms inside him had been defeated by the same creative energy that was burning itself into the trail of musical notes. It didn't matter, I thought. Maybe he'll fall in love.

—I'm not too interested in boys, I said.

—Oh?

He pivoted his head to look right at me. Not through me, as usual, but as if I were really there. He thought I was implying that I was gay.

—I'm not interested in anyone at the moment, I said.

That seemed to correct the impression, and he turned back to looking at the beach.

With Arnold in relatively good spirits I felt OK about going next door to make some kind of peace with Dorothy. It was already eleven, but my new parents were just getting up, toothbrushes poking out of their mouths, two glasses of bourbon and Alka-Seltzer fizzing away on the table. I couldn't believe it. Richard Solstice used to begin sculpting at sunrise, seven days a week.

Meanwhile, Dorothy had these red pajamas like a union suit with a square buttoned flap over the bottom that I had never seen. She looked like a female present stuffed into a Christmas stocking with

118

just the head sticking out. My naked father scuttled back into the bedroom.

—You should have come over a bit earlier, Dorothy said. You could have witnessed the primal scene.

I took one of the two glasses and poured about half of it down my throat without swallowing. Dorothy had a can of Raid and was spraying around the floor and corners of the room. The smell went right to my central nervous system and I felt the first twinges of paralysis starting in at the extremities.

—That stuff really stinks, you know. Can you imagine what it's doing to our lungs?

—Come over here, Dorothy commanded. You're going to get sprayed from head to foot.

I stood up and closed my eyes and put my hand over my mouth and nose while she disinfected me, culminating in a long blast under my hair.

—You should really get your hair cut, Penguin. You could bring in two hundred mosquitoes under there. They could be breeding in your hair. As a matter of fact, I shouldn't be letting you in the house at all.

—Letting me in the house? It's my home. It belongs to my family and it always has. Which is not *this* family. I'll come in here when I fucking want.

—All we want to know, Dorothy went on, is whether or not you are exposing yourself to any bodily fluids.

—Last night Arnold tried to bite me. But I escaped. I smear blood all over myself whenever I get the chance.

We were looking each other over like spies. She wanted to see in me the marks of my contagion and I wanted to see evidence of her midnight adventure with Virgil Varnum. But neither of these were visible to the naked eye.

Outside, the disorganized flock of sailboats had formed into the tight pattern of a race, all sails cocked at the same angle, crowding each other at the first buoy. The sun glinted off the chrome rails and stanchions of the club launch, which was decked out in red, white, and blue crêpe stringers for the Fourth of July.

I looked straight at Dorothy's mouth with its delicate and I suppose quite sensuous touch of dusk-colored hair on the upper lip. Luckily the phone rang before we could sink any further into this conversation. Richard picked it up.

—Happy Fourth of July to you, too, he told whomever was calling, which turned out to be Corkie Love, the annual president of the Squid Harbor Association. Corkie had called an Environmental Meeting for the following night to discuss the spraying issue. They'd found someone from a helicopter company who would speak to the group about details.

—There'll be a half-hour discussion, then a vote. Followed by cocktails.

—Well, I said. We don't have to go. Dorothy feels one way and you feel the other. That cancels you out as a couple. And I don't get to vote since I'm a dependent.

A mosquito, fattened with blood, landed on Richard's knee and Dorothy annihilated it with the Raid, leaving a spreading wet patch on the jeans in which the insect flailed away for a while, then died.

—Thank God insects don't write, Richard observed. I'd hate to be around if they wrote a history of mankind.

—Well, somebody has to write the history, Dorothy said. And we certainly don't want it to be the bugs. Just walk down to the Squid Harbor beach. Look at the children in their bathing suits. They don't know anything. You claim to be political, Penguin. Do you know what politics means? Politics means to watch over the lives of those kids, who are too small and innocent to know what is being done to them.

—What's being done to the children? I screeched. I'm not about to go down there and molest them.

—I saw you out there with the Varnum twins, Dorothy said.

It was true. I'd run into them on the Beach Road in care of this senescent old woman and I had shown them a sea urchin. I took it apart and showed them how the egg cases fit up inside.

The twins had names sewn onto their shorts so people could tell them apart. Aimee and Aurora. They were cute. I might even have one myself someday. But not two.

—Someone has to instruct the young, I said.

—Infect them, you mean.

—Jesus, Dorothy, Richard said.

—That's right, she said. Take Penguin's side. Her and your ex-wife. Big naturalists. Over in Belgium killing innocent minks. Sometimes I think you're too old, Richard Solstice. You think things won't affect you because you won't be around to see it or because you have already perpetuated yourself in the form of Penguin.

She held the Raid can about four inches from Richard's face, as if she were going to zap him right between the eyes. I had to say something to appease her.

—Listen, I said. I'll be careful. OK? I have some gloves.

—You say Joshua's coming back tomorrow. You can stop going over at that point. Until then you can just stay there so you're not traveling back and forth. You've made them your family as it is.

—It's mid-afternoon, I said. I really have to go back.

—What do you mean "have to"? What exactly do you do over there?

—I feed Cosimo. I feed us all.

—And you yourself eat from the same food?

—No. Arnold is on a special diet. He eats nouvelle cuisine.

—You're not going to go back after Joshua comes home. Either that or you can move in there for good. I have my politics too, which are the politics of survival. I did not happen to have been brought up in a beach cottage on Cape Cod.

—She has to find her own way, Richard said.

He spoke into midair so it wasn't quite clear which "she" he had meant. Dorothy flew at him.

—I suppose you're going back into your studio. You're an ostrich, you know that? You put your head right in the sand until it goes away.

—I have my own priorities, he said. Hysteria isn't among them.

121

He didn't continue. He took down the spare can of Raid from the shelf over the refrigerator and carried it out. We heard the studio door, then the crack of the arc welder as he switched it on.

14

Back on my studio couch at Joshua's again, I dreamed that there was a Texaco gas pump on the lawn of the Beta Sig house and Rebecca Crowell was there wearing dark green service station coveralls with a red star over one breast. One of the brothers came out of the house and said "Self-serve or full-serve, Ma'am?" and we sprayed the house with Extra Unleaded until it ignited itself into a single flame like an enormous birthday candle. Rebecca and the brother and I held hands and sang,

You can always trust your car
To the man who wears the star.

I felt a happiness that could have lifted me right up into the air, only it was dark, darker than I remembered night ever being, and a mosquito was buzzing right in the center of my ear.

I pulled the blanket over my head and it was gone. I had no idea what time it was, but outside the window it was totally dark and silent. Even the thrushes had not begun their day. Joshua would be here early. His nursing course was over. He'd be missing Arnold and he'd want to beat the summer traffic to the Bridge. Maybe he had already gotten up in his Cambridge apartment and begun to pack. As much as he talked about his book on the Mogul empires, his mind was on one thing only and that was the man sleeping in the other room, who was prematurely withdrawing and had already started to leave a vacuum in our lives.

I heard Arnold coughing, which was the first sound you heard in the mornings of that house. At first it was like someone coughing in his sleep, then louder, like a man awake, trying to cough something up and out of his heart that would not come. I heard the one bodily movement he made on his own, sliding from the slanted bed onto the open wheelchair and then clicking the wheelchair arm into position. You could not hear the chair rolling to the bathroom or being positioned beside the toilet, but only the flush, which came immediately, then a second flush, then the pause while he rolled back towards the bed and the click of the right wheelchair arm lowering to let him past. And, if the light went on, it meant he was giving himself one of the intravenous medications that perforated his forearms like a seam. He was supposed to be given the injections by me or Joshua, but I often heard him in there shooting it up alone. Much as he hated it, he knew it kept him going for his work.

The coughing started, then slowed down and stopped. Somewhere back in the marsh a night heron croaked and in the space afterwards I could hear water lapping right under the house the way it does when the tide is highest, under the new moon. Joshua's cottage was even further out on the beach than ours and the water seemed to surround it, lapping at the back and sides as well as the front, as if we were afloat. And we might have been afloat, the house might have been carried out and we might have already cleared the harbor buoy and sailed out into Massachusetts Bay. It had happened more than once on this beach, cottages floating away on the spring tide and having to be towed back to their foundations by the Coast Guard tug. Maybe the night heron was not croaking from deep in the marsh but flying past us over open water, astonished to see a house darkening the surface so far from shore.

There was a deep violet light in the window, then the hermit thrush singing right on top of me and I knew we were safe on land. I waited for Arnold to get up and begin his work. The thrush sang and paused, then sang again and paused, impatient, waiting for the piano to take its part.

I didn't wake up again until Uncle Joshua pulled up beside the house. I threw on the same Virginia Woolf sweatshirt and jeans I'd left on the floor and shook my hair out, trying to look as if I'd been up and around. Cosimo gave a long indrawn whistly whine and panted up to the door. His tail-stump vibrated with anticipation. He was like that old dog Angus at the end of the *Odyssey*. His master had come home.

Joshua carried his suitcase in one hand and a new black leather doctor's valise in the other, like someone who had just graduated from med school. He looked right past me when I opened the door, trying to locate his friend.

—He isn't up yet, I said. I just got up myself.

He dropped the two bags and headed for Arnold's room, then turned back, picked up the valise and took it in with him. I shut the door. I could see a half dozen mosquitoes in the room that Joshua had let in just by leaving it open for a few seconds. Over the summer their population always increased and grew hungrier, until by the end of July you could count a hundred of them on a single window screen, sticking their beaks through the mesh and pulsating with thirst.

I rummaged under the sink and came up with a can of 3M Wasp and Hornet Killer, which turned out to shoot a nine-foot stream wherever you pointed it. I aimed at one of them in the air and laid a visible stripe across the tapestry carpet that would not sponge off. I was trying to scrub it down with Ivory and cold water when Joshua appeared out of Arnold's room, looking tired and serious and dejected. He was pale anyway from his stay in Cambridge and he seemed to have lost weight. Around Uncle Joshua's mink-colored beard the bones of his face showed through the tight translucent skin as if he'd received some kind of radioactive treatment himself.

I asked him how Arnold was doing, and we went out on the deck to talk.

—He's tired, Joshua said. He's not keeping the nourishment in his body. It's passing right through him. It's just what they said would happen. That's the tragedy of it, everything the medical people predict comes true.

—He looked so much better yesterday, I said. His color, speech, breathing, all of it. I thought he was going to break out of here and go for a swim. Then last night he woke up coughing. I could hear him trying to breathe. He didn't work this morning. I missed it. I'm used to an hour of discord before sunrise.

—They wanted me to bring him back to the Clinic. They have some new things, they've increased the maximums for AZT, they could keep him going for this period or that period, depending on who you talk to. It's a way of making a gradual decline into death become even more gradual. I'd walk down the ward there, nurses with masks over their mouths, black janitors and Puerto Rican janitors sweeping the floor in masks and gloves, exquisite young men turned into tube-feeding vegetables waiting for the end but drugged into such a stupor that they wouldn't know the end when it came. I said to myself, Arnold Fratorelli is not going to turn into one of those.

He lit one of his Benson & Hedges and crossed his legs, smoothing his lemon yellow trousers and flicking a mosquito away in the same cultivated motion. I could picture Joshua Brand with the Ayatollah in a white Mohammedan courtyard, discussing Persian miniatures and illuminated versions of the Koran, with maybe some kind of socialist peacocks at their feet. I could not picture him walking the floors of the AIDS unit at the Massachusetts General Hospital. There is such a difference between what we are destined for and what actually becomes of us. Maybe I would stay on at Uncle Joshua's. Everything else had begun to seem unreal.

He let his face relax for a minute. He put his glasses on, which were hanging from a thin gold chain around his neck, and we both looked out over the harbor. There weren't any races on Mondays, so the Lasers rode upright and obedient at their moorings, and the only thing stirring out on the water was the crew of a small cruising ketch that had come in to anchor during the night. A man poked his head out of the companionway, pulled himself out on deck to look around, then urinated over the side as if no one else existed in the world. The sound of liquid hitting liquid echoed across the water for a few seconds, then the man disappeared into the hull. His wife came out on deck and began to hang diapers, one after the other, along the lifelines. The tiniest breeze scuffled the surface of the water and stirred the diapers like a row of signal pennants, all showing the same white message to the world. It doesn't matter, the diapers said. Life is always beginning. It doesn't matter what becomes of it at the end.

Arnold had wheeled himself out to the piano and was touching up his score with Liquid Paper. He looked wasted. I couldn't believe he was the same man who was eyeing the dock boys only a day before. There was a new white patch on his lower lip and his beard was coming in asymmetrically, which made the left side of his face look dead, like a field in which nothing can take root. The bones of his shoulders angled through the plaid blanket like coat hangers. It was as if he had changed bodies overnight.

—Fucking stuff, Arnold said. It's not really opaque. I put it on and the notes keep showing through.

Joshua came up behind us and laid a hand gently, almost gingerly, on the back of Arnold's neck.

—By the way, how was the Harvard commencement this year? Arnold asked.

—It was a historic event. For the first time in three hundred and fifty years it was worth attending.

—Why?

—Instead of God, the Chaplain invoked "the divine father/mother" in the opening prayer.

—That's silly, Arnold said. Everyone knows that God is male. They all are. Father. Son. Holy Ghost.

—You'll be a good Catholic to the end, Joshua said.

Arnold crossed himself in his wheelchair and dabbed another note out with the Liquid Paper, then his hand seemed to spring open by itself and the bottle fell on the piano keys, rolled off and onto his blanket, then hit the rug. It made a white circle just over the face of a Persian hunting dog.

—You did it, Josh darling. You made me lose my grip.

Uncle Joshua ran to the kitchen for a paper towel and some solvent and bent down over the rug. He got the white-out off, but there was a bleached spot now that would probably last forever. He didn't seem upset in the least. It was a material object. Things lost their value under the cool, even fluorescent light of death, a light that doesn't cast any shadows because it comes from all directions at once.

It was good, though, to know Arnold still had the strength to argue. I went to the back of the cottage to get my things, and Joshua called me from Arnold's room.

—Penguin.

I zipped up my backpack and went in. He had the doctor's bag open and was spreading out the equipment on the bed. It recalled all my sicknesses as a kid, when they'd call Doctor Ryder down from Wellfleet and he would touch the cold end of the stethoscope to my chest, then turn me over and inspect my back, running his finger like a small ship along the coastline of the purple and the white. When I'd come down from my fever with the bad germs all nicely cooked out of the bloodstream, I'd look in the bathroom mirror to see if the birthmark had been boiled away too. But it never had.

—You have to pay attention, Joshua said. Later we may have to run a feeding tube directly into his stomach through the nose. This is a bottle of ninety-percent oxygen with a respirator. We have to start him in on it tomorrow.

—I'd like to know what to do for a coughing spell like the one he had last night.

—In that event, we give the Septra by injection to get the infection down.

I looked at the box of Septra cartridges, neatly lined up the way watercolors might be arranged in their metal tubes. Joshua took a syringe from a needle assortment that could have been the prize possession of an addict.

—If you stay on, Joshua said, I'll show you about using these. Can you imagine? I wanted to be a physician at one point. It was what my mother wanted for me and it's come true. She had more influence than she thought.

—Is she still alive? I asked.

—She died nearly eleven years ago. Mother wanted a daughter, not a son. A daughter and a physician. And here I am.

I took up one of the smaller syringes, drew the plunger out, and forced it all the way down with my thumb.

—You never allow air into the chamber, Joshua said. That would be the end of it right there.

I had promised to go to the meeting with Sue Love, and I had a while to go before I met her. The asters had just appeared, and I walked down the beach road picking some purple and white ones for Joshua's table. I ran into Virgil's twins again, with their governess, who had tied them together with about a four-foot cord, I guess to keep them under better control. They had the gold-colored eyes but the Varnum nose hadn't appeared on them yet, and they were in fact quite appealing considering who they were from. I always expect the moral qualities of parents to show up physically in their kids.

The twins got excited when I stopped, and even more so when I took each by one hand and walked them to the tide line. The governess, Mrs. Baxton, seemed relieved. We dug for clams. I showed them how to tell the false clam holes from the real ones, which have a black spot. The other holes belong either to seaworms, which bite, or to razor fish, which you can't catch no matter how hard you dig. I showed them how to sneak up on the clam, press with your foot to see if it's near the surface, and dig down beside and under it so it can't burrow itself away. Of course the twins were too small to dig fast, but it turned out that working together and using all four of their hands they could catch the small slow-burrowing ones, and we had a pretty good pile going when Mrs. Baxton called.

—Wash up. Your father will be here in five minutes.

I brought them to her and tied the cord back up, which I had undone when we began to actively dig. They were like little prisoners again.

—You can wait, said Mrs. Baxton. Mr. Varnum will be glad to see you, I'm sure.

—I don't know, Mrs. B.

—I do.

She had a matchmaker look in her usually trancey eye. Mrs. Baxton had taken care of Virgil two decades before and I remember her as being exactly the same age. Old. I left. Not because I thought Virgil was interested. I just suddenly felt weird about being with the twins.

15

The Environmental Meeting was to be held at the Loves' house. Pig and Corkie. They were the copresidents that year. Pig Love was a bit chubby in a Republican sort of way but not as obese as you might expect considering the nickname, which he must have acquired before I came on the scene. Perhaps from inner qualities. His daughter Susan was skinny to the point of anorexia. Sue Love went to Mount Holyoke and dressed like an anachronism from the fifties with a citrus-colored skirt and a pair of brown shoes that were like leather boats that had been sunk to the seafloor by her feet.

Susan had been somewhat plump herself as a preteen, and also, for a string of summers, my best friend. Once we'd both been floating in the harbor on our backs, talking about the Bicentennial Parade, when Susan gave a scream and grabbed me in a death grip around the head. Charlie the lifeguard was there in about a minute on his board, and it turned out Sue had been stung by a Portuguese man-of-war jellyfish and right on the dock her left leg swelled up to double its normal size. *Cut it off,* she had commanded him. *It hurts and I want you to cut it off.*

They'd held her in the Chatham Hospital for a week. After that I never remember Susan consuming a bit of food. She still looked like a little girl with no physical development whatsoever, just that ubiquitous tan that looked like she had rotated herself all summer on a spit. I could imagine her in fifty years signing up for Elderhostel with the same absolutely sincere innocent smile on her face after having gone through the life cycle entirely without eating, like one of those dragonflies that live on air. Sue Love belonged to the class of people to whom everything has been given, and somewhere inside she had an immense tapeworm of guilt that ate everything she put into her mouth. She was as far from the Third World as anyone on earth and yet her body looked like one of those Ethiopian children on TV.

At the Environmental Meeting, Corkie and Pig Love had the folding chairs that rotated around the harbor along with the presidency set up in their living room around the cherry-red metal cone of their fireplace. They had a small Richard Solstice sculpture on a pedestal in one corner that depicted something like the wings of a hawk or seagull in flight, and that was it for fine art. The rest of their cottage was pure kitsch, if that's what the term is: ceramic loons and ducks with cigarette lighters installed in their backs, a green-headed mallard decoy containing a telephone, paintings of the ocean on black velvet in unnatural X-ray colors, a kitchen dominated by a gigantic microwave that could have nuked an ox. No wonder Sue Love was unable to eat.

P. T. Varnum showed up with Virgil right at his side, and the Yins came from their island. Their son Newton wasn't with them, though I'd heard he was actually around. Plus Pura Batrachian, whom I hadn't seen since the evening before the Fourth. She had a reporter's notebook and a small instrument dangling from a wrist strap that must have been a tape recorder. Richard and Dorothy came smelling of Cutter's repellent. The Steins were there, and Robin's parents, the Adlers, George Whipple and his wife with the bluish wig, and of course Jerry Perera with a woman I'd never seen: dark, interesting, Portuguese-looking. I couldn't tell whether she was a relative or a date. Possibly both.

Jerry was different from everyone there. He was someone who had earned his way into Squid Harbor through physical labor, combined perhaps with the high-risk operations of the narcotics trade. He came from another class, a class that couldn't afford to be either ethical or political, because it had to survive. Jerry had about a twelve-inch knife strapped to his belt in a camouflage-colored sheath that was also laced at the point around his thigh. He was not only a Vietnam vet but probably an ultra-right survivalist if you scratched his surface with that bayonet. I wondered if he recalled what he asked of me four years before, or whether he ever read my heartfelt response. He didn't look like he read anything. His eyes were farsighted, set deep in their sockets like the infrared eyes of a sniper, someone accustomed to seeing exclusively in the dark.

Corkie Love gavelled the meeting to order using her enamelled red tin fireplace like a Chinese gong. She was an earthy, competent-looking woman, always in tennis clothes, who had once served as mayor of their small Connecticut town. This was not a regular meeting, she said. That would be August tenth, as was the custom, at which time the Association would consider float maintenance, resurfacing the courts, and burying the water pipes below the frost line at least as far as the Adlers' so people could start living here year-round.

Tonight, she said, we are restricted to one subject, which we take up on an annual basis: mosquito control through spraying the Great Marsh by helicopter. Corkie had already priced a contract with Commando Aerochemical Services of Hyannis and they would do the job for nine thousand dollars, which would mean raising the annual assessment by two hundred eighty dollars per family.

A middle-aged man in a tight-fitting sky blue synthetic sport coat with matching tie who had been sitting beside her the whole time turned out to be the Commando pilot. They immediately began questioning this guy. Would one spraying do the job, or would it have to be repeated?

—It would have to be done at least once every year, according to the pilot. We spray in August at the peak breeding season, so you still have time. Ideally you also spray in April so you can kill the larvae in their two stages. The first year you could hope to reduce the population. Next year you get them all. Skip a year's spraying and they'll grow right back. You're basically talking guerrilla warfare. Mosquitoes are survivors. They're tougher than you are, they've been around longer, and they know the local terrain.

The pilot wore some kind of cologne that we could smell clear across the room.

—Essence of Agent Orange, Robin whispered. He was a defoliation expert in Vietnam.

The pilot also had a tic that pulled the skin of his face over to one side every two minutes or so, so that he had to stop talking and move his nose and mouth back to their original locations with his hand. Then he would light a cigarette, take a couple of puffs, and drop it into the hole of a Darlings beer can with a hiss. I imagined the mass of filters and beer and tobacco inside the can expanding until it took over the Earth.

—It looks like he sprayed himself in both stages, Robin said.

—This is at nine thousand dollars a hit? someone asked.

—Yes, Corkie said.

—What about the environmental impact? someone was asking.

—I'm not a biologist, the pilot said. I'll try to answer your questions. The tide flushes your swamp out twice a day, just like a toilet. So there's no long-term chemical buildup in the water, except maybe a slight residual in the back channels, which you are not likely to visit anyway.

—And what about accumulation in organisms?

This was Daisy Yin, who had a degree in some branch of science and talked as if she knew.

—The chemicals may linger in the food chain, said the pilot. You're not going to see it exactly, but I have to inform you that it is known to accumulate in clams and oysters and anything that feeds on them.

—We couldn't go clamming? Dan Adler said.

—They usually close clam beds for the duration of the treatment.

—And the birds? What about them?

—You may find a dead heron or two after we spray, answered the pilot. By next year they will have found somewhere else to reside. They're quite intelligent. They could migrate to the dunes in the National Seashore where they would not be sprayed because it is a designated refuge. The only animal species that might actually be poisoned would be those relatively high up on the food chain.

—Like us, somebody put in.

—There are Virginia rails in that swamp, Dan Adler pointed out. It's one of the only places in Massachusetts where they still nest.

—I don't know what they feed on, the pilot said. I've never laid eyes on one of those. I'm going to be straight with you. I don't beat around the bush. It's not 1960 any more. This is a different world. They stopped spraying DDT in America because it's supposed to kill wildlife. So what did you get? You got killer bees coming up from Florida and you have the African fire ants that can skin out a sheep in fifteen minutes. You have the ticks with the Lyme disease and you have AIDS. In my book human beings are more important than birds.

—But we know AIDS is not spread by mosquitoes, Daisy Yin said.

At that point I flashed on this poem we read in freshman English called "The Flea." It's about a bug biting two lovers and intermingling their blood. *It sucks me first and then sucks thee.* Carpe diem, that's what Professor Threadbee said it meant.

—It's your swamp, the pilot was saying. Your bugs, your birds, and your kids. Your decision, not ours. We run a pro-choice operation.

The pilot was answered by Daisy Yin.

—We've all been talking about *Silent Spring,* she said. I'd like to know how this would affect vegetation and wildlife.

Corkie Love interrupted.

—It's human life we're interested in preserving.

—What good does it do to be human, Daisy said, if there's nothing left around us? I'm a scientist and I am not hearing any proof. I will vote for the environment because that is real.

The pilot was somewhat subdued by this diminutive female Asian biologist who knew what she was talking about, while he was just unreeling a memorized sales pitch, hoping to capitalize on a few phobias so he could get nine thousand dollars for an afternoon of making believe he was back in Vietnam.

135

—I'll tell you, the pilot said. There's no such thing as a free lunch. You pay the price. It's your decision. If I have a contract, I carry it out. I don't make a moral issue out of it. I'm not a philosopher. I'm a professional. Take your choice. It's either birds or bugs, or I should say birds or no bugs. If you pick Commando, I assure you we will get the job done.

P. T. Varnum rose up and took the pilot's hand in both his hands.

—My man, you are just what the doctor ordered. So to speak. Get your helicopter over here and I'll pay for the first shot myself.

—You're out of order, P. T., Corkie declared.

—I move we reject the whole idea, Dan Adler said. We're forgetting our own values. We are the newcomers, all of us. The marsh has stayed the way it is since the Pleistocene. We saved it as a legacy for our kids and for their kids. We got together and paid what, George, three hundred thousand dollars for that piece? Collectively. The way we always do. Or used to. It's not a matter of money. If we kill the marsh at this point we can never get it back.

The pilot was collecting his cigarettes and sunglasses from the floor around him and getting ready to go home.

—It's your decision, folks, he repeated. I'll be in Hyannis when you want to call.

—He could be right, Marsha Stein-Mallow said. Maybe we ought to spray.

—Why? asked Dan Adler. Do you believe this guy with his scare tactics?

—No, I don't believe him. Maybe is all I'm saying. Maybe this year we ought to spray.

Now it was Jerry Perera's turn. People looked at him with an intense silent interest. He was a native with some mysterious connections. In summer he controlled their food and gasoline supplies. In the fall he winterized their boats and in the winter he ostensibly fished, but everyone knew he had something else going in order to support the extended Perera family and also build for his mother one of the costlier places on the shore. Jerry had made a lot of money in a very short time, which drew people's attention, even people like P. T. Varnum. He was obviously not scared by a few mosquitoes. He had arrived in a black undershirt with a heavy cross on his neck chain that could have been a weapon, not to mention the knife. Except for the little mustache he was close-shaven, but still the uncontrollable stubble of his face could have been used to smooth planks. I wondered what it would feel like to rub my cheek against that sandpaper surface. The woman hanging onto his leg as he stood up wore a thick layer of mocha-colored makeup. It was probably red underneath that, where he had scraped it raw. They had all the distinct appearance of distant incest. She played with her long single braid and then almost set it on fire lighting a cigarette.

—I vote to spray the swamp and get it over with, Jerry said. You folks will slide around on this all night. In Vietnam we hosed down a thousand miles of swampland and here you are worried about a hundred-acre patch. This year we spray, next year we'll forget it was ever any other way, then in a year or two from now we'll fill it and we'll have the most valuable property in the state. We'll cut a deep channel in there and we'll finally have ourselves a decent dock. Maybe a marina. I can see a restaurant . . .

I couldn't help what happened at that point. I had never spoken out at one of those meetings in my life, but I stood up and started screeching at Jerry Perera. It wasn't even my own voice I was speaking in. It sounded like a man-eating owl.

—You don't understand the first thing about this place, I told him. You've hung around here so long you can't even see it anymore.

I thought I would destroy him with the owl's voice and he would disappear, but he was still there, lifting one side of his mustache with this pseudo-ironic grin as if to say, "I'm on the pilot's side because we were both in Vietnam and saw things that left-wing feminist children like you could not even imagine."

What he did say was only a bit milder.

—Children of members can sit still and listen. But they don't get a vote. Besides, we all know your agenda.

—Agenda?

I got right up out of my seat and started to move towards him. It felt like winter and we were on the way to the Beta Sig house again, only this time it was just me, alone with a room full of sperm-driven males who just wanted to spray and destroy. Pig Love and the Pilot and the Brothers and P. T. Varnum all condensed themselves into that one dark Portuguese face with a drug-dealer's mustache and a survival knife strapped to his leg and this vacant-looking woman's hand hanging onto the sheath. I didn't know why I was doing it or what I was going to do, but all I could think of was that I wanted to seize him by the throat. His partner in incest put her hand up in a way that looked like she'd been trained in martial arts. Sue Love pulled at me, too, and Robin on the other side, so I sat down.

Corkie, the chairperson, tried to restore some order to the scene.

—Penny, we so much appreciate it that your generation is taking an interest.

Jerry had turned around to stare at me and I stared back. The infrared eyes sank deeper back into their sockets. The girlfriend put a hand on his bayonet to calm him down.

The members voted. Not counting the two abstentions, the vote went fourteen to eleven not to spray. Squid Harbor came through. A few fascists maybe but cultured and intelligent people on the whole. They weren't taken in by this guy with the blue plastic jumpsuit or by P. T. Varnum who might be a millionaire but had one vote like the rest of us. It felt good to live in a democracy. I hugged Sue Love beside me, which was like squeezing a swallow under the feathers with its delicate hollow bones.

—We won, I shouted. The swamp is going to stay the way it is.

—We'll form a committee, Corkie said, to study the situation. Pig will be on it, and Virgil Varnum, and Smokey Yin as chair.

Daisy's husband's real name was William but they always called him Smokey. As with the Loves, I had no idea what those names referred to. They had been given out at the same primordial moment as my own.

—All men, Daisy put in.

—All right, Daisy, you can be on instead of your husband. Smokey, you're off. I was just trying to get people who seemed neutral.

—Nobody's neutral, Daisy responded. I'll be happy to serve.

Dorothy threw her pack of cigarettes on the floor. She stood up and refastened her two scarves around her neck.

—For Christ's sake, Richard exclaimed. One outburst from this family is enough.

—No. If she has a right to be heard then so have I.

—The vote's been taken, Dorothy, Corkie reminded her. You can't get into it at this point. You get one vote as Richard's wife, which makes you an automatic member, and you could have spoken up during the discussion. We go by Roberts' Rules of Order. Which says that we are now all going to adjourn and have a drink.

Pig Love rolled out a portable refrigerator-bar on wheels and opened the top and began putting ice in old-fashioned glasses. Half the people had folded their chairs up and lunged for the liquor cabinet and half had gravitated towards Dorothy, who was by now speaking in tears.

—I'm telling you, Corkie, you have no idea what's going on.

—The meeting is over, P. T. said. Have a couple of drinks and no one will know what's going on.

Dorothy went on regardless.

—It's wrong. We're treating these insects as an endangered species and we aren't even protecting our own kids.

I couldn't believe I was being betrayed by my own family.

—*Richard,* I whined.

I sounded like a ten-year-old. There was going to be a public family scene. People began slipping away in embarrassment, including Jerry Perera and his incest victim of the week. This wasn't supposed to happen at Squid Harbor.

It was Daisy Yin who really took control.

—Dorothy, she said, why don't you just come out to Tobacco Island tomorrow and we'll talk about this in a smaller group. Virgil can come, Pig Love, and myself.

—Hey, Virgil said. Why don't we meet tonight?

—I'm chairing the committee, Daisy said. And I say no one is even going to mention it until tomorrow.

Virgil still had a glass in his hand with two ice cubes in it and nothing else. Pig Love reached him the bottle of White Horse over Dorothy's head and Virgil poured it in. The chairs folded up again as if by themselves and the meeting became a party. Daisy and Dorothy went off in a corner and of course no one talked about anything else for the rest of the night.

I stood out on the porch with Virgil Varnum and Robin. Susan Love came up and the four of us turned to look at the older generation inside. They were arguing away in there, but we couldn't make out a word. We could just see their mouths moving like a TV playing *Masterpiece Theatre* with the sound turned off.

I asked Robin who the woman was with Jerry Perera. She said she didn't know.

—I don't care, either, Robin said.

Her tone surprised me. I pulled her away from Sue and Virgil and away from the window light.

—Did you have anything to do with him? I asked her.

—Not really, Robin answered. But you know what I mean. I knew him.

—You had a physical relation?

—Not totally physical, she said. I guess you would kind of say it was oral.

—Oral, I said. What do you mean, oral? You mean verbal?

—That's what I meant to say, Robin said.

At that point a funny taste shot into my mouth and I needed a drink. I merely stuck my hand out and Virgil Varnum divined just what I meant. He gave me his, went in and got another, and returned. I didn't stay with him, though. The four of us—Virgil and I, Robin and Sue Love—moved apart from each other until we each

140

occupied a corner of the porch. The moon was in its first quarter, just setting over the invisible night activities of the marsh. It was the lurid artificial color of a Sunkist orange and it looked strangely deformed, as if in partial eclipse. In its bright path over the water I could see the fleet of Lasers riding at anchor and I had an impulse to swim, to start out at the float and just swim down the path of the moon to the furthest sailboat and stretch myself out on its deck and sleep forever.

16

Which I probably should have done. As it was, Robin Adler drifted off with her parents and Sue Love excused herself as soon as the bugs discovered us. That left Virgil and me staring at an increasingly romantic moonscape. Virgil went back in to get some more White Horse and ice. When he came out, he started reciting verses from Omar Khayyám. "And wilderness were paradise enow," he ended up. I said I never had known what *enow* meant anyway so those lines had always been lost on me. Hundreds of women had probably been seduced by that poem and if I believed in censorship it would be one of the first items on the list. There should be harsh legislation against using artworks for attempted rape.

Richard and Dorothy were still pantomiming behind the window. Virgil slapped a mosquito on my forehead and let his hand stay there for a second before he took it off, brushing the tiny corpse away as he did so.

—You have a lot of courage, Virgil said, compared to certain other women. Why don't I drive you over to our place? You can have the whole beach house to yourself. Nobody's using it.

I didn't have much choice. I had no car and certainly was not about to deal with Dorothy Dvorjak after our public falling out. I couldn't go barging into Joshua's house at one in the morning. I didn't think I had anything to fear on the part of Virgil, considering the sailboat incident and his recent vivid history with my new mother. He would be too embarrassed. So I hopped into the orange Rabbit convertible, leaned the seat back, took off my shoes, and propped my feet up on the dash. Virgil had an old Stones album in the tape deck that was saying *you can't always get what you wa-ant* as the Rabbit hopped in and out of the ruts, sliding basically out of control in the corners and gaining its feet again when the road was straight.

But you get what you need.

At one point a brownish bird appeared in the headlights and limped along the road, staying in front of us and making a histrionic display of pain.

—It's hurt, Virgil said.

—No, I said. It's faking. That's how she lures predators away from her nest.

—Predators? Virgil said through his aquiline nose.

—Yes. It's the female. She risks her life. She lets herself get eaten instead of her kids.

Suddenly the quail or partridge broke into flight. It whizzed up through the beam of our headlights like a battery-powered flying toy.

Virgil gave me a lecture on the Varnum beach house as soon as he had settled down next to me on the couch. It was in fact a converted boathouse from the nineteenth century. The multipaned floor-to-ceiling windows overlooking the Varnum's private float used to be doors that opened so that an eight-oared rescue boat could be launched on hearing an S.O.S. He showed me the old sign reading MASSACHUSETTS HUMANE SOCIETY that now hung over the stone fireplace. The only flaw was, Virgil said, the local citizens *wanted* shipwrecks so they could plunder the vessels when they ran aground. So the lifeboat sat there and was never used. The Varnums had had the boathouse towed intact by barge from Barnstable, which was twenty miles away.

Virgil opened a refrigerator that was concealed behind the facade of an antique wooden icebox. He made a couple of cocktails from rum and Pear Nectar and we put our feet up on a table with different kinds of knots embedded in its thick glass top: square knot and bowline and fisherman's bend and about twelve others. I asked

Virgil how they got the knots in there.

—I never inquire how things are done, Virgil said. I accept them as miracles.

I drank my Pear Nectar and asked him where he had taken Dorothy the night they'd passed me on the road.

—That was a miracle, I said. The two of you vanished right into thin air.

—Your stepmother wanted to know the names of the constellations, so I told her.

—I thought you said things were miracles.

—I told her their names, Virgil said. I didn't tell her how they were made. She's from New York City, where they never see the stars.

I formed an immediate picture of Virgil and Dorothy parked in the convertible at Oyster Point or the Bridge, the top down, looking up at the stars. I could see Virgil pointing out Vega in the constellation of the Lyre, which in the summer is extremely bright and high. I could see Dorothy leaning back until her spine impaled itself on the shift lever and Virgil suavely putting the clutch in and shifting it to reverse so she could settle herself across his lap in her attempt to see the midpoint of the sky. I could picture the three huge buttons of her light green surgeon's shirt coming undone of their own accord and of course she never wore anything underneath it so her chest would be lying there like a patient under the anesthetic. I could see Virgil paying no attention to this at first, just naming the stars: Cassiopeia, the Swan, the Corona Borealis. Then I could see him looking down and saying, *Well, what have we here?* I wondered if Richard thought anything at all about the external life of his new bride. Or was it just my dark side making it all up? I might have been jealous of Dorothy. Most of the time I myself didn't know what was going on inside the other half.

—All right, I said, it's two-thirty in the morning. In about six hours that meeting is supposed to start and I'm going to sleep.

—You're not involved in the meeting, Virgil said. It's me, Daisy, Pig Love, and your new mom.

—You're taking me with you. And we both have to get some rest.

He got me a pillow and sleeping bag and tossed them on the couch and left. I wasn't sleepy at all. I heard the door slam up in the main house and took off all my clothes. I walked out on the Varnum's float and dove from the board. The water felt so ephemeral that you could almost inhale it, and I wondered if seals could breathe both water and air or only air. I pulled myself back on the float and swished my feet in the water, which stirred up spirals of golden phosphorescent light. I wondered how they shined like that. It wasn't a miracle. That stuff about miracles was of course totally bogus, like most of what Virgil came out with. The answer was perfectly rational. Each of those little organisms must have had a little battery or generator or a small nuclear power plant inside, probably a generator, so when they got scared or excited they lit up. It was also probably sex. If there were just two of those things in a harbor or tide pool one could start flashing and they could find each other. The ones that didn't light up didn't get to breed. Darwin. Then, as I swished my legs around even harder so the whole water boiled with galaxies of light, I wondered if they had eyes. I couldn't imagine anything that microscopic having an eye. But if you couldn't see, what conceivable use would it be for you to give off light?

The minute I stopped moving my foot they just stood there and glowed in their fixed places like the stars. They were probably dying and reproducing all the time, I thought, and no one even noticed. Why do we make such a big event out of human death? Arnold would take off his body and give it to the viruses, seeing that they desired it so much, and then he would become a star. He would be located with other composers in the constellation of the Lyre and would experience music so pure that you wouldn't have to hear it, the way starlight is so pure that it has no color in it at all. Life is a bonfire, I thought, that you must walk through to burn off your imperfections. Even the little organisms in the water were yellow, not white. Impure. They were like me with my two colors. Good and not-so-good. We all had a step to go yet before we could transcend.

When I got back to the boathouse Virgil was standing there holding a red towel that said Darlings Beer.

—Just realized there weren't any linens down here, he said.

I walked straight up to him and stood on tiptoe and touched my forehead to the very extremity of his nose, then I worked my way under it and kissed him right on the mouth. I could feel the water sponging into his clothes.

—A body feels best when it's soaking wet, Virgil said, pulling me in then pushing me away. I shouldn't be caught dead with you. You're one of those high-risk groups. Haitians, homos, hard drug addicts, and penguins.

I looked right at him as I shook my hair out and dried myself off slowly, part by part, like a laborer cleaning and putting away his tools. I even let him catch a glimpse of my purple-and-white back. If everything was such a goddamned miracle on this Earth, what about *that*? I then wrapped the Darlings towel around my waist like a sarong and backed into the house.

When Virgil started to follow me through the door I waited till he got one arm inside and slammed it shut.

—Jesus, Penguin, he yelled, that's my fucking arm.

I opened the door to free his arm up, then closed it and brought the little prong down that secured the latch. I could hear Virgil standing outside the door.

—The least you could do is apologize, he said. You're homeless. I am doing you the favor of putting you up.

I fell asleep on the couch with nothing covering my body but the Darlings towel: red, white, and blue. I dreamed of the Beta Sig house again. It was a charred ruin and we were poking around the ashes with long sticks. I saw Jerry Perera's body in there, but I didn't touch it because it was still smoking and hot.

When Virgil showed up at eight-thirty to take his Whaler out to the meeting at Daisy Yin's, I was all dressed and waiting. Neither of us said anything about last night.

17

The Yins lived on Tobacco Island, which was a half mile off-shore, right in the mouth of Squid Harbor where our small protected inner cove begins to open out into the larger expanse of Wellfleet Bay. It probably got its name in Colonial days but it was also the place where you went as an adolescent to smoke your first coming-of-age cigarettes. So, as kids, the myth was that it took its name from us. Back then, when Newton Yin and his parents lived on the mainland a couple of cottages down from us, Tobacco Island was uninhabited, nothing but beach plums and high-bush cranberries and seagull nests right on the ground.

Virgil put the Whaler on full throttle, throwing a tail of spray behind us like a fire hose. If anyone had been anywhere near our wake in a canoe or kayak they would have been instantly sunk. Meanwhile, out beyond the island, Massachusetts Bay stretched out past infinity in absolute morning calm. It would have felt good to keep right on going past the Yins' house and the row of stakes leading out to the channel buoy and just go until the Whaler ran out of gas and we would drift, out of sight of land, in a place where humpbacked whales would be rising and sinking around us. I held that fantasy in focus until I remembered who I was with and tapped Virgil on the shoulder and shouted to him to slow down before he ran us up onto the beach.

The island was now totally void of all vegetation and rose only a few feet from the level of the sea. The Yin's house stood on the highest part, which had once concealed in its bushes the white bones of an old ship. Their house was all glass with a stainless steel framework and masses of large plants inside that made it look like an aquarium for tropical fish.

The Yins had three boats moored off their dock, which made me realize that they were rich, that since I was a kid everyone at Squid Harbor had become rich. I wondered if the force that made some people happy and prosperous was the same force that made others miserable and sick, or if there were two different forces, and whether they were connected, and whether it would be worse or better if they were. I was still on that thought when we roared up to the Yins' dock at a hundred miles an hour and Virgil whipped it into reverse so it stopped short. Our stern wave humped us about four feet into the air from behind. Smokey Yin fended us off with a boathook and tied us up bow and stern. He had already been in to pick up Pig Love and Dorothy, too, who was up there on the Yins' deck talking to Pig and Daisy with a cup of coffee.

—We didn't expect you, Smokey said to me. You and I will have to play Scrabble while the Committee meets.

The Yins' house was even more spectacular when seen from inside. There were no room divisions at all, just a kind of module for kitchen and bathroom in the center, and glass all around so there was water everywhere you looked. It was like being on an ark. There were no visible beds, and the floor was a layer of smooth stones like a stone beach, but they must have been imported because Tobacco Island was pure sand and nothing else. I knew that because we used to dig holes big enough to stand in, looking for the buried treasure of Captain Kidd.

We sat down on stone slabs raised a few inches above the floor. I didn't see any bedding or pillows either and I couldn't imagine where they slept. The Yins were a paradox. I had expected to see a houseful of computers like *2001* and instead there were no clocks on Tobacco Island, no books, not even a stereo. Just the stone floor and those Precambrian-looking plants. How they lived out there was a complete mystery. It was eerie to be surrounded by the ocean on every side.

When Virgil and I waltzed in together Dorothy looked ill and dove into her purse for her brown cigarettes and her lavender-colored Bic. I touched Virgil on the side of his waist with as much intimacy and possessiveness as I could manage, then drew some coffee out of a silver samovar whose feet had the claws of old-fashioned hawks or eagles, each holding a silver globe etched with a map of the world. It was the only ornate object in the Yins' Zen-like home.

It was a strangely comforting experience to sit on the cool stone, as if it could absorb your interior tension and replace it with a pre-human calmness of its own. Looking out on Tobacco Island at night you never saw any lights, and now it dawned on me that they didn't have any electric power out there. No plugs, no sockets, no light-bulbs, no TV.

—You must live by the sun, I said to Daisy.

She said yes. Meanwhile Dorothy hadn't spoken a word to me the entire time.

—We're going to call the meeting to order, Daisy announced. I have to ask Smokey and you, Penguin, to wander around for a bit while we talk to Dorothy.

Out on the deck, I asked Smokey about their son Newton, who was out in Palo Alto working on the Strategic Defense Initiative with a team of weapons geniuses, none of whom was over twenty-three. They were designing a satellite mirror to bounce narrow laser beams back down to Earth in order to fry the enemy in their individual homes. The specific problem of Newton Yin's team was how to keep the mirrors themselves from being destroyed by the laser beam.

I asked Smokey Yin how someone so smart and creative could be on the wrong side.

—Newton doesn't think in terms of right and wrong. His team at Livermore is given a mathematical problem coming from another team and their task is to solve their portion of that problem and pass it on. It's not moral, it's not political. It's neutral. They either solve it or they don't.

—I don't see anything as neutral, I said. Newton was such a great kid, too. He beat us all at Dungeons and Dragons. It's sad.

Smokey gave me this Confucian grin.

—It is not a father's position to pass judgment on the qualities of his sons.

All this time it had been clouding up outside and now the wind was bringing in a few drops of rain. Which turned out to be a good thing, since they took pity on us and Daisy called us back inside. I really wanted to take part in this decision.

On one level it was the Squid Harbor Environmental Committee deciding whether or not to spray the salt marsh, but this other subject had crept into the discussion too, which was the presence of an AIDS patient in a summer colony that had previously been troubled only by rumors of adultery or an occasional divorce. Like ours.

Pig Love was in there slurping on his pipe. Daisy, who had put a pair of wire-rimmed glasses on, looked old and grim. Virgil was playing with his Swiss Army knife, unfolding the big and small blades, the scissors, the hacksaw, the tweezers, the can opener, and finally withdrawing the toothpick and looking at it through the magnifying glass.

—It's good you came in out of the rain, Daisy said. You might be in possession of the facts.

—Facts? I love the marsh the way it is. No spraying. That's my vote.

—No, the facts about Joshua Brand's companion.

—What does *that* have to do with it?

—It seems to have entered the discussion. Whoever he is, he's part of the environment now.

—Why don't you ask Joshua? I said.

—We respect his privacy. Josh Brand is one of our own, after all.

—Well, I said, you should respect my privacy, too.

Pig took a huge watery drag on the black mouthpiece of his pipe.

—Why are they hiding themselves, that's what I want to know.

We're all friends here, we're the same kind of people, why doesn't he just come around and be straight with us?

—Take a good look at us, I said. Maybe we're not the same kind of people at all.

Pig Love took an extra deep slurp from the pipe, which had completely gone out and sounded like a pump sucking out the bottom of a bilge.

—Josh Brand is fine, he continued. However, there comes a time when we have to draw the line between members and guests. There are a hundred motels in Provincetown where he can stay.

—Pig, we've never made inquiries into members' guests before, Daisy said.

—Things are different now, Pig said. It's a new world. The old gentlemanly rules no longer apply. And you, Penny Solstice, you have a community responsibility. You've been at Squid Harbor from the beginning. You've grown up with these children. They are your lifelong friends. It's not friendship to let them be exposed like this. I remember you with Daisy's boy and Pete Schlessboom's boy as kids playing on rubber rafts and take a look at you now.

Pig took a look right at the center of my chest, which happened to say EAT C&A'S EXTRAORDINARY PIZZA.

—You're going to have children of your own, he went on. As Virgil already has. You know his daughters. I've seen you playing with them. That's excellent. That's what we want at Squid Harbor, the generations, the old teaching the young. But it wouldn't be wonderful if they got sick.

Pig Love banged a heap of wet sizzling debris out of his pipe, then stuffed it full. His face seemed to get fatter and pinker and one began to see how he had acquired his nickname.

—Look at my own kid Susan. She's your age, Penguin, and up at Mount Holyoke they've given them each two prophylactics in a little vinyl pouch. *Two prophylactics*. That's at a *girls'* school. What possible use would they have there for those things?

I thought of poor anorexic Susan Love, whose arms and legs were like Tinkertoy struts, lining up dutifully at the Mount Holyoke

Health Center to get her ration of contraceptives. In a way, Pig Love was right. It was a fucked-up world.

—It's just like Jonah and the Whale, I said. We think we can save the ship by throwing Joshua Brand over the side. Or Arnold. Or me. If we get Arnold Fratorelli out of Squid Harbor, the Earth will be normal again and we can go on with the Laser races and the barbecues. We think Squid Harbor is an island, but it's not. It's interconnected. If one person is infected, then we all are.

—That's what we're afraid of, grunted Pig Love.

It was what they were afraid of. They were afraid of being human. And they thought they could protect themselves from it the way Newton Yin and the Star Wars people thought they could protect themselves from the rest of humanity by erecting a huge nuclear contraceptive up in space. I thought of what my father had said, maybe we'd all have it someday, which would at least be equal, and then the animals could return and start evolving again towards something more humane than us.

We stopped talking and everyone took one of Dorothy's brown cigarettes and we looked out through the Yins' glass walls at the darkening sky. A big thundercloud had formed over the bay and you could see the top of it billowing up like a thermonuclear explosion. The water toward Provincetown was ash black. Over the shore you could see the kids tacking their Lasers in, racing the storm, people on their porches bringing in deck chairs and tables, rolling their car windows up.

Only at Joshua's was nothing happening. No deck chairs, no Windsurfers on the beach. That was my family: a Great Dane and two middle-aged men hiding in there with the shades drawn like the household of Anne Frank. Let them try, I thought, let them just try. One word to Cosimo and he would tear off their arms and legs.

—Perhaps Penny could talk to Joshua, Daisy said. She can tell him better than anyone else.

—Oh no I won't. They have a right to stay right where they are.

—If you won't tell him, Penguin, others will. And they may not be so diplomatic.

Already the wind had picked up and large drops of rain were batting the glass walls. It was time to get out of there. I had no desire to spend the day on Tobacco Island in a transparent house.

—I'm voting to let them stay, Virgil said.

God bless you, Virgil, I thought. Maybe there was a place between heaven and hell for people who were assholes only part of the time. I also noticed that his nose was less prominent than before. Virgil was becoming, in his late twenties, quite a handsome and thoughtful-looking man.

—I thought we were voting on spraying the marsh, Daisy reminded him. That was our official agenda.

A boat suddenly appeared out on the unsettled bay. Against the dark sky and dark water it was a supernaturally brilliant moving spot of white, growing larger as it came out, a big inboard with a canopy and fish poles sticking up on either side like the two antennas of a lobster.

—God, Virgil said. It's P. T.

In yellow oilskins and high yellow boots, P. T. Varnum walked up the shore path and opened the glass door without a knock.

—Well, P. T. said. It's eleven o'clock. What's your decision?

—As chair of the Environment Committee, Daisy said, and a biologist, I say we leave the marsh alone.

—We'll see about the marsh, P. T. said. And we'll see about the members and their guests.

Virgil, who had stood up, looked down at the smooth rain-beaten skull of his old man, which looked like one of those Easter Island statues that have been staring out to sea for a thousand years.

—Dad, this is the appointed committee. You might as well let us settle it. Penny was saying . . .

—Penny Solstice is not a member of this committee, P. T. said, and she shouldn't be out here. She's a college kid and she is ten feet over her head. We're not letting Squid Harbor become a sanatorium. Act graciously but carry the big stick, that's what T. R. said. I'm having one of the company lawyers as a house guest. He may have an idea of what to do. And another thing, Virgil, I can't let you go back in the Whaler in this weather. Anyone who wants to go with me in the Outrage, I'm leaving right now.

We didn't have much choice but to go back in P. T.'s boat. Dorothy and I walked down with Virgil, his father ahead of us, starting the big engine, revving it up, undoing the stern line. I was soaked to the skin the minute I went out the door.

—It's for the best, Penguin, Dorothy said. This way we'll all be saved.

Saved. It was the first word she had spoken to me all morning. There wasn't a single one of us who could be saved.

Virgil took Dorothy by the elbow and lifted her into the boat like a courtier, then turned to me. I jumped over the rail on my own and we were off. By then there were bolts of lightning out over the bay and the rain was so heavy that even with the big wiper sweeping the boat's windshield you could not see.

18

*I don't mind dying, I just don't
want to be there when it happens.*
                    —Woody Allen

In order to avoid further contact with the Varnums, I let
Dorothy drive us home through the rainstorm from the dock. She
dropped me off and headed on to Perera's to get supplies. When I
reached the house I found a note taped to the screen door:

DARLING
I'M OVER AT JOSHUA'S
LOVE
RICHARD

Obviously the "darling" didn't refer to me. I went to my room to
get out of the wet clothes and I found nothing clean, which did not
surprise me. I had been in the C&A's sweatshirt for three days and it
would have to be isolated and burned. I raided Dorothy's closet for
a pair of her white painter pants and a striped navy blue French sailing sweater that I knew she despised and never wore.

I went up and checked Richard's studio. The rain on the metal
roof of the studio sounded like one of those gamelans that have a
whole native village drumming on them at once. The aluminum
sheep or goat sculpture was gone; the truck must have taken it to
New York. Dangling in midair from the ceiling hoist was a new,
anthropomorphic construction made of greenish bronze with two
handless arms sticking straight out and a small tail, like a dog's. The

chain of the hoist was wrapped around its neck so it looked like a statue that had just finished committing suicide. Richard probably had raised it up like that so he could weld on the base. I thought it looked pretty good the way it was.

I flipped the hood back over my head and went to Joshua's. I hadn't seen Cosimo for a couple of days, and the Great Dane actually stood up and came over to show some affection, which meant that our eyes looked into each other from approximately the same height. I was proud that I had learned not to back off when Cosimo approached. As usual, I offered my hand as a sacrifice and he took one lick on it with his liver-colored tongue, which was exactly the length and shape of one of the beef tongues in Jerry Perera's refrigerated display of meat.

My father and Joshua were talking beside the vacant piano.

—Where's Arnold? I asked.

—In the bedroom.

I went in and sat in the wheelchair beside his bed. My hands felt quite natural on the cool stainless steel rims. I moved it a couple of inches back and forth. Maybe it would be my destiny to end up in one of these. I'd have a high-speed electric one and I would lead demonstrations of wheel-ridden people demanding extra wide toilet stalls and ramps.

Arnold looked half-asleep or drugged, as if he were not fully present in this world, even for him. I asked him how he felt.

—I don't feel anything, he said. Which is a blessing. How about you?

He spoke as if we were somehow both in the same boat. He said he was better but he looked actually worse. His face was white and narrow, like one of those eggshells that have become thin and brittle from pesticide, and the veins were so close to the surface that it seemed like the top layer of skin had come off. His lips were crazed with the same white lines only more pronounced than ever. He was freshly shaved, too. In places. It looked like somebody had hacked off his beard with a flint knife.

He held on with both hands to the satin edge of the white cotton blanket as if his bed were in fearful and violent motion, like a man holding the crossbar of a roller coaster.

—Nietzsche had syphilis, Arnold said. He got it on purpose. He went to a prostitute and deliberately exposed himself.

—Nietzsche was crazy, I said.

—No. He was a genius.

—Same thing.

—How long has it been raining? Arnold said.

—Since about noon. Can I get you something?

—I was in Venice once, he began. It was at the Biennale. I was premiering a piece, along with many others, in the New Music Section, which was at La Fenice. It rained so hard during the concert that the roof leaked, and sections of the white ceiling paint floated down on the audience like dying birds. Then we went out to eat. Listen, a waltz . . .

I waited for the next part of the Venice story, but Arnold was looking up at the ceiling as if he'd confused the two places in his mind, Venice and Squid Harbor, and the unfinished pine boards over his head were going to shred down on us in layers of veneer.

—You went out to eat, I prompted.

—Yes. As we ate we heard water lapping around our shoes.

—I thought it was the tides that flooded Venice, not the rain.

At that point, a drop of real rain broke through Joshua's ceiling and fell into a white porcelain pan in the center of the carpet, like a bedpan, only placed there for the leak.

—You see, Arnold said, it amounts to the same thing. That proves it.

—Proves what?

—It proves Joshua has been starving me. I know it. He hates me. It started weeks ago.

—What started, Arnold?

—The hatred. The starvation. He hates me because I'm athletic and he's not. You probably weren't aware of that. I can run the hundred in just under ten-nine. I could anyway before they zapped me with this AZT.

—Joshua doesn't hate you, Arnold. He cares for you more than anyone in his life.

—He never would have done this in Venice, Arnold went on. That's when we were in love. Nothing could touch us. We won seventy thousand lire at the casino and walked out on the beach. We could see the fishermen offshore, shining their torches down into the water to attract the fish. We had an octopus dinner right on the sand, with wine and bread, and now he won't give me anything to eat.

Arnold's body under the sheet had a long, thin, cold-blooded albino lizard look. It was consuming itself. No matter how much we fed him, he couldn't hold onto it. Yes, he had been an athlete. He had run track for his high school in Salem or someplace and had been some kind of champion. Joshua told me that. He had a choice of a track scholarship and going to music school. I stood there fervently wishing he could go back there and make the other choice and become a normal person and not this skeleton prodigy that was not even making reasonable sense.

—The Greenhouse Effect, Arnold said. Look. It's happening to you too. Your face is half green. It's turning us both into plants.

It wasn't worth it. No matter what music he had ever composed, it wasn't worth this.

—How is your oratorio going? I asked him. *The Keeper of Sheep?*

He gave me this blank look as if he'd forgotten his own work. I had a terrible feeling. What if his brain failed before he got it done? If we could only preserve the small fold or corner reserved for musical composition, we could let every other part of his mind and body perish. I thought it might help if I could get him remembering things again, like the stories of Venice. Joshua had mentioned a collection of personal effects, and I asked Arnold about it.

—Do you have any idea where it is?

—Maybe somewhere around the room. It's not worth it.

I followed his pointing finger and discovered a small cardboard box in the closet, under the pile of everything he'd brought down from Joshua's house in Cambridge. I got it out and put it on the bed next to his legs. In it was a conglomeration of photos, newspaper clippings, cassettes, and program notes, including the small book-like imitation leather binding that contained his Ph.D.

—It would be good to put some of these things in order, I said.

—You think I'm going to die, too, don't you? That's why you're doing this.

—I think it might help you with your work.

We went through a group of yellowy aging photographs first. The first picture showed his parents, who were these two dark Italian people posed stiffly in front of a stone cottage, the man obviously older and more worldly than the woman, but both still youthful, both in love in a formal, old-fashioned way. The man rested one of his hands on an obsolete-looking tape recorder the size of a big suitcase with two large reels.

—They had that taken in Sicily, Arnold said.

Arnold lapsed into an extraordinarily detailed, if somewhat disconnected family saga. He explained how his father, Raimondo Fratorelli, collected Sicilian folk songs as a hobby. He'd met his bride, Arnold's mother, Sylvia, on one of these trips. She married him, came to Massachusetts, and died of bone marrow cancer when Arnold was six. It was suddenly important to him for us to get these photos in the correct sequence, much as it amounted to guesswork on my part because, although he had all these images in his head, he was losing his sense of time.

—She never learned English, Arnold said. And I never learned Italian. They were afraid I'd have an accent for the rest of my life. Even Sylvia wanted me to be *tutto americano.* I lived with my mother for six years, and we never talked. She'd tell me long stories that I couldn't understand. But I'd know what she was saying without the words.

Then there was his father, in white tie and tails, standing beside a piano on the Charles River esplanade with a full-dress orchestra in the background. Raimondo had been the piano tuner for the Boston Pops. I knew that from before because Joshua had told me. There was a photo of two little kids beside each other on a piano bench:

Arnold and his brother Leo. They had been child prodigies, he explained. They gave a concert of piano duets in the Salem Town Hall when they were both under ten. Arnold went on in music, while Leo gave it up to eventually end in business school and become a real estate broker in California.

—Leo was more gifted than I was, Arnold said. But he was a year younger and it drove him crazy that whatever he did I had already done it. He thought he would never catch up. Now he's really going to have to hustle.

—Don't talk like that, I said. Or I won't listen.

Then we found an envelope mostly of brother Leo: Leo and his wife standing in front of their home in Santa Monica, Leo's arm around the stout shoulders of their Mexican gardener, plus their increasing number of kids playing around. There was one with two couples: Leo and his wife, plus Arnold with a woman, kind of an awkward smile forced onto his face. I had to laugh.

Another showed a happier Arnold in a open-topped sports car, beside a man with a scarf around his neck and a straw hat.

—My agent, he said. For my brief Hollywood career. I did the score for a movie of *Mrs. Dalloway*. The movie never saw the light of day.

Leo, it turned out, was a staunch Catholic who didn't even practice birth control. He got xenophobic about his brother's lifestyle and finally asked him to leave. Arnold was a "bad influence" on the boys, Leo had said. Los Angeles was enough like Sodom and Gomorrah without someone bringing it right inside the house.

A picture showed Mrs. Fratorelli only a couple of years after Arnold was born. She looked sad and homesick and ill, like someone whose energy is being drained off because she has silently set her will against her life. His father never remarried and never mentioned his wife to the two boys. It was as if he had brought them into the world himself.

—He brought us up in that Victorian home in permanent sorrow, with the living room curtains always drawn. He took the whole guilt upon himself. It was his fault. He had brought her from Reggio

Calabria and caused her bones to rot away from the New England fog. The only things left for him were his music and his two kids. He had us play for him every single night.

The next package we found consisted of old clippings of Arnold's amazing athletic career at Salem High, put together apparently by his father, which Uncle Joshua had also mentioned, but under the circumstances it hadn't seemed real up till now. Sometimes they were cut from the *Salem Evening News* or even the *Globe*, sometimes they were glossy, formal photographs of a dark thin wiry boy in a numbered undershirt holding a series of huge trophies, surrounded by track coaches in coats and ties. He made All-Massachusetts in the low hurdles and All-New England in the 100-yard dash.

—They offered me a track scholarship to Brown, but I turned it down for Julliard. Maybe I would have gone the other way. Maybe I wouldn't be dead. Maybe I'd be married and be selling office buildings and have five little boys.

—You don't get to do that, I said. Those other lives are illusions.

—It's not an illusion. It's my own brother.

—What about your music? When Leo gets through with his allegedly normal life, what will he have given to anyone that can compare with that? Isn't it worth it?

—Worth what?

—You know. Sacrifice.

—No, Arnold said. It's not. A piece of music isn't worth a thing. You can't photograph it, you can't fuck it, you can't live in it, you can't eat it, you can't hang it on the wall. It's air. It's temporary and invisible. As fast as you write it it ceases to exist.

—So what? I said. You still have to get it done.

We came upon a picture with his high school sweetheart, who was blond and pretty in the fifties sense of the term, so blond that in the old monochromatic photo her hair was totally white. Arnold's own hair had been dense and black at the time, not as it now was with its patches of suet-colored scalp. The young woman stood right next to him in front of a birch tree, her breast squished up against his upper arm.

—I tried, in those days, Arnold said. That was Valerie. She didn't last very long. I remember, when her brother took that picture, thinking he was the cuter of the two.

Which turned out to be true. There were about twenty photos of Valerie's older brother, who was a cellist. We came upon a bunch of programs from recitals he gave with Arnold, including the prize performance at the Pablo Casals Festival from 1965 at Carnegie Hall. Also a prize picture: Arnold with the cellist-brother, who had a longish, slightly equine-looking face exactly like Valerie's, and long, pale, steam-ironed sixties hair falling over the shoulders of his tux.

—Barry. Valerie was so jealous she left home. We did New York together after that concert. It was a horrible night. He found a third party in the hotel lobby, a minor league baseball player from some city in the South. "He has a Hellenic physique." That was the way Barry put it. He was incorrigible. He made us all stay in the same bed.

—Barry and Valerie, I said. Where do they live now?

—Valerie teaches English at Salem High. Barry is dead.

Whenever Arnold said someone was "dead" you always knew what they died of. If they had cancer or ran in front of a truck he would always say "he had cancer" or "he ran in front of a truck." Death was something else. Death was his. It was reserved for those who went in his own way.

The Victorian house in Salem appeared again, this time with Mr. Fratorelli seated forlornly on the front steps with a spotted dog. Arnold said his father never even dated another woman. He took some apprentices in the piano-tuning trade who would actually come to his house and live, but they'd get tired of the perpetual darkness and mourning and they would leave.

After that image he didn't seem to want any more history, though I think that trip into the past helped stabilize his thought. He motioned for me to put the collection back where we had found it. He then reached under the covers and felt around for the Pessoa book, which he kept always beside him, which he read because if his mind started gyrating out of control, the mild discipline of those poems could call it back. He seemed to be searching his own body for it, as if he kept the book in a personal cavity. He finally located it under there and pulled it out. Another huge raindrop fell from the bedroom ceiling into the white pan with its red rim.

It was a thin volume, too thin for somebody's entire work, even a poet. It made me think of life as a slow cremation, during which the body is turned into pure white ash from which a few pieces of paper can be made. Once Bondo had dragged me to this cult movie, *The Return of the Living Dead.* The star laid down on the conveyor belt of a crematorium and fed himself in. If a man's body were burned, the remaining ashes would weigh approximately as much as this book. Arnold put it in my hands and pointed out the passage I was supposed to read:

> *When I'm sick I must think the opposite*
> *Of what I think when I am well.*
> *(Otherwise I wouldn't be sick.)*
> *I must feel the opposite of what I feel*
> *When I am well,*
> *I must be sick completely—ideas and everything.*
> *When I'm sick I'm not sick for any other reason.*

—Are you going to set that poem to music also, I asked, as part of your final piece?

I'd let the word "final" slip out of my mouth without being able to stop it.

—How can I tell you? he said. You have no comprehension of sickness. If the truth be known, women have absolutely no comprehension of art.

—Come on, Arnold. Gertrude Stein. Dorothy Richardson. Louise Nevelson. Georgia O'Keefe. Irina Ratushinskaya. She was in a prison camp and scratched her poems on bars of soap because they wouldn't let her have a pencil.

—Those were not women, Arnold replied. They were angelic

beings. Angels do not belong to any sex. Look at a real penguin, for example. If you've ever seen one. Look closely between its legs. There's nothing there.

—Maybe you can't see it, but it's there. Penguins were never intended to be angels.

He stopped talking and stared at me, then he coughed one of the deep evacuative coughs I had heard only at night, and another, then a whole chain of linked spasms until finally something terrible came out of his mouth: a clot, like a small tea bag of jellied blood, just falling out of his mouth and lying there on the white towel that covered the blanket over his chest. Under the clot, a stain spread through the fabric like the darkest conceivable variety of red wine.

I ran out for Joshua. I could hear Arnold starting to cough again in the other room.

—Joshua, you have to come in. He should have a doctor. He should be somewhere else.

Joshua went in to him and I returned to the living room. Luckily Richard had gone. I couldn't imagine him standing in Uncle Joshua's house while his daughter was ministering to a dying man. I couldn't talk to him about it. But he must have known.

I was also starting to panic about my own health. I checked Dorothy's sweater and pants for splashes of blood. I looked at the backs of my hands and, in the mirror, my face. The mark across my neck looked blood red, as if the flesh were infected and throbbing beneath the skin. My face had this ghastly albumen color like a woman who has never been outdoors and has no destination in life but to age briefly and die.

I was still holding Arnold's book of poems. On its slick dust jacket was a single red drop the color of the world at sunset that was darkening and congealing on the glossy surface. It looked and acted like typical human blood. It hardened into itself as if to shield and protect a tiny wound on the surface of the book. Within that drop the red and white cells swam in a clear medium that would taste like a memory of the sea. It also contained the trace elements of poison, virus shapes hunting like submarines among the cells, trained to find and penetrate the vulnerabilities of their walls.

I held the book under Joshua's desk lamp to dry it up and bring the struggle to an end. That would be one way to stop disease and sickness in the world, for God or someone simply to hold it near the sun. I tried to remember whether the Earth's orbit was shrinking or expanding. I had gotten that question wrong on the final in Astro 12.

I touched the end of one finger to the half-coagulated blood, then brushed my forehead with it at a place above and between the eyes. This was my caste mark and my vaccination. I would need it to take me through the weeks ahead.

Through the doorway I could see Uncle Joshua preparing one of the syringes. He drew the plunger all the way out, broke the seal of a cartridge, inserted it, replaced the plunger again. His mother was right. His hands could have been the hands of a surgeon in their clear movements, with the brief deliberate pauses in between. Then I saw his whole body shudder in what looked like a brief spasm of horror or disgust.

—Do you need help? I asked him.

—No. I have it under control. We won't be needing you for the time being.

I splashed up to Richard's studio to watch him work. Somehow he didn't seem involved, either on Dorothy's side or mine. A man was deteriorating mentally and physically less than a hundred yards from his studio, plus his own wife was in hysterical reaction, while Richard Solstice kept on welding pieces of aluminum together as if it were all blue sky and seagulls like every normal summer in the world. I guess this was what it took to be an artist. You could even see it in Arnold, who was both in and above his own disease. It's not a state I wanted to achieve myself. If I was ever going to be really sick I would want to be there.

—How can you do it? I asked him.

—What?

—How can you just keep going when that's happening next

door? He's going to die and you just . . .

—That's why I do it, he said. Because we're going to die. Eventually, all of us. Even you. This work is all we have.

—You really think work can defeat death?

—No, work is just another form of dying, but it does allow you to participate.

—What's that sculpture you're doing in there, the dangling one?

—I'm calling it *Music*. It's going to be suspended over the sheep.

I couldn't believe that art was in any way an answer to the question raised by the body underneath that sheet. You could die alone or you could die with others around you or you could die in the cool, professionally trained hands of the medical coterie with its patriarchal hegemony of white-coated doctors and nurses with pale stockings that give them the legs of the dead. If you have to be there when it happens, you should at least be in the presence of someone who loves you and cares for you not because they are paid to but because it is also an inevitability of their own. Of course Joshua and Arnold would make the choice they had made. And my part was to be there, too, and shield them from the Pig Loves and the Dorothy Dvorjaks and the P. T. Varnums. Just for a little while I had to make a wall around that cottage, not to prevent the virus from escaping, but to protect that small community of sadness from the outside world.

Richard was humming Arnold's melody from the second poem of Fernando Pessoa. I recognized it because I'd heard it again and again as it was taking shape.

—Hey, that's our music, I said.

—A loss to the world. He was still young. He might have become a great composer.

Richard spoke in the past tense as if Arnold were already dead.

—All you can think of is what people make, I said. Don't you care anything about what they are?

—Who knows what anyone is? Richard said. I am, I make something, a few things perhaps, then it's all over. When you begin making then you cease to be.

—But you just got married. That's not ceasing to be. Or is that another participatory form of death?

He pulled on the double chain of the ceiling hoist until the hanged man was over the aluminum tent with the sheep in it. I realized the whole project was for Arnold. It was his version of the Keeper of Sheep. He must have known everything all along.

—"Whatever a man is intent on at the moment of death," Richard quoted, "he will keep doing in eternity."

I knew that. It was lord Krishna, from the Bhagavad-Gita.

But I didn't believe it. There was no heaven and, if there were, there wouldn't be music there, only silence, because everyone knows you have to have a body to make noise. Arnold said you had to have silence in order to make music, but then the silence has to be broken, and you can't break things in eternity. It's not permitted. I sat on a slab of raw aluminum about two feet from Richard's legs and I let myself cry. I cried for every possible thing in the neighborhood of my thought, like a little girl praying for everyone she can possibly think of, not just for Arnold and Joshua but for Rebecca and Jennifer and for Virgil, even though he was a dickhead in many ways, and for poor Dorothy who seemed too young to be twice married, and for the tall spectacled Chinese kid Newton who saw the universe as a Donkey Kong game, and for Jerry Perera, the best part of him left in a rice paddy somewhere back in Vietnam—and for myself also, the black-and-white flightless bird stuck in the center without really belonging there at all.

Richard reached down to hold me. I let it happen. I closed my eyes and willed my body to grow smaller and relaxed into his arms. For a few minutes I let myself not even remember where I was.

19

I am an actor, a member of the cast of Othello, *not a star but just a foot soldier in the Venetian army and we are fighting overseas, in Cyprus, against the Turks. I am a homosexual who sleeps with his arms around another soldier. Our beards smell of horses and salt pork. We look on without any emotion as the ravishing princess Desdemona, in a white robe, is strangled on a stone altar by the black general Othello, as if we were viewing it through swirly Elizabethan glass. After she dies, her body rises up on wires that draw her right up into the clouds. Othello is left alone to peel off his rusty armor in layers, like a striptease artist, underneath which he is shown to be a woman with large gravid black breasts. The army turns to fight against the Turks, knowing that without a commander it will be certain death. The soldier beside me takes out these colored photographs of famous architectural sites in Venice. The thing about these buildings is that they're all in flames. He explains that they look like the real thing but they are "parodies." He shows me a medieval-looking church or cathedral on fire and says:* There is the Burning Lamb.

I woke from that dream so soaked in sweat I thought I had urinated in my bed. It was hot and there were mosquitoes in the room. It was just beginning to be light. I lay there with only my forehead and my right arm exposed and waited for them to land. One did. Fat and red, she had already had breakfast but was greedy enough to stop for a little more.

I lay there thinking of the couple upstairs on the foam mattress on the floor of the sleeping loft. I had known Richard since the evening of my conception twenty-one years ago in Paris, at the Hotel de l'Opéra-Comique; whereas I had only known Dorothy Dvorjak for a month. In that period we almost worked through the predictable conflicts and became friends, but she was now in the inexplicable process of betrayal. Why? I wasn't sure. And yet I still felt closer to Dorothy than to my father, maybe because we were antagonists in this weird battle, maybe because we were also bonded as women in spite of everything. Like soldiers in some invisible battle, maybe we each needed an enemy. An enemy might make death easier to understand, death that was evolving as we evolved, that was inventing new weapons when the old ones were obsolete and, if they were too hideous to be shown abroad, tested them under the ground where He was king. Death who also crept in under the alias of love, disguised as a virus so minute that it could swim between the molecules of a condom. Death's agents were not monsters like Dr. Frankenstein, they were exemplary citizens like Dr. Newton Yin, who sat in his lab on the pedicured grounds of the Lawrence Livermore Laboratory working supposedly for the Government but not knowing who his real Employer was.

I hadn't understood the term "sacrifice" until that night. I had been to see the Vietnam War Memorial in Washington, which is a black slab with fifty thousand names on it designed by an Asian architect from Yale, a woman commemorating all those men. I had been born in the midst of that war and I hated it so much that the names of its dead seemed like inert things. Not even words: things on a black rock. And where were the stone monuments carrying the names of those who were raped like the little round-faced Dartmouth freshman in the Beta Sig house or the names of the AIDS victims like Arnold and God knows maybe Joshua in time and myself and the people we have yet to be with? They are the invisible statues in the nonexistent parks that allow us to keep going for another generation so perhaps we can find out, without having to nuke one another, what we are supposed to be.

Maybe the government would fund Richard's AIDS sculpture for the city of New York. More likely, some fundamentalists would shoot it down because it fails to uphold the values of the nuclear family. Maybe instead they'd circulate the vast quilt with the AIDS victims on it, which was growing so large it had to be displayed on a football field. It made me think of our pathetic little quilt back in Hanover. Castrate the Patriarchy. This was our struggle too, the struggle of women against the enemy. But I was no longer sure exactly who was the enemy and who was us.

Upstairs, I heard someone wake up and trudge around in a circle over my head. Dorothy was sleepwalking again. It is impossible to hate a somnambulist when they are actually in the act. I just lay there praying that she wouldn't crash over the low balcony railing and plunge headfirst down to the breakfast nook.

Finally she spoke something unintelligible and I heard Richard get up and lead her back to their double bed. I fell asleep too. When I heard her again it was completely bright out and she was down in her studio, my ex-bedroom, fully dressed, lighting a blowtorch to weld the legs onto another spider.

20

—You have to provide me with coffee, I said to Dorothy. No matter who I am.

The family was out of milk. She poured two cups of coffee and whitened them with Cremora and sugar. Dorothy had actually stopped drinking alcohol, at least before sunset if not after. I couldn't imagine why. The world was changing in the direction of abstinence but heretofore my two parents had definitely not been affected. Dorothy had once darkly hinted that she thought my own defective coloration had been caused by Katherine's being something of a lush while I was in the womb, and now the ridiculous thought struck me that in all that thrashing around upstairs my father and Dorothy Dvorjak had gotten themselves with child. That would be the last straw in my dispossession. It was too late for siblings. I'd be one of the homeless for good.

I observed her carefully as she bent back over the bronze spider, which was held in a vise, and lit the portable torch to braze on the next leg. There weren't any visible signs of change.

—I should weld your mouth together, she said over the roar of the torch. Then I'd weld your fingers together, and the bones of your spine. You'd make a pretty good statue. And you wouldn't be so much trouble. We could just stand you over in a corner along with Richard's other work.

—Why do you keep making the same thing over and over? I asked her.

—I'm looking for the essential spider. Also, I have to have a lot of work if I want a one-man show.

—One-person show, you mean.

—One-*man* show, Dorothy repeated. I haven't struggled all this time to become a "person."

—It's going to be nothing but spiders?

—*Arachnids.* I have thirty-seven. They'll be impressive when you see them all lined up.

—I can't wait. I like this one. I like the round things on the end of the feelers.

—It's a self-portrait, Dorothy said.

—They're all self-portraits. They are exact likenesses.

Then out of nowhere she made this surprising announcement.

—I'm getting ready to leave the Cape, she said. I can't put any of us at risk. I'm going back to New York City.

—It's your decision, I said. Richard and I can manage ourselves just fine.

—I expect your father will end up coming along with me.

—I hope so, I answered. It will feel good to have a little space around here. Maybe I'll get my room back if everyone's gone.

Of course I knew she'd never dislodge him from Squid Harbor before Labor Day. But I humored her. It would be nostalgic to have him to myself again. I paused a second, then asked her.

—What makes you so sure Richard wants to go to New York? He's worked here right through September for almost twenty years. Since I was one.

—He has to, Dorothy replied. It's the law of nature.

After this exchange I managed to get myself together with some raisins in black cherry yogurt, then I called Uncle Joshua on the phone. Our houses were so close I could hear his phone ring through the open windows, as well as some of Arnold's music playing in the background, which sounded eerie coming both over the phone and through the air.

—Is that a tape? I asked Joshua.

—No. Arnold is up and around.

He may have been up and around all right, working at the piano, but I knew that it took ever more massive doses of the antibiotic, which relieved the chest symptoms, but the body needed more and more of it to accomplish the same thing. The drug gave him a temporary, artificial immunity, but eventually it would cease to work altogether. The Pentamedine had some other side effects too, or maybe it was the AZT or the Septra or the TPN, he was ingesting so many things. One of the effects was a rash that spread over Arnold's neck and lower jaw like my own markings, only it varied, so that each day his face would have a distinct pattern of coloration, almost as if he'd become another person overnight.

—I have to talk with you, I said to Joshua. Alone if we can. Let's drive around.

On the drive we passed the Stein-Mallows' cottage and it was true, they were actually moving out. The whole family, babies and all, were shuttling suitcases and boxes through the downpour out to their gunmetal gray Dodge van. The Stein-Mallow kids, in yellow raincoats, passed the articles along in a human chain. Joshua honked and waved as we went by, but the Stein-Mallows looked up silently and did not wave back.

—That's a strange operation in this weather, wouldn't you say?

—They're going back to Cleveland, I informed him.

—Why?

—I don't know, I said. Maybe it's the environment. My stepmother is also talking of going home.

—My God, Joshua said. Are we going to soar out of the house and bite them?

—I don't know what they're afraid of. Maybe nature. Or maybe themselves. It's not a rational thing.

—We felt a little of this in Cambridge, Joshua said.

—Cambridge? I'm surprised. I thought that was a mecca of tolerance.

—I happened to rent from a couple with several kids who lived in the same building. One day my lease was up. I tried to get the Harvard Corporation to lean on them, but I haven't heard anything yet.

People weren't human, I thought. That was beginning to be quite clear.

All this time we had been driving slowly with the wipers on high and Joshua rubbing away at the windshield to clear off the steam that was coming from our breath. We reached the paved road, Route 6A, which goes one way to Provincetown and the other back towards Hyannis and civilization and New York. The uninterrupted line of traffic would have kept us from turning onto that road even if we'd wanted to. There were cars towing boats, long recreational vehicles towing little Samurais behind them, dune buggies, station wagons with human legs and feet dangling out of their windows into the rain, yellow-slickered motorcycle couples, and even a United States Military convoy with truck after truck of soldiers sweating under the tarpaulins in their helmets and camouflage suits. They were all on the southbound lane as if there were a massive exodus from the Cape, as if they knew something, like that there was going to be another Flood.

—I've seen this happen before, Joshua said. I was a child then, in another country. On top of everything else I also happen to be a Jew. But I would never have expected it at Squid Harbor. It's too bad. This was the one place where I was able to live like a normal human being.

—I know what you mean.

That was all I could find it in my heart to say. Then someone came up behind us and peeped courteously on the horn. I turned around. It was a big maroon car, which you could tell was a Mercedes-Benz from the peace symbol on the grille. It looked like Bailey Varnum inside, along with another well-fed capitalist, probably the beer lawyer from Providence. Joshua pulled over to let them by, waving out of habit as you always did on the Squid Harbor network of rutted and sandy roads. But P. T. passed us without any sign of recognition.

—I've known Bailey Varnum for years, Joshua went on. He used to be a sweetheart, in fact, which I could never reconcile with the man who floated up to the head of Darlings Beer. Maybe we're all different when we're on vacation.

—Maybe we're different when we come into power, I said.

I was on sort of a permanent vacation myself, I thought, and maybe at Squid Harbor I was different, too. But different from what? It probably took a while before you got to be a divided personality like Uncle Joshua. Or you had to be gay, or a huge corporate executive, before you'd have a public and a private life. I was of two colors on the outside but maybe I hadn't been divided yet within.

—How is P. T. different? I asked.

—Bailey Varnum has never feared anything in his whole life, but now that he's aging he has to face death like the rest of us. The difference is, Bailey thinks he can defeat it. Arrange a buyout. Offer a deal that death can't afford to refuse. Maybe he'll try leveraging us out too, Arnold and me.

By that time we had driven to the end of the Harbor Road and the Far Beach. Joshua stopped the car with the front wheels almost in the sand, pointing out over the water, the way someone would if he wanted to take you out Parking.

—I want to stop for one minute, he said. Just to look at the water. I've hardly been out of that house all summer except for Cambridge.

We could see all of Squid Harbor on one side, and the Great Marsh on the other. A blue heron was feeding in the shallows, taking a few steps as if she were bringing her feet down on an old and infinitely fragile fabric, then freezing in place and taking a stab into the water. Every so often she'd actually catch something and toss her beak so the prey was aligned head first in her mouth. You could see the throat wriggling as it went down, not swallowing so much as just letting the fish swim itself into the darkness, all the while probably thinking it had escaped.

The rain had subsided. On the tall wide-bladed sand grasses the remaining drops concentrated the first sunlight into points that almost could burn your eyes. The heron suddenly seemed to notice us and lifted herself upwards into their ponderous impossible-looking version of flight. For a moment I tried to think as Dorothy would have thought: here is this stepdaughter shuttling back and forth to an infected household, here is the wind blowing live viruses between Joshua's house and hers through fog so thick that the organisms could swim through it and still stay fertile, not to mention quadrillions of female mosquitoes carrying their cargoes of blood between the human children and their own, back and forth, weaving our own veins into the sinister circulations of the swamp. Nature was frightening if you happened to come from the city. It was probably best that she was heading back to New York.

Suddenly this big four-wheel drive truck with its headlights on and a row of yellow lights all over its roof came right up behind us and stopped about an inch in back of our car. I saw this through the rearview mirror and it looked like the scene in *Close Encounters* when that spacecraft with all the lights pulls up behind poor Richard Dreyfuss at the railroad crossing. Joshua didn't even seem concerned, but for a split second I imagined us both being pulled out of the car and raped. It could have been the Beta Sig Brothers coming to take their revenge. Then the vehicle backed up right into the sand and turned around and left.

—Who was that? I said.

Joshua finally turned around to look.

—I think it's the Perera boy, he said. He's an attractive fellow, perhaps a bit old for you, and not your type. His father was one of the best-looking men on the Cape. That was the legend.

—Oh, I said. It's only Jerry. I thought we were going to be killed or something. Worse.

—Death is bad enough, Joshua said, without trying to imagine anything worse.

Finally the rain had stopped. Beside me, so close I could have kissed his cheek without moving my body an inch, Uncle Joshua lit a cigarette and elevated his mouth to breathe a helix of smoke up through the sunroof. Out on the water, in the fleet of Lasers that had sat so patiently through the storm, someone was hoisting a bright pink-and-white striped sail.

21

Bondo was actually on the way. He called me from South Brewster, which was about twenty miles back up the Cape, to tell me his jeep had broken down and he was near the Jolly Roger Tavern on Route 6A. He would need a mechanic and there wasn't one in the vicinity. I told him I'd drive up to Perera's in Richard's car and see who I could find.

I was a perfectly good driver but I had never actually bothered to get a license so I stuck generally to unpaved roads. To go to Perera's meant less than a mile of public highway, though, and I felt confident. But it was a bad omen that Bondo hadn't even arrived yet and already he was in need.

—Bondo, I yelled, you weren't supposed to come on the Brewster road. You were supposed to come right down on the mid-Cape highway so you would get here.

—I wanted to take the scenic route. It says right here in the *Visitors' Guide to Cape Cod and Its Night Life* that that's what the tourist is supposed to do. And I am the tourist.

—You're not here to have a good time, I told him. You're here to help me see this through.

When I got up to Perera's I forgot to put the clutch in and the car stopped abruptly at a random spot between the gas pumps and the store. I spied a pair of boots sticking out from beneath this huge olive drab Ramcharger wrecker and my heart leaped up. Whoever was working on that thing could certainly fix a jeep.

177

One of the Perera girls came bouncing out to see if I needed gas. She was about fifteen and had the same passive-aggressive smile that I'd also seen on the woman who was with Jerry at the spray meeting. The myth was that the Cape Cod Portuguese settlers had brought black slaves with them when they first came, and that there'd been intermarriage, which might explain the exotic and untamable look of the Perera clan. I wondered if I was being a racist to have that thought.

Anyway, the girl at the gas pump looked like Jerry, in red high-tops and a Michael Jackson T-shirt. I realized she might actually be his offspring, if he had any, but Jerry had all kinds of relatives and the girl could have been anyone—she had a dark sexual gnostic look, though also completely innocent because she was totally unaware of it. I felt sorry for her: she'd probably have a husband and three kids by the time she was my age and would never leave the Cape from birth to death. I also felt, when she looked down to ask if I wanted gas, that compared to her I was a child who shouldn't even be behind the wheel. For once, I wished I had one sexual experience under my belt. Whatever it was, this girl had probably already done it a dozen times.

—I don't want gas, I told her. I need someone to go up to Brewster and fix a car.

—That's Uncle Jerry underneath the truck. You can have him if you can pry him out.

I went over and tapped the sole of Jerry Perera's work boot with my foot. He had grease-covered green pants on and he was lying on one of those little boards with wheels, like the ones used by people who have lost their lower bodies and have to move themselves around with their hands.

—Give me a pull, will you? Jerry said.

I gave him a minute to finish whatever he was doing, then I pulled on his legs until he rolled out from under the wrecker and stood up. He was shirtless. His body hair was soaked with oil or grease from the truck engine, which made him look mechanical himself, part of a big machine made up of grease-coated human chests.

—So it's Penny Solstice, he said. You've finally decided to go to Nantucket with me. Let me get cleaned up.

—Nothing doing. My friend's car is stuck down on 6A in Brewster and he needs some help.

—Your boyfriend from college?

—Roommate, I said.

—*Roommate?* In that case I haven't got time. I have to straighten a tie rod.

I believe Jerry actually thought I was attractive, even with the neck problem and the pallor from spending my life indoors. He had that undiscriminating look, though, like someone who'd eat anything in sight. No questions asked.

He lay down on the cart again and started to pull himself back under the truck. I grabbed his trouser leg and stopped him.

—We're strictly Platonic, I said. He really needs a mechanic. You have to come.

It was typically male to get territorial over someone they didn't even know.

Jerry seized onto my knee to boost me up into the passenger side of the wrecker, then climbed in on the other side. The first thing I noticed was a photo of the woman he was with the other night at the meeting. The picture was laminated in clear plastic on top of the gearshift knob. I saw it before he covered it up with his palm.

—I thought she was one of your relatives, I said. There is a family resemblance.

—Stella. She is an old war buddy. She used to be my second cousin, but we had it annulled. And she's not Platonic. I get nervous around Platonic women. You can't tell what they want 'cause they don't know.

He had a pair of luminous woolly dice dangling from the rearview mirror, along with a rabbit's leg. The leg was cut from a real rabbit and I felt the claws in it and the leathery foot pads and the long fragile bones under the fur.

—You eat any rabbit? Jerry asked.

We pulled out on the highway and he shifted the truck through about six gears, his hand smearing a layer of grease over Stella's plastic face.

—I don't, I said. I no longer participate in the food chain. I am a vegetarian.

Jerry reached across me to take a cigar out of the glove compartment and bit the end off, which he spat out the window. He had thrown on an olive drab USMC shirt with the Marine emblem on it, which was the snake of US imperialism coiling itself around the Earth. The shirt half covered the red-and-blue tattooed dragon on his arm. The dragon writhed in a clever, holographic way along with his arm muscles as Jerry steered the truck.

He lit the cigar and blew two tusks of blue exhaust smoke down through his nostrils.

—Vegetarian, he said. Platonic. And hanging around a couple of the boys in pink. Get serious, Penny. You're not in San Francisco. This is the United States.

—I can get out right here, I said. You can meet Bondo at the Jolly Roger in Brewster. He has a blue jeep with New Hampshire plates.

—You don't want to get stuck on the mid-Cape highway, Jerry said. You never can tell who's going to pick you up. Might just be somebody as bad as me.

He'd pulled out into the left lane and we were starting to pass people at this point, his foot hard on the floor and the motor rattling like it was about to self-destruct. I hoped he would handle Bondo's problem better than his own. We had to shout at each other over the engine noise.

—Valves, Jerry yelled.

I switched to the subject of the tattoo.

—I got it in Saigon. Excuse me, I mean Ho Chi Minh City. A tattoo parlor in back of a whorehouse. One-stop shopping.

—And you left some woman with an American baby to take care of and no legitimate means of support. You could have a child over there. She could be seventeen years old. As old as you were when you fathered her. She could be on the streets.

—It will improve the race, Jerry shouted back. Red American blood. When those kids grow up they'll lead the counterrevolution of Vietnam. They'll fly the Stars and Stripes again over Saigon. I'll go over and help them. I love to fight. I love war. I miss it. All this fucking peace gets on my nerves.

All the time he was going faster and faster while he yelled this. The Ramcharger's motor sounded like it would blow a rod. Then he slowed the truck down so we could hear each other and eased back into the proper lane.

—I'm a different person than you, Penny. You're the summer people. You had my old man clean out the cesspools every spring so things would be nice and sweet when you arrived.

—Come on, I said. Your family owned a store.

—We kept a store. You can't say you own it if it always belongs to the bank. My old man kept a store for two months in the summer when we made some money selling your kind of people smoked oysters and cocktail franks. We kept a store the rest of the year for Portuguese fishermen who had to live on credit from one haul to the next. What we made in August we gave away by Thanksgiving. We also had a scallop boat that went down in the hurricane of 1970. Edna. You might have heard. My father and my brother never came back.

—I'm sorry. I was three years old.

—I was a freshman at U Mass. I had two weeks of higher education when I got the news. I went home. My mother and sisters dressed in black. I stayed a month and signed on for Vietnam. I wanted nothing from the USA again. I wanted to get shot.

—Did you?

—No. I shot them first. What do you think of that, Ms. Vegetarian? I was eighteen years old. They told me to shoot all the gooks I could find and I obeyed.

He took his right hand off his girlfriend's picture and the other hand off the wheel, holding the palms up as if that would explain something he couldn't put in words. We were still doing sixty miles an hour. The wheel, then the whole truck started to shake. He wasn't going to steer until someone forgave him and under the circumstances it could only have been me.

—All right, I said. That's not going to bring them back to life. You did what they told you to. By the way, were they always soldiers, the ones you killed?

Luckily he didn't get to answer this. The sign read BREWSTER NEXT RIGHT and he had to put his hands back on the wheel to swerve off for the exit. I was wondering, if I'd been a grown male in 1970, whether I would have gone. To go meant you killed people, not to go meant someone got killed in your place. Some deal. Maybe the male me could have had a sex-change operation to avoid the draft and ended up exactly who I am.

Just after we hit Route 6A we saw the old blue topless jeep with the hood up and Bondo standing beside it forlornly like a cowpoke whose horse has a broken leg. He loved that vehicle more than a human being. It was parked outside a small motel with a miniature golf course called the Putt It Inn. I ran over to Bondo and put both arms around him and gave him a heartfelt squeeze.

—Cheer up, Bondo, I said. This is Jerry Perera. Bondo. Jerry. Jerry will repair your jeep.

Strewn in the rear compartment of the jeep were three duck-colored duffel bags probably full of dirty laundry that I was supposed to somehow get clean, along with a red climbing sack stuffed with paperbacks and a box of stereo components still wired together at the back, plus a great number of running shoes with the laces all knotted together so Bondo could handle them as a single entity. These things he showed to us one after the other, offering to take out the contents as if Jerry and I were customs inspectors at the border. Bondo is extremely polite.

Jerry began looking under the hood and Bondo bent over beside him. They were the same basic build and complexion, but that's where the similarities ended. Jerry went right for something bolted onto the engine, then something else bolted onto that, while Bondo looked like a man staring at an instruction manual written in

Chinese. Their bodies were different too. Jerry was fifteen years older, for one thing. Bondo was olive-colored because he was half Greek or something, but he was also greenish from never getting outside. All he ever did physically was to go over and lift things at the gym. Jerry was permanently tanned—not the surface tan you get from a summer on the beach but a tan that had evolved into his skin. Even the tattoos were baked on: the dragon on the right arm and the yin-yang symbol inside a pentagram on the left.

He talked to Bondo the way a doctor would lecture someone who'd let themselves get fat. He was condescending but at the same time man-to-man. It was completely different from when he talked to me. Even in his Vietnam story there was a hidden agenda, which is the way men talk to women, as if the words don't matter, they're just the prolegomena to something else.

—You don't take care of this engine, do you? This is a nice vehicle, a CJ-5. Custom seats even. They've stopped making this model. It's going to be good for a lawn ornament the way it's going. The oil doesn't show on the dipstick and the coil wire insulation is frayed off. Half your spark is going into the air. You also have a fuel line leak. Try turning it over.

Bondo got up on the front seat and cranked it. A low whining siren noise came out, like a curfew.

—Solenoid. I could haul it back to Wellfleet or I could go back and get a solenoid and put it in. Then you could drive it back.

—Which way is cheapest? Bondo asked.

—They are exactly the same. If I haul you back it is two dollars a mile. If I drive to get the part it is a dollar a mile each way, but twice as much mileage.

—Well, which would take longer?

—Exactly the same, Jerry said. If we haul the jeep back we go half as fast as if we just drive back for the part.

—I don't know, Bondo said. If there's no difference how am I supposed to decide?

—It's exactly the same, either way.

—You decide, Penguin, Bondo said.

—I'll just go to sleep in the back of the truck while you figure it out, Jerry said. Write me a letter.

Bondo kicked one of the tires of his jeep as if he were in a used car lot trying to buy his own vehicle from some sinister dealer.

—I'll stay with Penguin, he said. Mr. Perera can drive faster without us in the cab anyway. Isn't that right?

I had forgotten that Bondo applied the term Mister to all males older than himself. He must have grown up in a peculiar home.

—I'll be back in an hour, Jerry said. Thanks for the company.

—I haven't seen him for weeks, I explained.

—Oh yeah, you two were roommates, Jerry said. Penguin, why don't you ride back with me and let your roommate guard the jeep. You can show me the way.

—Forget it, I said. He might get kidnapped if we leave him here.

Jerry floored the accelerator. Black flames snorted out of the wrecker's smokestacks and he was off. I gave Bondo another hug, and arm in arm we waltzed over to the Jolly Roger Tavern. There were about ten unemployed-looking males at the bar, not poor but looking like people who made a sum of money doing one thing a year, probably with boats, drug-running or catching a single huge fish. And in fact there was a giant stuffed tuna over the vodka and rum bottles, its skin preserved with layers of shellac. Neither of us was quite twenty-one and we were of course trying to be nonchalant.

—Is that a real fish, Bondo asked the bartender, or a reproduction?

—That fish would be worth six thousand dollars, the man said. The Japanese pay fourteen dollars a pound. They fly those over in 747's. They take the seats out and fill up the fuselage with fish.

—Then they take passengers on the way back, another guy said, who had an admiral's cap saying USS *Narwhal.* That's why there's so many of them here.

—No, they take VCRs, the bartender said. Fish out, VCRs back. That's the balance of trade.

By that time Bondo had made his move and ordered a couple of beers. The bartender served us in a way that showed he knew we were underage but it didn't matter, because if Bondo had been in the service he could have been dying for his country and not be able to buy beer in his hometown. He had a small American flag stabbed through his shirt and he served us with a fixed patriotic smile.

—Thanks, Mr. Roger, Bondo said. I was dying of thirst.

I told Bondo everything. I told him about Dorothy and the marsh and the attack by moths and Mrs. Baxton and the twins, which suddenly seemed a hundred years back, and seeing the wheelchair and meeting Arnold and taking care of him solo for over five days. I told him that Joshua and Arnold shared an apartment back in Cambridge and they'd been together for years, though Uncle Joshua always came to the Cape alone. Finally, the summer before, he had brought him to Squid Harbor for a weekend and Arnold had fallen in love with it. Now Arnold weighed well under a hundred pounds, which was why I could so easily lift him out of his bed.

—Lift him out of bed? Bondo said. How?

—How else? With my hands.

I told him about Arnold's music and how he had studied at Princeton and had received a commission from the Julliard String Quartet. He had studied with this famous electronic composer whose name I could not remember, but Arnold referred to him as the Dean of the Synthesizer. He had taught composition part-time at MIT. When he moved in with Uncle Joshua in Cambridge, Arnold had come down with pneumonia in the winter and it wouldn't go away. He had started to cough blood and sleep twenty hours at a stretch, so he finally went to a men's clinic in Watertown and took the test. I told how they had brought him first to Mass General and even under intensive care he had almost died. They transferred him to a private clinic and then took him home.

I told him about the second attack, before Easter, and that Arnold stayed in the hospital and was in a room by himself, where he got lonely and tried starving himself by pulling the feeding tube out of his arm. I told him how Joshua described the ward, with people hooked up to catheters because they were constantly going to the bathroom without end. By then it was June, and they took Arnold down to Squid Harbor because he wanted to spend his last days in a natural context. That happened to be the morning Dorothy and I were out in the canoe.

Then I told him about the Great Marsh and the proposal to spray it to death from the air. I told him about the meetings and the Committee and P. T. and the lawyer and brought him up to the present time. And I told him what I had learned. I told him about helping Arnold to and from the piano and conserving his energies so he could compose as much as he could. I told him about trying to get him to take some of the strange liquids we put into him, and at the same time always keeping one eye on Cosimo whom I still did not fully trust.

I told him about the music, which I at first had hated but was beginning to understand. Its weird distortions were just like the world in which we lived.

I told him about strapping the oxygen bottle to the back of the wheelchair so he could put the mask on at any time. I told him I hadn't yet learned to give the intravenous injection, and that was when Bondo finally said something himself.

—What do you mean "yet"? Bondo said. I thought this was over. I thought it was just a temporary job till Professor Brand got back from Cambridge. And now he's been back for weeks. I thought you were a health freak. You are handling this man's food. And his person, his oxygen mask. You are swabbing his mouth out with Q-tips. This is not right. And even if you don't care about yourself, you're not alone in the world.

—I am alone, I told him. All I've got to my name is a father along with his child bride plus two suitcases full of dirty laundry. There are no washers and dryers at Squid Harbor. You better forget about those clothes back in the jeep.

It must have been an hour of conversation because Jerry Perera showed up and greeted everyone in the bar by their first names. In his hand he carried the new part.

—That must be the humanoid, Bondo said.

—Solenoid. That's going to be an even ninety bucks.

Bondo actually came forth with the money and placed it in Jerry's open grease-black palm. Their two arms were equally muscular and basically the same size, but Bondo's was the muscle of someone who worked out on a Nautilus, while Jerry's leaner sinews had come from work. Work and killing. A few massacred villages to make up for his lost dad.

Bondo and Jerry shook hands. Jerry offered the hand to me, then pulled it back.

—Almost forgot, he said. Vegetarian. You two sleep tight.

He had the solenoid installed in about five minutes, and it worked. He got back into the wrecker and stared down at us for a few seconds before he started it up. Twin flames shot out of his vertical exhaust pipes and he was gone.

22

I sat in the sling chair with my feet elevated to restore the circulation and watched Dorothy feed Bondo at the breakfast bar. She put a can of sardines out and asked him to please open them while she sliced the vegetables. Bondo found the little key under the can and twisted the metal band open and ate the whole can of sardines one after the other as Dorothy worked her way through a tomato.

—You shouldn't have turned your back on him, I said. That was your first mistake.

She opened the Italian bread and put the tomato and pastrami slices into it while Bondo ate the onion. Then he ate the sandwich. She cut a rectangle of brownie and heaped it with ice cream while Bondo was biting into a peach. Dorothy took the peach out of his hand and sliced the remnant of it onto the ice cream while Bondo forked the brownie out from under it. He ate the peach slices off the top, then ate the sundae.

—That was an awesome lunch, Mrs. Solstice. Penguin told me what a cook you were. I had taken it for an exaggeration. But I was wrong.

Dorothy rarely cooked food if at all and I had never told Bondo anything of the kind. It was more or less fend for yourself as far as Dorothy was concerned, whereas her precursor Katherine had made these vast Babette's-feast dinners that left everyone in a stupor by the end. I threw one of my sandals at Bondo's back. He had a short summer haircut that was almost military, so the hair on his head was the same length and density as the hair on his arms and legs, giving him the overall appearance of a black sheep that could be shorn, carded and spun into coarse monastic cloth or a hair shirt.

—OK, he said. I have eaten. Let's go to Provincetown. Mrs. Solstice, are you coming with us? You can have the front seat.

Dorothy quartered an apple and put it on the plate where the sundae had been.

—Some of us are not students, she said. The whole world is not on summer vacation.

Bondo looked around at all the spiders.

—You have plenty of statues already, Mrs. Solstice. You'll find that you have too many and you'll have to exterminate some of them. Think of the kind of decisions that will involve.

Dorothy had been gaining weight over the summer, and her arms had a Dutch look, as she bent over and poured, like one of those women by Vermeer who are meant to be doing whatever action they perform in the painting for their entire lives. I suddenly saw into her future. She would change from an artist into a housewife. She would get pregnant and robust. The factory of spiders would slow down and stop, while Richard would be out in his studio, working and working, drawing from her the energy that had once been her own. The two sculptors together: it was like a contest of insects, each drilling a tube into the other's soft abdomen, a painless injection, each trying to draw out the soft body parts in a slow, lethal pantomime that was also an act of love.

Meanwhile, Bondo had worked the upper half of his torso deep into the refrigerator, searching down in the vegetable bin for anything he might not have consumed. I pushed the door against him and held it shut. Death would take a day anyway, since I couldn't totally get it closed.

In Provincetown I would get my hair chopped just as short as his, or even shorter.

The hairdresser, Russell, at the Peaceable Kingdom Unisex Hair Center, had scaly flesh on his hands and his clothes smelled of the same medicines we fed to Arnold. I felt good with the haircut, though, and since I was nearly the same height as Bondo and we were almost equally dark, I felt like a twin. Which was supportive, even more than a brother or sister would have been. It felt like having a spare of myself, just in case.

—Twins are the worst, Bondo commented when I held him in the mirror of the antique shop next to the Peaceable Kingdom. Twins cause the problems of the world. Cain and Abel, for example.

—Cain and Abel weren't twins, I said. They were brothers. Brothers are a problem because they are both men.

—What's wrong with men?

—Nothing that wouldn't be solved by removing the testosterone gland. A simple operation. Then they'd be docile. It's too bad they outlawed the eunuchs and the castrati. Those were very practical ideas.

Meanwhile we were walking down Commercial Street in the height of the Provincetown season and it felt fine to be in a large anonymous crowd after the cozy isolation of Squid Harbor. I'd never live in a rural area any longer than I could help it. Nature is all right for a while, then it becomes a big green mirror which you end up seeing yourself in until you go crazy. That's why they have so many asylums out in the country. It's a known fact.

Bondo grabbed my arm.

—Look. Free merchandise.

On the corner of one little side street two men sat behind a huge goldfish bowl placed on a card table. They looked just like twins. They were losing their hairlines in exactly the same pattern and they had the same bodies in striped tank tops that resembled Victorian bathing suits. Each one had a gold ring in the left ear, the same cropped little mustache. They looked like another species, in perfect physical shape, petite, compact, all imperfections disciplined away, a species that had been mutated out after some terrible disaster and contained nothing but males.

What they were giving away from the goldfish bowl were Golden Sun condoms, each in an individual foil-wrapped package with a picture of a sunflower on it.

—It's better to be safe than sorry, one of the twin men said. When it comes down to sex.

The man addressed Bondo as if I didn't even exist. Bondo plucked one of the condoms out of the bowl like a blindfolded kid drawing a raffle prize. He drew out his wallet and slipped the Golden Sun into one of the plastic sleeves.

—I don't have any credit cards, he explained. I ought to have something to keep in there.

On another corner there was a small demonstration. Six or seven men and a couple of women had unfurled a banner saying AIDS RESEARCH NOW and another saying REAGAN, DON'T LET US DIE.

A young Episcopalian-looking priest stood up to address the group, which was rapidly expanding. He was up-front about things. The first thing he said in his streetside sermon was that he had tested HIV-positive himself.

—And if I've been spared temporarily, it's so I can continue my work a little longer before I go. You may wonder how a just God could permit such a disease ever to occur. It's a question men have been asking since the days of the prophet Job. Why should the good suffer? It has tempted some of our brothers and sisters to call it God's visitation on a lifestyle of which He disapproves. Let's pray for those people. Let's pray that their eyes and their hearts open and that they truly learn to follow in Christ, who Himself never turned His back on the afflicted. I've visited the homes and the bedsides of more than two hundred victims. I've been up close to the ravages of this disease and I have had young men take their last breath right in my arms. I've also seen the flowering of a miracle in the same places, which is the simple miracle of caring, the miracle of selfless and self-sacrificing human love.

He paused to allow himself just a moment of exhaustion, then raised his head again.

—We are a minority population. As a minority we have not always scrutinized our own behavior. As an oppressed class we've often taken our oppression as a license to do anything we want. Against the urging of our own hearts we've made the symbols of cruelty and domination into a badge of identity. Some of us have identified ourselves with the apparatus of captivity and submission, some have taken violence as a template for self-serving sexual goals. All this has changed. Something wonderful has taken its place, a miracle perhaps, like the honey in the carcass of the lion in Judges 14. We've found the divine energy of concern that was always within us, the caring and nurturing side that we so feared that we had hidden it under leather jackets and metal-studded vests. Under those layers of protective anonymity there were hearts maybe a little too open, a little too vulnerable. But now we are willing to take the risk. I have seen us caring about and caring for one another in unprecedented numbers.

He paused again, this time to make a gesture that brought the audience into a closer and denser circle.

—It is a calamitous scalpel that has opened us up and exposed something more beautiful than we ever suspected: the unfathomable love we have for each other as shown in the hundreds of volunteers, often putting their own health in jeopardy to comfort and care for and sustain not only loved ones but men who had been complete strangers. It is difficult to find a blessing in disaster, but in the midst of the epidemic the transformation of suffering and caring has allowed me to keep and even strengthen my belief in a God who is a stern instructor but whose first principle is Love.

The priest finished his impromptu sermon and stood there looking exhausted. He was almost unnaturally skinny and very tall, handsome in a somewhat decadent ex-preppy way, with an anguished Arthur Dimmesdale look, like someone who wore beneath his white collar and black-and-white clerical linen a rough undergarment of fleece. He'd attracted quite a crowd, mostly male couples with a few explicit lesbians and some regular tourists mixed in. When he stopped speaking, most of them took their pamphlets and drifted away.

Of course Bondo wanted to go right up and talk to him, but there was a circle forming around him, and they all looked more relevant than Bondo, with his denim cutoffs and the Nikes with no socks and the toes breaking through on every side. So I grabbed his arm with both hands and pulled him into the Baskin-Robbins and we each got a double scoop Fruit Special with nuts.

Bondo looked so upset when he took the first lick of it that I thought I might end up getting to eat both cones. He then threw his dollar seventy-five ice cream up in the air and watched it spiral down onto the sidewalk. It landed with the cone sticking straight up like a witch's hat.

—We can't do it, he said. We can't eat luxuries while this is happening around us.

—All right, I said. You threw that one away for them. Now you can share mine.

With death walking close by us on the sidewalks, working at the same ice cream seemed like a responsible thing to do. Maybe we were being spared this battle so we could struggle later with something even more unknown. We were all evolving, the ones who could eat ice cream and the ones too sick to keep anything down. As always the agent of evolution was another species, which was evolving too, an alien organism so small it was barely on the threshold of being alive. Here on the streets of Provincetown its work was clear, not only in the degeneration of those young faces and bodies but in the sense of ghosts walking among the crowd, invisible tourists who had already succumbed. It was an enemy and you wanted to hate it, but it was too small. It's hard also to hate anything that's not of your own kind. You couldn't exactly blame it on God because a responsible god would have to favor all creatures equally and would probably have to love each individual virus as much as a human being. If you had to hate anyone it would probably be the people who spread it but since they did that in the one foremost act of love, it was hard even to come down on them for that. The people with placards in the demonstration blamed it on the President, who is I suppose responsible for everyone and is much easier to blame than God, who is not an elected official but holds His territory more or less by force. I couldn't fathom it.

We took our joint cone down to the fish pier and sat on these ancient creosoted pilings way at the end. All around us were commercial trawlers, smelling of gull shit, diesel oil, thick tarry ropes, and every variety of saltwater fish.

—You have to work hard, Bondo commented, to see any kind of divine goodness in a plague.

—The Bible is full of plagues. God uses them all the time. It's the priest's business to find some good in them.

—I'd turn in my uniform if I were him. Some job. He has to defend a universe that sucks.

—I'm starting to have it figured out, I said. It's evolution.

—I don't see how people can evolve who don't have any offspring, Bondo said. That's not the way I learned it.

I had the thought, but I didn't quite know how to state it.

—Well, there might be a new kind of evolution, I said. Evolution without reproduction. There are species of lizards that have no males, you know, only the females. Out in the desert. And they are doing just fine.

—It's hard talking to you, Penguin. You're not always logical.

—Two thousand years of logic, I said, and look where it's gotten you. Now it's our turn.

I threw the remaining apex of the cone at him and it fell into the water behind the stern of a decrepit old fishing vessel called the *Sadie H. Rodriguez*. A big black-backed gull edged the other gulls aside and scarfed the cone up in one bite. Bondo threw a piece of celery that he had in his pocket and the same gull ate that also.

—That gull is going to survive, Bondo said.

On the pier head beside us a middle-aged woman with shorts on and sturdy cellulite thighs had set up an easel and begun to paint. Her watercolor emerged from the white paper like something coming out of the fog. There, right in her painting, was the *Sadie H.* There were the two red fish-houses with the long rows of white gulls on top of them, there was the hot-dog and popcorn vendor on the next dock with his red and white umbrella, there was the harbor and a few sailboats and the mist coming in from the open water and she was done. It was amazing how quickly you can create something and have it look even better than the original world. There were no bird droppings in her picture, no oil slick on the water, no hunger, no poverty, and no disease.

—Let's not go back to Squid Harbor tonight, I said to Bondo. Let's sleep in the dunes.

—But you've got the big meeting tomorrow. You have to be alert by eleven in the morning.

—It's OK, I said. We'll get up at the crack of dawn.

The priest was still at it when we walked past him on the way back to the jeep. There was still a crowd so we couldn't get near, but I felt close to him anyway. I could hear him in dialogue with another young man, who was upset and angry and looked even closer to death than Arnold, in spite of the fact that he was still walking the streets.

—Christ does not want us, the sick man was saying. He doesn't want us and we are not among the groups of people who He loves. If He did, He wouldn't have visited us with this fucking plague. You're either deceiving yourself or you're trying to deceive us. There's no room in His kingdom, Father, for people like you and me.

—You're wrong, the priest said. The Church has no outcasts. Let me tell you something. Humanity itself is a sexually transmitted disease. It has carried its original sins of pride and disloyalty through the chain of bodily fluid that has come down since Adam. The only man not to have been conceived by human semen was Jesus Christ, because He was not born from the sexual act. Now, because it is among us, He has taken it upon Himself. If the sickness exists in our bodies, it is in His body too: the mystical body of the world that is His church. That's what it means for Him to take upon His own back the cross of our sins. The sickness will not kill him because He is immortal, but He will suffer from it exactly as we suffer, and because He cannot die, His suffering will be that much more acute and will continue in His body as long as it remains with us.

The man crossed himself and turned back to the guy he was with. The priest, tired, looked for an opening in the crowd to get away.

We're both in the same business, I thought. We are outcasts. But we're putting our different shoulders to the wheel.

23

We had a splurge dinner at the Sea Floor restaurant with one and a half lobsters apiece, then went to this movie called *Prick up Your Ears.* I'm so inherently dense as to double meanings that Bondo had to explain the title to me twice.

—Prick up your rears, Bondo said. Get it?

—Oh.

Maybe it was just that as a female I'd been shielded all my life from that level of macho hermeneutics, so I was not trained to understand. Prick up your ears.

The movie was about a playwright in London who grows famous and then his male lover kills him. It was like *Sid and Nancy,* the one about the Sex Pistols where Sid Vicious kills his girlfriend Nancy in a heroin fit. Afterwards we just sat in this little park and tried to make sense of this stuff, why you would engage in cruelty to the exact people you are supposed to love and support in the face of mutual enemies like global capitalism or microbes that have targeted the entire human race.

That brought up our parents and the parents of everyone we knew. Bondo's parents had just divorced each other after twenty-one years of such uninhibited warfare that they would throw books and even small electrical appliances at each other, such as their Water Pik.

—It would have been much better if they'd just gotten together and conceived me and separated the next morning, Bondo said.

They spent two decades staying together so I would turn out normal and look at the result.

I recalled Katherine and Richard at their worst. Once she took one of the small wooden sculptures he was creating in those days and put it in the driveway of this house we were borrowing from someone up in Vermont and drove back and forth over it until it resembled a Belgian waffle. I remembered my mother saying, "Here, you're an exhibitionist. Try exhibiting this."

I remembered Richard refusing to eat for a whole day and Katherine setting the table and the plate of food growing cold while he sat right in the chair with his eyes closed, not opening his mouth even to speak. I remembered one of the fights over Fritz the Furrier when he hit her across the face with the flat of his hand and her cheek turned so red I thought the capillaries had burst and she would bleed to death under the skin.

Richard and Dorothy were still in the romantic phase. The fighting and lying had not overtly begun yet, and I hoped it wouldn't, but of course I knew it would. I did tell Bondo about my stepmother's adventure with Virgil in the Rabbit. Of course we'd never know what really happened that night or if Dorothy told Richard either an edited version or nothing. The worst of what people did to each other were the deceptions, because when you love someone you control their version of reality, and if you lie to them, that's like making them autistic, so what they think is the truth is not their true situation at all. I lied from time to time myself, so I knew what that kind of control was about. But if I were ever to actually marry someone I'd do it right, at least in the beginning. There's no use starting off on the wrong foot.

We were the new War Babies, born under the napalm-colored star of Vietnam, raised in the seventies, learning the theory of deconstruction by watching our families get divorced. We were allowed to be kids until the Catastrophe, then we were older than both parents put together, and we were supposed to turn around and bring them up. Virgil Varnum's five-year-old twins for example were emotionally about three years older than their alleged father. And when I lay there in my bed listening to Richard and Dorothy flapping around in the storks' nest over my head, I felt like a housemother, always on the verge of telling them to knock it off and get some sleep.

Bondo let me drive the jeep up to the foot of the Provincetown monument. I'm not much with a stick shift, but we got there and paid our dollar-fifty to climb the dark circular stairs up to the top. You could see the lights of Cape Cod stretching all the way back to Barnstable and Yarmouth, the lights of boats on the ocean and even the faint lighting of Plymouth back on the mainland beyond the Canal. I tried to imagine what it was like in the seventeenth century when the Pilgrims got here and there were no lights at all, just the two different darknesses of the land and the water, and the stars randomly distributed across the sky.

Bondo claimed the lights made it more beautiful. He said the world was better off with civilization, because it had come up with things like electricity to improve the night.

—Men are anthropocentric, I said.

I wanted the electric power to fail, right while we were up there, so the original night would come back and we could feel the true shape of the land rising on both sides of us out of the sea.

Bondo said there would still be the head and taillights of cars, but the power failure I had in mind would extinguish all electricity, even batteries, and probably extinguish the people too, except maybe the few Native Americans down in Mashpee and Sandwich, whose ancestors had been around since the Ice Age and who would be allowed to have kerosene lamps.

The harbors on the arm of the Cape made little circles, like diamond necklaces. One of those circles was Squid Harbor, in which one of the diamonds was Richard and Dorothy's, and one was Uncle Joshua's, where Arnold Fratorelli was dying in his room, and one was the estate of P. T. Varnum, who would be sitting over a bottle of White Horse with the company lawyer, preparing their tort for the meeting tomorrow morning.

The National Seashore entrance gate was closed with a locked iron bar. Bondo thought he could pick the padlock with this little wire prong he got out of his toolbox, but of course it didn't work. So he changed the gearshift into four-wheel drive and had me go out and turn these little knurled things on the front wheels, then we drove around the gate through the brush. It was a good feeling to be the only car in that massive parking lot, and to be the only ones walking on the beach with our feet in the cool sand.

We threw all our clothes into a pile with my white sweatshirt on top so we could find them on the beach when we came out. It was dark so I wasn't embarrassed and with my body out in the open air I felt like an indigenous part of the night. On the way into the water I could feel something like rays of darkness penetrating my skin. We swam. Or I should say *I* swam, because Bondo fundamentally walked out until the water was up to his neck and rotated in a circle. Although I could not see him do this, I could tell from his voice as he kept talking that he was turning his head around like a lighthouse so the sound alternately increased and grew faint. The whole time I was backstroking past him in laps, from time to time blowing a few squirts of water into the night sky.

I had never taken my clothes off in front of anyone who wasn't a doctor in my life, but at night I was invisible and therefore the same color all over like anybody else. It was a wonderful feeling. I wished we were nocturnal animals or lived in an all-night climate like the Arctic, only more tropical so it would be possible to swim.

Bondo finally floated up to me and stopped.

—I wonder how whales manage to do it, he said. You'd think the female would drown underneath the male.

—Maybe they don't use the missionary position. And besides, whales can hold their breath for half an hour.

—Did you ever try it while you were holding your breath?

—I never tried it at all, I said. Remember?

—Oh right, Bondo said. You're in original condition. I almost forgot.

Naturally Bondo had no towels or anything so we ran up and down the beach to get dry. A late moon had risen, divided almost in half, so I began to see a little, and it was worth the whole expedition to watch Bondo's penis flap up and down when he ran, as if it were trying to shake itself free and take off on its own. I can't say that I blame it. I wouldn't want to be attached to a man my whole life either. Of course Freud was a sexist and totally unscientific with his utter fallacy about penis envy. I had no more envy for Bondo on those terms than I envied Cosimo for having a tail. It was an anachronism like the appendix and it would eventually wither away. I looked deep in my heart and couldn't find envy at all, nothing but sympathy for something so awkward and vulnerable as that. Freud should have talked to a woman before exposing himself in print.

Back in the jeep Bondo lowered the two seat backs to let us stretch out. The moon was so strong that it obscured the stars. You could almost have read by that much light, even though it was well past full. Gibbous, Bondo called it, a word that always sounded to me like monkeys.

—Bondo, I said. Exactly how many women have you violated in your life?

—I slept with Rebecca and Jennifer once, all in the same bed. But I didn't do anything.

—Well, did they?

—Who knows? Bondo said. It's hard to tell when you're asleep. And what about you?

—I told you out in the water, I said. Never. And I'm not going to.

—Penguin, he said. That's unnatural. You're never going to evolve.

All Bondo had in the jeep was this half-empty bottle of Paisano red wine, but it wasn't right anyway to drink much before the meeting. We passed it back and forth, watching the orange moon set over the dunes and talking about our lives. Bondo concluded once again that he was normal, then fell asleep. Of course I would have freaked out if he'd done anything, like tried to climb on top of me, but he didn't and I felt an odd disappointment that kept me awake for a while after Bondo began to snore. I thought of whales next to each other, and it passed into a dream, and I dreamed of whales trying to mate but as soon as the male swam over the female, his body would plug up her blowhole so she would start drowning and it wouldn't work out.

By the time I had my eyes open Bondo was already talking to one of the cops. The blue lights were strobing away and I got an instantaneous fourth-degree headache. The cop who wasn't talking to Bondo had one fat hand wrapped around each of my ankles so I couldn't move.

—I'd advise you, he said, not to try anything cute.

I looked away from the flasher and saw the first light of dawn up in the sky. The cop had picked up Bondo's trousers and was foraging through his pockets.

—What's this, he said. Ned! The boy's got a rubber.

—Naturally, my cop said. We could use it as evidence.

—I live at Squid Harbor, I said, and my parents have their own corporate lawyer. So everything that happens here is going to come out.

—Lady, he said, you're in a national seashore. We are from the Department of the Interior. We are forest rangers.

He released me so I could sit up. I turned my head around slowly, like an owl, to see where we were. Forest rangers. There wasn't a tree around for miles.

24

Bondo eventually managed to talk his way out of that situation while I watched from the passenger seat. We were wildlife observers, he said. We were waiting for dawn so we could photograph the birds.

—Black-bellied plovers, I yelled out.

—They're starting their fall migration, Bondo explained.

Of course the forest rangers wanted to see his equipment. To my surprise, since he had never showed any interest in nature whatsoever, Bondo actually produced this canvas rucksack out from under the seat that had a Nikon camera with a tripod and a huge telescopic lens, so they let us go. Not that they had believed him about the birds, but they'd set it up so that if Bondo came up with the camera there wasn't much the rangers could say.

—There's a lot of weirdos in here, the man said. Next time you better get a permit. He gave the Golden Sun condom back to Bondo, who slipped it back into the credit-card window of his wallet. In plain view.

In a couple of hours we were having breakfast while Richard and Dorothy were just starting to move about. The spidery sculptures had turned into a mound of newspaper-wrapped objects in the center of a floor littered with sports pages and comics.

—We're serious, Dorothy said. We're packing to leave Squid Harbor.

Richard had taken the cheese slicer and begun to section his hard-boiled egg into yellow and white cubes. Uncle Joshua always called him a Cubist, and maybe that's how a cubist sees his world, he puts order into his life by cubing it, and I wondered if he saw people—me, for example—as cubic too, like those Picassos where you can hardly tell it's a human being. When he looked at me, maybe I came out as a purple-and-white cubic penguin. God knows how he saw Dorothy. There wasn't an angle anywhere in her body, yet if he ever sculpted her she might turn out as an arrangement of blocks. It's hard to know what anyone else is seeing unless you can somehow find your way into their eye. Especially artists, who can go blind in a way from having to see so much.

—What about you? I asked my father. Are you going with her?

—I haven't decided.

—Oh yes you have, Dorothy said.

—You don't own him, I said.

—We own each other, Dorothy said. We're married. We are a family. That's what a family is.

Richard's expression showed that she was right. The chiseled planes of his face were mushed together as if she'd gone over him once or twice with her welder. Here was one of the prominent people of our time and this woman my own age almost could lead him around like a sheep. It was, I suppose, love, which is at best a mutual enslavement, mostly enslavement of one, usually the woman, though in this case it looked like Richard was wearing the ball and chain. It was discouraging. I grabbed a banana out of the fruit bowl and headed for the house next door.

Joshua looked terrible. He was thin-faced and his eyes had an aqueous look and his skin was puckered the way it would be if you held your face underwater for a week.

—His fever is up, Joshua said. For two nights now we haven't slept.

I went right into Arnold's room. His eyes were wide open but he looked like he couldn't really see.

—It's me. Penguin.

—I know, Arnold said. I've been dreaming. I've had my eyes open but I can't turn off the dream. I dream that they're burying people inside pianos. I try to open the pianos and look into them, to see who's in there, but the lids are screwed down.

—They aren't burying people, I said. It's summer. The kids are sailing. Everyone is alive. What can I get you?

—Nothing, Arnold said. I can't think of any desire. When I was sick, as a child, I would make a list for my old man. I would write everything I could think of that I wanted and I'd give it to him when he came into the room. I'd put a number beside each want, and there'd be maybe thirty or forty things on the list. Now I can't think of anything.

—Anything within the possible, don't you mean?

—Anything. You'd think I would put on the list: No disease. A new body. Physical health. The chance to work again. Or else just for it all to stop. You don't know what it is not to want anything. Not even love.

—You shouldn't be talking so much, I said. Nobody's going to love you if you're never quiet.

I sat beside him and put my hand on his forehead. When I rubbed at the hairline, small packets of hair came off right in my hand. The body's calendar had gone wild and all the age signals were taking place at once. I had seen this program about relativity where Peter Ustinov had gone into space and had returned an old man while back on Earth his twin brother was still young. It was like that for Arnold. He was in the space capsule already. One of these days my words weren't even going to reach him, because he'd be in a different kind of time.

His eyes were still open, he was still talking to me, but he had also been having another dream.

—It was my own body, he said, it was lying on the bed—not this one, but my bed in Salem. I was above it, just a few feet in the air, looking down on it, and there was a kind of musical accompaniment, in a split rhythm, like thirteen over seven, fast and slow beat at once.

I could see his two hands take up the rhythm underneath his sheet.

—Don't talk, I repeated. Don't drum. Those things exhaust you.

Arnold was straining for breath just to say a few words, then in the middle of his breathing he'd be caught by a cough, so it seemed he would suffocate as he spoke. The amazing thing was, as he got physically better his mind seemed to go astray, while in the midst of his worst coughing attacks he would be supernaturally alert. He'd have these lurid irrational dreams with his eyes open, then he'd come around and describe them in detail.

—I'm going to go now, I said.

I waited for him to get his breath under control before I left the room.

When I got out on the deck, Uncle Joshua sat me down for a talk.

—I got a call from a man named Barney Kohlfeld.

—I've never heard of him.

—He claims to be an attorney from Darlings beer.

—He was the other guy in the Mercedes.

—Yes, and he proposed that if we could just find another home for Arnold, they wouldn't need to raise the issue today and they might not even campaign to spray the marsh. It's a bit of a plea bargain before the annual meeting.

Already I could hear traffic bouncing over the primitive Squid Harbor roads on their way to the clubhouse. I thought of witch-hunts in the Middle Ages and of lynch mobs putting their hoods on in the Mississippi night. It didn't matter if people were educated or professional or rich, they acted the same when confronted with the Unknown. It didn't require the exchange of bodily fluids for the transmission of fear or panic; a phone call or cocktail party was all it took.

I was ashamed for the Squid Harbor women, too. Women are supposed to be the courageous ones where human suffering is concerned, but they were participating in this epidemic right to the hilt.

—I shall wait here, Joshua said, or maybe we should dress Arnold up and wheel him over. They could behold the monster with their very eyes.

It was one of the first times I'd known Uncle Joshua to be angry. You could see the red network of veins light up under his skin. It made him look healthier than I'd seen him all month.

Bondo drove us to the meeting in his jeep. On the way we picked up Pura Batrachian, who was back from New York. She was walking along in long pants and eight-inch combat boots and a Banana Republic bush hat with the mosquito net pulled down over her face. She looked at me, then at Bondo.

—I'm covering this for the *Voice,* Pura said. It's going to be the story of the summer. I can see the headline: BEACH COMPOUND PANICS.

Then she noticed Bondo.

—So what's this? she said. Where have you been hiding him?

—He doesn't emerge in the daylight hours, I said. His name is Martin Bond, he's a classmate. Bondo, this is Pura. She's a reporter.

—Dartmouth, huh? I plan to cover that story too. Penguin is becoming my muse.

—I didn't know reporters had muses, Bondo said.

—Everyone has one. But Penguin is the best. She's totally altruistic. Most muses take fifty percent for themselves.

The clubhouse was built on one end of the Squid Harbor pier. It was a single-room frame building with a brick mantel covered with silver trophy cups and exposed rafters in the ceiling peak, which was dimly illuminated by a pair of eye-shaped Japanese style windows. The place had been there since I guess the sixties, but it still managed to keep the resiny smell of fresh-cut pine. It had an old vertical piano for the one chamber music concert we had every summer, along with a Ping-Pong table and a bookcase overflowing with mildewy old yachting magazines. On the wall was a large nautical chart of Cape Cod that gave all the locations of shipwrecks with little illustrations of each ship going down and the sailors swimming and drowning in the waves. We had these wrecks memorized when we were kids.

Most of the Squid Harbor cars were already in the lot, while at the water end of the pier there was all kinds of activity, since this was also the day of the Junior Regatta and the children were down there in their Lasers hoisting and checking their sails in preparation. Of course with the Stein-Mallows gone, the race would have about half its participants. But they had the pennants up anyway out on the flagpole, a gaudy triangle of alphabet flags in the late morning breeze.

It was a good day for the kids' sailing race, but in the clubhouse the ambiance was grim. After people were seated, Virgil Varnum and Pig Love slid the big boathouse doors shut to close us in. They did this as if it were preorchestrated and the whole course of the meeting had been planned out. They wanted it to look as much like a courtroom as possible, so their junta takeover of Squid Harbor could have the appearance of Law.

The sun still blazed into the windows, so of course immediately the confined area started to heat up. Barney Kohlfeld, P. T.'s corporate attorney, turned out to be a stout, sweating, bald-headed man with a white shirt unbuttoned at the throat and a tie loosened around it. His neck and forehead veins stood out like a man far underwater whose blood pressure was straining to equalize with the depth. When I looked at his tie closely, it turned out to be strewn with little red embroidered cans of beer.

Wearing a pair of half-frame topless reading spectacles, Bailey Varnum sat next to his lawyer at the portable table. P. T. was in his element too, deep down there where prehistoric fish eyed one another in the dark. Even Pig Love looked shrunken and timid behind those two, and needless to say, Virgil Varnum in the presence of his father wouldn't dare open his mouth. The audience was composed of the rest of us, Squid Harbor old and new, with one of the charter members distinctly absent: Professor Brand.

Corkie Love, who was supposed to be copresident, sat in a regular seat, next to Lydia Adler, and Dan Adler was there, and the old Whipples with one of their sons, Adam or Nick, I'm not sure which, a man already elderly himself. Jerry Perera was there with his widowed mother, old Mrs. Perera, who ran the store when we were children and used to buy Fudgsicles there. I noticed that the dark woman on the shift knob wasn't with him, also that he looked smaller and more obedient beside his mom. Jerry motioned me into the chair next to his, but there was no place for Bondo so I found another seat. I didn't want to give Jerry any ideas. I did locate myself on his right, though, so if he happened to want to look he'd at least notice my better side.

Richard and Dorothy showed up late, in the company of a couple I'd never seen, who were definitely New People, and another couple who were young married yuppies with embarrassed smiles, looking around for others like themselves, of which I realized there were more than I had thought. George Whipple went up to the newcomers to begin introducing them, but P. T. Varnum had already begun to call the meeting to order and George's wife hustled him back into his seat.

Bondo was sitting with me and Pura in the very last row, nearest the door. The meeting commenced and we went rapidly through some ordinary community business such as the burial of water lines and the annual rise of the dues. Corkie Love chaired it modestly from her seat and it all went pretty much like a New England town meeting, which I suppose it had aspired to at one time. When we came to the special items, however, the helm shifted to P. T. Varnum and his hired gun.

—This is Barney Kohlfeld, P. T. boomed out, of Kohlfeld and Holder in Providence, Rhode Island. Barney will help us through the legal complexities of the upcoming issues. It is the first time we've ever needed professional assistance, but times have changed and we have to keep up with them.

—I represent Mr. Bailey Varnum, whom all of you know. I have worked with Mr. Varnum at Darlings for over nine years.

—He helps maintain the liquidity of the firm, P. T. said.

Down on the water I heard the first gunshot signaling ten minutes to the preliminary race. This was followed by two blasts of the horn that the sailing master used to organize the regatta. The younger couples obviously had kids participating, since they pricked up their ears and strained to hear the race at the same time they listened to Mr. Kohlfeld. Out of the corner of one window I could see the boats grouping themselves as they approached the start, first heeling in all different directions, then the fleet coming together onto a unified tack.

The lawyer coughed once and started his presentation. He had some kind of difficulty speaking, maybe the vestiges of a harelip or cleft palate, and much of his power came from constantly having to overcome the threshold of human speech.

—You have two issues before you, Kohlfeld began. One is a bit simpler. It involves insecticide spray over the wetlands area.

—We voted that down already, Dan Adler reminded him.

—I understand. However, you have had time to reflect on it and the outcome may be different this time. The other issue bears upon the freedom of association and the right to restrict visitors whose presence may be detrimental to the community. You are fortunate in having explicit bylaws on this subject that are much clearer than the average legal statute.

—They were written by a poet, P. T. said proudly. Who is unfortunately no longer among us.

Right next to his lawyer, both of their chairs distinctly elevated above the others, staring straight forward with his hands on his knees like an Egyptian, Bailey Varnum nodded in affirmation as Barney Kohlfeld raised his copy of the Squid Harbor Association bylaws into the air.

—The law is, he said, the immune system of civilized society. He read from the text like a minister with the Holy Word.

—*Rule Eleven B. Conduct of Guests. The behavior of guests becomes the direct responsibility of the Association member whom they are visiting. Any guest who is found to disturb the tranquillity and order of the community . . .*

P. T. seemed to fill up with a bubbling sense of nature as Kohlfeld repeated the phrase "tranquillity and order."

—. . . may be requested to leave until the problem is settled to the satisfaction of all parties.

Pura Batrachian, her net folded demurely under the brim of the safari hat, had a small notebook out and was taking down every word. I wondered what P. T. Varnum would have said had he known it was all going to appear in the *Village Voice.*

One of the newer community members raised her hand to speak. She had a somewhat throaty and commanding voice and looked like she was on a torture diet of roots and grains to keep the skin taut across her cheekbones.

—I have just paid three hundred thousand dollars, she said, for a summer cottage that has essentially become a prison, and that we are also about to place on the market for sale. If anyone would buy it, now that the community is coming apart. And they won't even let us spray the swamp because they claim it is so full of their precious storks.

Outside, in the sunshine, you could hear the three blasts of the horn announcing that someone had crossed the finish line of the first race. Bondo had borrowed a pen and paper from Pura and was beginning to scribble something himself, which was a good thing. If we ever wanted to write about this, we'd have a record. Or in case they actually went through with bringing it to court.

Putting a hand up to his mouth again, as if he could twist the words into shape, Kohlfeld the lawyer was finishing up his case.

—Your terms "order and tranquillity" mean that you have a right to the pristine and natural environment that you expected when you bought your property, and not a life under a constant threat. It is your right as landholders to spray your wetlands and, if necessary, to ask one of the members' guests to leave. You will simply need a motion from the floor.

—I so move, P. T. said. I move both of those motions. They're sound ideas. I move we make them one motion.

—I second the motions, said the three-hundred-thousand-dollar woman.

—It's been discussed, moved, and seconded, Kohlfeld announced. Now you can vote.

—Take back Squid Harbor, someone said.

I think it was Mr. McAllister, though he sat at some distance from his wife.

—Richard, I said. Say something. You can't let this happen.

Dorothy reached over and clamped her hand onto his knee.

—*Don't you dare,* she hissed at Richard from behind her copy of the rules.

Another gunshot from the end of the pier: that would be the start of the main race for Lasers. The wind was picking up, too. There'd be a few capsizes. I could remember the feel of too much wind in the sail, the boat heeling over, the incredibly cold first impact of the water.

Richard took Dorothy's hand for a minute and held it, then kept holding onto it as he stood up to speak.

—You're not in order, Solstice, P. T. warned. Isn't that right, Barney? Discussion is over.

He stood up over Kohlfeld as he asked him that. He showed the gold eyes of the dominant wolf. Kohlfeld's neck sort of disappeared down his white collar. The corporate hierarchy was pretty clear, and we were fast becoming part of it ourselves.

—Right, Kohlfeld said. Discussion's over. Vote.

—The hell it is, said my father. That rule about disturbances has nothing to do with the present case. No one is disturbing the peace around here. No one is being disturbed. Besides, we can't vote on two motions at once. There's the spraying. And there's the invasion of a man's private situation, one of our own, without a shred of evidence. Freedom of association works in the other direction, too.

—Discussion is over, sir, Kohlfeld repeated. I have to ask you to sit down.

P. T. spoke to my father in gentler tones, as if they were by the fire at a men's club and not at a public forum.

—Things have changed, Richard. It's not the same old people anymore.

P. T. was right. Faces I didn't recognize were nodding in agreement. Let's spray. Let's take back Squid Harbor for ourselves. For whom? I was glad Uncle Joshua wasn't there. He wouldn't have recognized it either.

Meanwhile, Dorothy was pulling at Richard's pant leg, trying to get him back into his seat. But my father continued. I think he was somewhat oblivious to reality, which was that P. T. hadn't even needed the lawyer. The majority were the new people, and they were already mostly on his side.

— . . . no evidence that anyone in this community is at risk. We're wasting the summer. We're lucky enough to have the gift of life. Let's make a statement of apology to Josh Brand, and I'll take it over to him myself.

—Out of order, Kohlfeld said. There's already a motion on the floor. Two.

—There's no floor, Richard answered. Those rules are a joke. We made them up five years ago so we could get a tax easement on the marsh. We're not a government. We're human beings living on a beach.

—The law is no joke, Kohlfeld said. It must be respected even in the remotest corners of the earth.

—OK, Barney, P. T. said. This whole damn thing is out of order. Just get them to take their vote.

—Right, Richard said. Let's vote. Let's vote this fascist motion out of existence and enjoy the rest of this gorgeous summer day.

—Great, I said.

I love the word *fascist* when it's used correctly.

—You're out of order, Miss Solstice, P. T. said. This is not a family affair.

At this point Dorothy hit the complete roof. She pointed through the windows of the sliding doors out to the harbor. She was more agitated than I'd ever seen her. The large silver hoops of her earrings flailed around as if they were about to tear themselves off.

—Turn your heads around and look, Dorothy cried. Look at those kids out on the water in their boats. They're not old enough to

213

know how vulnerable they are. It's up to us. I'm packed already. And I'd advise every mother who has children here to do the same. Or is pregnant.

At that point Dorothy collapsed and sat back down and then crushed herself against my father's shoulder and began to sob.

My God, I said to myself, no wonder. They've done it. They're going to reproduce.

For some reason I immediately thought of the two men back in their cottage together, married in their own way and equally in love, while death nourished itself like a dark embryo inside their bodies. Pregnant. Dorothy. My father. Maybe with any luck it would turn out to be a sister. In another twenty years there might be someone to talk with about the Family. It was just what I needed to complete my life.

Twenty-nine people were present. Eleven proxies had been given by phone. There were twenty-three votes to spray the marsh and also request the departure of Arnold Fratorelli, with seventeen against. The motions had carried.

Bailey Varnum sat back and took out a cigar. He undid the wrapper and looked out towards the water through the circle of the cigar band, like a telescope. The horn sounded twice. The kids in the last of the three races would be just rounding the seaward mark.

Bondo offered Pura a ride back in the jeep, an expedition I didn't want to join. Pura looked ecstatic. She didn't care how it turned out. She had her story.

I took my time walking back to the house, drifting along the beach instead of the road. I took my shoes off and walked in the shallows, stepping on clam holes that would squirt up between my toes. The sand looked dead, but there was a lot of invisible life under there. The invertebrate activities of the shore made me miss the twins and even Mrs. Baxton, along with the beginning of summer, when things had been a lot simpler than they were now.

Dorothy would be triumphant. In the holy name of pregnancy and reproduction, she'd be directing the police to wrap Uncle Joshua's house in yellow tape, a house where another kind of birth was taking place. That birth was the microscopic footprint of Arnold's pencil making its way across the page, as random and hesitant and uncertain as somebody just learning to walk.

The doorknob wouldn't turn when I got home. Nobody locked the door at Squid Harbor unless they were making love or maybe taking a shower, so I thought maybe they're doing it again but then I saw Richard's head up in the studio window so I knocked. Nothing. I knocked again. Finally Dorothy showed up, but instead of opening the door for me she kept it locked and stood behind it and shouted.

—*No!* You don't live here.

—For Christ's sake, I said.

I rattled the door. I knew where the spare key was anyway, and when Dorothy actually stood there like an apparition without opening it I reached under the steps and got the spare. Dorothy held onto the knob so I couldn't turn it.

—You are being REALLY INSANE, I said.

—You're not a member of this household.

She actually had the strength in those child-sized wrists to keep me from turning it even though I used both hands. I put the key back and went up for Richard. He shut off the welder and cocked the helmet back to show his face.

—You have to help me. Dorothy's locked me out.

—Give her a few minutes. She'll cool down.

As he said that the joint he was welding changed from white heat down through red to the color of ordinary steel.

—That's not the point, I said. It's my own home.

Richard came down with me and used his two hands on the door. It was still locked. Dorothy was staring at the two of us through the pane. I got the key.

—You're stronger than she is, Richard. I'll just unlock it while you twist.

—You better not, Dorothy warned him through the glass.

—You have to, I said. She's crazy. You're my father. This is where I live.

—Some husband, Dorothy shrieked. Why don't you elope with her? That's what she wants! Can't you see it? Oedipal little witch. She takes after her mother. She wants to break us up.

She had the big yellow-handled pliers that she used to break off the legs of her spiders. She'd gripped them onto the doorknob from the inside so it couldn't be turned.

—You're not coming in either. As long as you side with her. Go live at Joshua's. You can all die together. The four of you.

—You can go back to New York, I shouted. You don't belong here.

—I will. I'll go back to New York and go on welfare and raise this child by myself. I've got all I need from your side of the family. One Solstice sperm.

—OK, I said. I'll move next door. Just let me in to get my things.

—No you don't, Richard said.

He gave the doorknob a sudden wrench with both hands that caught Dorothy off guard. I heard the yellow pliers fall on the floor and he was in.

—Bastard, she said.

—You have no right . . .

Their voices faded as I walked up the driveway to the road. I'll just move in with Uncle Joshua, I thought. Who needs it? Then I thought, it was my house more than Dorothy Dvorjak's, no matter how many children she had managed to conceive. She could take her army of spiders and go home.

When I got back there was this slow seismic vibration coming from upstairs that sounded like a washing machine in the spin cycle. But we didn't own one. It was just the postnuclear couple making love.

25

A young girl gets on the airplane between her mother and her father, who zip her into the soft blue sleeping bag and tighten her seat belt snugly over her lap. They are flying to Paris, France. She has been allowed to stay up until midnight because that is when the plane leaves the John F. Kennedy Airport. Almost as soon as they take off the sun suddenly rises from the ocean ahead of them just like a welder pulling one drop from a pool of white-hot molten steel. Below her the icebergs seem like an immense fleet of sailing ships, all fleeing from Europe to discover the United States.

In the little village she can't understand the language of the children who dance around her, making faces and laughing at her shoes. But she is given a whole cottage to play in while her parents talk with the old sculptor in his garden. In the cottage is a room with a toy circus that the sculptor made himself. A clown is jumping out of a burning house while two other clowns catch him on a trampoline. A lady in a bright red bathing suit straddles two dappled horses, while a man rides a one-wheeled bicycle overhead on the high wire, his miniature fingers curled around the balancing pole. When she feels lonely, she talks to the circus people and they tell her the secret stories of their lives.

The other room of the cottage is a library of picture books she can spread out on the floor and trace on tissue paper with a set of pastels the old man gave her for being so well behaved.

It is too rainy to be outside and her parents are drinking sherry with the old man in his big studio house. She asks to be excused and walks under her umbrella out to the library. There is an old book called The

217

Boy's Illustrated Natural History *with engravings and stories from the whole animal kingdom.*

She turns to WOLF.

It is the story of Mrs. Boganski and the Wolves. Mrs. Boganski had to take her children from her small Russian town into the city of St. Petersburg. It was a freezing arctic night and she bundled each child in a separate blanket and arranged them in back of her on the sleigh. When she got halfway to the city, on the open steppes, she heard the howling of wolves, and as they moved nearer, they appeared in the moonlight silhouetted against the snow.

Unless Mrs. Boganski did something, the whole family would have been eaten by wolves. Their pale eyes formed a circle around the sleigh. She could hear the hunger growling in their bellies. All her children would be lost if the pack attacked them. She separated one bundled child from the group and threw it to the snarling carnivores. They paused for a moment over the warm meal.

The Russian mother lashed the horses towards St. Petersburg. Soon the wolf pack was on them again, however, surrounding them, and another child had to be thrown out. The lights of St. Petersburg made a dim glow in the air, or was it the pale arctic dawn? Again the wolves appeared with their cold golden eyes. Again a child was thrown out, and again. When she reached the outskirts of the city there was but one child left, the youngest and the woman's favorite, but the wolf pack was upon her and she had no choice. The last bundle was thrown down to the snow and she whipped the horses on ahead. The citizens of St. Petersburg opened the gates for Mrs. Boganski just in time for her to slip inside.

For the hundredth time the young girl reads the wolf story and then she sleeps. She dreams of the noses and tongues of wolves. She wakes and reads the same chapter again.

Over her head, in the old sculptor's library, one of his red mobiles swings slowly as if a breeze were flowing right through the house. She goes into the next room. Besides the bareback lady and the three clowns, the third ring of the toy circus contains a group of wolves. One of the wolves has a clown's hat on and the others are sitting on their haunches in a row, like pupils waiting to be taught.

218

It is time to leave the sculptor's village for Paris. Then she and Richard will fly back to New York. Her mother, Katherine, will take the train to Brussels, where she imagines them eating tight little green vegetable spheres that taste like turds. Katherine will return in summer, when they will go up to Cape Cod together as a family.

On their last morning in Saché, the old man gives her a present, a little she-wolf in a nightgown with a stocking hat, which she still has.

The next morning I asked my father where the Calder wolf toy was. To my surprise he climbed up and produced it from one of the boxes in the sleeping loft.

—Take care of him, Richard teased. That's all that's left of your inheritance. The rest goes to the new family tree.

I put it on a shelf over my bed just like a kid, with a little shrine around it made from the Pessoa book Arnold had lent me and the empty Tequila bottle that I salvaged from the fire. The Mrs. Boganski story I could never figure out. Of course she should not have thrown her children into the wolf pack, but would it have been better to throw herself? The children could never have managed the sleigh all by themselves. They would have been eaten long before they reached St. Petersburg. Or she could have done nothing and let the wolves pick and choose for themselves while she drove along. Considering the alternatives, maybe what she did was for the best. She could at least perform one act of human choice, which was to name the order in which we will be eaten. Sometimes that's all that can be done.

I thought there might be hard nights coming, but having both a wolf and a penguin in my room would get me through.

Bondo was still sleeping on the living room couch with his body turned away from the light and burrowed into the foam-rubber bolsters. He looked like a man with no face or front parts at all, only a back.

Dorothy was in the final stages of packing. She was stowing her embalmed spiders in red and yellow plastic milk crates and gathering up the quantity of gas tanks, welding heads, and bundles of brass rods from her studio. She did this with a single-minded determination and without speaking, as if the rest of the family weren't even there.

If Dorothy left, my father wouldn't have a choice. She was incubating my little stepbrother or stepsister, which in their eyes took precedence over anything that might be going on back here. I remember my mother Katherine screeching at him about how he was never around when I was an infant, he was in his studio or at the Cedar Tavern with That Fucker André or with some other artist at another bar but not at home where he was needed most. That discourse went on over my playpen before I even learned to speak.

Of course Dorothy was not alone in her departure. Every once in a while I would hear a car pass on the road, not bouncing gaily over the ruts the way midsummer cars do, but slowly, burdened with luggage and vacillation and with the dry sadness of people moving out. Before long, it would come down to me and Bondo: me and Bondo and the man dying in the next house. I felt like Mrs. Boganski with the predators closing in around the sleigh.

I never thought I'd see the day when members of my own family teamed up with a capitalist like P. T. Varnum in his restrictive schemes, though in the long run maybe it wasn't much different from my mother and Fritz the Furrier. It was heavy opposition, but it didn't matter. We'd get a lawyer ourselves. All I wanted was for Arnold Fratorelli to have a tranquil space for his last work. A baby could be produced by any of us, but *The Keeper of Sheep* was unique. For that reason we had to shield him from what was happening at Squid Harbor, which was supposed to be a Democratic Town Meeting form of government but was in fact a combination of imperialist anarchy and mob rule. If they wanted to close down the community before summer was over, it was their own decision. It would make Arnold's surroundings that much more serene.

Bondo groaned as if in a bad dream and pulled the sleeping bag over his head. I threw a shoe at the lump.

—Get up, Bondo. We're going back to Provincetown. Cover your nakedness and come have some bananas and Muesli.

—Come have some mucilage, Bondo said.

It was so foggy that morning I couldn't see Joshua's cottage from our own porch. No boats, either, and no water, only a vapor so thick that your lungs sponged through it like a pair of gills. The fog came into your head, the way the ocean must be inside a fish as well as outside, circulating itself through the body, so it can equalize the pressure.

I went over to Joshua's. Arnold was up, in the wheelchair, with a blue oxygen mask over his face.

—His breathing seems better when he sits up, Joshua explained.

Arnold had had a bad night. I could hear the air trying to find a way through the congestion into the working surfaces of the lungs. He was like a man laboring up the vertical face of a cliff, his whole body twisting itself around the thread of oxygen that flowed from the yellow tank. He breathed his own dense fog at all times.

—It's good that you're here, Joshua said. You can relieve me.

—At what?

—We are watching the indicator on the top of the oxygen tank. It's nearly depleted. You can tell from the hollowness of the sound.

Joshua had me rap on the tank. It sounded empty until you got to the bottom, then it changed tone. There was just a bit left.

—When the indicator shifts over from white to red he's going to need a new tank.

I took over the watch while Joshua fixed something to eat. Cosimo was stretched out on his braided rug in the corner looking dead. He didn't even get up when I came in.

I fixed my eyes on the window of the brass regulator, waiting for the change. Arnold relaxed his breathing for a minute. Around the edges of the oxygen mask I could see the muscles of his face trying to work themselves into a smile. I moved over beside him and he reached out and touched the back of my head, the fingers sensitive as a man reading the world in Braille. When everything starts to go, I thought, maybe touch is the last sense you can trust.

Even with Joshua right in the other room, I felt alone watching the oxygen tank. It was like being deep under water, like that movie about the sub, *Das Boot,* watching some kind of pressure gauge that might explode at any moment, and send all the water in. All I could think of was the Jimmy Cliff song:

> *Pressure drop*
> *Pressure drop*
> *Pressure gonna drop on you.*

Joshua stood watch again over the tank so I could call Bondo and get him over. He was still barely awake when he showed up. Joshua gave him a whole mugful of espresso and I forced his head down so he would focus his attention on the valve. Meanwhile, Arnold continued his oxygenated climb through altitudes that no one else could see.

With Bondo taking over the pressure gauge vigil I could walk out with Joshua onto the deck. I told him that the Association had voted to spray the swamp and to evict Arnold as a disorderly guest and that Bondo and I would go to Provincetown to get a lawyer. The lawyer would hold off the action so Arnold would have plenty of time.

—Plenty of time for what? Joshua said.

He had a numb look, as if he'd forgotten the plan.

—Time for him to finish his piece.

—Time for him to die, isn't that what you mean? Isn't that what you're waiting for, so you can close up your house like everyone else and go back to school?

—I thought we were all waiting for the same thing, I said. That was the way I understood it. I thought it was going to be over after his piece got done.

Joshua was angry and his face flushed red underneath the tan. Now that Arnold's work was nearing completion, Uncle Joshua was getting a weird petulant tone that made me worry about the living will. After all, it was meant to pass the decision over someone's life span to a sane and competent person, which was supposedly Joshua Brand. However, this was no longer the cool Joshua of a month before but the beginnings of a desperate-looking man. I put an arm around his shoulders, which seemed to collapse together as I held him, like the soft wing bones of a bird. We stared into the blindness of the fog.

Suddenly Bondo yelped from inside. We ran in so fast that even Cosimo stood up and stared. Arnold still had the mask over his face. I could see the red warning inching its way across the indicator window, like a parking meter's red violation flag.

—We have to change bottles, Joshua said. There's only a few minutes left.

Joshua showed us how to prepare for the change. The protective cap had to be removed and the flange nut loosened so the new tank could receive the valve. Then the bronze valve was removed from the old bottle, tightened part way, placed over the new tank, and screwed on. Finally the new assembly was tightened with a wrench. It screwed on backwards compared to how screws normally went.

—I've only done this in the hospital. With someone else helping. This is the first tank we've been through. There's a transition when no oxygen is passing, so we have to work quickly once we take off the valve.

He was instinctively talking to Bondo and not to me, even this professor, who was so cultivated and I suppose as much the opposite of masculine as a man could get. How many generations would have to pass before men addressed women as equals? And the worst thing was, I accepted it. I trusted Bondo to get the procedure. Even my generation would have to die off as well, before things could change. While I just stood there, it was Bondo who loosened the fitting, taking it slowly so some oxygen would continue to pass through the breathing tube, even though it had already begun to hiss out.

—I've even shut off the pilot lights on the stove, Joshua said. There can't be open flames while we do this.

The same thing had to be done with the fresh tank. With Bondo holding the old tank and me holding Arnold's hand, Joshua unscrewed the valve. There was a rush, then a silence. I could feel Arnold tense up.

—OK. Now I am screwing it into the new fitting.

You could see Joshua knurling the valve down into the new bot-

223

tle. It seemed to go smoothly. There was a slight pop when the valve in the tank opened. Joshua screwed it on down.

Then something went wrong.

The new tank ripped itself out of his hand, wide open and hissing, taking the valve off the tube. It shot over near Cosimo. The dog snorted and jumped, then galloped across the room. The bottle found its way into his corner and spun around. Bondo made a leap for it and held it, the oxygen hissing through both of the valves.

—Take it outside! Joshua yelled.

I made a leap for the door, opened it, pushed Bondo outside. He threw the tank into the bushes. It lay there hissing and invisible and diminishing like a python in the agonies of its death. In a couple of minutes the noise had entirely stopped.

Bondo dove after it.

—That's poison ivy, I shouted.

There were the unmistakable triads, the reddish green gloss of the leaves. But he came up with it.

—We unscrewed the valve off the tube, Bondo said. While we were screwing it on the tank.

We took it back in. It was useless: no pressure, no oxygen, an empty canister of nothing. This was the stuff that made life possible, that got us out of the choking sea into an atmosphere which we could breathe. It was the first thing we needed in our blood and Arnold could no longer synthesize it for himself. His body rooted in one place, his mouth started to turn and seek sustenance in the air. It was not a human movement, more like the blind light-seeking behavior of a plant.

His chest would heave, stop completely, then start to heave even more. He had turned himself half out of the chair trying to see what was happening, why his lungs were expanding but not bringing anything in. They were a separate and sightless organism, a jellyfish swallowed inside him and striving to escape.

—Get another tank, Bondo ordered.

Joshua stood transfixed.

—That was the only tank, he said. We don't have any more.

—Then call the emergency squad, Bondo said.

Squid Harbor didn't have 911. I was already at the phone dialing O.

—The Wellfleet police officer, I shouted.

—I'm sorry, the operator said. You'll have to spell that. I'm located in Nashua, New Hampshire. I'm not familiar with your locale.

—*Wellfleet, Massachusetts.* Get the police. Or the emergency squad.

It was a male operator, who like all male operators didn't have any idea of what he was doing. There was probably some kind of a strike.

In a minute another voice was on the line.

—This is the Barnstable County Chief Deputy Sheriff.

—I want the Wellfleet police.

—He's not at the phone. He's fishing. We'll have to radio him in. Give us your number and we'll call you back.

Joshua was removing the mask. Arnold turned his head frantically as if there might be more air in a different direction. Bondo was screwing the fitting together, trying to figure it out.

—I've got it, he announced. Now we just need another tank.

The phone rang. It was the sheriff again.

—Look, he said. My department understands there is an AIDS patient down there. That's not the one you're talking about, is it?

—What difference does it make? We have to have someone from Wellfleet. We need an oxygen tank.

—Lady, you're going to have to wait on this. It takes special equipment. If they'll come down there at all. Those are all volunteer squads around there. You know what that means. They're not paid to have that kind of exposure.

—Then what the hell good are they? I screamed into the phone.

I slammed the receiver down onto its hook.

—Get my father, I said.

—He's gone.

—Dorothy has an acetylene welder, Bondo remembered. She'll have an oxygen tank.

We crashed out the door. Cosimo followed us. He arrived before we did, leaping and pawing at the door. His claws lacerated the screen.

—*Down,* Bondo yelled. *Down!*

We could hear Joshua calling him also from inside the house.

Bondo pushed him aside and pounded on the door. Dorothy was taking her time with the lock.

—We've got to get in. We need oxygen.

—What do you mean, oxygen?

—Your tanks, Bondo said. For the acetylene torch.

—Forget it. They are underneath everything. I put them in the bottom of the trunk because they're heaviest. It took me all night to pack that thing.

—Well, get them out.

—Bondo. You'll have to explain why.

—You have to give us the oxygen, I said. Arnold's not breathing.

—I told you that man oughtn't to be here. You shouldn't be taking care of him. He belongs in a hospital.

I seized two handfuls of Dorothy's oversized Icelandic sweater and pulled her back and forth like an inflatable toy.

—Get the bottle, I told Bondo. Go through her stuff if she won't help and find it and get it out.

—Find it?

—Dorothy, where is the oxygen?

—Penguin, I'm not getting anything if you push me around. Now, what is the story?

—Arnold needs the oxygen because the valve broke and we lost Joshua's only bottle.

—And I'm supposed to supply it?

—He is a human being, Dorothy, just as much as your supposed baby who is not even alive yet. Now WHERE IS THE OXYGEN?

—It's underneath the *Arachnids.*

We dove into the steamer trunk filled with newspaper-wrapped metal spiders.

—I'll get it, said Dorothy. One at a time.

She handed them up one after the other and Bondo piled them on the rug. I could see the colors of the tanks emerging beneath. I grabbed down through the objects and hoisted one out.

—That's acetylene, she said. You want to set him on fire?

She fished her way down to the other bottle, the green one, and lifted it out.

—I've been working with these materials for years. I could have showed you how.

—Well, come on over and help us.

—I can't, Dorothy said.

—You're not going to catch anything. There's no blood splashing around. Just come over and help us install this tank.

—Penguin. Don't you understand anything? I'm not myself anymore. I'm pregnant. You can't ask me to go.

Bondo grabbed for the bottle and we took off. Cosimo, who was waiting, crashed through the boundary of alders like a moose.

We got back to find Joshua massaging Arnold's chest. His breathing was so shallow we couldn't hear it or see it. The jellyfish in his chest seemed to have given up its attempt.

Bondo went for the valve.

—You have to hold the top part steady. While you screw in the bottom. Look. It's going to fit.

The same preliminary hiss came from the bottle. Bondo held the valve with one hand and bore down on the nut with the other. The hissing stopped and the valve indicator finally went white. Joshua replaced the blue mask over Arnold's face. The indicator stayed in the white zone, then trembled back into the red.

—Jesus, Bondo said.

Arnold choked up even though he had the mask on. The oxygen wasn't getting through. He pulled the mask up over his head and gave me this paralyzed look of someone who is drowning in the open air. I grabbed the tank and hose and mask in both arms and took them outside. I don't even know why I did this. But there was Dorothy standing on the path through the small thicket that separated the two houses. She had a large wrench in her hand.

—Bring it, she said.

I brought her the tank. Dorothy unscrewed the valve again and tapped something inside it with the wrench and screwed it on. She then put the wrench over it and had me hold the tank while she tightened it backwards with both hands. I thought of her hands on the door handle the night she locked me out. Their strength surprised me. The pressure indicator moved to the white again and stayed.

—You did it! I shouted. You saved his life. He'll be able to finish.

She didn't say anything and turned away.

I shot back in the house, slammed the tank into its wire rack on the wheelchair and replaced the mask. His lungs took this one tremendous breath and then collapsed. They then breathed and contracted again and he was alive. Slowly he began laboring again on his ascent.

Fifteen or twenty minutes later the Emergency Vehicle came, strobe lights flashing all over its roof, the rescuers striding down Joshua's driveway with an orange tank.

—We didn't want to park too close, a man said. We didn't know what to expect.

They had on complete waterproof yellow outfits with yellow boots and gloves, and they wore Halloween masks over their faces. Two of the masks were werewolves. One was a yellowish rubber likeness of Ronald Reagan.

—This was what we could find, the man said. You can't be too safe with this thing.

—You're too late, Bondo said. We fixed it ourselves. You might as well leave us the oxygen bottle and go home.

We watched them return to the ambulance. Two of them lowered their masks as they backed out, but it was impossible to make out their features in that light.

26

Somehow I managed to get Bondo up early and inject some coffee into his veins and load him into the canoe. It seemed like decades since I first paddled in with Dorothy. The marsh had changed. Already the grasses were turning from their deep June green to their late-summer decadent greenish brown. Around the first turn in the channel we surprised a mallard trailing seven or eight adolescent ducks. She tried teaching them to fly on the spot, but all they could do was flap their wing-stumps and run desperately on top of the water. The mother, already in the air, made a tight quacking circle over our heads, then landed and flapped alongside the ducklings, urging them on. We stopped to let them get ahead of us.

—I grew up in Chicago, Bondo said. I never . . .

—Shh. There are rules against talking in the marsh.

A great blue heron glided down out of the rookery and landed a short distance away. I tried to imagine what it would be like to stand on just the bones of my legs: no flesh, no muscle, only the skeleton of the foot resting on the delicate aquatic roots.

Bondo let himself lean backwards from the bow seat until he was lying on the floor of the canoe. I paddled forward. The heron didn't even move as we went past. It just observed us from behind those black, uncanny eyes.

I tried to see the heron the way it would see me. I tried to clear my mind of everything human, the names of things, the knowledge of history, the fact that in the future we are going to die. I tried not to know the name of the heron, not to know Bondo's name or

Arnold Fratorelli's name or my own, or that I had stood in a court-room and heard myself sentenced to the Women's Reformatory in Concord. I saw a woman propelling a canoe with a wooden paddle, a man with dark hair and dark eyes staring straight up at the sky, a cloud forming up on the horizon exactly the shape of a bull walrus with a single enormous tusk. I tried thinking that the little embryo in Dorothy Dvorjak's stomach would never ripen into another Solstice and that it would always be the twelfth of August. But then this tiny bat-pitched alarm sounded on Bondo's watch: it played a synthesized, Taiwanese version of "Heartbreak Hotel." It took him a full minute to locate the button that turned it off.

—We have to turn around, Bondo said. We have the lawyer's appointment in an hour.

The heron must have heard the alarm too. With huge, slow wingbeats it rose up and disappeared into the swamp. I would have followed it. I would have stayed in there, safe from the whole thing. It was Bondo who had to turn the canoe around and steer us out.

The office of the Gay and Lesbian Emergency Action Alliance occupied half the upstairs space over the Wharf Theater. On the stage, the Provincetown Players were rehearsing a scene from *The Curse of the Starving Class*. We had a few minutes and we watched them: mostly actors our own age, probably still in college them-selves, with one older professional-looking person playing the mother.

—I could never be an actor, I told Bondo. I can't imagine being anyone but myself.

—Penguin, you are always acting. You played a Radical Feminist last year, now you're the Courageous Nurse.

—Those aren't roles, I said.

—Those are causes, Penguin. Even Arnold is a cause. They're not you.

—Jesus, Bondo, I am them. We're them. We're not anything ourselves. We are so fucking privileged that we don't even exist. The whole middle class doesn't exist because it has lost any history it ever had.

—That's what that Japanese guy is saying. Fujimora. History is over.

—For us maybe. For most of the world history is just getting underway.

Bondo reached one finger deep into his ear and pulled something out of there, like a bug, and looked at it intently.

—I exist, he said. Look at this. A Brazilian fire ant crawled into my ear.

—You don't exist, Bondo. You're dead. That's why the ant is in there. It knows. You're going to be a yuppie. It's inevitable. The termites are going to colonize your brain.

Luckily at that point a woman in a GLEA T-shirt appeared, who took us into a side room and introduced us to the lawyer, Stephen Smith. The touch of the lawyer's skin when he shook hands was just like Arnold's, his hand spoke with the same desperate Braille. I wouldn't have been surprised to learn that he was sick. He practiced law in both Boston and Provincetown. He had also run for Congress once and lost. The newspaper clippings of his campaign hung on the wall in a row of plastic Jiffy frames. There he was shaking hands with Edward Kennedy and with Paul Tsongas and with somebody in the penguin-colored uniform of a priest.

—We want to make sure our friend doesn't get evicted, I said.

—Just give me five hundred dollars, Smith said. If anyone tries anything on your friends you can call me up.

On the way back in the jeep, cruising the mid-Cape highway with the wind in what was left of my hair and the sand dunes all around us, I had an impulse to tell Bondo just to forget the Squid Harbor exit and keep on going. It had been a hermetically sealed summer, a summer spent as a voluntary companion to the doomed. There was another feeling, a rebellion, a thrust towards freedom growing inside me like a blind tuber under the layers of asphalt pavement. The jeep's gas tank was full and the road went forever.

—I've forgotten the turnoff, Bondo shouted over the wind.

I couldn't do it.

—Exit 12W. South Truro. Wellfleet.

In a minute we were on the Squid Harbor road and the jeep was hunching itself over the ruts. Whole sections of the road were covered by drifts of dry white sand.

—One more windstorm, Bondo said, and this is going to be impassable. Even for us.

—I wanted to keep on going back there. I didn't want you to make the turn.

—Where would you go, Penguin? Back to the Antarctic? Remember, you've been expelled.

—Out west. Kansas. Oklahoma. A city just large enough to have a football team.

—You don't know anything about football. You think a first down is something you find in a sleeping bag.

—Team sports are dumb. But I like to watch the audience gathering for a game.

Stopping at the post office, we pulled the day's mail out of the two boxes. In our box was a letter for me, from Virgil Varnum. I went right into the bathroom when we got in and opened it up. It had a check made out to Penelope Solstice for a thousand dollars, and a note.

Your side may need something for expenses. You can send back what you don't use.

When we went over to tell Joshua about the money, we heard Cosimo's bass-clef howl, along with the exploratory notes of music being composed. Arnold, his mask off and hanging over the arm of the wheelchair, was seated at the piano.

I went back next door to see if I could help pack Dorothy's stuff into the Civic. She wasn't taking any assistance though, even from Richard. She made trip after trip in silence, each time taking another plastic milk crate and fitting it into the back. She had the car radio tuned to an antiquarian rock station that was playing "Yellow Submarine" and her head wrapped up in her huge Guatemalan scarf that dangled almost to the ground. She looked like a teenage runaway with a precocious amount of luggage. It was amazing that she could fit it all into that tiny car.

She was already behind the wheel when we lined up to say goodbye. She kissed Richard and said she expected him in New York as soon as he could shut down the studio. She'd make arrangements to get the subtenant out of his loft so he could resume work right away. He had a show coming up at Blum Helman anyway, she reminded him, which would be a lot easier to set up if he was in the City.

Then Dorothy turned to me.

—Penguin. I'll miss you.

—I guess I'll miss you, too.

—You guess.

—Look, I said. I understand. You're pregnant. But you could have left without tearing everything down.

—Tearing it down? This was my honeymoon. This was supposed to be my house. When I was a teenager I had a six-month marriage with a drunk. Now I have something halfway meaningful and look what happens. One of his children inside me and another one driving me out.

It was hard, as a woman, to stand there screaming at someone who was pregnant. I reached through the window to kiss her on the cheek. She pulled away.

—Maybe sometime, she said. Not now.

She even gripped Bondo's arm and pulled him towards the car for an affectionate hug. All she could do with me was take my sleeve and press it theatrically against her mouth, pulling away at the same time, as if my clothing endangered a whole generation of upcoming sisters and brothers. For a month Dorothy had been avoiding me physically. I knew what it must have been like to have had the plague.

The little Civic was packed full. There was a milk carton on the passenger seat beside her, strapped in with the seat belt and containing a half-completed spider with one stainless steel feeler reaching itself up through the newspaper.

At the end of the driveway Dorothy's car stopped short, her tail-lights flashing on. Virgil Varnum's Rabbit hopped past her with the top up, throwing off a wake of dust and sand. Without even waiting for the air to clear, she drove away.

I put one arm around Richard's shoulder, the other around Bondo's waist, leaning on both of them and letting them drag me along.

—It will be nice having just the three of us, I said. Maybe we can hire a cook.

27

I am in a biology class taught by the famed anatomist Doctor Joshua Brand. The students are all women and we're dressed in these newspaper bathrobes covered with headlines about a war. We are to each dissect an insect on a brightly colored plastic tray. Mine is a giant earwig the size of a lobster, with pincers at the rear end of it at least three inches long. We have to cut them open down the ventral strip when Professor Brand signals by lighting a candle. He strikes his match and the candle flares up with this supernatural light that almost blinds me even in the dream. I cut my earwig open and find that it's packed solid with small wriggling larvae that crawl in all directions over the table and start dropping on the floor. The word pregnancy *writes itself on the blackboard in red chalk.*

I woke up and turned on the light over my bed. It felt quieter with Dorothy gone. There was no sleepwalking, no erotic activity right over my head. But I felt something weirdly alive in the quality of the silence around the house. I held my breath. Voices were moving beyond and to the right of my window, behind Joshua's house.

—*Christ,* somebody whispered. *A light.*

I switched it off and lay there breathing in the dark. I bit the back of my wrist to see if I wasn't still in a dream. It hurt. But I could also have been dreaming that it hurt. How were you supposed to know when something is in fact a dream or if it's real? Maybe one day I'd wake out of the whole summer. Maybe I'd wake out of that and find myself a totally different person. I used to think I'd get up one morning and find myself with a normal body like everyone else.

I opened the screen and stuck my head out to see around the corner of the house. Right where the voices had been, a small flame smoldered in the grass, almost like a firefly only larger and a different color, more orange. It flared up and then died. Someone spoke.

—Shit. Went out.

I put my jeans on and a sweater and cracked open the kitchen door to see. It was quiet, but it also felt like people were still around. I stepped lightly on the deck and down. The grass was wet on my feet. The fog made things two-dimensionally layered, unreal. I felt two-dimensional myself, a shadow lurking among the shadows of things, under the fog-blurred moon.

Other shadows were out there besides my own. They had started some kind of fire and it died on them. They would be waiting to come back, to finish their work. I knew. If the fire hadn't caught down in the Beta Sig house we would have gone back into that cellar and tried again. Could there be people who hated Joshua and Arnold as I had hated the Beta Sigs, not even knowing them personally but liking the idea of them in flames? I don't think you would set someone on fire who you actually knew.

I was stock still. The mosquitoes found my face in the darkness and closed in. I had to endure them without moving, like a Native American being tortured in the woods. Someone was coming back. They crept back to the place where the fire had been and picked up something and moved it closer to Joshua's house. It must have been what I'd noticed from my room. If it was some kind of slow fuse like our kerosene-soaked string, I could wait till they were gone and put it out. But if it was some kind of bomb or explosive, there wouldn't be time. I had that hermit crab feeling again. It was not me standing in wet grass in the middle of the night and about to be blown into the sky. It was a member of another species, without a past or future, whose antennae reached out into the fog without a sound.

The light flared up again. I could make out a vague face, but I didn't recognize it. The man headed up Joshua's driveway towards the road. The fire was traveling along through the grass like a burning snake, towards the windowless back wall of Joshua's house. Cosimo, I thought, you have failed. This is exactly what dogs are supposed to hear with their sixth sense, and you're not sounding the alarm.

I ran through both blackberry thorns and poison ivy and stomped once with my bare foot right on the flame. Amazingly, like those people in California who walk over the glowing coals, I didn't feel burned. However, the fuse didn't go out either, so I groped ahead of the spark and found the fuse and pulled it away from the house. I snuffed the end of the fuse out like a cigarette in the wet grass. By this time Cosimo had finally woken up inside the house and started barking, a baleful, serious bark unlike anything he had ever said. A light went on in Joshua's room. I could hear a truck engine revving in the dark. I couldn't see a thing, so I figured I couldn't be seen either, and I walked towards the truck sound. Suddenly their taillights came on and their wheels spun a cloud of invisible sand and they were gone. I saw in the flash of red light the last two digits of the license plate: 39.

I woke up Bondo and related the whole thing.

—Don't bother calling the police, Bondo said. They're probably the ones who did it. The same guys who came down with the Reagan masks.

—It's attempted arson, I said. We can't just let them get away.

Bondo reasoned that the dog would have scared them off and they wouldn't be back. I looked to see if Joshua had come out, but he hadn't. The lights had gone off over there and the next-door cottage sat quietly undamaged in the fog.

—The best thing we can do is go back to sleep, Bondo said. In the morning we'll be able to scope it out.

The rest of the night I spent in a confusing hypnagogic state in which I was the one burning Uncle Joshua's cottage, then I was burning my own home, then unknown people with animal-headed Egyptian masks were setting fire to the pyramid on a dollar bill. By sunrise I didn't know whether I was sleeping or awake.

I dragged Bondo outside as soon as there was light enough to see.

It was a professional-looking fuse, nothing like the length of package twine we used on the Beta Sig house, and it led up to a white plastic bag tied off at the neck and placed right under the wall of Uncle Joshua's cottage. Bondo thought there might be a bomb in there, but I could smell kerosene. As a former incendiary I knew just what it was.

We pulled the bag out from under the house and carried it to the shore. I tore it open. It had a thoroughly saturated purple sweatshirt in it with the arms tied together in a knot. We checked the neck to see if it might have anyone's name on it. Then we committed it to the sea, which was not exactly ecological, but we didn't want the thing around. It floated out into Squid Harbor surrounded by a growing oil spill with all the colors of a prism catching the rising sun. There was a snowy egret a few yards offshore, and the ripples spread under its legs, so the white bird was reflected in a petroleum rainbow. Sometimes the worst things in the world are also the loveliest to behold.

Bondo went inside. I stood there a while longer, absorbing the white bird's image in the incandescent slick. I was beginning to think that events, too, had reflections as well as things. Whoever had tried to burn Joshua's house might have known about me too, might have thought that I lived there. I who had once done the burning could in this case have been the burnee. I had thought justice was the victory of the good, but maybe it was just a kind of symmetry so the world balanced out in the end. We didn't get the Beta Sig house, and they didn't get Uncle Joshua's. Which was all right with me.

Bondo came out with a thermos of coffee and we got into the jeep to cruise the road, hoping and not hoping that we would find the truck. We got up to Route 6A and turned right, not towards Provincetown but towards the village of West Wellfleet, where a number of fishermen lived, probably including the ambulance drivers who had shown up the other day.

Then we got low on gas and turned around. It was still so early that Perera's wasn't open, and we had to wait at the pump for someone to show up. Next to the familiar wrecker were a couple of other pickups that Jerry also seemed to own. One of them had the plate number *485-739*.

—This is starting to get creepy, Bondo said. Gas or no gas, we are on our way out of here. Now.

We made it back home on empty and woke up Richard. We told him the whole story over breakfast.

—I always knew that dog wasn't much good, he said. A hundred pounds a day he feeds it and it can't even keep watch.

From the next cottage I heard Cosimo's low howl and a chord or two from the piano. They were up. Richard wanted to immediately phone the police. Again, Bondo said no. It probably *was* the police.

—Then try the state troopers.

—They're not going to do anything, Bondo said. They're brothers. They're a fraternity. They have a code of silence. Cops stick together all over the world.

I couldn't believe Jerry had been involved in it. He wasn't just a native any longer, he was a full member of the Association. But there it was, hard evidence, one license plate number out of a hundred. I tried to picture him in a room with the deputy sheriffs, who probably also assisted him in the drug trade, the curtains down, planning to set fire to Uncle Joshua's home. I couldn't. Jerry was an asshole but not to that extent.

—I'll talk to Jerry Perera myself, I said.

I don't know where I got the courage. Maybe it was the sympathy I felt for what they had done or tried to do, a weird collusion in the same species of crime. I was with Joshua and Arnold now, but I had also been one of the others; I too had planned a forbidden action in a room with the shades drawn and taken it into the world and watched it sputter and fail.

I found the sweatshirt I had worn under so many layers the night we went to the Beta Sig house in the snow. I washed my hands and face and for the millionth time in my life I tried to scrub the purple stain off my neck, but as always the friction only increased the contrast.

—You're crazy, Bondo and Richard said at the same time. Stay out of it.

—Don't think I'm going to drive you, Bondo added.

I drove up to the highway myself in Bondo's jeep. Jerry Perera was on a ladder up against the store window painting LOBSTERS in large white letters on the glass. The truck with the sinister license was still there.

—Gas? Jerry shouted. One of the girls will fill you up.

—It's you I want to talk to, I said.

He took great pains in finishing the *S,* then took me into the cellar of his store. He had a desk down there with a telephone and a computer on it, plus a couch with buffaloes on the slipcover that looked like they were being driven over a cliff. So this was where Jerry Perera brought his women. Pura Batrachian and the other one who looked like an incest victim and the ones who hung around the store who were about twelve years old. I looked for signs of them, like a ripped fishnet stocking or a black bra, but he kept it pretty well cleaned up. Naturally. He wouldn't want them to find traces of their predecessors lying around under the couch.

It was still early in the morning, but Jerry offered me a beer. I noticed my hands were numbed out and felt disconnected from my arms, so I took the beer just to give them something to do. Jerry swiveled himself around in his chair a couple of times and stopped abruptly.

—I'm a busy man, he said. How can I help you?

—Someone tried to set a fire over at Joshua Brand's house last night.

—Could have been anyone, Jerry said. They're a very popular couple.

—It had to be someone with a certain license plate number. I thought I'd talk to you before we take it to the police.

Jerry spun once more in the desk chair and leaned back so I could see the snow-tire patterns on the soles of his boots, then came forward until his face was very close.

—I'll tell you who would be the first suspect, Jerry said, *if* they held an investigation. Think about it. Someone right close by to Professor Brand who happens to be on probation for attempted arson. They know what that means. People who do that never stop at one.

—They're not going to arrest me if I'm the one who calls them.

—Try it and see, Jerry said. They're professionals. The first suspect is always the one who phones in. They know the criminal mind. It's just like their own.

Jerry went up the half-flight of stairs to the bulkhead door and locked it, then reached down to switch on his answering machine.

—Just so no one disturbs us, he explained. Now, how much do you really want to know?

—I'm trying to get something done over there. And I want to know what's going on.

—Suppose some of the local citizens were interested in the continued health and welfare of their community. Suppose they had lived here for generations and didn't want to be contaminated by outsiders with lifestyles other than their own. Suppose there were highly influential persons who dropped the hint.

—Suppose there were, I said. Someone like you wouldn't go along with them. You're not the type.

—Someone like me, Jerry said. And how would you be knowing what type that is? You've never exactly taken the time to find out. You and your roommates. But suppose something else. Suppose someone went along to make sure things didn't go too far. Suppose that person was the one who made that fuse, saying there was a fuse, and suppose he installed a dead spot in the middle so it would fizzle out.

—What does that mean? I said. We're supposed to be grateful for that? You're talking about criminals. You're not the native any more selling groceries to the summer trade. You have a house here. For that matter, why didn't you turn them in to the police?

—Suppose that meant I'd have been turning them in to themselves?

Jerry got a tinfoil package out of a drawer and a green plastic parakeet mirror and poured some of the white powder on the glass. I had not seen cocaine in the flesh before but I knew instantly what it was. With a single edged razor blade he arranged two lines of it side by side.

—No thanks, I said.

I had accepted dope only once in my life, back in the Morrelsex days. Marijuana. It was of course all over the fraternities at Dartmouth but at 36 Chestnut we never used it. We were in a revolution, and we didn't have time to waste fooling around with our minds.

Jerry scraped one of the lines back into the packet and left it open on the desk. He sniffed the other through a short brown coffee-stirring straw with a long sensual inhale that drew his eyes inward and turned them into dark metallic circles that had been dug out of the Earth, like Etruscan coins. On second thought it seemed worth trying. I put my face down to the mirror just to sniff up the dust on its surface, then he made a half-sized trail of it for me. It took about a second to sniff it through the tube and in that time I felt I was betraying every person in my life.

I glanced at the locked bulkhead door.

—Don't worry, Jerry said. I can wait as long as you can. Longer. I live here. How many years have I waited already? Five? Six? Ever since you've been ready.

—I'm not ready yet, I told him. Even if I did believe you about the fuse.

—If you're planning to be a nun, he said, you better get the right clothing. That way nobody will mistake you for something else.

I got up and turned myself at a right angle so I was facing the door. The geometry of the room shifted ever so slightly from the cocaine, forming a non-Euclidean space that shrank down until Jerry's body filled it from edge to edge. Then he leapt right through the wall and did something to the bulkhead door that let the sunlight in.

—A word of advice, he said. Just let this pass. They won't be bothering you again.

—That's a promise?

—A promise. I always keep my promises to women.

I guess I was supposed to feel this flood of gratitude at this point, but I just felt that the stairs were slanted at such obtuse angles to each other that someone had to help me climb.

My head got somewhat clearer in the summer light and I realized I had to get back to Uncle Joshua's and help. I bought some gas from one of the Perera girls, then checked the scene in the rearview mirror as I waited for a gap in the mid-Cape highway traffic. The road seemed to reflect light so that the cars swam in a slightly liquid air, a mirage effect which could have been outside or inside, it didn't matter. That was what it was all about, the underpaid natives slashing down coca trees in South America, the drug czars and dictators flying over the Caribbean in military transport planes, the black men and little black children drowning in addiction, all for this slight shift in reality that meant you didn't know whether something was outside or in, whether I was holding the steering wheel or it had its own strange grip on my hand, and if my DIVEST NOW sweatshirt had grown little tongues on the fleece of its lining or the tongues were on the inside of my breasts trying to lick their way out. There seemed to be a question and maybe Jerry could answer it. He was the expert. I turned to find him, but he had gone back to working on his sign. He had completed the *S* on *LOBSTERS*, and underneath that he was writing *$6.95 a pound.*

28

When I got home, Bondo was helping Richard to dismantle his current piece of sculpture so he could fit it into the U-Haul truck. This one was called *Bell Buoy,* and it had a greenish bronze sphere at the base, which represented the part of the buoy that's under the water, then a spray of greenish ocean-colored steel rods jutting out from the top, which I think was supposed to represent the sound of the bell emanating through the fog. But it might also have been music. The edges of these rods were so jagged you could cut your hand on them; they cut the air with their rawness like the chords that came towards us from the house next door. The sculpture was very much like an iceberg, or a human being, so much of its mass was carried under the surface in order to keep it upright.

Richard had to unweld the rods from the base, and we both put on helmets so we could watch.

He started the arc welder and cut into the piece like a dentist, slicing one rod after another away from the central knot. As each rod was chopped off it bent over like a dying stalk of marsh grass and finally clanged onto the cement studio floor. The ends glowed white for a second, then red, then eased down to their regular color. We carried the rods out after they had cooled. Because of the edges Richard made us all wear leather gloves. We then skidded the base onto Richard's little electric forklift and forked it up into the truck.

We took a break and the three of us sat on our big boulder at the water's edge. From the house beside us an occasional chord would come forth, and though my ears were still blind compared even to Cosimo's I could tell that the hand was weaker and more uncertain than before. Arnold had begun to tell me that he was no longer choosing from an infinite source of musical ideas, but that his mind felt like a room that was being moved out of, with only a few pieces of furniture remaining, which made the music even at that distance seem unbelievably vulnerable and sad.

Joshua and Arnold had no idea that behind their cottage a slight, crooked trail of scorched grass marked an attempt to blow them prematurely into the afterlife. Which might have been for the best, in that they would both have gone at the same time, but that kind of judgment was not ours to make, not the Reagan-headed Deputy Sheriff's and certainly not mine. My task was to draw a protective circle around that couple until their work was finished, both the musical labor and the other labor of death, which was also unequal because one person gets to depart while the other has to carry on alone. I had always thought death was democratic because it treats everyone eventually in the same way. But it's not. Death is a monopoly. It's like any other dictatorship.

I no longer even remembered the reasons why I'd decided to join them. The reasons weren't important. Their life had already become my own.

We were just sitting there, Bondo and Richard and I, listening to the music and the water's silence, when this blinding mechanical roar appeared out of nowhere and it was good old Peter Schlessboom practically running his thousand-horsepower Evinrude up on our beach.

—Cookout tomorrow night, Peter announced. I'm spreading the word.

—It's not even the middle of August, Richard said. The cookout isn't supposed to happen until Labor Day.

—This year it's different, Peter said. Some of the members have decided to leave early, so now is when we're going to have it.

He shot off in the speedboat before I could ask him where his son Sleezy was keeping himself. I hadn't seen him since Bondo arrived, or Susan or Robin either, for that matter. My world was shrinking, and I was also losing my sense of time.

The three of us wandered down to the pier like people taking the last walk of summer. There was absolutely no wind and no one was out in the boats except Peter, racing from cottage to cottage over the glassy harbor with his invitation.

That year's sailing master, who was a tanned, preppy, anonymous kid with Docksiders and no socks, came down and said hi to us and started the launch. He powered out to the nearest of the Lasers, unhooked it from its mooring, and tied it to his stern. He then went to the next one and hooked its bow to the first, then to the next. When he had all nine of the Lasers strung out behind him like a line of midsummer ducklings, he headed across the bay towards the Oquosset Boatyard, which was their winter home.

Up at the clubhouse, we could see the Loves, Pig and Corkie, lowering the flags and taking them off the white wooden mast: the Stars and Stripes and the state flag of Massachusetts and the local club flag, which was navy blue with a somewhat creepy squid in the center. They spread them out ceremoniously and then folded them in smaller and smaller triangles down to the size of a handkerchief. Pig Love then brought out the blank pistol that they used to start races with and fired it into the air. Finally they drew the bay doors into each other and locked the building with the brass padlock that only came out on the last day of the season. It was a strange sound to hear on a midsummer afternoon.

The end-of-the-year party took place at the Schlessbooms' on the fourteenth of August. You could not miss the noticeably grim and ironic tone compared to the usual Labor Day festivities. As always the Schlessbooms' house looked like it had just been dry-cleaned for the occasion. Even the sand around the house looked commercially bleached. The Schlessbooms tore down their cottage every few summers and built a new one on the same site, like those primitive tribes that burn their possessions every year. The current Schlessboom estate was an expensive-looking postmodern stained cedar edifice perched right on top of their personal dune.

The first member I bumped into was Sally McAllister, whom I

had seen only at the annual meeting. Sally was wearing one of those pullovers that kept slipping off her shoulder. She'd pull it up again and it would fall off on the other side. She wasn't much older than I was, but you could see that she accepted the Philadelphia-bourgeois life of her husband's family with the fanaticism of a convert.

She confused me with Dorothy.

—You must be Mrs. Solstice, the woman said.

—I'm not.

She didn't hear me.

—What a terrible way to end the season. Of course it's different for you. You don't have any children.

—I am the children.

She stayed oblivious.

—We're going home early, Sally McAllister said.

—Home where?

—Bala Cynwyd. It's outside Philadelphia. My husband's family has a farm there, and we live in one of the outbuildings.

An uncharitable picture flashed into my mind of a long row of cow stalls with Sally McAllister in one of them, her head between those iron rungs, ardently waiting to be milked. She was a woman too, supposedly one of my own. I wondered if I was losing my feminism to something else, another kind of anger whose objects, like Richard's *Bell Buoy*, were still ninety percent concealed.

At that point Bondo walked by on his way to the cauldron, and I brushed the tips of his fingers as he passed.

—That's my dear friend Martin Bond, I confided to Sally McAllister.

—Yes, she whispered back. I completely understand. I always thought it would be difficult having an older husband.

I pulled out from under her and followed Bondo over to the center of the room. Virgil Varnum, in black tie and cummerbund, was ladling out cranberry daiquiris from a white cauldron with small icebergs and lime halves floating on the surface. I looked at the icebergs carefully. It was true. Nine-tenths of them were submerged and barely discernible in the antifreeze-colored alcoholic sea.

When Virgil saw me he stopped, picked up another half gallon of rum, and inverted it over the drink.

—The mixture's not rich enough for you, Penguin. Say, I saw you talking to Sally McAllister. She's one of my oldest pals.

—You've shown her the guest house?

—I gave her a tour of the whole grounds, Virgil said. It's a pity you didn't get to do it. The full expedition can take several hours.

—I'll bet it can. By the way, Virgil, thanks for the financial aid.

—I am a pragmatist, Virgil said. I enjoy seeing the best side win. Has your stepmother left already?

He bent over and beaked his nose into my hair just over the left ear.

—She's been gone almost a week, I said. Richard is following her as soon as he can pack. What about the twins? I miss them. Aimee and Aurora. Such beautiful names.

—Gone, he said. Flown to Poughkeepsie. In the company plane.

Bondo had already found Robin Adler and Sleezy. He had his arms around them both.

—We're working in Provincetown, Robin explained. At the same restaurant. The Motif. I'm a waitperson and Chester takes people's money. Chester. That's what we're calling him now. It sounds more dignified.

—And we've got an apartment.

Sleezy pecked at Robin's cheek like a man on his twenty-fifth anniversary. Chester. They had become a couple. They were a perfect match.

—Yeah. We saw you in town, Sleezy said. You and Martin. We pounded on the glass, but you didn't turn around.

—Snobs, Robin said.

—Snobs. That's what I said. You two should move into town. Seriously. This place is depressing. It's like *On the Beach* around here. Postnuclear war. My parents are leaving. Robin's parents are leaving. They don't even know why.

Robin pulled me aside.

—I hope you don't hate my parents, she said.

248

—No. Your father opposed the whole thing. He never wanted them to spray the marsh.

—They're so worried about Eliot. He's only eighteen, and he has a boyfriend in New York.

—So what? Your parents are actors. They're in the theater. They must be used to it.

—It's different now, Robin said. They think it's a death sentence.

I turned around and there was Newton Yin, towering over Smokey and Daisy, crew-cut, in a sweatshirt that said LIVERMORE QUARKS SOFTBALL.

—Penguin Solstice, he said. Do you remember who I am?

—How could I not? I thought you were blowing up the world.

—Hardly. Our goal is to make sure that it never happens. Or if it does, that it happens in space where nobody will get hurt.

—Space is the only clean place left on Earth, and you want to go up there and trash it. Besides, they're planning to bring the cold war to an end. Haven't you heard?

—It's not coming to an end for us, Newton Yin said. We don't listen to the news. It's too ephemeral. Countries come and go, but war is eternal. Our task is to make it as beautiful as possible, like a distant display of fireworks. We're even thinking of having it on the Fourth of July. We'll put satellite cameras up there, so you'll be able to watch it from the comfort of your home. In fact, I'll tell you a military secret. We may be able to combine SDI and the stealth bomber so that World War Three would be entirely invisible. No one would know it was happening until it was over.

—Great. How are we supposed to know who won?

—We'll tell you, Newton said. Public relations. That's a big part of our job.

Then I saw Bondo actually talking to P. T. Varnum. I had to go up and see what they could conceivably have to communicate. Bondo was talking about politics at Dartmouth.

—We forced our trustees to divest their holdings in South Africa, Bondo said.

—And where are they going to keep their assets? In the library? It's a global economy. There isn't anything that's not tainted if you look at it long enough. I buy malt from Communist China. I buy aluminum from Paraguay. That's a military dictatorship. Money transcends politics, that's what I say. That's why it's going to save the world.

P. T. gave me a faux-Japanese bow when I approached them and said, "Ah so. The Mystelious Femare." He stepped over to the cauldron and poured me a chivalrous glass of punch.

—I already have one, I told him.

—Well, you should have two, P. T. said. These are the dog days. It's been a rotten August. And there's a rotten time coming in the world. We work our rear ends off—excuse me—to make something right in this nation, and there are always people around to queer it up.

—Are you going to stay? I asked him. Or go back to Providence?

—Certainly I'm going to stay. This is my summer home. I fought in the Pacific theater. We lost many a battle but we never ordered a retreat. There were insects on Corregidor carrying germs that could kill you in an hour and a half. I'm sixty-six years old. What the hell have we got to lose? Our sex life?

I didn't exactly know who P. T. meant by *we*.

—I misunderstood, I said. I thought you were the one who was really the most freaked out.

—Marines don't "freak out," P. T. said. But they are known for being loyal to their unit.

P. T. looked at me with a new interest, as if he was seeing me for the first time and maybe had an idea.

—What are you doing with yourself, young lady? I understand you had a little trouble up at your school. That kind of adventure takes guts. I know. I was in demolition myself.

—It got me expelled, I said. I don't know what I'm going to do.

—Who needs formal education? P. T. said. Ninety-nine percent of that stuff you can pick up on your own. Shakespeare. "There is a tide in the affairs of men." You can read it in the evening, after work.

If they don't need you then you don't need them. Take me. I quit college and joined the service. I was at Guadalcanal. A Jap sniper shot me in the leg.

P. T. rolled up his pants leg on the spot and showed me this immense hairless calf with some kind of suspenders holding up his sock. There was a bulge in his leg with a dark spot under it and a hole, like a quahog living there under the sand.

—And it still hurts, P. T. said. After forty-eight years that son of a bitch still wakes me up in the night. They were about to amputate. I told the guy with the knife, I am going to need that leg in the future. And if you cut it off I will find you and kill you when I get well. He didn't. And it healed all by itself. I figured what the hell. I would be better off dead than strapping on a prosthesis every morning. I never got a degree. You know what my major was going to be? Latin. If I'd gone on, I would have taught school. I'd be a retired schoolteacher on social security. I got a job selling beer for Joe Schlitz, and I've been in beer ever since.

—I guess there's not much further to go when you're the President, Bondo said.

—There's nowhere to go when you're sixty-six years old. Don't waste your youth. Don't finish at Amherst or wherever you were. Those guys are lackeys and they stay lackeys right to the end. Go to night school, take an accounting class, and then call me up. I'll give you a job. You can start in stirring the vats and work your way up. Learn by doing. God knows the company could use a few good gals to keep us honest.

—I'll look you up, I said, in a few years.

—In a few years I will be dead. You may be too, if you don't take care of yourself.

P. T. went over to his wife, a tiny white-crested creature with a red beak. She was getting her clothes on to go: full yellow oilskins even though there wasn't a cloud in the night sky. It was the signal for everyone. This wasn't going to be one of those endless farewells. P. T. was going and the rest of us were content to follow him out. For the first time I noticed that Bailey Varnum walked with a slight limp.

Bondo had gone on ahead of me to the car, with Robin and Sleezy, when Jerry Perera came up out of nowhere and took my arm. He gripped me a wee bit harder than necessary, in fact hard enough to twist me around so I had to face him. His skin looked almost black against the white formal jacket and shirt.

—Are you under a contract to go home with that group?

—I'm under my own free will.

—I'm a student too, Jerry said. I'm a specialist. I've been studying the same girl for years.

—*Woman,* I said.

It was probably the wrong moment to correct him. That would take a thousand years, along with a brain transplant. Learn by doing. I broke away and jogged to catch up with the others in the Schlessbooms' parking lot. My arm hurt above the elbow where Jerry had grabbed it. I hoped it would be a lifetime bruise to add to my own markings, a radical hand-printed masculine-violence tattoo.

We stopped at a point on the road halfway between the Schlessbooms and home, and we looked up at the sky. It was the time of the Perseid meteor shower, Bondo said, and we actually saw one. It transformed from green to orange as it fell and seemed to set the stratosphere on fire with its passage. I made a wish. I wished for the instantaneous evolution of the male half of the race into human beings, so we would have some company in this world. I wished that Arnold would get well and live a natural life into old age. Then I changed that because it doesn't make sense to wish the impossible. I wished he would just get to finish his piece before the end.

Bondo had gone on ahead of me and I caught up. In the light of the moon refracted through the beach-plum and cranberry bushes around us, and the Perseid meteors, I took his hand. That contact seemed to erase what had happened a few minutes before. Thank God, I thought, now that the century is over we are beginning to see a few human men.

Robin and Sleezy had started on ahead. Chester. By the time

Bondo and I caught up with them, Chester had stepped off into the beach plums to regurgitate.

—He always does that, Robin informed us. Despite his appearance he has a highly sensitive stomach.

I told Robin they'd be crazy to try driving back to Provincetown and that with Dorothy gone we had plenty of room for them to spend the night.

When we got home, a light was still on in Joshua's house but the curtains were drawn. Richard was already upstairs in the sleeping loft, snoring blithely away.

I showed Sleezy and Robin the two cots in Dorothy's empty studio. Bondo announced he was going to crash. He shook the sand ritually out of each shoe and organized his sleeping bag on top of the couch. I went into my room and opened Fernando Pessoa.

> I wrap myself in a blanket and don't even think of
>   thinking.
> Feeling creature comfort and dimly thinking.
> I fall asleep with no less purpose than anything else
>   going on in the world.

Robin interrupted my reading by knocking at the door. I said to come in.

—You mean you guys don't even sleep in the same room? Robin whispered.

—It's not that kind of relationship.

—We live and learn, she said. You two looked like the romance of the late twentieth century.

She closed the door. I lay there considering ways to kill Jerry Perera without actually hurting him, thinking about Arnold next door in his endless climb towards death, and wondering what it would taste like to sleep with someone who had just thrown up.

253

29

It came to feel like we were the only family left. People didn't know why they were leaving, whether it was the risk of disease or insect spray or simply the first unpleasantness that had ever crept into a place built on the sand-castle fantasy of seasonal human perfection. Although they supposedly came there for the solitude, their boatless harbor and traffic-free roads turned out to be too quiet. It was nature with the human element removed, the way the Garden of Eden would have been if God had actually killed Adam and Eve for eating the apple the way He had wanted to at first. Reality had broken into the little circle of cottages and life had ceased to be fun. They weren't leaving because of fear, but because they had seen themselves in an unexpected mirror and even in August it wasn't summer any more.

From my perspective the atmosphere was right. We were in the last act of a play where the bad minor characters had eliminated each other and only the King was left, plus a few loyal companions who had lasted to the end. In many ways I would have liked Bondo and Richard also to disappear, who were not a hundred percent devoted, so it would be just me and the two solitary men who never came out of their gray house. The seals would return to the harbor the way they do in autumn, and I could take my clothes off and wade out towards the deep midharbor channel where they fished. It wouldn't matter if Joshua and Arnold saw me. We already knew each other down to the bone.

I had been sitting for hours by Arnold's bed, listening to the stories he'd started to dig up about Salem, Mass., and his childhood in the old Italian quarter. As Arnold's mind started to waver in the present tense, he put forth these childhood reminiscences with a hallucinatory realism that made me feel like kind of a phantom sister who had been beside him all along. At first I just listened, then I started to write them down.

When he'd fall asleep I would leave him to join Bondo down at the pier. We'd sit on the unused diving board and watch a pair of terns swoop down for minnows among the empty orange moorings. When the late-afternoon sky would darken under a black storm cloud over Provincetown, the terns looked supernaturally brilliant, as if their bodies contained skeletons of light.

The birds would take turns flying and fishing. One tern would hover over a spot, then dive completely into the water so you couldn't see it and reappear with the fish in its beak, while the other circled around it and screamed. It was a dance without audience or choreographer, in which the dancers were not mentally conscious but simply alive. It had gone on before even the Mashpee Indians had camped here and would continue when the cottages were just a row of overgrown foundations on the shore.

Bondo had studied the Middle Ages. Back at the last millennium, he said, around the year 1000, in the time of Plague and massive concern about the end of the world, whole villages would uproot themselves and wander the countryside. It was like now, only a thousand years earlier. One village would meet another village in the medieval landscape and there would be immediate total debauchery followed by the extremest forms of penitence and self-flagellation, whipping one another with the dried tails of cattle or walking to the next city on their knees. They would single out individuals, too, and ostracize them as carriers of demons and disease. A thousand years of alleged Western civilization and things hadn't changed an inch.

—That's going to happen again, Bondo would say. People will turn to bizarre leaders. Itinerant actors will come to occupy the positions of state. Whole governments will be replaced by theatrical companies. Then people will forget there was ever anything else.

Sometimes Uncle Joshua would join us. With Arnold sleeping or trying to write music, Joshua would light one Benson & Hedges after another out of his slender Italian leather purse and tell us about the masked carnivals of Venice and the hermaphroditic taxi drivers who had taken him into the secret neighborhoods of Teheran. He told us about this Sikh or Sukh club in the back canals of Venice that staged a ball with eighteenth-century costumes, the husbands with swords and capes, the wives in white wigs and long period gowns, only underneath it, all of the participants were men. I didn't dare ask whether Arnold and Joshua had actually dressed up. It was hard enough to imagine them happy in the first place without trying to guess which of that couple would have appeared in public as the Wife.

Even the water seemed vacant since the Yins closed down Tobacco Island and left for Billerica. Despite what he'd said to me at the party, P. T. Varnum followed his wife to Providence, and Virgil took off for Saratoga Springs to confront Viola and be closer to his girls.

One morning Richard and I stood outside with coffee and just breathed in the seasoning of the air, sharpened with salt and with pungent trace minerals drawn from the sea surface by the rising sun. Before long, Bondo joined us, trailing this ratty bathrobe he had found in the rest room at the Motif. We looked next door and saw two figures on Joshua's deck. Arnold had finally come out. Swaddled in Joshua's Persian blanket and wearing the blue oxygen mask draped around his neck like an amulet, he gave us this El Greco wave with one thin elongated arm.

Fearless in the absence of boats and swimmers, the snowy egrets came out of the marsh and at low tide fed in the shallows directly in front of the house. The weather changed too, as if it too were a participant in the pageantry of departure. By the middle of August it had started to feel like October. The air thinned to a perfect transparency while the harbor darkened and grew red as if someone had laced it with Chianti.

—Midsummer autumn, Richard would say.

With his sculpture and tools packed away so he couldn't work, my father became a different person. For the first time since I knew him, he seemed to participate in life on its own terms without immediately having to hammer it into Art. He'd tell us about Paris and Greenwich Village in his Bohemian days and even his hitch as a military artist when he sketched court-martials in Seoul.

—I'm glad to be here, he'd say. It's like twenty years past, when we'd carry you down to the water so you could get your feet wet. Katherine and I, one on each side of you. Of course you'd be totally nude.

—Save us from the details, I would say.

Before too long, though, Richard grew quieter. Dorothy was getting to him, calling him away from us and back to the new family. The phone would ring first thing in the morning and again in the afternoon. She'd reorganized the apartment and had gotten the tenant out of his loft. When was he coming? Was there another woman there? How many women? How much was it costing them to have that U-Haul truck parked at the studio door? "Get one of those other women on the phone," she would say, "I want to talk to her. There's a few things she'll probably want to know." All the way from the deck we could hear her voice lacerating the phone.

I loved having Richard with us. I loved the extended evenings when Joshua and Arnold would be talking quietly on their deck and the three of us on ours, and the sounds of the two conversations would meet between. There was a sadness, too, as in midautumn, as if when Richard left I wouldn't see him again, ever, and the same even with Bondo. I realized the close presence of death was affecting us all, making all movements seem final, and I suppose they were. The next time I saw Richard he'd be the father of another family, and the previous family would be fictional and extinct. Richard felt it too. He was kind and reflective rather than obsessive with arc-welder energy.

But he was only half here. The other half was already forging little bronze animal figures for Dorothy's forthcoming infant back in the apartment on West Fourth.

One day I answered a phone call from Dorothy myself.

—Penguin, she said. You're still alive. I suppose your father is next door, in the infirmary.

—Come on, Dorothy. We need him. He's Joshua's best friend. He's my best friend. He's holding us together.

—In two days I'm filing for divorce, tell him. I can raise this thing myself. He can stay there forever. Just tell him to send child support. Or I can sell off his pieces one by one.

—OK, I said. We get the point.

That evening we steamed up some clams in a mixture of half beer and half saltwater and carried the last of the tools into the truck. Joshua came over and brought a present: an illuminated page from the Koran with a border of geometric shapes.

—Thanks, Richard said. I'll have to hire someone to read it when I get back to New York.

—You should.

—Why? What does it say?

—It prescribes the times when you're not supposed to lie with any of your wives.

Bondo and Joshua walked down towards the water to leave me alone with Richard. He leaned against the U-Haul truck with one hand on the door handle and said we should all go to New York. There would even be room for Bondo, if not at West Fourth, then in Richard's studio down in the old Laight Street warehouse.

—You've done your part, Richard said. Why don't you come home now and let things take their course?

—I can't. I've gone too far already.

—You have a family down here, Richard insisted.

—This is my family, I said. Right here. You and Arnold and Joshua and Bondo and me. You can desert us if that's what you think is right. Katherine deserted me. You might as well make it complete.

—We're not supposed to look backwards, he said. We'll turn into pillars of salt.

It was ten o'clock at night when he finally put the U-Haul into gear and plunged it forward into the ruts. I watched his headlights flash through the sand moguls till they were out of sight. I stood there like a pillar of salt for about five minutes and then turned back to Joshua's house, where I found him on the deck alone.

—Don't worry, he said. It's not going to be long.

He sounded desperate and bitter, as if we were betraying him, as if there were something that could be done that the people around him were refusing to perform.

—He went home to his wife and embryo, I said.

—It doesn't matter. We're all going. Arnold is going, too.

I realized he had a right to be sadder than any of us. It was one thing to go back to New York, another to leave the Earth forever. The truly abandoned one was Uncle Joshua. His bitterness extended even to Arnold himself.

—He's a musician, I said. His timing is perfect even in this.

Meanwhile, Bondo was back in the kitchen dragging the last clams out of their broth, pulling the foreskins off their necks and slurping them down. I put the lid on the clam steamer, then shut off the porch light and pulled him out on the deck.

There was one light over on the Oquosset shore and then that was extinguished, leaving the sky moonless and only the harbor buoy blinking its one letter in Morse code. Dot dash: A. Not for Achievement or Arson or political Action, but for the name of a sickness that one of us carried by himself through the dark, which in another sense we all carried: P. T., Richard, Bondo and I, the new Solstice child sleeping in Dorothy's womb, even Jerry Perera, despite the fact that he was a homophobe and was probably out there abusing some innocent woman on his boat.

Then Bondo grabbed my shoulder and pointed up. In the north, right above Provincetown, a green light was just appearing in the air. It started like a thin line of writing on a computer screen, and suddenly shot up into the sky. It turned off completely for a moment and then started again from the top. It flashed from a spot right overhead and shimmered downward all the way to the opposite shore. It filled all of outer space with this green radioactive light.

259

—It must be the aurora borealis, Bondo said. This is a time of great sunspot activity. I read that in the *Boston Sunday Globe*.

It left me speechless. I had never seen anything like it in my life.

Joshua shook me out of my stupor by lighting a cigarette over on his deck. The match looked unnaturally orange compared to the northern lights, as if there were two species of fire: our own human controllable fire and a cool greenish flame that would never be ours, though we were allowed to see it, and anyone reckless enough to follow it would have to be willing never to come back.

—They saw those every night in the winter of 999, Bondo said, under Ethelred the Unready. Entire villages would leave their huts and follow them into the north. Then they would freeze to death and monks would find their bodies scattered in the snow.

—Another decade, I said, then it will be us.

The whole northwest sky turned to an intense green in which fronts of darker green would flash up over our heads and back down towards the trees in back of the house.

—And the thing is, Bondo went on, they're not really lights at all. The light doesn't even exist. It's an illusion.

—It's not, I said. You can see it. It's totally real.

When we'd finished the last of the martinis and clams and also the dregs of the wine and dredged the last final warm Rolling Rock out of the studio, we went inside. The Aurora was still up there, but it had become blurry and had started to spin somewhat nauseatingly around the Pole.

I grabbed the sleeping bag out of my room and climbed up the ladder to the loft. No wonder Dorothy had to leave, I thought as I climbed those vertical steps. This house would be an uninsurable menace if you were pregnant. Especially if you also happened to be a somnambulist.

I asked Bondo to bring me my book of poems along with three or four aspirins and a Tab.

—And bring your sleeping bag, too, I added. If you think you can handle all those things at once.

30

Once he discovered them, Bondo had gotten immediately friendly with Robin and Chester, which as I said was what we were calling Sleezy at this point. Bondo gravitated towards the known and familiar rather than my own risky companions. He would go off to Provincetown every morning in the jeep, which was useful since he could do all the shopping. Then one day they hired him for the lunch shift at the Motif. That was good. We needed the money and it gave him something to do while I gave more and more of my energy to Arnold. Joshua had grown so lugubrious that he could hardly be counted upon to help.

Bondo would come back with these paper bags full of surplus fried clams and fried shrimp and whole uneaten portions of battered sole. Some were legitimately left over and some he scraped right off of customers' plates who couldn't bring themselves to eat that stuff. We'd have them for supper and freeze what we didn't consume.

—It's ecological, Bondo would say. Otherwise it would all go right into the dumpster. Perfectly good food.

Arnold was focusing his strength to finish *The Keeper of Sheep*. Joshua grew more gloomy and tired-looking every day. He didn't even go out much on his deck. I would end up feeding both Cosimo and Arnold as well as handling the oxygen and the medication. Joshua had shown me how to tie off the arm above the elbow until the vein stood out and pierce it with the fine needle and push the Septra or TPN into his bloodstream. After I learned this operation I was always the one who performed it. As I think back on it, Uncle

Joshua seemed phobic about that part from the beginning. Despite the medical aspirations of his mother.

Following these injections I would have the strangest desire to shoot something into my own arm in the same way. I wanted to feel it go in and spread through my system and make me larger or stronger or more immune to the smell and the pain of Arnold's room. And I learned something about contagion. If you are close enough to a diseased person, you end up wanting to have the disease too. I don't know why that is. Maybe another weird ramification of love. I know that I had an increasing desire for physical sickness so I could stab or insert something into my body that would make it well.

Arnold wasn't getting any better, and he knew it. He hated the capsules and shots, and he hated the fiction that was hidden behind them: that he would get radically normal again, that he would live free from pain and compose music and hear it performed and be able to care about another human being. When you are sick, the universe of your sympathy shrinks into itself like one of those slowly collapsing stars.

—I want to finish my piece, he would say, and then I want it all to stop.

—If you don't take the medicine, I would tell him, you're not going to be able to breathe, let alone compose.

I would lift him out of bed with my bare arms like one of those seances where you put your fingers under someone and they rise up in the air. He had a strange buoyancy, an absence of physical weight, as if the bones that had already become hollow were dissolving under his flesh. I would put him in the wheelchair and take him to the piano and steady his hand as he made the notations slowly and deliberately on the endless parallel furrows of the staff.

—Does that part work? he would ask me. Is that the right progression?

I would have to laugh because I knew nothing about any kind of music, let alone his, which was increasing in dissonance as if he were trying to depict the condition in which his body was tearing itself apart. Arnold would laugh too, until the laughter mixed itself up with coughing, and I had to rush a handkerchief over his mouth so the blood droplets wouldn't stain his score.

He would then try the chords out on Cosimo or call for Joshua, who had started to spend more and more time alone in his study with the door only slightly ajar.

—Joshua's writing a new book, Arnold said one morning. It will be extraordinary when it's done. But I won't live to see it.

—You will see it, I told him. You have to hang in there for Joshua's book.

I was even lying to him myself. I couldn't help it. I was going to have to learn how not to be able to lie.

Arnold would work ten or fifteen minutes and have to be wheeled into the bathroom. I'd back the chair next to the bowl and close the bathroom door to wait outside. He would call me when he was through. I would open the door and flush the toilet for him and lead him out. At times he'd be too weak to clean himself and I would have to help him. I would wash his legs and buttocks with a white towel and then wash the towel out in the sink.

This is the worst, I would think while I was cleaning him. This is the most grotesque thing a person can be brought to do. It is what a mother does for a child, or a nurse does as part of her profession. But I am not related to this person and I am making no money and I don't even have any Hippocratic Oath about helping my fellow human. And yet it was specifically after those sessions in the bathroom, when I had wrung out the white towel in the preliminary Clorox bath and was soaping it in the sink and hanging it with the others to dry, that I'd get this feeling of weightlessness, as if I could rise right up over the toilet bowl and the bleach bucket and the rack of damp towels and float out into the other room. I understood what the terms humility and service meant, and had always meant, especially for women, and why someone would put on a black-and-white penguin costume and become a nun.

Arnold took my arm one morning after I had cleaned him and put him back to bed.

—We have to get a nurse, he said. No one should have to do this for anyone else.

—The nurse would be someone, too, I reminded him.

—Nurses are supposed to, Arnold said. Cleaning people up is their art form.

—No nurses. A nurse would take one look at you and have you dragged back into the ward.

It was true. He had lost even more weight and the exposed skin was so dry that the lines around his mouth were starting to bleed. His face had taken on the complexion of animal bone.

It would have been easy to get out of it. Joshua could have hired a nurse and I could have just come over and read poetry to Arnold like Walt Whitman in the Civil War and helped him with his music sheets at the piano. The nurse would clean around the toilet and give him his injections and change the cloth diaper we put over his chest when he began to cough blood and that we half the time couldn't get off because it had already fused with the skin sores. The nurse would commute to Squid Harbor from one of the Portuguese families on the back streets of Provincetown and be paid to see and smell things we would rather not conceive. She would be like the black soldiers we send out on our little military adventures so we don't have to suffer the inconvenience of death with our own middle-class bodies. If she got the disease herself, that would be an acceptable sacrifice. It was her work, after all, her calling, her chosen occupation in this world.

After these sessions in the bathroom I would wheel Arnold back to the piano. I'd go back and work on my own journal, which was coming to be less the history of coeducation at Dartmouth and more the story of Arnold Fratorelli and this young woman who for some reason felt compelled to see him through.

When the lavatory experience left him too weak to compose, I'd wheel him over to his bed. Then, lying there with his eyes staring at something a thousand miles beyond the plywood wall, he would tell me about his life. He would talk for a few minutes, then get so incoherent I'd have to stop him. Then I'd go into my study and write it down. A life shouldn't go unrecorded, I thought, especially of an artist whose importance might not get to be fully witnessed by the public eye.

One day Arnold had me get out the box of personal things again, which we had not visited since the time we dug out the photos of Mr. and Mrs. Fratorelli and his house in Salem and his brother in L. A.

—I want us to make a scrapbook, Arnold said.

He sounded like a kid occupying himself while he recovered from chicken pox or the mumps. That night I asked Bondo to bring back an album and some double-sided Scotch tape when he returned from Provincetown. The scrapbook occupied much of my time with Arnold from then on. I'd show him each piece and between us we worked things into a semblance of chronological order. We started with the little orderly pile we'd constructed before and went from there.

We grouped all the athletic clips and trophy poses together, which brought us through high school, then we cut his page right out of the 1972 yearbook for Julliard School. There were a couple of other men's pages sliced out already, which Arnold must have done sometime before. After Julliard, Arnold had gone to Princeton to study electronic music. There were several photos of a studio that looked like the cockpit of a space shuttle, only with a keyboard in place of the steering wheel, plus a photo of Arnold receiving his degree, and another with a man whose face even I dimly recognized, who turned out to be the famous conductor, the late Matthias Falk.

—Matthias passed for straight, Arnold said. He had a wife, a son, he lived a complete double life. The public never knew. He managed to get his death passed off as TB.

There was also a draft card, classified 4F.

—I just walked into my draft board and told them the truth, he said. Three aging American Legionnaires. "What'll we put down?" they said to each other. They checked some box and I was free. I wasn't even a protester. I never cared for politics. I'd look at the demonstrators, and I'd look at the soldiers, and I'd realize I wasn't either one. They would have put me in the trenches. I could have died in Asia instead of here.

His first compositions were recorded in 1976 and 1977. He had miniature reproductions of the record jackets. *Seven Movements for Seven Instruments* and *Doktor Faustus,* which was a chamber opera for tenor, bass, mezzo-soprano, and transistor. I pasted the review clippings next to the titles. "One of the luminaries of electronic neo-romanticism," a reviewer said.

Another critic, in a clipping from the *New York Times,* said Arnold had "an infinite future in the contemporary scene." He laughed to the coughing point when I read him that.

—"His death marked the high point of postcontemporary music," Arnold said.

Meanwhile, he had stopped eating altogether. I offered to spice up the gruel-like substances we fed him, but he wouldn't bite. Joshua wasn't eating much either. I'd end up finishing both their meals. For some reason I had grown ravenously hungry and even at times felt like shovelling in the remains of Arnold's antibiotic puree.

There was a program from the opening of the new wing at the Los Angeles County Museum, where they premiered Arnold's *Homage to Jimi Hendrix,* which was billed as a "bicultural break-through" at the time, because it opened electronic music to rock themes.

—You won't believe who came that evening, Arnold exclaimed. Rock Hudson. I'd never seen his movies and I didn't even know what he looked like. The man next to me on the platform had to point him out. He wasn't a cause yet at that point. He was probably HIV positive and didn't know it. No one knew anything at the time.

We pasted in a picture of Arnold, the agent, and Matthias Falk, standing beside a color TV that displayed the American flag.

—Falk the Cock, Arnold said. It was two o'clock in the morning. The station was signing off. The three of us stood there as they played the national anthem and saluted the Stars and Stripes. Totally nude.

There was a tape, too. Arnold had gotten a research fellowship at MIT. He worked with a molecular biologist to compose music based on the genetic patterns of DNA. The tape was the *Recombinant Symphony,* for men's chorus, synthesizer, and percussion. I pulled Arnold's blanket up to give him a rest, then took it into the living room and played it. It sounded like the wind whispering through the metallic vegetation of another planet, cold and ethereal, a wind not of air either but something colder and brittler than air, like swimming down through a microscope tube into the world of giant molecules. Cosimo stood up when I played the *Recombinant Symphony* and listened, as if only an animal could truly hear it, his ear tips vibrating at a supernatural rate.

If they could recombine bacteria to eat oil off the ocean and grow ten-foot tomatoes, then why couldn't they recombine something that would feed on human viruses and do some good in this world? Of course I'm not a scientist, but I wondered if they were working all that hard.

We pulled a plastic hospital ID bracelet out of the box. It wasn't even broken. Arnold had grown so thin at Mass General that he was able to slip his hand in and out of the purple ring at will.

—I was living with a computer programmer at that point. Jason. He taught me some technical things. He was so tall his feet and ankles hung out over the end of the bed. I had to get up in the night and cover his legs.

It turned out that Jason the Programmer was given to bringing home strangers in the small hours of the morning. There was a weird photo showing a couple of black guys who had brought a bicycle up to their apartment. The flash lit everyone's eyes up, like those pictures of nocturnal animals surprised at a water hole. Arnold declined to tell me what the bike was for.

In that period also, he composed a piece for Janet Keeler, the soprano, called *Immortality.* It was a setting of six poems by Emily Dickinson. When Janet Keeler sang it, in the Fogg Museum, Joshua Brand was in attendance. It was their first meeting. Arnold himself had accompanied Janet Keeler on the piano.

—When I saw this guy in the audience, I blushed. I thought: He's the one. He made me lose my place in my own score.

Almost immediately after they met, Arnold had taken an extended trip to Venice with Uncle Joshua. He had a whole package of photos from that trip, including one blurry shot of the two of them squeezed into the first-class lavatory of a 747, six miles over the Atlantic. They took it, Arnold explained, with the self-timing device.

There they were in a gondola being serenaded by a pair of accordionists in front of a Venetian palace. There they were in St. Mark's Square, with a couple of pigeons sitting on Arnold's shoulder. There they were under the Bridge of Sighs, shopping on the Rialto, dining alfresco with an American poet in an enormous bat-winged hat. The poet was the one who introduced them to the work of Fernando Pessoa.

There were no photos of the notorious masked ball, but one did show the two of them lounging around on the porch of the same five-star hotel where *Death in Venice* had been filmed.

—The Grand Hotel Des Bains. They had a long brass telescope pointing towards the ocean, Arnold said. There were several attractive boys out there on the Lido beach. You can't see them in the picture. We tried to find one who could play the role of Tadzio in the story.

The Venice pictures took up the last few pages of the album, leaving only one page for a poem, from *The Keeper of Sheep*.

—That sums it all up, Arnold said. That poem more than anything, the one about the pirates.

He had me read it to him for the dozenth time:

Pirates and Piracy, ships and the moment!
That maritime moment when the prey is seized!
To be as one with all those armies, to be part and parcel
Of all those raids on ships, the massacres, the rapes!
To be, in my bondage, the woman having to serve them all!
And feel it all—feel all these things at once—through
    to the backbone!

. . .

Slow ship, pass by, pass away and don't stop here . . .
Leave me, pass away out of sight,
Take yourself out of my heart,
Vanish in the Distance, the farthest Distance, the mist of God,
Disappear, follow your destiny, leave me behind.

—I don't know about the rape part, I said.

—Rape is extraordinary if you understand it.

—You mean if all parties are willing.

—Then it wouldn't be rape, would it? Arnold said.

I shut my ears. On some issues we have to draw the line.

After that little interchange, he had one of his worst attacks. I dropped the book and pulled the oxygen mask over his face. His lungs heaved like a man trying to breathe in the vacuum of outer space. After a long while he finally put down the mask.

—One day I'm not going to do that, Arnold said. One day I'm going to go as I am.

—What do you mean by that?

—You know what I mean. I'm not going to put on the mask. I won't let anyone force me to, either. Maybe a time when Joshua isn't around.

—I'm not going to force you, I said. Nobody else will, either. Joshua knows the arrangement.

—You I can count on. As for Joshua, much as I love him, I am not so sure. The ones you love are not always exactly the ones you trust.

I knew what he meant. I had begun thinking myself that Joshua might not go through with it, might fail at the last moment and call in the doctor and start the whole hopeless round of hospitals and medication again. It was natural to extend someone's life as long as you could, especially someone you loved, especially when like Uncle Joshua you had nothing else in the world except for Cosimo. It was natural to want to keep him with us, but it was more humane to let him go.

It turned out that Arnold hadn't seen his father in all this time.

He'd sent him tapes, records, even scores. But he had kept Raimondo Fratorelli out of his personal life.

—My father had come to live like a monk. He hadn't had sex in thirty years. How could I have expected him to understand?

By December, Arnold had grown weak, depressed, and uncreative. He'd been trying to compose at his usual rate, although he could hardly get up and walk across the room. He had left MIT and stayed around the apartment all day while Uncle Joshua went to work. He tried working out on Joshua's Nautilus but he couldn't lift even the lightest weight. The rash returned, this time on the soles of both feet so he couldn't wear shoes. By this time he pretty much knew what it was. He had known about the disease for years. He had known people who had it, who had died from it or had friends who died from it. But he hadn't applied that knowledge to himself. It's amazing how much reality you can deny if you put your mind to it.

—I thought I was exempt, he said. All the symptoms pointed in the one direction I refused to see. I woke up one day feeling like a fugitive. I forced a pair of slippers onto my feet, took a taxi to Mount Auburn Hospital, and turned myself in.

The test was positive. That letter, a little typewritten note from the Commonwealth Laboratory, was in the souvenir box too. I didn't want to paste that one into the album, but Arnold insisted. He wanted the scrapbook to be real.

He had waited three weeks before telling anyone, even Joshua.

—I didn't believe it myself, he said. I used to take the note out of its envelope every morning after Joshua went off and just stare at it, hoping I could make it change. As long as no one else knew about it, then it wasn't real.

He had been going in to Mount Auburn every week, however, taking every drug they'd prescribe for him, including the then-novelty drug AZT, in increasing dosages.

—I felt like an addict. I felt the virus mutating inside me, becoming my own, evolving away from whatever medicine they'd put in next. You can feel it inside you, you know, like a city, like foreign citizens living in your streets, only after a while they're not foreign anymore, they're you. I lived like an experimental animal. I was a pink, radioactive, hairless laboratory mouse.

He had been dining with Uncle Joshua at a Thai restaurant one evening and Arnold just blurted out the news. Joshua walked out into the night. Arnold hired a cab, had the driver cruise the streets until they found him. Arnold offered to move out, which Joshua accepted at first, and they went to a private clinic. The clinic turned out to be so dismal that Joshua took him home.

—Wasn't he worried that he'd get sick, too?

—He thought if he wasn't positive by then, he wasn't destined to be. And he loved me. For a reckless little period back there, he wanted to have it, to share it with me and die with me if need be. And I wanted that too. It seemed at the time like Tristan and Isolde, a Liebestod, the end, the utmost possible human form of love. Now we know better.

At first Joshua had been overwhelmed by it: the pain and crying, as well as the medical routine. So they returned to the clinic, where Arnold lived for three months in the late winter and early spring.

—They were dying around me, he said. I'd get to know someone and the next day they'd be taking his body out. It must have been that way in Vietnam. We'd managed to avoid the war with our little problem and now we are here. And the worst of it was the music. One guy next to me was a Boy George freak. You think Boy George just sang the chameleon thing. Wrong. Boy George recorded *hundreds* of songs. I couldn't get anything done. You can't compose music without silence. You can't see the stars when the sun is out. There's not enough darkness between the notes. And they were of course losing their hearing, so they'd turn it up louder and louder. I'd cry out and the nurse or the volunteer would come running over and I'd say "The agony is all right, please just stop the fucking noise." I used to pray that God would strike me deaf.

There was one picture from this period that Arnold made me cram into the album. It was of a young man with a scared, birdlike look, a writer. The picture was actually torn from the dust cover of his book. He'd been next to Arnold, and he had died. They had carried his body from the clinic in a saffron-colored bag.

—His mother came in after he'd gone, the very next day. Of course the staff had cleaned everything around his bed, and they were ready to bring someone else in, but she wanted to make sure there was nothing of his left. She brought me a book. It was a coincidence: the book was the same *Selected Poems* of Fernando Pessoa that Russ Hart had given us back in Venice.

After pasting the picture in, I read him another:

> *There are sicknesses worse than sicknesses,*
> *There are pains that do not ache, not even in the soul,*
> *Yet are more painful than all the others.*
> *So many things exist without existing,*
> *Exist, and linger on and on,*
> *And on and on belong to us, and are us . . .*
> *Over the turbid green of the wide-spreading river*
> *The white circumflexes of the gulls . . .*
> *Over and above the soul, the useless fluttering*
> *Of what never was, nor ever can be, and that's all.*
> *Let me have more wine, life is nothing.*

Joshua had brought him a Casio synthesizer so he could compose in the clinic with headphones to blot out the noise. Two days after the young writer died, Arnold had begun *The Keeper of Sheep.* He asked Joshua to take him home again so he could write it.

It was early spring in Cambridge, just about the same time that we were up in New Hampshire getting tried. Arnold was living in Joshua's place on Hilliard Street and Joshua had enlisted in a volunteer carepersons' program at Mass General. That was the point at which they'd made out the Living Will: after he finished the piece, if he was not better, all life-supporting mechanisms were to be removed, even if Arnold wasn't conscious enough to make the decision himself. Joshua signed it. I was a signer too, not on paper exactly, but in my heart.

They would probably have stayed up in Cambridge except for

one last extremely unpleasant thing, which had no place in our scrapbook but should be told.

The sparrows had started their nests in the trees around Joshua's house, the days were warming up, and Arnold was getting his work done, at least in the shrinking periods of time when he had the strength. Besides Joshua, a volunteer had been coming morning and evening to help out. One day at noontime the downstairs neighbors, who owned the building, handed Uncle Joshua a letter asking them to find another home.

—Wasn't that illegal?

—It doesn't matter. We didn't have the heart to resist.

That was when they decided on Squid Harbor. They'd been there once before, on Labor Day weekend, and Arnold had loved it. It was the place he had most wanted to call home.

Arnold had one last thing to do, before they went, which was to find a way to get up to Salem and see his father. The volunteer drove him up, no advance warning, but Arnold knew Raimondo would be home. Where else would he have been after all those years? The old widower was inside in his hermitude, still with the shades drawn, after a whole lifetime still in black mourning and alone.

—I had to introduce myself to my own father. He had no idea who this person was. "I have all your recordings," he said. "You have done very well." He looked so completely frail and vulnerable, I didn't have the heart to tell him what I had. I climbed back into Jack's car and we drove off.

The next day Joshua had come down to Squid Harbor to prepare the house. The following week they arrived with Arnold before breakfast in the gray van. They already felt like fugitives. It was the morning Dorothy and I were just offshore.

31

The harbor had been fogged in for three days without a breath of wind, only an intermittent warm rain that clung uniformly to the leaves of the high bush cranberries as if they'd been coated with life-like shellac. The sand had darkened into mud. We were all lucky that Bondo was making his commuter trips to Provincetown in the jeep, since he could bring back the Rolling Rock beer and baskets of jumbo fried shrimp that kept us going. By *us* of course I mean Bondo and me, since Richard had gone and neither Arnold or Joshua seemed to consume anything at all. Arnold couldn't keep anything down but the clear feeding plasma that seemed to pass right through him. Joshua didn't eat either. I didn't know whether that was out of homeopathic sympathy or just sadness, or that Uncle Joshua was growing sick himself, which was one of my greatest fears of all.

On the second day of the rain I had tried to go up to Perera's in the Volvo and gotten stuck. I had to wait for Bondo to return from Provincetown and pull me free with the jeep, and even the jeep began to dig itself in with all four wheels so Bondo had to attach the winch to an anchor, which he pitched into the wet sand. The winch pulled the cable taut, burying the anchor so you couldn't even see it, then it caught hold and cranked both vehicles halfway onto the road. Ultimately the winch failed too and we had to leave Joshua's Volvo where it was. This is the Flood, I thought, this is the way it must have started back in the Book of Genesis, with people throwing anchors out of wheeled vehicles so that you no longer knew whether you lived on water or on land. The new moon was also bringing unnaturally high tides that would lap right under the pilings of the house and cause us to wonder if they'd recede or if they'd keep on rising and submerge Cape Cod back to an undersea reef as it was in the Pleistocene.

That evening we ran out to the shouting of invisible men in the harbor and the scream of diesel engines at full throttle with their propellers flailing the surface of the water.

—Throw her in reverse, one of the voices said.

—Watch out!

—Check the sounder.

—*Shit. Balls.*

The engine noises stopped. Their colorful sailors' language continued to perforate the fog.

Bondo and I followed the voices out with our canoe. A large motor yacht emerged out of the fog like a ghost ship as we came up. It dwarfed everything around us—or what would have been around us if we'd been able to see. The yacht was longer than any of the houses and its wheelhouse was higher than any local mast. It must have become disoriented and run aground. Squid Harbor wasn't deep enough for anything like that. It was like a lost vessel from a giant planet whose citizens were four times the size of human beings. The white-uniformed crew had to look down with their binoculars to make out the local savages arriving in their native craft.

—We're going to need help, said the captain. We can't get off the bottom.

Bondo offered to tow them free with the canoe.

—You wouldn't kid around, pal, if you knew who was aboard this thing. Where are we, anyway?

—Squid Harbor, I shouted.

The uniformed man seemed to be consulting a chart.

—Squid Harbor. Fuck. We'll have to wait until the tide floats us off.

Way at the stern of the boat someone leaned over the polished railing next to a brass ornamental cannon. Whoever it was had three-quarters of their head wrapped in a shawl, with dark glasses and what looked like a white dinner jacket with a black bow tie. Another figure appeared at the side of the first: the same dark glasses, the same shawl around the head. They appeared to be a couple but you couldn't tell from that distance what gender either of them was. They looked aloof and happy despite their wealth and position, like people from some century before Marx and Engels when you could still be both innocent and rich.

Then an astounding thing took place. Beside the couple in white appeared a third figure, familiar, dressed in the same white formal way but not so innocent-looking by any means, this one obviously a male and holding a champagne glass in his hand, who looked to me fleetingly similar to Jerry Perera. Or was it my condition to see him everywhere? The three figures looked down at us for a moment, then turned away from the rail to drink and talk. Back on the stern piazza, they seemed totally oblivious of the frantic embarrassed crew up on the bow. I half-waved to Jerry, then I checked myself. Maybe it wasn't him. Or, if it was, maybe he didn't want to see us. If Jerry Perera *had* been aboard, how could he have let the ship run aground right in his home port?

—Look, I said to Bondo, isn't that someone we know?

By the time Bondo looked, the fog had rethickened and buried the ship again. We heard a sound like winches lowering one of their small boats to the water, then another engine. Maybe they were trying to pull themselves off. We couldn't see anything. We set out for the shore in the canoe. There was no hint to give us a direction. I was in the most familiar place in the world, and I might as well have been in the middle of Hudson Bay.

We heard a chord sequence from Arnold's piano and paddled straight for it as if he had sent us a radar fix. In a few seconds the beach appeared, and the two cottages above it, like a photograph developing in a tray, gaining contrast and outline, until the canoe crunched up on the sand.

—Who do you suppose they were? Bondo asked as we were getting out on the shore.

—Who knows?

In an hour or so, after we'd had six cold fried shrimp and a pot of coffee, we heard engines starting and the sound of their hull sucking itself out of the mud. There was no break in the fog. The ship got out of Squid Harbor almost unseen.

That was the twenty-first of August. Bondo went to work and I didn't go next door all morning. I heard the piano and didn't want to disturb him. And now Joshua called.

—Penguin, we won't be needing you today. He's finishing up the last few measures and what he needs most is not to be disturbed. Why don't you give yourself the afternoon off?

I went up to the sleeping loft and crashed.

By the morning of the twenty-third it had all changed. The wind came sharply from the direction of Provincetown over the small village of Oquosset across the bay. The sky was a clear blue cerulean stained-glass window with thin high clouds like clippings of white wool. And for the first time that summer it was cold. Bondo and I were each zipped up to the throat in our respective sleeping bags, and we had even worked the bags up against each other during the night. I wriggled off the foam pad and rolled twice inside my bag to get over to my clothes without showing myself to Bondo. With the exception of that brief moment at Virgil's, no one since Katherine had ever actually seen my back.

Outside, the bay had whitecaps and the air was filled with little groups of beige-colored sandpipers flying south, already migrating for the Caribbean and Tierra del Fuego, driven by the northwest wind. Way out beyond the entrance buoy and straining at its anchor was the yacht that had run aground. It looked minute under the new immensity of the sky.

I picked a quick pint of blackberries, left half for Bondo, and brought the rest over to Joshua's. Arnold was in the wheelchair listening to a tape. He seemed to be breathing OK and his mask was draped over one handle of the chair. Joshua wore this elegant maroon robe with "JB" monogrammed on the pocket. A couple of logs were blazing away behind the glass door of their green Swedish stove.

—Something to celebrate! Joshua said. We've completed the last movement.

Arnold had the score to *A Keeper of Sheep* spread out on a board across the two arms of his wheelchair. He raised his hand and Joshua immediately punched the pause button on the open-reel deck. Arnold made a change in the notation, tapped the pen twice, and Joshua started the music again. It played for a minute or two, then came another pause, a chord on the piano, a few more notes revised. He was playing as a solo the duet he would never play with an actual woman's voice.

Suddenly Arnold was seized with a series of dry spasms, followed by a cough that seemed to pull his body out of itself from some point deep in the center. His head and chest heaved forward almost into the open strings of the piano, then collapsed and doubled up over the score. I ran over to fasten the oxygen mask on his face. I stayed for a minute with my hands on his shoulders, righting and steadying the body that was convulsing under my hands.

Joshua had rushed into his bedroom for a syringe and was getting ready to give him a shot. Arnold usually rolled up his sleeve by himself at this point, but this time he didn't move. His breathing had subsided and he let the mask slip down around his neck.

—I can't work with that stuff in my system, Arnold said. It makes undersea noises in my head, like the cries of the humpback whale. Try it and see.

He turned and spoke to me in a low bronchial whisper that Joshua was not supposed to hear.

—Remember the agreement, he said. You are the one who has to help.

Why me? Maybe he saw me as my father's child, maybe because I had burned an enemy stronghold and he saw in me the capacity to destroy. Joshua was pro-life, I suppose, and I was pro-choice. What Arnold wanted was like an abortion, only at the end not the beginning, and a person should also have the right to that. Especially an artist, who would want to create the shape of his life in aesthetic terms. If you thought about it, death might be a kind of a creation, too.

Arnold went back to working on his score. Scattered around the clusters of notes there were red drops bleeding into the paper like the tracery of another unwritten song.

—It has to be right the first time. I don't get to hear it rehearsed.

He spoke with a strangely modulated heaviness, as if he had been given a certain allotment of words or sentences, a daily ration, and once he used them that would be it for speech.

—Of course you're going to hear it in rehearsal, Joshua said. And in performance. We'll call Janet Keeler and she can make the arrangements.

Arnold turned to me. He was wearing the same look he had when I first met him, as if his eyes went right through my head like X-rays and embedded themselves in the wall.

—He's started lying to me, Penguin. It's already begun.

—We're both behind you, I said. We're all going to be there when it gets performed.

It was almost impossible to look Arnold Fratorelli in the face and tell the truth, which was that the drugs were substituting for his wrecked immunity, and if he stopped taking them his body would immediately fail. I knew that when I felt his shoulders shaking under my hands. His flesh had not even seemed to be attached to the bones, and the bones themselves felt as brittle as the hollowed-out white crab claws I would show the twins in the detritus of the high-tide line.

He might not even hear the piece rehearsed, let alone in performance. Which meant he would never hear it with the words. The logistics would be impossible. Would Janet Keeler come to Squid Harbor? Would they rent a hall somewhere on the Cape and bundle Arnold up to hear the rehearsal? Would they try to drive him to Boston? You could tell he neither cared nor needed to hear it. It was done. Richard used to tell me the same thing about his sculpture. When he'd finished something he didn't want to see it ever again.

Sell it, get it out of the studio, begin something else, the way a crustacean sheds its previous shell and travels on.

—It won't be necessary, Arnold said. I know what it sounds like. I just need to know that eventually it will be sung.

—It will. Joshua and I will make the arrangements.

—Good.

He continued to work with the mask on: listening, pausing to breathe a lungful of pure oxygen, penciling in a revision, signaling Joshua to stop and restart the tape.

The next morning I stood on the deck with a cup of coffee. There was a new sound from the bird life around the cottage, not the territorial songs of adult breeders or the hungry, insistent chirping of the young, but the anxious whistles of migrants about to start out. The old birds might remember where they were going, but the new ones would be heading into the Unknown. There was a new silence from Joshua's house, too. No howling dog, no discord. *The Keeper of Sheep* was complete.

The first thing I wanted was for Arnold to play the whole piece for us, if he had the energy. I wanted Bondo to hear it, too. For once Bondo was up earlier than I was and the jeep wasn't in the drive. In a few minutes he showed up.

—I've been to the mailbox, Bondo announced. You have a postcard from Michelle. She's still in Arizona. And something for you from Dartmouth.

The Dartmouth letter was from the Dean of Students.

Dear Miss Solstice, it read. *Over the summer the College Disciplinary Committee reconvened to consider the circumstances of your expulsion. These were reviewed in the light of recent administrative and policy changes at the College and blah blah blah blah blah. We are happy to welcome you back for the fall term.*

—Assholes, I said. They can't even stand by their own position. It was true, though. We would all be readmitted. We could get our old house back. We could finish the castration quilt. I could crawl right back into my life where it left off.

—All right, I said. I have to give it time to sink in. Now I want you to come over and hear Arnold's piece.

Bondo hadn't set foot in Joshua's house since the oxygen tank disaster. I hadn't forced the issue, either. Arnold could no longer deal with more than one person at a time. But just this once it was different. His work was finished. There was something to celebrate.

—I have to get to the Motif, Bondo said. I'm on vegetable prep today and I'm late.

—You have time. This is important. He's completed his work and you have to hear it.

—You can bring the tape over here.

—It's not a tape, Bondo. It's the real thing.

—Penguin, I've got red spots all over my hands.

—Bondo, you asshole. That's poison ivy.

—Listen, I have to get back to the Motif or they're going to fire me. They're already watching me for stealing too much food.

—Then you might as well keep going, I said. Just take your sleeping bag and zip your precious carcass up in it and leave.

—OK, OK. I'll go over to Joshua's and hear the music. I didn't know it was such a big metaphysical thing.

—Forget it, Bondo. It's too late. You don't deserve to listen anyway. Go punch your time clock so your manager doesn't mark you tardy again for work.

Bondo bounced off towards Provincetown in the jeep. I had to get someone else to hear Arnold's score. Joshua and I were not an audience. We were family. There had to be a more objective ear. I ran up the driveway in the cloud of Bondo's dust and headed for the intersection of the Harbor Road.

At that point Rita's Taxi drove up beside me and skidded to a stop in the sand.

—You look like a vagabond, Rita said.

—I need an audience.

—Don't we all? I'm working.

—I'm serious. Is anyone around?

—Jerry Perera's down at the fish wharf.

—I don't think he's exactly the one I need.

—You never know until you try, Rita said. Get in.

Down at the waterfront Jerry Perera's lobster boat was tied up at the float on the end of the swimming pier. Rita dropped me off and I ran down. It looked like there was nobody aboard.

—Jerry! I called.

—What?

He was down in the engine compartment, under the cockpit floor. He slid out backwards, his dragon tattoo writhing around with the effort, his clothes and hands coated with engine oil.

—Crack in the cylinder head, Jerry said.

I had always wondered where he concealed that stuff.

—Listen, Jerry. It doesn't matter what you're doing. You have to drop it and come up to Joshua Brand's. We need an audience. You just have to lend us an ear.

—Take one. They screw right off.

He reached out and handed me a wrench.

—It's no time for fooling around.

—Right. I'm going right up there, dressed like this, and shoot up some of their drugs.

—Come on, I said. A man is dying and he's going to play his last piece of music. Bondo refused.

—Your roommate won't be there? In that case I'll go.

We drove over in the blue truck with the shift knob woman, bouncing so hard on the dirt road that my head nearly banged against the roof. The radio was tuned to WCNT 24-hour country. I switched it off.

—You're going to hear real music, I told him. You've got to get that stuff out of your head.

—Jesus.

—You'll feel right at home, I said. Hey, you're Portuguese. Did you ever hear of Fernando Pessoa?

—I can't stand Portuguese music, Jerry said.

—Not music. Poetry.

—Poetry? My old man wouldn't let poetry in the house. He had this old Portuguese superstition. "Poetry spoils the fish."

Of course Uncle Joshua was appalled when I dragged the Perera boy in instead of cute old familiar Bondo, and Jerry was wiping his hands over his pants and looking for a place where his oilskins wouldn't destroy the upholstery. Arnold waited at the piano. Much to his credit, Joshua got his composure back, found the rain tarp that he used to cover the firewood, and spread it out over one of the white couches so Jerry could sit down. I sat beside him.

Arnold drew himself up in the wheelchair with an aspiring vertical energy I hadn't seen for weeks. He began the piece. There was no singer of course, but I could hear the words of the first poem in my head.

> I'm a keeper of sheep.
> The sheep are my thoughts
> They are my eyes and ears
> My hands and feet
> They are my nose and my mouth . . .

Thin as he looked, pale, sick to the point that his eyes seemed to be the only living element in his face, he played chord after chord, melody and accompaniment at once, as if all of a sudden he had three hands. Cosimo stood up and stared. The early morning fragments I had heard all summer came together. I heard the thrush's clear song amid the dissonance, and I thought of the poet, the keeper of sheep, getting his flock to line up, to organize themselves, to be counted once and for all. Jerry put his hand on the dog's shoulder, leaned back, and closed his eyes. Even if he hated it he was at least being amazingly polite. Joshua leaned forward intently, his head resting in his hands.

This music was different from the metallic synthesized music on the Recombinant tapes. It was softer, more filled with feeling, as though a channel had been cut open between the brain cavity and the heart. It was both warm and uncompromising. It was open and

283

final at the same time. It had both sickness and the sense after sickness that you could break through into another place. Without knowing a thing about music, I more or less understood.

When Arnold finished playing, he made a long, convulsive exhalation as if he had been holding his breath for the whole time. He closed the score and slumped his head forward. Jerry leaped up to go over to him but Joshua stopped him.

—Why the fuck are you sitting around listening to nothing? Jerry yelled. The man's gonna die.

—He'll come around, Joshua said.

Joshua cupped the blue oxygen mask over Arnold's face and he breathed in.

Jerry looked down at his coveralls and patted Cosimo on the head. The dog actually licked his arm. They got on like pals. Then Jerry walked over to the piano bench and shook Arnold's hand. They looked like two different species: Jerry in his sleeveless USMC shirt and his highly developed arm with its tattoo, Arnold pale, masked, sunless, his hair falling out in patches, his hand sticking out of his bathrobe sleeve like a claw.

He must have seen men dying in Vietnam, I thought, he must have taken their hands that way to say good-bye.

When I went next door again I found Bondo actually moving out.

—It's OK, I said. It's over. I found someone else to hear the piece.

—I'm leaving anyway, Bondo said. I'll move in with Robin and Chester in Provincetown.

We were in the process of loading his few worldly possessions into the jeep when I heard the phone ringing inside our house. It was Uncle Joshua. I had to come next door right away.

I went and Arnold was slumped over again. The mask was half red and hanging loose to one side. The music was all over the floor. He had been vomiting blood.

—We have got to get a physician, Joshua said. We can't handle this alone.

—You said we were not going to do that. Remember? Not after he'd finished his work.

Joshua paid no attention to the arrangement. He went right for the phone and called Doctor Ryder, who treated everyone at Squid Harbor and was about eighty years old. I remembered him leaning over my bed when I was a kid, putting the thermometer in my mouth, probing my stomach for the appendix. They had a long conversation.

—He won't come, Joshua said. His secretary says he's sorry. They say he has a previous engagement.

I was trying to rescue the music from the red and beige bodily fluids that had come up from Arnold's chest. I tried always to use the latex gloves for this kind of contact but in this case there wasn't time. Maybe Bondo was right, I said to myself, maybe I have a break in my skin somewhere and the virus will crawl in and in five or six years I will lose weight and die. Maybe I am a natural victim like all women everywhere and this is the form it will take: Virginia Woolf in her trout stream and Sylvia Plath in her oven and me inoculating myself with this.

Meanwhile Joshua was just standing there passively next to Cosimo's inert body and Arnold was holding the mask on with his hand, wheezing into it as if he had a rock lodged in his throat. The music was stained but intact. Thank God, I thought. I could still read the little penciled notes even through the overlay of blood. It was all right if Arnold's physical body passed away. *The Keeper of Sheep* was done.

—What's wrong with Doctor Ryder? I asked. Is he coming or not?

—No. He says try the clinic in Provincetown.

—Joshua, no one's going to be able to get down here. The ruts are a mess. Your Volvo is still blocking the road.

—What about the jeep? Joshua asked.

Bondo would be half an hour getting to his restaurant. We moved the patient into his bed and cleaned him up. Joshua gave him another injection. Arnold was too far out of it to resist. He breathed in and out of the mask as if he were being drowned.

I tried to call Bondo at the Motif. I reached Robin Adler but Bondo hadn't arrived. Back in the bedroom I heard the attack again, the long heaves as the body tried to empty itself of everything that was poisoning it from within.

—Here he comes now, Robin said over the phone. He looks pissed. You sure you want to talk to him?

—Put him on.

—Bondo, I said. You have to help us. You have to get a doctor down here in the jeep.

—I thought you weren't going to do that, Bondo said. I thought after his piece was done . . .

—Joshua's not going through with it, I said. He's the executor. I can't do it by myself. I think it's against the law. It might even be homicide. I'm on probation, don't forget.

Bondo obeyed. In less than an hour the blue jeep churned through the mud holes around the Volvo and deposited the doctor on Joshua's deck. He was surprisingly young, looking no older than Bondo or me, skinny, red-haired and his face was so pockmarked from leftover adolescence that it resembled the surface of the moon. He had a Hawaiian shirt and red jeans and looked as if he'd just come from a beach party. As it turned out he'd been working for three nights and days straight.

He fired some questions at us right away.

—How long has it been since Mr. Fratorelli tested positive?

—Almost a year.

—How long has it been since he's had medical attention?

—Two and a half months.

—I don't know why you called me down if your strategy is to let him die. You have to choose one or the other.

Bondo went back to wait in the jeep. The doctor was alone with Arnold for fifteen minutes. He took a deep, sighlike breath, collapsed into Joshua's Arabian armchair and introduced himself. He was Bruce Stevenson. He had a dozen patients on home care in the Provincetown area and he saw all of them at least once a week.

—He won't survive another attack like that. Either you get him back into the hospital or you're going to lose him.

—And if he goes back?

—Who knows? He has pneumocystic pneumonia. His glands are swollen under the arms and on both sides of the neck. He may have picked up something else over the summer. With care, he could live five weeks or five months. He might live a year. Without . . .

The doctor didn't even complete that sentence, just let his voice trail off to instill his meaning. We walked back to the jeep. Bondo had his feet up on the steering wheel and was listening to the Dead.

—He's made up his mind, I said to the doctor. They've been all through it. He has a living will.

—His friend isn't so sure, Doctor Stevenson said. And he is the one in charge.

The doctor got in the jeep and Bondo drove him off. Back in the house, Arnold was sedated and sound asleep. I walked out with Uncle Joshua on the deck. The sky was a luminous afternoon blue and there wasn't a cloud in it. The yacht with the unknown people aboard was gone. Out on the bay, a fleet of sailboats from the Oquosset club was heeled over and roaring towards some invisible mark. Everywhere else in America it was still the climax of summer, the stock market was at a record high, God was on his throne, and there was finally some kind of relative peace in the world, as if all the wars had gone inside.

—Did you hear that? Joshua said. He might live another year. They might have found something by then. They're testing a vaccination.

Maybe Joshua was right. Maybe we should forget it and keep him alive even as a vegetable, hoping they'd find something, or even if they didn't because Joshua loved him anyway, whether he continued to be himself or not. How could you make a choice for someone like that? As long as they can still think they have to be able to decide that for themselves. But then, how could you even tell if someone had ceased to think? The answers to these questions kept being questions. But then I would look at Arnold and I'd know.

Right over the harbor an osprey hovered above a fish, with her wings beating and her body held absolutely still. Then the wings closed and she dropped into the water and emerged with empty claws. She hovered again and dropped and failed once more.

I had come to love Arnold over the summer, like the older brother I never exactly had. And as I came to know that, in those days of caring and listening, I also accepted that he would be gone. The love and the September sense of loss had grown together, as the same feeling, as if the beginning and end of summer could come at the same time.

We had helped Arnold finish his piece, we had sustained him, and now it was time to set him free. I had planned to assist Uncle Joshua in this, as I had assisted him all along. But if Joshua wavered I would have to do it myself. My whole life seemed like a long preparation for this event: my body marked from birth as Cain's was, my determination shaped by setting a house on fire.

—We made a promise to Arnold, I said. We have to carry it out.

Joshua offered me a rum collins and a cigarette from his little leather purse. We sat and stared out over the water. The osprey was still diving and this time she came up with the fish alive and moving in her claws. That is the way the angel of death would come, as a part of nature, with neither attachment nor mercy. I imagined what it would be like to be the mackerel or herring up there looking down on the pointless human houses and feeling the talons in my side, my gills trying to find oxygen in the unbreathable air.

—I don't know any more, Joshua said. I don't know.

The osprey flew right into the sunset with her prey still thrashing around. You could see the warm light glistening off its scales.

32

Bondo stayed up in Provincetown that night, with Robin and Sleezy in their cozy room. It felt creepy being by myself. I lay there on my back staring straight upwards with the wind threatening to take the house apart, but it was so clear it looked like there was nothing between us and outer space. Over the skylight the stars cruised among thin clouds like schools of luminous fish. Twice, a meteor broke out of its place and tore across the small square of darkness above my head. I could see how primitive people would have thought they are actually falling stars. They just detach themselves out of the heavens and drop, and if you look back where they came from you can see the blank place they left in their constellation. One of these windy nights the stars could come down all at once and leave the sky vacant, the way a blind person sees it, and you would feel totally alone.

Anything could happen in such an unprotected place. Someone could die in their bed and be drawn up through the chimney in a thin column that no one would even see. Even in the warmth of the sleeping bag I felt the individual veins of my body like a map of sinister back roads. And between the veins and arteries there were soft indeterminate places like hills scattered with owls and nocturnal deer. Several times that night I woke and went back to sleep and dreamed of a voice singing dissonant music, then woke up again to find nothing in the whole house but myself.

In the morning Joshua was standing on his porch next to Richard's cube sculpture exactly as I'd seen him on the original night. I walked down to the beach to put my feet in the water and he joined me. Arnold was still sleeping. He'd given him two shots during the night and at dawn one of the new BDT capsules Doctor Stevenson had brought, which were part of an experiment and not even released to the public yet. Of course the government had to wait through about a decade of irrelevant animal tests and homophobic red tape before anything got to the human beings it was supposed to help.

—We don't want anything like that happening again, Joshua said. When the road dries I'll leave you in charge for a morning and go up and arrange for a proper kind of nurse.

—Have you consulted Arnold about that? I asked.

—I don't think Arnold is competent to make that kind of judgment. From now on the decision falls on me. I am the executor. I have to do what is right.

—Remember, we all agreed, I said. He wants it to be over. His work is finished.

—What do you mean, over? We have to fight for his life. And whom do you mean by "we"?

—I'm in it too, I said. Look at him. What is it we're fighting for?

—Love, Joshua said.

—No. He's letting go at his end. We have to learn to let go of ours.

At that point a strange look crept onto Uncle Joshua's face that seemed stern and rigid almost to the point of cruelty.

—I am a better judge of that than you are. You've done an excellent job. Now the situation calls for a professional careperson. You have some salary coming. You and your friend can go somewhere for the rest of the summer.

—I won't be traveling with Bondo, I said.

—I'm sorry to hear that, Joshua said. He strikes me as a very attractive young man.

From then on Joshua didn't want to leave me alone with Arnold for a minute. He called Doctor Stevenson for a list of visiting nurses and the name of a long-distance ambulance service for the trip back to Mass General. "We can't give up hope," he went around saying. "Just yesterday they had a breakthrough in Geneva." Or it would be Paris or Stockholm or Beijing, anywhere they were working on the disease. He'd go into his room in the evening and watch the television news. Brandy in one hand, cigarette in the other, he would sit all the way from Tom Brokaw through MacNeil-Lehrer, hoping one of the anchorpeople would announce a cure.

One evening he pushed the mute button on the TV remote control and turned to me.

—Cucumber root, he said. Cucumber root will bring him back.

It had become impossible to explain to Joshua what he knew was really taking place. Arnold lay drugged and sedated, most of the time now with his face hidden under the mask. Doctor Stevenson came down again and brought our nurse. Those two installed a nasal-gastric feeding system so we could force the liquid nutrients directly into the stomach. The four of us crowded around this completely mummified shape as they taught Joshua and me to find the measuring mark on the long tube and snake it into his nose, down through the esophagus, and beyond. Arnold's muscles would resist in kind of a vomiting action, and we would have to stop. Then, when the vomiting instinct had subsided, we resumed pushing the tube down until it came to the mark. The tube was connected to a red "KANGAROO" pump and the pump was in turn connected to a feeding bottle. When he indicated hunger we were to start the pump and it would channel the food along the tube. If he didn't indicate anything, we were to do it anyway every four hours on the hour. The nutrients were in three bottles on a rack over the pump. They looked like different flavors of Kool-Aid, made not from water but from low-fat milk, like the somewhat slimy rennet pudding they used to feed me as a kid.

—When he improves, Doctor Stevenson said, we can get him back on his own feet again. Don't expect any symphonies, though. There's a tendency for this stuff to fog the mind.

—He doesn't need to compose any more, I said. He's done.

The nurse was from Provincetown. Her name was Ingrid Costa. She had ash brown hair with a green tint to it and a white starchy blouse that contained a down-filled pillowy bosom. Her arms swelled out of the white short sleeves like the trunks of trees, the vaccination marks looking like raw spots where the branches had been ripped off. Maybe I'd been among men too long in that house. I felt repulsed by the physical parts that made her female. Or maybe I was repulsed by the human body, which was constructed with all these entrances for death.

Ingrid would arrive at eight, supervise the patient's care and feeding until five, then scribble a page of instructions so we could get him through the night. She would lift Arnold bodily into the bathroom and close the door, then emerge with him in her arms again, place him in bed and reconnect the tubes. I felt an odd pang of jealousy as I'd watch her do this, as if she had come in and usurped my place.

Back when I was alone with Arnold all those days and nights, he'd told me the history of his life. After Ingrid Costa came into the picture, he never opened his mouth. I could see him trying to complain, trying to signal me, but Joshua made certain we were never alone.

—You ought to go to nursing school, Ingrid told me during one of those silences. You seem so interested in health.

One day around the first of September she stopped me on the way to her car.

—The sick take care of the sick, she said. I think Professor Brand has it, too.

—What makes you so sure?

—I have a dozen of these cases. I can tell.

—And what about you? I asked. Aren't you afraid?

—The Lord gives special protection to the healing professions, Ingrid said.

She then dragged out of her bosom a silver crucifix that must have weighed over a pound.

—This I wear day and night. It lets me go into the valley of the shadow of death without any evil.

She paused.

—You should have something too. I know you are not a believer, but you should wear something because you are in a dangerous place, and you have no protection at all. I'll see what I can find for you on my next trip.

I went over one morning to find Uncle Joshua fully dressed and sound asleep on the couch. I entered Arnold's room. It had a new sanitary hospital smell, which was far worse than the old smell of disease.

—Read something to me, he said in a voice that was new, higher in pitch, and almost supernaturally clear. The one sentence drained his capacity for speech.

I took out the Pessoa book from the small collection of things he kept under his sheet.

—I'll read something, I said. It might help purify the air.

What I chose was the third poem he had set to music.

From the highest window of my house,
With a white handkerchief I bid good-bye
To my poems going off to humanity.

He pulled one of his hands out from under the covers as if it had been lying in there by itself. It held a piece of paper, a note, which I unfolded and read:

HELP ME. THIS IS NOT WHAT I WANT

He had signed it and printed his name under the signature the way a child might sign their first-grade drawing: ARNOLD F. I recognized the paper as having been torn from the margin of his music sheets because it too was marked with droplets of dried blood.

The following day was Tuesday and Ingrid's day off. Joshua had already asked if I'd help out and I had said of course.

I had to do some serious thinking before I began that day. I was to be at Joshua's at eight so I got up extra early in order to launch the canoe and take it up into the marsh. There was a pact or conspiracy between me and Arnold that could not be spoken aloud or thought out together but had to be formed by each of us separately in our own way. By now we were so connected it was like one of those tubes leading from Arnold's nasal cavity was connected on the other end right into my own.

As I paddled across the open water toward the swamp channel I could almost feel Arnold's presence in the bow, weighing it down and stabilizing it against the small morning waves. All summer I had wanted to load Arnold into the canoe and take him up into the marsh, so he could say a kind of good-bye to the natural world. Joshua would never have allowed it because we might have been seen.

Already the high swamp grasses were dying down and the tips of the cranberry leaves had taken on a color of dark autumn fire. Of course there had been no frost yet, so the mosquitoes were still out in force in the early morning calm. I vibrated my face to swish them off and kept paddling to protect my hands.

I felt the strange mechanical drumming of a helicopter, first in the pit of my stomach, then as a direct slapping against my inner ear. It came in from the direction of the highway and like an inflationary insect lowered itself over the marsh. From its belly a mist descended over the far border of trees where the heron rookery was.

I waved my paddle.

—*No*, I shouted. *Don't spray!*

I took the two paddles and made an *X*, but he either didn't see me or was not about to respond.

Row after row the helicopter laid down its grid of insecticide. I stepped immediately on the panic button, leaped over to the other seat of the canoe, and started to snake my way back out through the maze of channels. Two black-crowned night herons croaked desperately past me, which you never see during the day, then a pair of blue herons that actually crashed into each other in flight, plus a whole flock of egrets fleeing the toxic rain. They circled the harbor in confusion, then flew towards the Oquosset shore.

The helicopter was tracing its spray pattern closer and closer to where I was. I looked up and could see the word COMMANDO in neon orange letters on its side. I waved again and shouted. I threw the spare paddle up in the air and it wheeled like a rotor blade into a patch of pampas grass. The machine clattered right over me about fifty feet above my head and I lay on the floor of the canoe and held my breath and buried my face in my hands. I could feel the poison coating my body like hair spray. When I couldn't hold my breath any longer I exhaled and then vacuumed it in. In the complete void of that moment I heard a male voice out of a TV commercial say, *Gee, your hair smells wonderful tonight.*

I managed to unfold myself and find the paddle again and perform enough water-beetle movements to get me out from under the cloud. My eyes started to function again in the clearer air. The helicopter stopped spraying and rose abruptly, then left over the highway. It must have run out of chemicals for the moment. I was dizzy but I could still paddle, and I found my way back into open water. For a while everything I could see was the same color, and the canoe seemed to rotate slowly around the axis of my spine. This is good, I felt myself thinking, great, this is what it's like being an insect. This is the way we die after we've been sprayed.

I remembered the pilot at the Loves' meeting, with the word COMMANDO stitched over the breast pocket of his blazer. I guess he had finally received his orders from P. T.

—You're not going to believe this, I told Joshua when I got back. There's not a soul left in Squid Harbor and they are up there spraying the swamp.

—I heard. Perhaps when they've finished they will come and spray us.

—They already got me, I said. Look.

The chemicals had dried over my hair and clothing into a mesh like a fine layer of cobweb that was impossible to remove. I felt like one of those insects wrapped up and stored by spiders, to be devoured at some future time. I went in and scrubbed the places on my body that I could reach with disinfectant soap.

Arnold seemed to have gained strength from the tube feeding and from Doctor Stevenson's new drug. He had the bed cranked up at a decent angle and when I arrived he asked me to help him into the chair. I wheeled him into the living room and Joshua poured two cups of his thick espresso.

—That's what I'm going to miss, Arnold said. Coffee.

—You'll be drinking it again, Joshua said. Look. You're breathing without the mask.

He was, but after a minute his lungs sounded like they'd been filled with sawdust. I slid the mask gently up over his face.

—I'm going up to Perera's for supplies, Joshua said. You take care of things here. See if you can get some nourishment into him.

His mood varied exactly with Arnold's condition. He was in pretty good spirits. He seemed also to be trusting me again, as if he thought I had also seen the light.

I hadn't. I knew what had to get done.

—I need everything, I told Joshua. English muffins, cheese, tomatoes, granola, and beer.

He added my items to his list. Poor Cosimo went to the door as if he'd be taken on the trip. Joshua reached into the jar of Dog Truffles and fed him a treat. Then he slipped the list into his pocket and left.

I waited till the sound of his Volvo was lost in the lapping of the sea, then I switched on the tape of *The Keeper of Sheep.* Arnold slipped the mask down from his face and let it hang around his neck. He breathed deeply and his breath sounded clear, then started clogging again. I reached for the mask, as I always had, to put it up over his face. His hand just touched the back of my hand with the fingertips and I stopped. He breathed like a man underwater, a man trying to drown by holding himself submerged. His face turned from its usual ash white to an ultramarine blue. I tried to move the mask back into position. Arnold pushed it away from his face, even though he was strangling in the air. His breath stopped altogether. Then he fumbled for the mask again, the hand trying to save the life of the body against its will. I put my hand over his and pushed it down so that the oxygen mask was crushed against his chest. He had no resistance. It was like pulling an infant's fingers away from her mouth. I put both of his hands in his lap and wrapped the satiny edge of the blanket around them. I unfolded the mask the way you would rearrange a flower and I laid it on the desk board over his score. You could hear the oxygen hissing out into the air.

Arnold took a breath that seemed to expire halfway through, jerked his hand out from under the blanket, and reached it out into the room. The hand groped autonomously for the oxygen mask. I took it and pressed it hard against my breast and held on. His respiration came fast and shallow, like the minute terrified breathing of a bird held in your hand.

Then it just stopped. In a moment of complete silence his head and chest slowly collapsed onto the opened score.

Nothing in my life had prepared me for what happened next. His whole body convulsed once and a blast of plum-colored liquid shot out of his mouth. I pulled the score out of the way and put it on the piano. Over in his corner Cosimo started up as if a stranger were at the door. It was the first time I had heard him fully bark.

I turned the volume of the tape deck to its lowest level. This should have happened at night, I thought. But it hadn't. The afternoon was full of late summer color and the harbor light sparkled with whitecaps. Then there was this tremendous racket, like something inhuman coming down out of the sky. The helicopter of the Commando Aerochemical Service made a pass directly over our roof. Instinctively I hit the floor, as if we were being bombed. Then the door blasted open and it was Uncle Joshua. He must have forgotten something, or suspected us, and turned around. He looked at Arnold, turned to me, and shrieked.

— *Bitch!*

He ran over to Arnold while I was in the act of standing up. He picked Arnold's head up and tried to uncrumple the mask, which had slid under his face. Then he put the mask down and grabbed for Arnold's wrist to check his pulse.

—Bitch, he repeated. Fix the mask.

I stood there and did not obey. Joshua straightened the mask out, tried to cup it so it would fit over Arnold's nose and mouth. I faced him directly and seized both of his wrists. He kept repeating the word *bitch,* over and over, which had the effect of making me hold tighter. I am not particularly strong, I'm not an oarsperson or anything like Jennifer, but I felt another strength adding itself to my own, a strength which must have come somehow from Arnold himself.

Joshua spat at my face.

—Bitch.

The liquid felt venomously warm running down my cheek but I held on. I realized Joshua was weak, so weak that he couldn't twist away or resist, and we just faced each other without moving, while behind us Arnold's head slumped back onto his chest.

Suddenly Joshua yelled *Cosimo,* and the Great Dane leaped up barking. This is it, I thought, tear my arms off, this is what you're trained for, but he didn't attack. He just barked and barked while I held firm. After a while Uncle Joshua's body collapsed down onto the floor, so that he knelt there, my hands still clutching his wrists, and his face started to wash itself with tears.

I let go and Joshua didn't move. I went to the phone beside the piano and called Doctor Stevenson.

—I think it's over, I told him. You better come down.

I went and got one of the Dog Truffles out of the jar and gave it to Cosimo. Then I kneeled down beside him and put one arm over his back. In about five minutes I heard a siren up on the highway, then saw the red lights of the ambulance and the blue rotating light of the police.

Doctor Stevenson was the first person to enter the room. He found me with my eyes closed, still kneeling beside the dog.

The door of the big Provincetown ambulance van was open and

its two-way radio was crowded with different voices. Two men with yellow oilskins and masks and yellow plastic gloves handled the body. They spread out a dark-green vinyl-looking sheet like a garbage bag and laid him down on it and one of them did something to his mouth. It looked like an uncomfortable posture with his arms and legs strangely twisted around. I started forward to adjust them and then stopped. He couldn't have been uncomfortable, because he was dead. The tape of his composition was still playing. He had disappeared into his own music and this corpse had simply come around to take his place.

Two attendants were holding Uncle Joshua by the arms. He was crying and trying to pull himself free at the same time. His face was streaked with tears. I could finally see for sure that Joshua's Hollywood tan had been cosmetic and that beneath it the skin of his cheeks was as pale as Arnold's if not worse.

—She killed him, he hissed. The little deformed bitch. She murdered him. She was planning it all along.

Doctor Stevenson pushed me back against the kitchen counter so the two men could pass bearing the stretcher with the dead person on it. Joshua was wiping his cheek with his sleeve and the makeup was coming off in a thick smear. They carried the body in its green shroud past him up towards the ambulance and he followed it for a few steps before the police car showed up and two yellow-gloved Provincetown cops held Uncle Joshua back. I was behind the counter at this point with one foot in Cosimo's water bowl. Doctor Stevenson was standing in front of me, blocking me from Joshua's sight. Joshua went over and lay next to the dog. He put his arm around him and held him as a woman would hold her husband after having a bad dream in the night.

—We will have a few questions for you, the big cop said. When there's more time.

The ambulance had gone and one of the police cars had followed it, with Uncle Joshua riding in the back. I refilled Cosimo's water dish and poured him a substantial amount of food. The big cop and his sidekick had remained. The smaller one took out a small portable tape recorder and a notebook.

—We just want to go over this, the big one said. We want you to start at the beginning and tell us how you came to be here with the deceased.

I started to tell the story but Doctor Stevenson kind of moved in front of me with his own version.

—She did everything anyone could, he said. The man was a terminal AIDS patient and Miss Solstice was helping to care for him. From my preliminary examination and his previous history I can attest that he died of pneumocystic pulmonary congestion and there was nothing that could humanly be done to prevent the death.

Doctor Stevenson went over to the wheelchair and straightened some of the music sheets on the piano. The mask was still crumpled up and hissing on the floor. He shut off the flow of oxygen at the tank and casually straightened the mask, which he then detached from the hose and popped into his leather bag.

—He seems to have damaged his own oxygen mask in a spasm, he said. At any rate he won't be needing it any longer.

—And what relation are you to the deceased, young lady?

—She's the next-door neighbor, Doctor Stevenson explained. You can see her family's cottage right through that window.

—We'll have to know the next of kin, the police chief said. What relation was that other man?

—I don't know what you would call it exactly, I said. I guess you should just put him down as Friend.

33

I woke with an insecticide hangover that burned like a six-inch needle probing the center of my brain. I was alive in my own bed and standing beside me was my aluminum penguin, silent as always, but reliable because he never slept. Richard had taken the night flight from New York to Provincetown as soon as he heard the news. He was still sleeping up in the loft.

Bondo had come back, too. He had driven my father from the airport. They were getting to be great companions, and I think, in some way that kind of scared me, my father even approved of him. Bondo was prostrate and snoring on the couch. The hermit thrush was once again singing its morning flute carol, but there was no point to it anymore. Its heart was not in it. Its territory was an empty concept, a false memory of July. Its children had grown to maturity and set out on their own. And there were no further answers from the piano.

The day before I had assisted in someone's death. Perhaps I had killed him. It was someone who wanted it to happen and wanted me more than anyone else in the world to be present, but that did not change my hand's memory of the crushed mask and the slight shoulders that had finally ceased their aspiration to breathe. I touched my breasts and my stomach and went over the contours of my face to see if anything felt different. I had the same fleshy beak, the same featherless female body. Therefore I was the same person. Nothing had changed at all.

Someone was knocking at the door and I threw on a shirt. It was only eight on the digital clock over the stove and neither of my men had even stirred. The person at the door was Doctor Stevenson.

—I drove Professor Brand home with me last night, he explained. I brought him back and now he's over in the house. Neither of us got any sleep at all.

I covered my naked frailty with Bondo's long black Grateful Dead sweatshirt and walked with the doctor along the access road in the direction of the beach. Everything looked like autumn. The beach plum leaves were brown and dried out and brand-new clumps of purple asters had sprung out of the sand on the shoulder of the road.

—I could have saved him, I said. I could have easily forced the mask back over his face. He could be in there right now playing the piano.

—What would he be playing?

—I don't know, maybe he could have started something new.

—Don't think about it, Doctor Stevenson said. You can't go back. It's over. I signed the certificate giving the cause of death as cystic pneumonia and the secondary cause as AIDS.

—I thought they were going to arrest me again. The way he was accusing me. I wanted to be arrested. I believed everything Joshua was saying. It was the truth.

—It's all right, Miss Solstice. The cops didn't pay any attention. People accuse nurses, doctors, whoever happens to have been there at the end.

—I wasn't just "there," I said. I stopped him. Physically. I held his arms.

Doctor Stevenson halted in his tracks.

—You want to go to a hearing over this? Haven't you already done that this year? That's what Professor Brand told me.

—Was it this year? It seems like another century.

—Once is enough, Stevenson said. Don't say anything more about it. The witness isn't available for questioning.

—What about you? I asked. You're not judging me for it?

302

—You made a decision, Doctor Stevenson said. You acted on it. You carried it through.

—I guess I need forgiveness, I said. Something like that. I have to stop playing that scene over in my head.

—I can't do that for you, Miss Solstice. Nobody can. You'll have to find that in yourself.

It was what Doctor Stevenson must have said to dozens of bereaved persons, male and female. It was a lie. You can't forgive yourself any more than you can lift your feet up with your hands and fly. You could perhaps be forgiven by the one you offended but what if they're dead? I saw the doctor to his little Yugoslavian car.

Uncle Joshua was out on the deck in his maroon robe with the monogram, leaning on Richard's sculpture of the two cubes, as if he couldn't fully stand up on his own. Over the harbor a column of gulls was riding a morning thermal and the white birds stretched upward in a spiral as far as the eye could see. He was studying them like a naturalist looking for an unknown species. I looked up, too. Any one of them could have been a human soul, unaccustomed to its new plumage and trying to shake it free.

I wanted to speak to Joshua but he didn't want to listen. He was the one man who could have said, *It's all right, I forgive you,* but his mouth was sealed shut like the white lips of a clam. I wanted to tell him something, too, that it was the right ending and it had been designed by Arnold just as he had written the ending to *The Keeper of Sheep* and stopped. The word *wake* kept flashing into my mind. In Ireland or Japan they would have had a party, they would have sat around like in that movie *Ikiru* and got drunk on saki and told wonderful stories about Arnold that would help him make his way up through the ionosphere. But America was still an unorganized culture and nothing like that would happen. The word was still true: a wake. Now we could wake up again, we could reopen our lives. And Arnold would also be wakening, when he finished his trip, in a germ-free location where the only substance they have to breathe is light.

Richard and Bondo felt the same way. Bondo had been reading

to Richard from the *Tibetan Book of the Dead* and he said that since Arnold had dealt with all the Wrathful Deities here on Earth he would be going directly to heaven without having to waste time in another life. I didn't believe that stuff, which was invented by male priests to take advantage of the bereaved, but if it made those two feel better about things, it was OK with me.

The three of us picked up a pint of Jim Beam at Perera's and just started driving on Route 6A until we stopped in Eastham at the Crown and Colony Inn. This was a weathered old mansion on a forgotten lane that had been the King's Highway at one time. We splurged on dinner. Richard ordered Medallions of Veal with a white wine sauce and Bondo had Maine Lobster à la Captain Nickerson, who turned out to be the original owner of the house. I had a Blue Crab in its shell. Its eyes made me uncomfortable on their stalks, but I turned it around to face Bondo and was able to approach it all right from the rear.

After we'd eaten, our table got a little morose.

—Sometimes as I get older, I start to believe in God, Richard said, then He does something that shows He isn't in control at all.

The waiter overheard this and came running over as if to defend his faith, but he ended up just refilling our wine. From my point of view I didn't see how God entered into the picture, whether He existed or not. Arnold was dead. Uncle Joshua would never forgive me. I couldn't blame him. It was for Arnold that I acted, not for him.

The memorial service had been scheduled for Tuesday up in Salem. That afternoon old Raimondo Fratorelli, Arnold's father, had appeared out of nowhere in a black suit with these tiny pointed shoes that threatened to sink into the sand. He had already made the arrangements. He was dressed for a funeral. He had probably looked that way ever since his wife Sylvia died: waiting his turn. He'd glanced around Joshua's house and tapped a couple of strings inside the piano. "Rinaldo was a gifted musician," Mr. Fratorelli had said.

So Arnold wasn't his given name. Rinaldo was lovely. No wonder he became a neo-romantic.

Mr. Fratorelli had looked at a page of the score without seeming to notice that it was almost illegible from the blood.

After dinner we retired to the bar. I ordered dessert. Richard and Bondo went for snifters of brandy and a couple of big phallic cigars.

—This may be it, Richard reminded me. This may be your last dinner as an only child.

—Then I'll go to Brussels and live with Fritz and Katherine, I said. It is pointless to expand the population of this country. It has too many diseases. And too many broken homes.

Bondo lifted his snifter and flicked a thumb-shaped glowing ash from his cigar.

—Here's to Mr. Fratorelli, Bondo said. He was a very talented man.

I took Bondo's cigar and plunged the burning end of it right to the bottom of his brandy. The snifter instantly filled with hissing steam.

—You have no right to even pronounce his name, I said. You wouldn't visit him on the last day he was alive.

—Penguin, Richard said. Wait till we get out in the car.

—I'm not a child. Bondo is a complete asshole. He is afraid of his own skin.

The waiter reached over to remove the ruins of the Courvoisier. He came back with three more.

—Compliments of the Crown and Colony, he said. Our sincerest condolences to your family.

I stood outside in the parking lot while those two finished up their meal.

At Uncle Joshua's the lights were out and his Volvo was gone. He had left a note tacked on his door. *Please care for Cosimo,* it read. *I'm driving Raimondo back to Salem.*

They never would have met in Arnold's lifetime. Now they sounded like a couple of old friends.

Back home, we had a nightcap with Richard. Then he climbed the ladder up to the sleeping loft, where only two weeks ago

305

Dorothy had walked in her somnambulistic dreams.

—I'm too old to keep up with you, Richard said. I have to save myself for the children.

I poured the rest of Richard's martini into our glasses. It was half past twelve but I wasn't tired at all.

—I can't go to sleep yet, Bondo said. Let's take the jeep out into the dunes. It's the only reasonable thing to do.

I was still furious with him but I agreed.

We passed Perera's store on Route 6A and I noticed a light shining from the open bulkhead door. At one in the morning Jerry was at work, doing whatever people do in the drug business. I pictured him sorting white powder from large seagoing burlap containers into small envelopes, or counting stacks of brand-new fifty-dollar bills.

We headed right across 6A instead of turning right or left, which brought us in at one of the smaller entrances to the National Seashore. We drove over a sand fence that had been previously leveled by someone else's passage, and Bondo put the jeep into four-wheel drive. In a minute we were in the dunes. Except for the faint glow of lights from Perera's corner, it could have been the Kalahari desert.

The road was obscured by night and the drift of sand. There was nothing but pure sand underneath us, and the jeep slid over and around its contours like a skiff. The radiance of the headlights illuminated the wake churned up around us by the wheels. Finally the engine overheated and we stopped. The radiator ejected from its blowhole a column of ultraviolet steam.

The moon and stars were invisible. A low cloud cover reflected the highway lights. The sand surrounded us with its cool nuclear glow: sand under the wheels, sand mountains on every side, the low sand-colored clouds. Bondo put on *Songs of Liquid Days*.

I leaned across the gearshift levers and tried kissing Bondo on the mouth. He tasted decadent, like our dinner at the Crown and Colony, an afterimage of shellfish and brandy and cigars. The memory made me angry and I stopped. The ambience of death was still too close. I thought of Arnold's last minutes and I couldn't get his face out of my mind, the mouth trying to breathe and my own hand holding the mask away, responding not to natural bodily sympathy but to the voicelike demands of the will, like holding someone's face underwater until they drowned. I tried to bury that image in the pungent sweetness of Bondo's face but it kept returning. I chewed his tongue. It didn't matter who he was. I was a cannibal dining on human flesh. Bondo was kissing the evil markings on my neck and shoulder as if to say he accepted them, they were forgiven; like death, they were a natural event.

But they weren't.

—You can't kiss that away, I told him. It's there for keeps.

Somewhere, still close, the door Arnold had passed through remained open. A wind from that door blew over the sand hills and over the jeep and I sheltered myself from it against Bondo's chest. That wasn't enough. The wind still blew against my unprotected back. I had to be wrapped completely in the skin of another person. It was a nonpersonal desire, cold as the night sand. It didn't matter in the least whose skin it was.

I dragged Bondo on top of me so I'd be covered. I was so used to handling someone with hollow bones that he felt heavy, as if he had an invisible second body stuffed inside him.

—If people can die, I said, we can at least do this.

I lay underneath him in the reclining seat like a patient waiting for her operation. I wanted to be asleep or drunk or anesthetized but I was wide-awake. I was partially a woman having her first lover and partially someone standing apart and watching, a voyeur, if you can be a voyeur of your own self. The Philip Glass tape ran out. A memory of Arnold's discordant music played in my ears.

Love is eternal innocence, one of his songs said.

I wasn't innocent but I was hoping someday to get there. I didn't love Bondo, either, but there was no one around to know that, so it was for him that I unfastened my sweater and blouse. My light cotton skirt with the purple irises on it offered no resistance whatsoever. Meanwhile Bondo was doing something irrelevant in the

faint light. He was unwrapping a candy bar or pulling the cellophane wrapper from a cigar. No. He was opening the foil package of
the Golden Sun condom he had pulled out of the fishbowl in
Provincetown and he was putting it on.

—Jesus, Bondo, I said. You're not actually going to wear that. I
mean, shit, this is the first time.

—This will take just a minute, Penguin. We won't regret it.
You'll thank me for it in the morning.

After it all happened pretty much as it had been described in lit-
erature and Bondo had cried out like someone being strangled and
then stopped moving, he fell asleep. For a second I feared Bondo
had died too but I felt him breathing. I buried my hands in his hair
and prayed for Arnold but it was ridiculous, praying for one man
with another one on top of you, so I slid out from under him and
stood up in the sand beside the jeep.

The moon was breaking through oyster-colored clouds and I
could look back and see Bondo sleeping in the seat where we had
just made love. The sand had already drifted around the wheels,
making the jeep look like it had been there for a week. Arnold was
already lost in space, back there somewhere on the path of our orbit
where we had been yesterday afternoon. We were continuing on at
over six thousand miles an hour, but he had stopped. I knew it
would be cold and dark for him but there would also be the pure
intergalactic silence that he loved. Arnold considered silence to be a
form of music. He used to stop me and make me listen when nothing whatsoever was going on.

I thought: Arnold, I've done the one thing I could to try and
catch up with you, but it didn't work. I am still around.

I felt clammy and somewhat violated inside. Unknown substances were oozing down the upper part of my leg. That wasn't
supposed to happen. The thing Bondo had used to protect himself
from me was lying on the dashboard like a freshly dissected eel. I
picked it up. It had substantial openings at both ends, and all this
Ivory Liquid was drooling out. The Golden Sun must have burst
from the huge pressure of Bondo's love.

I did what I could to clean myself up. The sand felt cool and innocent under my feet, so I walked. I walked away from the jeep and my sleeping lover and towards the road, which was still glowing with the light from Perera's store. Overhead, night-migrating song-birds were calling to their mates across the dark. *I'm still up here*, they were saying, *how about you?* Back in the National Seashore I could hear the surf crashing on the shore. All around there were strangely familiar sounds.

My feet followed the track we had made coming in. I just let them control me, and they found the way. I got to the Seashore road, then it was easy to hike back up to the store.

I couldn't see whether the cellar door was still open, so I crossed 6A onto Perera's parking area. Compared to the sand, the pavement was still warm from the day's sun. The two gas pumps scrutinized me as I crossed in front of the store. I thought of the punch line to this Martian joke some boy had told me back at Morrelsex:

Just a couple of guys standing around with their dicks in their ears.

Prick up your ears. That one too had taken a week before I got it.

The gravel felt sharp and unnatural underfoot. I stood in front of the open bulkhead and looked down. Jerry was awake in his office reading a magazine with a grizzly bear on the cover that stood on its hind legs while somebody blasted at it with an AK-47. His feet were up on the desk. He had on brown, military-looking socks. The radio was playing some quiet blues. No bags of cocaine, no money any-where in sight.

—I saw your light on, I said.

—That's what it's for, he said. A lighthouse for lost ships. Especially if they have interesting cargo. So come on down.

A white cat with patches of raw bare skin jumped out from under Jerry's desk and ran out past me into the night. Jerry folded the book on his lap and I went downstairs. My leg felt like a skin graft where all that liquid had congealed.

—I was thinking of Arnold, I said. I couldn't sleep.

—I don't sleep either, Jerry said. I haven't slept since 1971. Welcome to the club.

I shivered. Jerry took the buffalo-coated bedspread off the couch and wrapped it around me as if I had walked out of the snow. He kissed me on the forehead like an older brother, then followed with a hard incestuous kiss on the mouth that made our teeth scrape. I wondered if he could taste Bondo, but he kept our mouths together for a long time, so I guess if he tasted anyone he thought it was me. He sat me down on the couch, still shivering and still wrapped in the spread.

—I thought you might come around tonight, Jerry said.

—I came because somebody is dead and I can't find him. I came to ask why you didn't speak to me when you were out on that yacht.

—Yacht? Jerry Perera said. What yacht?

He stood behind me and pulled the buffalo robe off. He pulled down my blouse, which was half-unbuttoned already and slid easily down. He ran his hand over the purple shape on my back and traced the outline of it with his finger.

—It's perfect, he said.

—You're the first person who ever got to touch it.

—Shit, Penny, that makes you beautiful. It's a natural tattoo. I've paid good money to have those things put on.

He turned the light off and I moved over to make room for him on the couch. The cellar bulkhead was still open and I could see a handful of stars between two clouds. He's finally resting, I thought. His work is done. The open door, the one Arnold had gone through, was beginning to swing shut. I took the rest of my clothes off under the buffalo robe and relaxed. I was tired. But the three bodies in my life had at least for the moment become one.

34

I dreamed about spiders, which had taken over the rooms of my house because I wasn't there to defend it. Sometime in the night Jerry must have left the cellar because he wasn't around when I woke up. The survival mag was still on the desk where his feet were resting when I came in. The bulkhead door was closed. I guess he didn't want his extended family to see me when they opened the store.

Already there were sounds of people upstairs walking around, getting the meats out of the freezer, cranking the awning into position. I slipped back into my one and only skirt, which I had slept under as a blanket. I peered out and then opened the door. The sun was already hot and blinding, like a nuclear furnace, which I suppose it is. After my eyes adjusted I snuck around back of the store where the trucks are kept and followed the dunes road back towards the jeep.

Bondo was just stirring around in his seat. I shouted "Hey, Bondo," and kept walking. After three serious sand dunes, I approached the beach.

NO PHOTOGRAPHY

RESTRICTED AREA

NUDE BATHING ALLOWED

Even though it couldn't have been much after seven, there were two extended families of nudists there already. The naked parents and grandparents had set up a card table and were starting a game of bridge. The men had thick white fur on their chests like servings of angel-hair linguini. The women had large pendulous breasts that interfered with the game. It was probably a good idea, I thought, for God to have made people wear clothing right from the start. But the little bare children were lovely. They were playing some kind of nudist tag with two beach balls, trying to knock each other off their feet. The whole crowd seemed as happy as a herd of seals. Only their cocker spaniel moped off to one side, obviously uncomfortable in that company, looking as though he wanted to be shorn.

I went right to the waterline and took off all my clothes. For the first time, amidst the nudists, my purple-and-white coloration made sense. It was not a hideous deformation but just one of the accidents that happen in the change from a conception to a reality. I was not a hermit crab inhabiting a foreign shell but a woman wearing a body that seemed to fit. I stood for a long time feeling the sun warm my dark patch like a forgotten garden. Then I went in.

I floated around weightless the way they do in the space capsules, rising and falling with the waves, my legs dangling down, opening and closing like jellyfish tentacles under the surface. A fish coming between them could have been instantly stung to death.

The day before I had been a virgin, one of the very last. Now I had two lovers, one more or less a child and one very definitively a man. The fluids from both of them were probably mixing together with the sea. Bondo's condom had broken and Jerry hadn't performed any birth control routines at all. Neither had I. I'm not even sure I knew any. I remembered some disgusting practices from Sex Education, which were like life-saving techniques. You could pass an exam on them, but in an actual emergency they wouldn't do you that much good. Of course I had gotten an A in that class.

I had tried to use Bondo to fill the vacancy left in the world by Arnold Fratorelli, but it only grew worse. The night sky over the sand dunes had seemed like one vast human cavity as I walked away from the jeep. I had to put Jerry in there, too, a member of the enemy, before I could let go of Arnold and finally sleep.

I could just imagine myself pregnant. I could see taking the baby home to West Fourth and raising it alongside Dorothy's, waiting to see whether it turned out plain or Portuguese. I would be Dorothy's baby's sister and she would be my baby's grandmother. Dorothy's baby would be my baby's aunt. They'd grow up hating each other like a pair of twins.

Back on the beach, a Land Rover had arrived and let out some more nudists. They were unfolding aluminum chairs and reading the *Boston Globe*. I carried the ball of my clothes right through the center of them and they didn't even lift up their eyes. They were like polished copper skillets, while I was half carbon paper and the other half papier-maché. Nudists are wonderful. They have seen the human body in its beauty and its deformity, and they have learned to forgive it for both. I had read *Paradise Lost* in the original language, but there were some things Milton forgot to include. Adam and Eve must have had wicked suntans with not even bathing suit marks, but what about the angels that visited them from heaven where they are eternally wrapped up in robes? Angels are of course perfect physical specimens, but they also must have been as white as ghosts.

I was a ghost. I was a black-and-white angel fallen into a nest of human beings.

I felt funny dressing in front of that group, so I walked over a sand dune to put on my clothes. I hiked to the top of the next dune and looked around. Bondo was nowhere in sight. I couldn't see the jeep or the tire tracks.

I shouted BONDO at the top of my lungs.

Why should he have heard me? I couldn't even be faithful for one night.

I would go back to the nude beach until he found me. I tried retracing my steps over the sand dune, but they had all filled in. I went over another hill and looked down but there was no beach, just another dune, and beyond that more dunes in every direction. I was lost. Arnold Fratorelli might have been dead, but at least he knew where he was. I sat down in the sand like a child and prepared to starve. I was only a little ways behind him. Perhaps, if I moved fast enough, I could catch up. The black-backed gulls could have my body. The small clam-boring sandworms could have my bones.

There was a sound off to the right like someone blowing a ram's horn. More weird activity from the nudists, I thought, but it could lead me to the beach. I got up and followed. It sounded again. I ran over a hill and looked for the sea, only it was Bondo, stuck in the valley between two dunes and leaning on the horn button of the jeep.

He was stuck hard. He took the anchor as far as the cable would allow, buried it in the sand and winched forward. Then I carried the anchor another cable length and he winched forward again.

—This is how the mammoths pulled each other out of the tar pits, Bondo said. In their last days.

It was true. Every time the jeep stopped the wind would blow new sand around the tires. If we had left it for a day it would have been extinct. I remembered Richard telling me how a beached schooner had been swallowed by the sand. The ship lay inside there for a hundred years, then during a windstorm it had emerged in perfect condition, ready to be sailed away.

Finally we worked the jeep onto solider ground. There was sand throughout the vehicle and every object inside it, making the whole thing look partially digested. When we started it up, the transmission made this hideous grinding noise.

—The jeep from hell, Bondo said.

—I want to drive. Just show me how to work these levers.

I drove us up to Perera's along my own trail of footprints from last night. I stopped in front of the pumps. The bulkhead door was open and the same B. B. King tape was playing down in the cellar.

If you want to keep on flying
Don't look back.

It made me think of the burning cities in the Bible, and my father warning me of the woman who turned herself into a pillar of salt. I thought: keep flying, Penguin, there's more room up ahead than there is behind.

Bondo pumped gas from the self-serve island and I went in to get some beer. All the Perera women had their shorts on and I felt weird in the semiformal attire left over from our night at the Crown and Colony. Jerry came up from downstairs, which I had hoped for, and when he had organized himself behind the counter I asked for a six-pack.

—We carry a number of different brands, Jerry said. Which would you like?

—Molson, I said. We're heading for Canada.

—You might want your sweater up there. It gets quite cold.

I saw one of the Perera girls poke the other in the ribs. Jerry went downstairs and came up with the sweater, folding it deftly as he came up. He put it on top of the Molsons and pushed my money away.

—You've been awarded one of our revolving accounts, Jerry said.

By that time the Perera girls openly stared. I looked back at Bondo in the jeep, but there he was, innocent as always, trying to screw the radio antenna back into the fender with not the least trace of suspicion on his face.

I took one of Jerry's charge slips and wrote down our phone number at 36 Chestnut. He turned it upside down and gave it a cross-eyed look.

—I'm illiterate, he said. What good is this going to do me?

I hoisted myself up beside Bondo in the jeep. The late-morning traffic was thickening on the mid-Cape; everybody heading home after the weekend. I wanted nothing more in the world than to be part of that human flow.

35

Fly bird, fly away; teach me to disappear!
                                    —Fernando Pessoa

We went back to say good-bye to Richard and get our things. We could take two days getting up to Hanover and still be there in time for registration. When we got back to the cottage, though, Richard had already left. *Had to go home,* the note said. *See you in Salem. You'll have to close the house yourselves.*

Salem. The funeral. Joshua and Raimondo were going to try to get Janet Keeler to sing *The Keeper of Sheep*. It would be outstanding, voice and piano conversing in that quiet place. But I wasn't going. If you're the one who did it, then you don't get to attend.

I'd closed the cottage down with my father a dozen times. I could certainly do it myself with Bondo's help. We shut off the water supply and took the glass fuses out of the electrical box. I stripped the beds and folded the sheets in the cupboards between Dorothy's studio and the kitchen. I stood on the ladder and unhooked the Calder mobile from its wire and packed the red and black ovoids individually in newspaper, then wrapped the small, skeletal Giacometti in a square of foam. I stored them both in the deep locking drawer under the record cabinet.

The wildlife had already grown brazen. A gull sat on Joshua's chimney grooming its feathers. A blue heron stood right outside our house. They were waiting for the humans to migrate so their season of dominance could begin.

One day, I thought, we really would be gone. Our picture

windows would be cracked from the winter storms and our roofs would have caved in. The greenhouse effect would cause ice-blue glacial water to rise over the floorboards. Blue crabs and sea anemones would cling to the kitchen chairs. Egrets would reside on the chimney tops like the storks of Holland. An osprey would construct its nest on the diving board at the end of the club pier. Even the Varnums' white stucco estate would break into fragments. It would become a tenement for foxes and a habitation for pale snowy owls.

But not yet. We were still in the competition, and we had to fortify the house. We drained the sink fixtures and emptied a can of antifreeze into the toilet. We unplugged the appliances so they wouldn't be destroyed by lightning. We left a bottle of Wild Turkey on the deck for the local hunters who would be down in a month to shoot sea ducks. In the spring there would be green shotgun shells under the deck boards, but there would also be no vandalism, no arson, and no broken windows. The Wild Turkey was a form of mafia protection, or a small sacrifice to the gods of the locale.

I went into my room alone and stood a moment with one hand on the shoulder of my aluminum penguin. I took a bedsheet and wrapped it around its body three or four times and pinned the end. One of the wings still stuck out so I unwrapped and redid the whole thing until it looked like a mummy, and no one could tell that anything living or valuable was inside. A penguin would not mind the winter. That was their specialty. I closed the door and left it for another year.

Bondo was already revving up the jeep. I started over to Joshua's just to check things out. Amazingly, a woman jogged past the driveway up on the Harbor Road. It was Pura Batrachian.

—Pura! I called.

She stopped and walked back. She was sweating under her headband and had a ripped undershirt on that said NINTH AVE 6K OPEN. She was the picture of New York health.

—I thought you were gone, I said. I thought everyone was gone.

—I'm doing the story. I just came back to check the facts. Maybe you can help me.

—It's not a story, I said. It happened. Someone is dead.

—Of course it happened. That's why we're telling it. We're a newspaper. We are committed to the truth.

I turned back towards Joshua's house without even saying good-bye.

It was early evening by then and the sky was darkening towards purple over the marsh. In the other direction there were already stars coming out over the bay. One was a big bright one like a planet and the others looked like part of Orion, which always signified the coming of fall.

It was kind of an uncanny moment, like an eclipse, as if day and night were happening at the same time. I walked up on Uncle Joshua's deck and stood next to Richard's sculpture of the double cubes. I saw what they were now and why he had called them *Chance*. They were the height of a man standing, but they were in fact a pair of dice, same as the ones hanging off the mirror in Jerry's truck, touching each other like an hourglass at just one point. I heard Arnold's voice in my mind saying "*alea*, the Latin word for dice. Die." You could have thrown them in the air with your hand full of desire but they'd come back down in a pattern of dots as random as the affiliations of the stars. No matter what number the dots said it would add up to the truth, not the truth Pura was talking about in the *Voice*, but the way things are in the actual world before you alter them by saying what they mean. The space between how we want things to be and how they are has exactly the human shape in which we live.

Even with the tube threading his nose, even in his blue oxygen mask, Arnold had committed himself to live in that space and had kept filling it with music until he died. Then he became an object and they put him in the evergreen-colored bag. The stars were objects, too, because no one lived on them and they were thrown randomly over the sky like hundreds of black dice. It took the whole weight of our human desire to shape them into swans and scorpions and the remote solitary hunter with his dog.

I was just going to peek in the window to see that everything was

318

OK. Then I remembered I was supposed to feed Cosimo. The shades were drawn and it was too dark to see inside, so I felt for the key over Joshua's door and went in. I waited for my eyes to adjust to the dim light. There was the piano, the priceless carpet with the stag-hunting motif, the philosophers climbing their two mountains of jade. There was also a wheelchair with a yellow oxygen bottle and the Persian blanket in which Arnold had spent his last month. I tripped on something and almost knocked over one of the Chinese statues. But there was no dog lying on its mat, and, when I whistled, nothing the size of a horse came leaping out. Joshua hadn't come back to get him and no one had been in. I flipped the light switch but the power had been turned off. I found Joshua's silver table lighter and used it to look around.

On the glass-topped coffee table there was a note:

I came to remove the nutrients and the pump. I am so sorry about the dog. It got by me so fast there wasn't anything I could do.
Ingrid N. Costa, R.N.

On top of the note she'd left a green metal crucifix on a string. Tiny as it was, if you squinted you could make out the nail holes in its hands and feet plus a painful-looking wound across the stomach that had the appearance of a cesarean section. I slipped it over my neck but it felt snug. I could imagine the cord shortening and strangling me as I slept. I put it back. It was too late anyway to be of any use.

I thought of Cosimo running in the night. Maybe he'd found his way to the beach and was making up for lost time. Maybe he'd found a female, though I always suspected he was fixed. Maybe he didn't know he had been fixed. Maybe he was trailing Joshua the way dogs do, nose to the ground, working his way towards Boston. I didn't know if they could keep the scent over a bridge.

I felt sorry for Cosimo. He was too large and fierce-looking to be loved. He had been close to Arnold for a whole summer. His long, liver-colored tongue had licked everything in the house. He too could be sick. He could be transporting the virus into the canine world.

I felt sorry for Uncle Joshua. We had deserted him, Richard and I, and even Cosimo. Arnold, in a sense, had betrayed him too.

I thought about it as we turned onto the mid-Cape highway and headed west. I could have reshaped the oxygen mask and put it back over Arnold's face. He would have resisted for a second maybe, then relaxed and breathed. Even that half-dead body had its own instinct to survive. Time would be very different in that case. Arnold would be in his slanted bed, gathering strength for the trip back to the hospital. Ingrid Costa would be bending her archetypal bosom over his thin chest like the Venus of Willendorf, drawing the feeding tube out through his nose. She would have been replacing it with another, hooking it to the pump, sponging his scab-covered hands and feet.

That picture was from a universe that did not exist. If Arnold had been alive, Bondo and I would have had to be dead. All the people in all the cars circling the rotary with us on Route 6 would have had to vanish out of their clothes. The weight of the world's being was too much. He couldn't stop it. Its thoughtless dance went on revolving without him.

At the peak of the Bourne Bridge over the Canal, we passed a Greyhound bus going the other way. Its windows were lighted and I could see a young woman in one of the window seats who was heading almost to the end of the Cape and who was politically active but didn't know the first thing about sex or death. I might have warned her, but already she was too far off.

We stopped at a turnout after we passed Plymouth and I took the wheel. I had never driven on a freeway before and it was exhilarating to go sixty miles an hour through the darkness in that open jeep. I had it floored. If it had been able to move any faster, I would have. I would have passed everything on the road.

We stopped at a shopping center when we got down to a quarter of a tank. We were somewhere in Massachusetts, heading north. We went into the Walden Twelve Cinema Complex to see *Platoon*. I thought of Jerry Perera shooting civilian families in Vietnam and wondered if that was what kept him up all night reading his hunting magazines. I squeezed Bondo's arm with my fingernails until they struck bone.

We got a bucket of caramel popcorn on the way out.

—That was a dorky picture, Bondo said. The good sergeant and the bad sergeant and the innocent young private. Wars aren't so simple. Especially that one.

—How would you know? I said. You would have dodged the draft. You would have gone to Canada and sat it out.

Bondo couldn't answer. He would have. He knew it. And I would have, too, if I had been a man, because neither of us were anything like heroes. Jerry had volunteered. He was on the wrong side in the Vietnam War, but at least he had believed in something and acted on it. Jerry and I had killed people because of a belief. Bondo never would. Walking ahead of me in the empty parking lot in his plaid shorts, the caramel popcorn in his hand, he looked about eleven years old. I didn't exactly know much at that point about love, but I knew it wouldn't be with someone who was still a child.

We drove north on the back roads until after midnight. We were in New Hampshire or Vermont or even Maine. There were serious mountains casting their shadows at us and the shapes of evergreens on both sides of the road. The Molsons we'd picked up at Jerry's had run out. Bondo used his phony ID and got two quart bottles at a store that had deer heads sticking out of the wall. It was about to close. The man behind the counter had six fingers on his right hand.

—I saw them, I said to Bondo. There were six.

—I wasn't keeping count of the man's fingers, Penguin darling. I was there for the purpose of buying beer.

We found a campground in a stand of virgin forest with sites pleasantly concealed among the trees. Bondo put on an Indigo Girls tape, but it sounded unnatural, so we talked and listened and tried to identify the sounds of the night. The wind in the high branches was something you never hear on the Cape because there aren't that many trees and the ones there are all gnarly and deformed from having to live in sand.

I continued the story of Arnold's life in explicit detail.

—I thought you said he was getting senile at the end, Bondo remarked. How did you get him to tell you all that information about his life?

—He would have these amazing moments. He would ramble a while, then grow silent, then it would start to pour out. I have sixty pages of solid notes. It was the same way when he was composing. And the amazing thing is, he knew when his mind wasn't right, and he'd have me scratch those parts out when he got lucid again. He didn't want us to write down anything but the truth.

Bondo was trying to figure out how the down bags zipped together so we could both sleep in the same reclining seat. He got the prong of one zipper into the socket of the other, but it placed the bags head to foot. That was all right with me. Bondo assumed from what had happened that things would continue between us, but I had a different history of last night than he did. Of course I knew I was lying to him, but I was relearning what I knew already, that lying is a kind of freedom, that a person has the right to be the only one knowing the full history of her life. This knowledge freed me from both Bondo and Jerry, too. And in having helped Arnold escape from his body, I was perhaps freest of all. A part of myself had gone with him, and that part was now in orbit, beyond whatever could happen here on Earth.

We had given up on the bag conjunction and were about to sleep in the two seats of the jeep when the forest silence was split with this tremendous roar. It was a gang of four motorcycles that parked in the next site. We couldn't see them exactly, but the voices were all male.

—We need a fire, one of the voices said.

—There ain't anything to burn.

We heard them pulling small limbs off the trees and then jumping up to hang from the larger ones and bounce up and down to crack them off.

—I need a joint bad, one of them said.

—You can have mine. I got it sticking right out in the air.

When they got the fire going, we could make them out. They

had vests over their bare bellies and full beards plus earrings and nose rings that glittered as they moved in the firelight. They put one of the picnic benches on the fire and it blazed right up.

—Creosote, one of them said. It fucking burns.

They put the other picnic bench on the fire and the night was like day.

—There's a jeep over there, one of them said.

—So what? You ever fuck a jeep?

—Ollie fucked a sheep once. I was there.

—You bet your ass you were there. It wasn't no sheep either. It was you.

—Up your ass.

—Up yours.

The bikers put a country tape on and started to dance. It was Dolly Parton or somebody singing a slow, mournful waltz about a blue motel. There were four male couples holding each other in the orange wood fire glow, like teenagers at the last dance of a prom, their beards on each other's shoulders, hands around the waists, bellies pressed tight into a single drum. They danced through the Dolly Parton and a whole Waylon Jennings album until the fire was so low we couldn't see.

If Jerry Perera had been there instead of Bondo, we would all have become friends. He would have compared tattoos with them and admired their rigs. With Bondo, I was still a prisoner of my class. I felt scared, restless, and angry as I tried to sleep. I thought of Arnold. Before too long they'd be gathering up in Salem for the ceremony. Arnold would be there in a hermetically sealed casket, thinking of nothing at all. His mind would be like a TV set with the power turned off, or the night sky without any stars. I have tried many times to think of nothing, but I have always failed. You get the mind down to one item and you try to remove that and meanwhile something else has crept back in. The dead have succeeded in emptying their minds, which is why we can never know precisely where they are.

Old Mr. Fratorelli would have been at the site for hours, tuning the piano down to the last tenth of a vibration. Uncle Joshua would have been with him, impeccable in black, arranging the chairs and flowers. They would be trying to give some visual elegance to the lobby of the funeral parlor, because they probably don't let you bury AIDS victims in the Catholic church. Janet Keeler would be riding up from Boston on the commuter train with her accompanist. The two of them would be frantically poring over the bloodstained score.

Already that segment of my life was receding. Arnold had left the Earth three days before, and we'd come four and a half million miles since that time. That was all I remembered from the Sun and Planets course in the fall term of my freshman year. The Earth travels a million and a half miles a day and it does not slow down or stop for any individual person. So when someone steps off, you do leave them rapidly behind. I pictured him floating in a place where there are no colors at all, free from the blue mask and the yellow oxygen tank and the red gastric food pump forcing nutrients around the back of his nose. Those tubes had linked him to a physical world that had betrayed him to the extreme. He would be much better off without them.

As I imagined Arnold happy, I also felt free and disconnected, like someone who could breathe freely again after a long constriction. The night sky over the treetops had an intense, ink-blue pigmentation that made me think of gathering food and provisions into a protected place. I could already feel over the open top of the jeep a dry, clarifying wind. It was a wind out of the future, a wind from the direction of autumn.

I thought of Jerry Perera, too, who would be down in his cellar probably, sleepless, studying a *Soldier of Fortune* mag or looking up through his bulkhead at the stars. That was OK. I could forgive him. I was kind of a student of fortune myself.

Bondo was snoring. Even the motorcycle men had quieted down.

We woke up to find all eight of them sleeping right on the bare ground of their site. It was almost noon. Their arms were around each other and they were fully dressed. The rivets on the backs of their jackets spelled out PARADISE ISLAND CC. Wherever *that* was. We tried not to wake them as we pulled out.

We appeared to be in the Franconia section of the White Mountain National Forest and we found our way back to Route 2. The cars around us mostly had "Live Free or Die" license plates, which made me feel immediately at home. We headed west on 2 through East Jefferson and cut down on State Highway 117, which bypasses Littleton and follows the river down through Franconia and Sugar Hill. We went through the villages of Bath and Woodsville and reached Route 10 at Piermont. There was a Clock Museum just before you come into Piermont, but it was closed.

—Too bad, Bondo said. Some of those old clocks are awesome.

We got a box of Poptarts for brunch and a Tab. The road fed into the Interstate at that point, and we couldn't escape it. We went north instead of south, however, just to keep rolling, and nearly reached the Canadian border before we turned around. We got to Hanover just as the sun was setting beyond the Connecticut River in Vermont.

Jennifer and Rebecca and Michelle had been readmitted in the same way and had been in Hanover for weeks. They had already laid out an issue of the *Id*. They were planning to rush all-male fraternities in the fall and develop sex-discrimination cases that would go all the way to the Supreme Court. The Merrill Lynch lawyer had even told them he would help them out for nothing. They grabbed me and Bondo when we arrived and crushed us alive like Boa constrictors. I had forgotten how physically strong Jennifer was.

—We'll finish the quilt, Michelle said. And you can be Associate Editor of the *Id*.

—This is where you can stay, Jennifer said.

She showed me this microcloset where we used to keep all the skis. They had fixed it up with crêpe stringers and had squeezed a foam mattress onto the floor.

—They raised the rent on us, Rebecca explained. So Michelle's going to move in, and you and Bondo can live here, too. We can split it five ways.

—Becky and I will be upstairs and Michelle gets her own room because she is the Editor and she needs to think.

I lay beside Bondo in the little closet and, amazingly, I felt like making love. It was a new discovery that hadn't quite worked yet and I wanted to try again. I nudged him, but he seemed to be asleep.

There was a bicycle with no wheels hanging from the ceiling above us next to the light. It looked like the skeleton of something that had fallen into a South American river and been eaten by piranhas down to the bone. It would be a tremendous labor to reconstruct a living creature again from that yellow frame. Maybe if you put someone in a bath of acid you could dissolve their infirmity and their disease. Maybe a sculptor working from the armature of bones could give them life. I could register for my classes in the morning. I needed Beowulf and the Romantics plus Four Female Philosophers for the Women's Studies Concentration. Next week I could invade a segregated frat house and become an Amendment to the Constitution. I could sit down to a liter of margaritas with Rebecca and Jennifer and sew the finishing touches on the quilt.

CASTRATE THE CAPITALIST PATRIARCHY

I could sew a little sheep into one corner to represent the summer at Squid Harbor and Arnold Fratorelli, who would no longer have to be castrated because he was dead.

I found the ball of my clothing and unfurled it and slipped it on. I knelt over Bondo and kissed him once on each eye and once in the furry mammalian patch just below the navel. I tiptoed past Jenny and Rebecca, who had passed out in their chairs, and retrieved from our pile the one bag of things I would need. I went out through the back door and down the alley behind the Scorpion Secret Society and into the night.

I walked over to check out the Beta Sig house, which I hadn't seen since we attempted to burn it down. There it was, in perfect condition, the back porch newly rebuilt and painted where the fire had managed to do some damage before it got contained. I stood in front of the Beta Sig house for a while. I guess I was waiting for something to happen, some signs of life. Finally a light went on. One of the brothers got up, put on a shirt, shut the light off again. I felt like a Peeping Tom. The light then went on in a small upstairs room that must have been a bathroom. Then it went on downstairs. I got closer so I could see inside: a guy was in there lifting weights. He had his back up against a slanted board that had the same angle as Arnold's reclining bed. The guy's face got purple as he pressed the bar up and the veins of his neck stood out. He would rest the bar on its holder, then lift again. Finally his light went out.

The sky was just starting to brighten over the roofs of the white classroom buildings on the row. It formed a series of purple and roseate bands that, like a Mark Rothko painting, seemed to glow from within. The clock on the library tower said quarter past four. I crossed the green towards the Hanover Inn, where the 6 A.M. Greyhound would stop and I would get on. *Vermont Transit.* The clock chimed once as if only one person were awake on the entire dark half of the world.

Born and raised in New England, William Carpenter earned his B.A. from Dartmouth and his Ph.D. from the University of Minnesota. He began publishing poetry in 1976 and four years later won the Associated Writing Program's Contemporary Poetry Award. In 1985 he received the Samuel French Morse Prize and a National Endowment for the Arts grant.

His poetry has appeared in many magazines, including *American Poetry Review, Pequod,* and the *Iowa Review.* He has published three books of poetry, entitled *The House of Morning, Rain,* and *Speaking Fire at Stones. A Keeper of Sheep,* his first novel, made its debut in Germany in 1993.

Carpenter moved to Maine in 1972 to help found the College of the Atlantic, a school dedicated to human ecology and the environment, where he remains a faculty member. He lives with Donna Gold and their son, Daniel, in an old former inn on the Maine coast.